BRYCE

BRYCE

VINCENT BIVONA

HAMMERMILL

This book is a work of fiction. Names, characters, places, and incidents either are products of the author's imagination or are used fictitiously.

For more information on the author or future books please visit www.VincentBivona.com

In memory of Paul A. Teta

Forever in our hearts

PART 1

SPY GAMES

CHAPTER 1

That's what neighbors are for.

It's amazing how five simple words can change someone's life forever. Joe Panza had been lying on his bed, debating whether or not he should go to the track and get in shape for spring tryouts, when the phone rang. He could tell who the man on the other end was without even looking at the caller ID—the way the caller spoke his name, enunciating each syllable, was as identifying as a fingerprint: *Joe-seph.*

The voice brought a smile to Joe's face. He'd been so busy, he hadn't realized how fast time could pass you by. He supposed part of it was Amanda. When you had a girlfriend, it was easy to spend your days with her rather than do anything else.

Joe reasoned that was why he hadn't seen Luke since the time he brought the movie over to his apartment. Sometimes, time just got away. Therefore, he was glad that Luke had made the effort to call him.

"Hey, Luke," Joe said, eager to hear what his old neighbor had to say. "What's up?"

"Not much," Luke said. "Are you home right now?"

"Yeah, I'm in my room."

"Good. I need to ask you for a favor. Go to your window."

Joe did, curious as to what he might find. He almost expected to see Luke standing in the street, waving to him. Instead, the only thing he saw when he peeked out his blinds was the sun and the normal scenery of a dull suburban block.

"I'm there," Joe said, half disappointed. "What am I supposed to be looking for?"

"Look at my house."

My house, Joe thought. Luke was still referring to it as his.

"Okay . . . ?"

"Is there a car in the driveway?"

There wasn't. Joe was about to say so when Luke added: "A *white* car?"

Suddenly, everything began to piece together: the white Mercedes. He was talking about the white Mercedes. Joe still felt a bit guilty that he'd had dinner with Bryce, and decided to play dumb. "No, there's no car in the driveway. What's this about?"

There was a pause on the other end of the line, and then: "I think it belongs to the guy Crystal's seeing."

Joe could understand how Luke must feel. It couldn't have been more than a few months since the separation. Luke had a right to be pissed. Anyone in his situation did. But as much as Joe disliked what had happened to Luke, he had to admit that he thought Bryce was a pretty nice guy.

When Joe didn't say anything, Luke interpreted his silence as surprise. "I know," he said. "Fast, right? Almost *too* fast. Makes me think this guy might have been in the picture before I was out of it, if you know what I mean."

"Luke, I—"

"Don't worry about it. There's no way you could have known about him. But there *is* a way you can help me."

Joe bit his lip, unsure if he wanted to hear what it was.

"I need you to look out your window every half hour and call me if that car shows up, okay? He'll most likely park in the driveway."

Now Joe was *sure* he didn't want to get involved. The only thing stopping him was that he couldn't just say no, not after all the times Luke had helped him out with his car. And not just any car, either: his *first* car. Every teenager's vessel into freedom. He also remembered what Luke had said when he'd tried to thank him for his help: *That's what neighbors are for.*

Those five words echoed in Joe's head now. Therefore, instead of saying *no* like he wanted to, Joe knew he had to pay his old neighbor back.

"Sure . . ." he said. "No problem."

CHAPTER 2

An hour passed before Joe actually looked out the window. He was walking into the kitchen when he saw the white Mercedes parked in the driveway across the street. He debated whether or not to eat something first, but then, after remembering how Luke had sounded on the phone, he decided to call him back.

Luke answered after the first ring. "Joseph. Is he there?"

"Yeah. He parked in your driveway, just like you said he would."

There was a grating sound on the other end of the line, as if Luke was grinding his teeth. Then: "Is his the only car in the driveway?"

Joe thought it was but peered out the window again just to make sure. "Yeah."

"So nobody's behind him?"

"No."

"Okay, good. Do you own a pair of binoculars?"

The question took Joe by surprise. "Binoculars?"

"I need you to read me his license plate."

"His— Oh . . ." Joe didn't like where this was going. He wondered if doing such a thing was even legal. He almost asked Luke, and then stopped himself. Not because the question would sound dumb, but because he was afraid of the answer.

"I have a friend who's a police officer," Luke said. "He can run his plate and tell me exactly who this guy is."

Joe thought about telling Luke who Bryce was himself so he could save Luke the trouble, but then realized if he did, he would reveal that he knew more than he'd let on earlier. He'd already played dumb and acted as if he'd never seen Bryce before. Now he had to keep up the charade.

Getting the plate number wasn't the problem—his mother kept a pair of binoculars in the kitchen drawer for watching the birds on the birdfeeder—the problem was that when he envisioned himself looking through the lenses, spying, he felt sick, almost slimy.

"You would be doing me a huge favor," Luke continued. "You might think I sound crazy asking you to do this, but that guy's over there with my little daughter, and I have no idea who he is. Don't I have a right to know? Crystal didn't even have the courtesy to tell me she was seeing someone, and now she's brought him into the house where my daughter sleeps. Can you believe that?"

Joe *was* starting to believe it. If Crystal had foreseen how Luke would act, then maybe she had done the right thing. Who knew what Luke would do to Bryce in a bout of jealous rage? That was another reason why Joe was so hesitant about getting the plate number: he didn't want to be an accessory. Nevertheless, Luke did have a logical argument: Luke *didn't* know who Bryce was. It wasn't enough to convince Joe, though. What convinced him was the fact that Luke could just as easily get the information himself if he was around. Plus, if Joe did this for him, then he and Luke would be even, and that would be that.

"That's messed up that Crystal didn't even tell you she was seeing someone," Joe said, trying to put sympathy behind his words. He thought he did a pretty good job. He also thought that was what Luke wanted to hear.

It was.

"I'm glad you agree, Joseph. I hope you never have to go through what I am. I hope you and Amanda stay together."

"Thanks," Joe said, distracted. He was already rummaging through the drawer for the binoculars. He pushed aside a pair of scissors, a few scattered pens, and other assorted knickknacks that found the drawer to be their final resting place. When he came upon the black leather case, he pulled it out the way a claw does in one of those stuffed animal arcade games. The binoculars inside were made out of sleek black rubber with the word BUSHNELL written across the barrel of one of the scopes. Joe put the binoculars to his eyes and peered out. The kitchen clock leaped out at him, the numbers so big that they were blurry. He adjusted the little knob between the barrels until it cleared.

Guess they work, he thought.

"I'm sure you and Amanda won't have any problems," Luke was saying. "She seems like a very nice girl. How's everything between you two?"

"So far so good," Joe said.

"Good. The first few months of any relationship are always the best. Cherish them."

"I will. I have the binoculars, by the way."

"You do? Good. What's the plate number?"

Joe carried them over to the window and put them up to his eyes again. This time, instead of everything being blurry because it was too close, it was blurry because it was too far away. He tried adjusting the focus a second time, only to find that his efforts were in vain. It was his vision, he realized. He didn't need an eye chart to tell him it was time for a new contact prescription. The letters and numbers on the plate blurred together to form one incomprehensible jumble.

"I can't make it out," he told Luke.

"Try adjusting the focus."

Joe did, even though he knew it would get him nowhere. "Still blurry."

"What kind of binoculars are they?"

Joe looked at the name on the barrel again. "Bushnell."

"Must be one of the lower-end models. Something you can pick up at a drugstore."

"My mom's not exactly 007," Joe said. "She uses these things to look at birds, not spy on the president."

"Do you think you can go outside for me and get a little closer? Even if they're not the greatest binoculars, they should still be better than your normal eyesight."

Joe thought about this. He was already treading water he didn't want to. If he did this, he'd be doing laps in it. But then he thought about what Luke had said earlier—how he was worried about his daughter—and knew he couldn't just tell him no.

"Yeah," he said, a little reluctantly. "Just let me get my shoes on."

He decided to use the back door and go around to the gate instead of opening the garage. He did this for two reasons: The first was because going out of the garage would be too obvious, especially with the binoculars in his hand. The second was because he didn't want his mother to hear the motor and come out looking for him. He had a feeling that if she caught him spying on Bryce's car, he would never hear the end of it. More so, nobody *else* would hear the end of it. When your mother was a certified gossip, that's the price you were apt to pay if you weren't careful.

He slipped out of the house like an eel, careful not to make a sound, and did the same when he came to the gate. He paused, looking for a place to hunker down, and decided on one of the bushes next to the driveway.

"Did you get the plate number yet?" Luke asked in his ear.

"Not yet," Joe said. "I'm trying to get into position." God, he sounded more like a spy than ever. He might as well talk to Luke in code in case an enemy was eavesdropping.

"Okay," he said after he'd scurried over to the bush and crouched down. "I'm looking now."

The back of the Mercedes looked closer, yet the license plate was still blurry, the letters and numbers indistinguishable. This was the closest he dared to get and was about to abort the mission, when he decided to try adjusting the focus one last time. Slowly, with each turn, the picture within the two circles became clearer. The view was still a long way off from being considered HD, but it was enough for Joe to make out what he needed.

He read the letters and numbers to Luke as he tried to steady his hands and stop the world from trembling (through the binoculars it looked like it was in an earthquake). When he finished, Luke said, "Let me read it back to you."

Joe confirmed all but the last digit before everything went black. For one horrible second, he feared that God had struck him blind for being sneaky and underhanded. Then he lowered the binoculars and saw that it was much worse. A tall and brawny man stood over him, silhouetted against the sun.

"Hello, Joe," Bryce said.

CHAPTER 3

"Is the last number right? Joseph? Joseph?"

Joe closed the phone, cutting off Luke's voice. He looked up into the dark shadow and saw nothing but Bryce's gelid eyes. Joe had no doubt those chips of blue ice would be sparkling in the sun if their positions had been reversed.

"Hi . . ." he said, fighting to keep his voice even. A million thoughts buzzed through his head. What did you say when you were caught red-handed? Did you confess? Make something up? Pretend you weren't doing anything wrong?

It turned out Bryce saved him from having to decide, because he said, "Your mother invited Kendra and me over to play with Snowball."

Luke's daughter, Kendra, stood next to Bryce, her arm raised high above her head so she could grab onto Bryce's pinky finger. Joe had been so full of fear that he hadn't even noticed she was with him. She wore a little orange sundress and smiled cheerfully at the mention of Snowball.

"Hey, Kendra," Joe said, still feeling a bit shaky. "Got a high-five for me?" He raised his right hand. Had his left been resting on the Bible, it might have looked like he was about to be sworn in as a witness. In an absurd sort of way, he *was* swearing, swearing to himself that this was the last time he'd ever sneak around.

Kendra struck his palm, and Joe shook it, mock-hissing as if it hurt. Kendra giggled. The joke never got old.

"It's good to see you again," Bryce said. The tone of his voice was level and unrevealing. It was impossible for Joe to get a read on it. Bryce extended his hand, and Joe stood, shaking it for the second time in his life. At first it was a normal handshake—Bryce had a firm, yet gentle grip—but then it started to tighten like a vice. Joe felt his bones shift to accommodate the stress. Just before pain should have erupted, Bryce stopped and let go. Joe looked into his eyes, but they hadn't changed one bit. Neither did Bryce's complacent smile. He just stood there as if he were happy to meet Joe again. And maybe he was, Joe thought. Maybe all this sneaking around was playing tricks on his mind. If you acted enough like a secret agent, you almost expected to get tortured when you got caught.

"It's good to see you, too," Joe heard himself say.

"Is your mother in the house?"

"Yeah, I think so."

"Thank you," Bryce said. "Hopefully you'll join us when you're done out here. You know how Kendra loves you."

As if to confirm this, Kendra giggled. Bryce gave her arm a gentle tug and led her to the front door. As they walked away, Joe couldn't help but watch, wondering what Luke would say if he knew this man was walking around with his little girl. Joe thought about telling him, then thought about how he'd felt two seconds ago when he'd gotten caught, and decided that some things were best left unsaid.

What Luke didn't know, wouldn't hurt him.

CHAPTER 4

School made the weekend feel as if it had passed in the blink of an eye. Once more the sounds of bells ringing, feet clunking down the hall, and a conglomeration of voices fusing together to form a solitary drone of gossip replaced the sounds of nature, iPods, and televisions. Classes replaced going to the movies and hanging out with friends, and the discoursing teacher replaced the lecturing parent. The halls turned into runways of the latest fashions, and the spoiled students modeled them while those less fortunate stood back and admired. Almost as if they had never left, school and its routines returned.

Joe stood at his locker during the break between first and second period, spinning his combination. Usually the lull between sports left him feeling a bit depressed by this time of year, but now he felt depressed for another reason. It wasn't that he had been bored—with his car, Luke, and Amanda, he'd had plenty these past few months to keep himself occupied—and it wasn't because his mother didn't think dating was a good idea and that he should focus on academics and sports and scholarships. It was because he felt like a piece of himself was missing. And whenever he tried to identify what that piece was, it slipped by.

His locker popped open, and he exchanged his English textbook for social studies. The hall filled with the sound of students echoing his actions: open locker, switch books, close—a timeless song that would go on repeating itself until college.

He walked to his next class and sat next to a tall, lean-muscled boy with sandy-colored hair. C.J. snuck a peek at him out of the corner of his eye, and Joe did the same. Not long after, Miss Teta handed out a test. About a quarter of the way through, Joe noticed that C.J. was peeking again. Not at him this time, but at his *test.* He thought about covering it better, or maybe putting down the wrong answers on purpose and going back to change them later, but then decided to do the complete opposite: he made his test *more* visible and answered correctly.

At lunch he watched as C.J. sat at a packed table, boasting about some girl he scored with and the ones in school that wanted him. Joe sat alone, wishing that someone else he knew had off. He was just about to push his lunch away and bury his head in his arms, maybe take a nap, when Timothy Rogers pulled up a chair.

"Don't you look like the poster child for an antidepressant?"

"Hey," Joe said, brightening a little. "What's going on?"

"Same shit, different day. You know how it is. What's up with you? Why so glum?"

"No reason."

"Everything okay between you and Amanda?"

Joe thought of Sarah, and how Amanda had no clue what they were up to. "Yeah," he said, "we're good."

"So then what's bothering you?"

Joe looked at C.J.'s table again. The be-pimpled Ian Richert, the point guard during the fall, had everyone in stitches standing on his chair and mimicking the actions of a monkey (no doubt doing a lanky impression of some ugly girl that wanted C.J.). Seeing Ian act this way made Joe's lips slightly rise in a smile, but when C.J. started to laugh, Joe frowned immediately.

Tim saw where Joe was looking. "Ahh," he said. "It all makes sense now."

Joe turned to him. "What does?"

"You and C.J."

"What about us?" Joe asked, more defensively.

"It's obvious. Why don't you guys make up already?"

"It's complicated," was all Joe could say.

"Come on, are you guys really never going to talk to each other again?"

After what happened four periods later, it seemed like the answer was yes.

Dr. Zamer, the principal at Farmsville High School, had promised the students at the beginning of the year that the teachers were going to attend special weekly meetings to discuss classroom functions. The purpose of these little gatherings, he had said, was to improve student performance by not overwhelming them with work. Teachers were supposed to collaborate with one another and plan their schedules so tests were spread out, and limited to no more than two per week.

Just like the president had lied during his campaign, so did the principal. Joe had had three tests last week, and another today. Mr. Rugerdy was already handing back the most recent one when class started.

Joe took his seat next to C.J. but made it a point not to look at him. Enough was enough. Tim was right. If they weren't going to make up, he might as well move on with his life. He had more important things to deal with anyway, like spring tryouts. He was sure he'd make the team—he'd always made it before—but if for whatever reason he didn't, he had no idea what he'd do, didn't even want to consider the outcome. He knew he needed a scholarship to get into a good college when the time came. Plus, sports had always been a part of his life, and if he couldn't do them, he had an idea that the little bit of emptiness he was feeling now would expand until it swallowed him whole.

Mr. Rugerdy snapped him out of his thoughts by placing last week's test facedown on his desk. Joe flipped it over, not sure what he expected to find. He hadn't studied as long as he should have—more or less gave his notes a cursory glance—and had taken it in a daydream, where numbers, exponents, and parentheses tried to attack him from the page. To his surprise, the number at the top told him that he had passed with an 83.

Beside him, C.J. groaned. Joe couldn't help but peek. C.J. had his paper held out in front of him with both hands as if he intended to rip it to shreds. The number at the top was circled in red ink: 63.

While the rest of the class groaned or breathed out sighs of relief, Mr. Rugerdy walked up to the chalkboard and began writing a problem. Several students exchanged uneasy glances, and by the time he finished, the room had fallen silent. It didn't seem to faze him in the least. He stood in front of the board, covering the problem.

"Okay," he said, addressing the class, "we're going to do something a little bit different today. I want everyone to clear their desks and take out a pen or a pencil, a piece of paper, and a calculator."

"Are you serious?" whined Keith Hemosh, a beefy-looking kid who sat at the back of the class. More than a few other students echoed his displeasure. Another test was unthinkable, almost inconceivable. Joe was even shocked. He heard a bunch of kids to his left whispering and decided they were either planning on lynching Mr. Rugerdy, or going down to the principal's office after class to complain.

"Yes, I'm serious, Mr. Hemosh. Now please, don't call out. Everyone, clear your desks."

With reluctance, everyone did. When there was nothing on them, save for the accouterments Mr. Rugerdy had asked for, he began talking again.

"Like I said, we're going to do something a little bit different today. I've written an equation on the board. The first person to properly solve it will receive an extra five points on their test."

Now instead of moaning, everyone looked up with wide eyes as if trying to figure out if this was a joke. It might have been, had it been April—Mr. Rugerdy was known for his April Fool's pranks—but April was still two weeks away, and he didn't look like he was joking.

To confirm this, another student, a pale girl named Jessica Lambert with about a thousand rings in her ear, asked, "For real?"

"Yes, *for real*," Mr. Rugerdy replied. "I'm in a good mood today and decided I would be generous. But . . . if you don't want the five extra points, then I can just as easily . . ."

At that moment, the classroom erupted into a burst of pleas and hands pressing together. By the looks of things, Joe assumed not everyone had done as well as he had.

When they quieted, Mr. Rugerdy continued. "I don't want anybody running up when they're finished. I had the oversight to allow that this morning and had Nurse Patty screaming at me. So when you're finished, raise your hand, and I'll come over to you. You have one shot at this, so check your work *before* you raise your hand. Are there any questions?"

Keith Hemosh raised his hand.

"Yes, Mr. Hemosh?"

"Can I go to the bathroom?"

Mr. Rugerdy shook his head and sighed. "In five minutes. Are there any other questions? Preferably about the problem?" When no other hands were raised, Mr. Rugerdy stepped away from the board, uncovering the problem, and said, "You may begin."

There was a scurry of pencils as everyone copied down the problem. Joe got to work immediately, moving numbers from one side of the equation to the other. He found it surprisingly easy and wondered if anyone else did, too.

He discovered that C.J. didn't, because, like in social studies, C.J. was looking at his paper. Joe felt a flash of anger. How many times was C.J. going to cheat off him? At the rate things were going, it seemed like he'd do it every opportunity he got. There was no doubt that C.J. was taking advantage of him, acting as if Joe *owed* him. But Joe didn't owe C.J. anything, which was why he purposely wrote down the wrong answer and made a poor job of covering his paper.

A minute later C.J. raised his hand triumphantly. Immediately after, Joe did the same.

"Okay," Mr. Rugerdy said, walking over. "Let's see what you have, Mr. Galeno." He bent over C.J.'s paper, checking his work. As he did, Joe heatedly erased the wrong numbers and replaced them with the right ones. Mr. Rugerdy nodded, and then frowned. "I'm sorry, but you're not correct. Good effort, though; your work is improving. I see that extra help session this morning paid off."

Someone on the other side of the room snickered, and C.J. shot them a venomous look. They instantly fell silent.

"You raised your hand next, Joe, right? Let's see what you have." Mr. Rugerdy bent over his paper, and when he raised his head, he was smiling. "It appears we have a winner," he announced. "Very good. Five extra points. I'll change your grade in my book, Joe. You may do the same on your paper, if you choose. Congratulations."

"Thank you," Joe said, feeling the weight of twenty-seven pairs of angry eyes on him, all of them annoyed and peevish, but only one suffused with such a rage that they were nearly set ablaze. Joe tried to ignore C.J. as best he could, but each time he happened to glance his way, he found him glaring.

He was still glaring when class ended and he followed Joe out into the hall, slamming him against a locker. C.J. was tall and would have loomed over any other eleventh grader, but Joe was equally as tall and stared straight back. He didn't know if C.J. would try hitting him or not but knew he wouldn't hit back.

"What the fuck was that all about?" C.J. asked him. His voice was unpleasantly coarse and his breath smelled like the peanut butter and jelly sandwich he'd eaten for lunch.

"What was what all about?"

"Don't play dumb with me. The extra five points. You knew what the answer was and you wrote it down wrong on purpose!"

"You're right," Joe said. "I did." He tried to push past C.J., but C.J. slammed him into the locker again.

"Why the hell did you do that?"

"You wanna know why? Because I already let you cheat off me in social studies. That's why. Once is enough, okay?"

"No, it's not okay," C.J. said, and slammed Joe against the locker for a third time. "I needed those extra points more than you did. Because of you, I failed that test. If I fail another, Coach Heck might not let me play baseball this season!"

"That's if you even make the team," Joe said vehemently. He had tried to be nice, had even tried to walk away, but enough was enough. He wasn't going to stand around being bullied.

C.J.'s mouth twisted into his patented jester's grin, an expression Joe recognized as a precursor to a fight. "What did you say?"

Joe held his ground. "You heard me. You didn't play so great last season. Maybe you should just stick to basketball."

C.J. raised his fist, but before he could drive it forward, Mr. Rugerdy stepped out into the hall. "Joe, C.J. What are you two still doing here?"

"Nothing," C.J. said. "We were just leaving."

"Yeah," Joe agreed.

Before Joe could turn away, C.J. put an arm around his shoulder and pulled him down the hall. To anyone they passed they would have looked like two friends, but Joe knew what that hug signified: it was an enemy's embrace.

"Listen," C.J. said when they were out of earshot, "we're done. You said so yourself. So if you're not my friend, then that makes you my enemy. Got it?"

Joe got it, all right. He got that C.J. was a selfish prick.

"And if you show up for spring tryouts, I'll kick your ass. Last thing I wanna do is see your ugly face on the team." He pushed Joe away and slipped into the throng of students drifting by. Joe thought about shouting something back but then decided to brush his shoulder off instead. It felt dirty.

CHAPTER 5

Joe still had C.J.'s words echoing in his head when school let out. He stood leaning against the snack machine, swinging his key ring around his finger while he waited for Amanda. He hoped that with each revolution, he was closer to driving C.J.'s words away. No such luck. They were louder than ever, making Joe want to tear the hair out of his head. He turned around and pulled his foot back, preparing to drive it into the snack machine and take out some of his anger, when he spotted Amanda and felt some of the tension release. He couldn't stay mad, not with her in his sight. He loved the way her auburn hair swished over her shoulders as she walked. Next to her beautiful smile, her cute dimples, and her emerald eyes, it was his favorite thing about her. He drew in a deep breath and slowly put his foot down.

"Mad at the machine?" she asked.

"Mad at something," he said, after they kissed.

She threw him a coquettish smile. "Better not be me."

"It's not. Just something that happened today."

"Tell me about it?"

He considered but decided not to. "It's nothing."

"Are you sure?"

"Yeah."

He took her hand and weaved his fingers through hers, leading her outside. The student parking lot was just beyond the cafeteria. Together they walked past a collection of cars in contrasting states: some right off the showroom floor, their chrome glistening under the sun, and others older, looking as if their next stop might be the junkyard. Joe's car fell somewhere in between. It was secondhand, but thanks to Luke, it looked new.

"Are you *sure* you're all right?" Amanda asked after they exited the lot and came to a stop at the second traffic light.

Joe gave her a quick look before it turned green. "Yeah, why wouldn't I be?"

"Because you haven't said a word since we left."

"Really?" He hadn't noticed. All his attention was focused on what C.J. had said.

"*Really*. Now are you going to tell me what's bothering you, or what? Because you can't say it's nothing."

"Are you sure I can't?" he joked.

"Joe, I'm being serious."

"Okay, I'll tell you. It's about C.J."

"No surprise there. What did he do?"

"He was being an asshole."

"You mean he was being himself?"

"He was mad I didn't let him cheat off me, so he threatened to kick my ass if I showed up for spring tryouts."

"See? What did I tell you about him?"

"You were right," Joe admitted. "He's not a nice person."

"Not at all. So, what are you going to do?"

"About tryouts? Go to them."

"No, about C.J."

"What do you mean?"

Amanda looked at him seriously. "You're not going to go to an administrator?"

Joe shook his head.

"Why not? You can't let him get away with it like that!"

"He didn't really do anything, and it's kind of my fault he's mad at me in the first place."

"How's it your fault? What could you have possibly done to him?"

"Because. . . . Hey, do you hear that?"

"Joe, don't change the subject."

"No, I'm serious. Do you hear that?"

Amanda strained her ears. Now that she thought about it, she *could* hear something. It was faint but definitely there; a distinct rattle, almost as if something was clicking.

"Hold on, I wanna try something." Joe pressed on the gas and accelerated. He brought the car up to forty and then eased off. "You're kidding me," he muttered.

"What?" Amanda said.

"I'll show you."

He pulled over to the side of the road and popped the hood, careful not to touch the hot engine while he rooted around inside. Amanda stepped out and looked on from beside him.

"Not exactly the cleanest part of your car," she observed. The engine block, the hoses, and basically anything else under the hood were coated with a thick layer of grease. It had been this way ever since Joe had gotten the car. He'd thought about cleaning it once but dismissed the idea when he realized how much effort the task would cost him. The only part that was clean was a two by three inch section of metal that looked like someone had rubbed up against it. Joe had never noticed it before but assumed it had either been him or Luke during one of their Mr. Fix-it sessions.

"Do you know what you're looking for?"

"Not exactly," Joe confessed. "But I have an idea." He pushed aside a few things, the way a surgeon might push aside organs. Then he paused. For a moment, he was struck with a sense of Déjà vu. "See that?"

Amanda peered into the engine, looking at what he was pointing to. A thin hose, about as thick as a garden snake, twisted its way in front of the engine block before disappearing again. "Yeah. What about it?"

"It's rubbing against the fan. That's what's making the sound."

"How do you know?"

"Because it's happened before. Luke zip-tied it for me, but I guess it broke."

Sure enough, sitting to the right of the hose, trapped between a wire harness and a temperature sensor, was a lime green piece of plastic. It stood out so sharply against the black grease that Joe was amazed he hadn't noticed it sooner.

"And look what I found," he said, holding it up.

"I'm guessing that's the zip-tie?"

"Yup, it—" Joe brought it closer to his eyes, unable to believe what he was seeing. He had initially assumed it had melted due to the heat of the engine, or at least swelled and cracked, but the plastic was still as thick as ever. In fact, it would have still been an unbroken circle had there not been a diagonal slash separating it. If Joe didn't know any better, he would have said it looked like someone had cut it with a knife.

"What?" Amanda said when she saw the intent of his inspection.

"Nothing, it's just, well . . . look at this. Doesn't it look like it was cut?"

She took the broken zip-tie from him and turned it over in her hands. "Yeah, so?"

"That's what I thought."

Then, understanding dawned. "Wait, you mean by a *person*? But nobody could have done that, right? I mean, it was under your hood. Don't you need to have the keys to your car to open it?"

Joe thought about this and knew she was right. The simplest explanation was usually the most logical. Something on the road had probably kicked up and cut it, or it had gotten caught on one of the engine's moving parts. Yet, if this was the case, then why did he feel so uneasy?

Joe tried as best he could to block out the sound of the rubbing hose while he drove home. If he kept the car below thirty-five miles per hour, he found that it didn't rub too badly (the last thing he wanted was for something inside the engine to break the hose).

When he turned onto his block, there was a man on the side of the road sweeping away the sand the sanders had thrown down during the icy winter. He didn't see any of the big orange trucks the town sent out, so he assumed the man must be one of the neighbors. But he knew all of his neighbors and didn't recognize him. Even from down the block, he could tell that he had dark hair and pretty broad shoulders. All his neighbors were either old, fat, or skinny. If Luke hadn't moved away, he might have assumed it was him—even if it didn't particularly look like him—because the man was in front of Luke's house. In fact, now that Joe thought about it, it looked like—

And that's when he realized who it was.

As Joe approached, the white Mercedes came into view, sitting in the driveway.

"That's Bryce," Joe said. "That's the guy I told you about."

"You mean the one who caught you playing detective?" Amanda said.

Joe playfully cuffed her. "Hey, I wasn't *that* bad."

"Oh no? Just be thankful you weren't spying on a foreign embassy. I doubt *they* would have let you go in favor of playing with Snowball."

"What can I say? My Labradoodle wins the hearts of many. Dogs are becoming a big part of the spy industry these days."

Amanda laughed. "Yeah okay, James Bond."

Bryce waved when he saw them coming. He stood off to the side of the street with his broom, holding it in one hand like a sailor grabbing onto the mast of a ship.

"Hi," Joe said when he slowed the car to a stop.

"Hey, Joe. How are you doing?"

"All right. Yourself?"

Bryce wiped a hand across his forehead as if to exaggerate the extent of his labor. "Can't complain. Just sweeping up some of this sand. Seems it only wants to pile up in front of Crystal's driveway. Guess she's one of the lucky ones."

Joe looked and saw that it was true. The street before Luke's old driveway sloped just enough to catch all the sand. He wondered how Luke had ever dealt with it with his back the way it was and assumed he had always hired someone.

"So, is this your girlfriend?" Bryce asked, putting down his broom.

"Oh, sorry. Bryce, this is Amanda. Amanda, Bryce."

"That's a lovely name," Bryce said. He rested his forearms where the car's window retracted into the door and folded one arm on top of the other. Then he leaned into the car, staring.

"Thank you," said Amanda a little uneasily.

Bryce leaned in closer, fixing his cold blue eyes on hers. "It's nice to meet you."

"You, too."

"So, do you and Joe go to the same school?"

"Yeah, that's how we met."

Bryce leaned in even more, eyeing her lustfully. A little *too* lustfully. Joe had seen guys look at Amanda this way at school but would have never expected it from Bryce; not at his age. Now he was beginning to think that maybe Luke had a right to be worried about Bryce being around little Kendra. He could pretty much *feel* Amanda's discomfort, and was about to save her by telling Bryce they had to go inside when he saw something that drove all the air out of his lungs. Bryce had shifted and his elbow pushed against the side mirror. Joe thought nothing of it at first, other than the fact that he would have to readjust it, but then Bryce shifted again, pulling his elbow away, leaving a circular smudge about as large as a silver dollar. For a moment Joe didn't know where this little black bull's-eye had come from, and then he saw Bryce's sleeve.

What should have been white with brown pinstripes was black with grime, the type of grime that looked oddly like engine grease. *Joe's* engine grease. As in the grease that had been wiped away on the little section of sheet metal under his hood. The fact that it was on the part of Bryce's sleeve—the part that would go unnoticed until the shirt was taken off—disturbed Joe even more.

CHAPTER 6

Any thoughts that Joe had had of C.J. were completely gone by now, replaced by Bryce and the zip-tie. He lay on his bed with Amanda, staring at the ceiling and playing with her hair while she rested her head on his chest.

"You're quiet," she said.

"Sorry."

"Don't be. Just tell me why."

He didn't want to trouble her. This was something he needed to think about. So he said, "I'd rather not."

Amanda huffed, then rolled over so she could look at him. He hadn't heard that cute sound come out of her in a while and smiled, remembering the way she'd done it when they first met.

"What's so funny?" she asked.

"Nothing," Joe said, his smile growing wider.

"Come on, tell me!"

"You huffed."

"I what?"

Joe imitated her, and she slapped him playfully on the shoulder. He took her hand in his and pressed his palm against hers. The tips of her fingers, delicate and thin, only came up to Joe's first knuckles, and he closed his hand over hers.

Now it was Amanda's turn to smile, her cheeks dimpling.

"Did I ever tell you that I think your dimples are cute?"

"You really think so? I'm a little self-conscious about them."

"Why?"

"Because I never had them before."

"What do you mean?"

"I broke my jaw once, and I guess it healed weird."

"Ouch," Joe said. "How'd you manage that?"

"I'll tell you one day. Right now I want *you* to tell me something instead."

"And what's that?"

"Tell me why you were being all quiet before."

"I don't know what you're talking about," Joe lied.

"Come on, Joe; I can tell when something's bothering you. Was it the way Bryce was looking at me?"

"So you noticed that, huh?"

"Uh, yeah! Are you kidding me?" She mimed sticking a finger down her throat. "Vomit zone."

"Did you also notice what was on his sleeve?"

"No. What was on it?"

"Grease."

"Grease?"

"Yeah, grease. As in the grease from under my hood."

It took Amanda a moment to process what this meant. "Wait, so you think *he* cut your zip-tie?"

"It would make sense."

"Why?"

"Because he caught me spying on him. You said it yourself: 'Be thankful you weren't spying on a foreign embassy because *they* wouldn't let you go that easily.' Well, what if he *didn't* let me go that easily? What if he was pissed and wanted to get revenge?"

"On a teenager? You're nuts. He may be creepy, but he's still an adult, and adults don't do those things."

"Yeah, okay," Joe said sarcastically. "Just like adults don't look at little girls?"

"Hey, who are you calling little? I'm almost seventeen. I've got an ass and everything."

"Not you. Kendra. Little girls her age."

Amanda stiffened. "He looks at Kendra like that?"

"I don't know, but I know Luke had me check on him because he didn't know who Bryce was and didn't trust him around her."

"And you don't trust him, either?"

"I did at first—he seemed really nice—but I don't know now. He *did* look at you like his tongue was going to roll out of his mouth, and there was grease on his shirt."

"That could have been from anything. He was sweeping when we said hi. What if he was working on his car before that?"

Joe looked at her seriously. "You really think *he* works on that car? It's a Mercedes."

"I have no idea. I'm not a car person. Besides, I thought you said he was nice after he caught you?"

"Why are you trying to defend him?"

"I'm not. I'm just thinking logically. Was he nice after he caught you or wasn't he?"

"He was, but . . ."

"But what?"

"I don't know. When he shook my hand it almost *felt* like he wanted to hurt me, if that makes any sense. Like, I could almost feel him wanting to squeeze until it broke."

"But he didn't."

Joe confessed that Bryce hadn't. Then added quickly: "But maybe that was only because Kendra was with him."

"You're letting your imagination run away with you."

"And that's a bad thing?" Joe asked playfully.

"Maybe in this situation, but I'm glad you're capable of imagining a few things."

"Like the night we babysat Kendra?"

Amanda nodded. "Yes, like that night in particular. You know, I had fun going mini golfing and all, but it was really that night that made me fall for you."

"Really?" Joe asked.

"Really," Amanda said, and kissed him.

Joe kissed her back. She took his hand and placed it on her breast. He got the hint and kissed her again.

CHAPTER 7

Joe stared into his engine, looking at the piece of metal that had been wiped clean. It was located in such a place that someone who might have been trying to stick their hand into his engine would have rubbed their elbow up against it. Sure enough, when Joe tried to get at the place where the zip-tie had secured the hose, his elbow *did* rub against it. He also discovered that the mark was definitely made by an elbow. He tested this the way those guys did on C.S.I., by rubbing his own elbow against a similar spot under the hood and finding that it left the same type of streak in the grease: clean in the center where the bone made the most contact, and smudging around the edges.

He thought about calling Amanda and telling her what his detective work had uncovered—ha! turned out he wasn't that bad of a detective after all!—but he'd just gotten back from dropping her off and didn't want to bother her. They had hung out in his room, watching television and playing with Snowball until time, as it had a way of doing, slipped away. Now she'd either be finishing up dinner or placing one of her long, slender legs into a leotard as she dressed for dance.

Joe decided he could wait until later to tell her and dipped his head into the engine, looking at the hose more carefully. He knew there was more here than what met the eye. There always was in those detective shows, and if they proved anything, it was that diligence paid off. Already he'd confirmed that someone had tampered with his car. What he wanted to find out next was if—

And that's when he saw it. About a third of the way along the exposed part of the hose, right at the spot where the zip-tie had secured it, was a little slice. Not something that stuck out, but something so small and superficial that it would have gone unnoticed if nobody had been looking for it. It was about the length of a fingernail and as thin as a hair. Joe only noticed it because he was bending the hose back and forth until it came into view. It was enough to confirm his suspicions: it could only have been made if someone had used a razor to cut the zip-tie and had applied a little too much pressure.

Joe pulled his head out from under the hood, unable to believe what he was seeing. Almost at once, his heart went from beating moderately to thrumming wildly in his chest. He inadvertently wiped a greasy hand through his hair and looked up into the sky as if in hopes of finding a single answer to the million arising questions. It turned out all he had to do was lower his gaze. Standing across the street, next to his white Mercedes, was Bryce. He saw Joe look at him and waved. Joe raised a numb hand and waved back. In fact, it felt like his whole body had gone numb. He was staring at the man who had tampered with his car. The evidence practically confirmed it. First the fact that he'd caught Joe spying on him, then the smudge on his sleeve, and now the zip-tie and the hose. Joe remembered Amanda's warning not to let his imagination run wild—there was always the possibility that the zip-tie had been cut by something in the engine and everything else was just a coincidence—but she hadn't been there when he'd been caught. She couldn't have felt what he felt. Bryce had stared at him with those icy blue eyes. And, even if his wave had come off as friendly, his eyes hadn't. They were the eyes of someone who sought revenge.

Joe tried as best he could to appear calm. He knew if he betrayed any emotion Bryce would know he was on to him, and he couldn't have that. He had to make it seem like he didn't know anything. For that reason, he walked down to where his driveway met with the street, as if he had nothing to hide.

"Everything all right with your car?" Bryce asked.

No, Joe felt like shouting back. *You cut my zip-tie! I don't know how, but you did!* What he said was, "I don't know. There's a weird sound coming from under the hood." He was surprised at the evenness of his voice. He'd expected it to waver or tremble, but it came out sounding calm and untroubled, like nothing was wrong. He told himself he'd be pretty good at theater and made a mental note to try out next year if he ever got bored.

"Rubbing, huh?" Bryce said, walking down Luke's driveway to meet him.

No, don't come over! Joe pleaded. He didn't know how much longer he could keep up this charade. He was doing fine now, but he had no idea how he'd do under pressure, and he'd have plenty of that if Bryce stood next to him. Already he felt sweat beginning to form on his brow. On second thought, scratch theater. It would be too hard. He couldn't do this.

To his consolation, Bryce stopped at the foot of the driveway, the street separating them like a river. For a moment, Joe imagined him as a vampire and hoped that he'd try to cross the running water so he'd die.

"Yeah," Joe said. "It sounds like something's loose."

Bryce stuck his hands into his pockets, looking . . . looking almost *pleased* with himself. "That's too bad," he said. "I hope it's nothing serious."

"Me, too."

"How are you enjoying the migratory birds?"

"The what?"

"The birds that pass through here this time of year. You like bird watching don't you?"

It took Joe a minute to realize what Bryce meant. Binoculars. You used *binoculars* to look at birds. He *had* noticed. He wondered what Luke would say if he told him this.

As if this thought had summoned him, Joe's phone rang. He barely had to glance at the caller ID to see that it said:

Call from . . .

Luke

He wasn't surprised—life had an odd way of producing coincidences, especially at inopportune moments. He took one look at Bryce and felt the beads of sweat on his forehead turn into pools. He quickly wiped at them before they could drip down his face. His phone was already out of his pocket, which meant he couldn't put it away. He had to answer it or Bryce would get suspicious. Struggling to keep a neutral expression, he lifted it to his ear and accepted the call.

"Hello?"

"Joseph," Luke said on the other end. "Can you—"

Joe overrode him, speaking loudly so Bryce could hear. "Hey, Amanda. Can you hold on for a second?" He pulled the phone away and cupped a hand over the lower half, thankful for an excuse to get away. "Sorry," Joe said to Bryce, "it's my girlfriend. I'll talk to you later."

"Not a problem," Bryce said.

Joe expected him to walk away, but he didn't. All he did was stare inquisitively as Joe turned around. Joe could even feel Bryce's eyes boring holes into his back as he walked up the driveway.

"Sorry," he told Luke when he brought the phone back up to his ear.

"Trying to get away from someone?"

"You don't know the half of it." When he got to his car, he turned around, half expecting to find Bryce still standing at the foot of Luke's old driveway. But when he turned, Bryce was gone.

"Joseph? Joseph, are you there?"

Luke's voice slowly crept into his head, pulling him out of his daze. He had no idea how long he'd been lost in thought, trying to figure out where Bryce had gone. It had only seemed like a few seconds that he'd had his back turned to him, surely not enough time for Bryce to walk back into the house. Yet, that didn't change the fact that he was nowhere in sight.

"Huh? Oh, sorry," Joe said. "Yeah, I'm here."

"Okay, good. I need you to do me another favor. Are you at home?"

"Yeah, I'm out front with my car."

"Ah, the car," Luke said happily. "How's it treating you?"

Joe could have told him about the zip-tie and the little slash he'd found in the hose but decided not to. He didn't want to get Luke worked up, especially if he told him that he thought Bryce had something to do with it. No, this was something he'd have to keep to himself. If he told Luke, Luke would flip out and confront Bryce in an instant. If he was messing with Joe's car—Joe, a neighbor—that was enough proof for Luke that Bryce was also messing around with Kendra, who slept in the same house. And if Luke confronted Bryce, Joe was as good as dead. No, it was better not to tell Luke anything.

"The car's running fine," Joe said. "Everything's good on my end."

"Good to hear," said Luke. "Can I ask you to do me that favor?"

For a moment Joe wondered what would happen if he told Luke he couldn't. Just hung up and never answered his phone again. Would the sabotage, if that's what it was, end? Would Bryce, if that's who was responsible, leave him alone? He had half a mind to find out but remembered that haunting phrase—*that's what neighbors are for*—and grudgingly said, "Sure . . ."

"Thanks, Joseph. It means a lot that you're helping me. At least I know there's one person I can depend on. Listen, I need you to tell me when that white Mercedes is in front of my house."

"It's there right now," Joe said, keeping his voice low as he scanned the front yard for Bryce.

"Is it really?"

"Yeah. It's been here all day."

"I see."

If he closed his eyes he could imagine Luke scratching his chin, deep in thought. He wondered if Luke had called Crystal and asked her some question or another about Bryce, perhaps if he were over the house or not. If that was the case, then by the sound of it, she had lied.

"Okay, thank you. Can you do me one more favor?"

"Sure," Joe said, this time a little more enthusiastically. The conversation was dwindling, and he could hang up soon. He liked Luke and loved talking to him, but now whenever Luke called, there was always an element of espionage present, and Joe didn't like that.

"I need you to call me when the Mercedes leaves."

"Sure," Joe said again.

"Thank you, Joseph. You don't know how much of a help you are."

Joe hung up. He found a bright orange zip-tie in the garage—Luke had given him a whole carton of assorted colors—and secured the hose with it. The two pressed up tight against a wire harness, locking into place. Joe looked from the lime green zip-tie that had been cut to the bright orange, and couldn't help but think of Sarah and her colorful shirts. He also couldn't help but think that it was bad that Luke kept asking him to play secret agent. He needed to stop before something got out of hand. All he had to do was look at the slash in the hose to know that.

CHAPTER 8

The next day, Joe slowed his car to a stop, pulling up against the curb in front of his house. He still felt a little uneasy doing what he was doing and tried to reassure himself that Amanda wouldn't find out. He unbuckled his seatbelt and turned to the girl in the passenger seat wearing the neon yellow shirt.

"We're here," he said.

Sarah looked at his house, and then back at him. "So *this* is where you live. Funny, I always imagined you lived in a castle."

"Why's that?" Joe asked.

"Aren't you Amanda's knight in shining armor?"

Joe forced laughter. It sounded fake, even to his ears. "Come on," he said, getting out. As he walked around to Sarah's side he tried telling himself that everything would be all right but found that he couldn't do it. He needed to hear it from someone else. "Are you sure Amanda won't find out about this?" he asked, a bit nervously.

"Relax," Sarah said. "You worry too much. Didn't you tell me she's at her grandmother's today?"

"She is."

"Then we're fine. There's no way she could have seen you pick me up. Besides, I'm certainly not going to say anything to her. Are you?"

"Are you kidding me?"

"See? Then there's nothing to worry about."

Joe was trying to convince himself that Sarah was right when he felt a vibration in his pocket and pulled out his cell. "It's her," he said, shocked. He felt almost certain she was watching him.

"So pick it up," Sarah said. "If you don't answer, she might suspect something."

Joe looked at her with an expression of horror. "Do you think she suspects something already?"

Sarah shook her head. "I doubt it, but there's only one way to find out."

Joe wondered how she could be so calm while he was so anxious. He took three heaping breaths, enough to make his head swim, then answered, hoping he sounded normal.

"Hey! What's up?"

"Not much," Amanda said on the other end, "just sitting on my grandma's couch being bored, wishing you were here."

"Aww, I wish I was there, too, but I wouldn't wanna rob your grandmother of a chance to see you."

"Right, because there won't be plenty of time for that when we go shopping."

"Where are you going shopping?" There was always the possibility that they would visit the Sun Valley Mall in town. It wasn't a far drive from where her grandmother lived, and if they did go there, there was no way of telling where else they would go. What if Joe and Sarah bumped into her by chance?

He felt a lump appear in his throat when she said, "The mall."

"Which one?" he asked, barely able to get the words out.

"Bayview."

Joe felt instant relief. Bayview was a lot farther away, and she'd be heading in the opposite direction. He was safe.

Sarah must have seen the look on his face because she mumbled something and pressed her head next to his to hear the conversation.

"Who was that?" Amanda asked.

"Who was what?" Joe shot Sarah a poisonous look and searched his mind for an appropriate answer.

"I heard somebody say something."

"Oh, that was probably Luke."

"No, that was definitely a girl's voice," Amanda said.

"Must have been Kendra then. We're at Little Vincent's right now getting some pizza before we work on my car. Remember that rubbing sound we heard the other day?"

Amanda said that she did.

"Yeah, well, Luke is gonna help me fix it."

He silently thanked God he hadn't told her he'd already done it.

"Oh. Okay. That's good. Tell Kendra I said *hi*."

Joe pulled the phone away from his ear and said, "Hey, Ken, Amanda says hi."

Sarah raised her voice to sound like a little kid, making a happy little shriek. Joe winced at her horrible acting skills. Surprisingly, they turned out to be satisfactory enough because Amanda said, "She's sweet. You think we'll ever get to babysit her again?"

"Sure. If not, we can always go over to Luke's apartment when she's there."

"You don't think he'd want to spend the time with his daughter instead?"

"Just like you're spending time with your grandmother now?" Joe said sarcastically.

Amanda laughed. "Quiet. I told you we're going to hang out in a few."

"Sure, sure. Anyway, let me go. Kendra's eyeing my pizza, and if I don't eat it soon, she's gonna shove her face into it."

"Okay, I love you. Tell her I said goodbye."

"I will. I love you, too. Talk to you later."

He ended the call and held the phone in his hand, staring at it. He wasn't surprised to find that the lump that had appeared in his throat earlier had grown several times larger. It made him feel sick.

"You don't look so good," Sarah observed.

"I don't feel so good either," Joe said. He set his phone down on the roof of the car and sat on the bumper, bringing his hand up to his head.

"You're not going to faint, are you?"

"No," he said. "I don't think so."

"Okay, good. Last thing I need is for you to pass out on me." Sarah looked him over just to be sure. "Here, try drinking some of this." She handed him the Snapple from her bag. "The sugar should help."

Joe accepted the bottle and took three large sips. It seemed to work. He kept his eyes squeezed shut, focusing on his breathing, and felt the world come back one particle at a time.

"You know, you worry too much," Sarah said. "Every relationship has its secrets."

"You're right," he said. "It's just . . . it's just that I never thought I would lie to her."

"Ever?" Sarah asked incredulously.

"Nope. Not until now."

"Are you sure you still want to do this then?"

"Yeah," Joe said. "I'm sure." He pushed himself off the bumper and stood. He swayed a little but managed to stand. He hadn't felt like this since Coach Heck had put him in for two back-to-back shifts and was amazed to find that the fear of getting caught in a lie could make him feel even worse.

He tried handing Sarah her Snapple back but, when he did, he either let go too soon or she didn't have a firm enough grip on it, because the next thing he knew, the bottle was falling to the ground. He tried to scoop it up before it hit, but it was too late. It struck the asphalt and shattered in a spray of liquid and glass.

"Shit!" Sarah shouted, jumping back as some of the tea hit her shoes.

"Sorry," Joe said. "I'll give you the money for it. Or if you're still thirsty you can have something inside."

"No, that's okay. It was almost empty anyway."

"Are you sure?"

"Yeah. It was just unexpected, that's all." She bent down to pick up the pieces. Joe helped, knowing that if he missed one it might end up in his tire.

"Wanna go inside?" Joe said when he was sure they hadn't missed any.

"Sure," said Sarah. She shifted the pieces of sticky glass from one hand to the other. "Do you have a garbage in there?"

Joe looked down at the pieces in his own hand. "Yeah. Let's get rid of these things." He led her up the driveway and around the side of the house. After all the excitement, he was happy to discover that he didn't feel that uneasy anymore.

CHAPTER 9

Amanda sat in Honors English the next day, barely listening to Mr. Stevenson talk about the use of coincidences during the Victorian period. Since they had just read *A Tale of Two Cities*, he used Dickens as the prime example, citing Sydney Carton's and Charles Darnay's physical resemblance, Miss Pross's discovery of her long-lost brother, and Defarge's discovery of Manette's letter denouncing the Evré-monde family. The discussion was supposed to be interactive—students were to chime in with their comments or observations—but Amanda felt distant today. She just stared out the window, looking at the world on the other side of the glass. The weather was warming, birds were romping, and tiny buds were beginning to bloom on the trees, announcing that spring was on its way, but it did nothing to lighten her mood.

Ever since Joe had ignored her last few texts and hadn't called her to say goodnight, she had been deep in thought. It wasn't like him. He usually responded within minutes, and if for whatever reason he was busy, an hour. Two at the longest. He had never flat-out ignored her. Never for this long, at least. And never until last night. It made her wonder if something had happened. The last time they spoke he had told her he was working on his car with Luke, and she wondered if something had gone horribly wrong. She knew how dangerous cars could be. Just look at what had happened to Luke's finger. Joe had never told her how Luke had lost part of it, but she didn't need to be a rocket scientist to make the connection: *mechanic + moving parts = disaster.* What if something like that had happened to Joe? On that logic, what if something *worse* had happened? What if he was lying in a hospital bed right now? The fact that he hadn't picked her up for school didn't help to ease her mind. Now, she would have to wait until fourth period when they crossed paths to dismiss that horrible thought. Although, truthfully, she didn't think she could wait that long. She was already finding it hard to concentrate. Mr. Stevenson's words were merging with the birds' song from outside, forming one incomprehensible blend of noise. The real world was growing hazy while the horrible world her imagination created—a world in which Joe might be hurt—became startlingly clear.

Amanda decided that if she was ever going to get on with her day, she had to look for someone who knew Joe. Maybe they could tell her if he had come in. If he had, then she could relax. She was sure there was a logical explanation why he had ignored her. There always was. Maybe he lost his phone. Or it broke. Or . . .

Or he doesn't love you anymore, a cruel voice inside her head whispered.

No, impossible. Joe would never stop liking her. They were the perfect couple. Yet no matter what Amanda did, she couldn't stop that horrible thought from creeping out the back of her mind.

When the bell rang and Mr. Stevenson dismissed the class, she scanned the hall for Joe's friends. Faces upon faces floated by, but none she recognized. It seemed that whenever you were in dire need to find someone familiar, they were never in sight.

It was by pure chance that she bumped into Timothy Rogers. She had kept her head turned as she walked to her next class, scanning the faces that passed, when she collided with him.

"Sorry," she said. "I didn't—" And that's when she noticed who she had bumped into. With his towering height and almost midnight-black hair, Timmy was impossible to miss. "Tim! Thank God it's you!"

Timmy first gave her a startled, then an inquiring look. "Hey, Amanda. Everything okay?"

"That depends. Have you seen Joe today?"

"Joe?" Timmy shifted his eyes so they almost looked into the back of his head, as if he'd find the answer there. "Actually, yeah," he said when he rolled them back. "I saw him on the way to social studies. Why?"

Amanda breathed a sigh of relief. "No reason. I was just curious." That meant that Joe was okay. She scolded herself for getting so worked up. His phone had probably broken, after all. She was just about to thank Timmy and walk away when she remembered that he worked at Little Vincent's. "So, how'd it feel making a pizza with anchovies?" she said jokingly.

Timmy gave her an odd look. "What are you talking about?"

"Joe," she said. "He only eats his pizza with anchovies."

"Yeah, I know, but why would I have had to make a pizza with anchovies?"

"Because— Never mind. I thought you worked during the week, that's all."

"I do. Three to nine."

Now it was Amanda's turn to give *him* an odd look. "Were you working yesterday?"

"Yeah . . ."

"Then you should have seen Joe. He came in with his neighbor."

Timmy shook his head. "Nope. One of the guys called in sick, so they moved me to register all afternoon. There's no way I could've missed him."

Amanda suddenly felt like she had been sucker-punched. That cruel voice came back, whispering the same horrible thought: *He doesn't love you anymore.*

"Are you sure he didn't come in?" she asked.

Timmy shook his head again. "Sorry. Why, did he say he did?"

"No . . ." Amanda struggled to keep her composure. "No, it must have been a different day. My mistake." She thanked Timmy and left, grateful that there was a bathroom close by. Just as Joe's world had spun the other day, Amanda's began to spin now. She stumbled into the first stall, feeling like she had to vomit. When the urge passed, she sat down on the rim of the toilet and buried her face in her hands. It couldn't be true. Timmy had to be wrong. Maybe Joe had come in when Timmy had to get something out of the back room. It was always possible. Amanda kept telling herself this because she was unable to accept the alternative—because the alternative was inconceivable. Yet, no matter how hard she tried to persuade herself otherwise, that cruel voice spoke up again: *He doesn't love you anymore.*

CHAPTER 10

The wind picked up and blew his wet hair back, making his skin ripple with goose bumps. It had been warm all day, but it felt like there was a cold front moving in because the temperature was dropping fast. Joe looked in his gym bag for a towel and dried his hair. The walk from the gymnasium to his car wasn't far, but he didn't want to catch a cold. Not with spring tryouts right around the corner. He had spent the last two and a half hours with Coach Heck in what he called his "Afternoon From Hell," a specialized pre-tryout workout guaranteed to either get you in shape or kill you in the process. Several other students had showed up, including C.J., who kept giving Joe sneering sidelong glances from his treadmill. C.J. might have made a comment to Joe about showing up after he'd told him not to, but by the end of the workout, he could barely breathe.

Joe only got through it by thinking about Amanda. He hadn't seen her all day and couldn't help but wonder why. The best explanation he could come up with was that she was probably home sick with a stomach virus or some other twenty-four hour bug. But every now and then, a more malignant thought crept its way into his head: what if she knew he had lied to her? What if she was avoiding him? If he'd had his phone he could have texted her to ease his mind, but after dinner last night, he realized he had lost it. It wasn't in any of the usual places: on the kitchen counter, his dresser, or the top of the television. In the end, he reasoned that he had most likely left it at Amanda's again.

In any case, now that the workout was over, he could finally find out why he hadn't seen his girlfriend all day. His intent was to go home, take a quick shower, and go over her house like they had planned, but what happened next changed that.

His car was sitting at the far end of the lot, looking lonely. He made it a point not to park near people because he knew how careless kids were with their cars and didn't want to get his paint chipped. Not after all the hard work he'd put into buffing out the scratches. He also made it a point to park under a lamppost since he knew it was one of the safest spots in the lot. It provided protection from collision, and when it got dark, it would light up the car and deter any burglars. Even though he knew it wouldn't get dark for another hour or two, he still parked there out of habit. And it was there that he opened his door, tossed his gym bag into the back seat, and slid in behind the wheel.

He checked his face in the rearview mirror and started the car. He was pulling out and tuning the radio when he realized something was wrong: the car was drifting to the left. Luke had told him it might do that sooner or later—he said front-end alignments usually got thrown off after driving a few thousand miles—but he said it would only do it slightly, and this was by no definition slight. If Joe let go of the wheel, the car would eventually draw a circle on the pavement.

He stopped and got out, checking to see if maybe he could diagnose the problem from outside. It turned out that he could. His front left tire was completely flat.

"Are you serious?" he said, exasperated. He looked around to see if anyone was watching, almost hoping they were so they could confirm that this wasn't really happening, but he was in the back of the lot and there was nobody around. Besides, he didn't need anyone to confirm the horrible truth anyway. All he had to do was look at the way the deflated tire was squished under the rim.

Joe's first impulse was to find out what had caused the flat. He dropped to his knees, inspecting the tread. He wondered if he had missed a piece of Sarah's broken Snapple bottle after all and ran it over on his way to school this morning. Then a worse thought: What if it was Bryce? His body went rigid, and he looked around again, making sure he was alone. For a second he could have sworn he saw someone hiding behind one of the lampposts, but it turned out to be a plastic bag blowing in the wind.

Calm down, he told himself. *You're letting your imagination run wild.* But was he? No. He thought it was perfectly rational this time. He could find no broken glass in the tire, and if he squinted hard enough, he thought he could make out another slash mark, like the one he'd found on the hose in his engine. But then again, that really might have been his imagination.

Joe stood, running his hand through his hair and wondering what he should do. He could call a tow truck, but knew that would probably take forever, and that was not an option if he wanted to get to Amanda's house at a decent hour. Time was not his friend right now. He needed to get there as soon as possible so he could find out why she hadn't been in school. Each minute that ticked by he became more certain that she knew he had lied to her, that she *had* been in school, and that she was avoiding him. No, the tow truck was definitely out. He thought about calling Luke, but then a better idea occurred. Even though Luke had never shown him how to change a tire—not with his back the way it was—Luke had *told* him how to do it, and that was just as good.

After looking around the lot again and confirming that no help would arrive, Joe popped the trunk. The jack and a tire iron were off to the side, and he pulled them out. The tire iron was a no-brainer to operate. The jack, however, proved to be a little more difficult. After toying with it for a minute, he figured out how it worked. The spare was next. It was supposed to be in a compartment under a flap in the trunk, but as Joe prepared to lift the flap, he became aware of a sinking feeling in his stomach: What if Mr. Lancaster had taken it out? He had never checked to see if it was there. Holding his breath, he pulled the flap back. To his relief, the spare was there, looking like a black rubber doughnut. He pulled it out and set it next to the tools.

"Need any help?" a raspy voice asked after Joe had jacked up the car and removed the flat tire.

Joe looked up to find a dark face peering out at him from the open window of a rusty pickup, the Farmsville High School logo emblazoned on the door in fading vinyl.

"No, thanks," he told the groundskeeper. "I pretty much got it." It was true. Once he started, Luke's instructions came back to him and he found the task extremely easy.

"You sure?" the groundskeeper asked, getting out. He had on a pair of dirty coveralls that hung from his shoulders like the skin of a man who has just lost a lot of weight. "Be no problem."

"I'm sure," Joe said. "Really."

"Okay. If you insist."

Joe thought he'd get back in his truck, but he didn't. He just stood there, watching. When Joe realized he wasn't going to leave until the tire was replaced, he continued.

The procedure was easy from here. All Joe had to do was reverse what he'd done to get the tire off. In minutes he had the spare on, and the car resting on the ground again.

"Not bad," the groundskeeper said, inspecting his work. "You do this before?"

"First time," Joe said, a little proud.

The groundskeeper nodded. "Well, looks like everything's on tight. Have a safe ride home."

Joe thanked him and watched as he got back into the rusty pickup, puffing purple exhaust as he made his way to the equipment shed behind the school.

Now it was Joe's turn to survey his work. He stood back, taking in the sight of the car with the spare on it. It looked almost comical the way it leaned to one side, as if it had had one too many drinks. He remembered hearing that you couldn't drive too fast or too far on a spare and now realized why. There was no way that thing could handle the normal stress of driving the way a regular tire could. He considered going straight to a gas station to get it replaced but then thought about Amanda again. If she still expected him to come over, then he was already late—it had taken him about thirty-five minutes to change the tire—and he didn't want to be any later.

Amanda didn't live far from the school. Thankfully for him, she didn't live on any main roads either. Joe didn't know the limitations of the spare and didn't feel like testing them. He kept to the backstreets and a steady twenty miles per hour, twenty-five when he grew impatient. It took him another twenty minutes to get to Amanda's, and by that time, he was almost an hour late.

He parked by the curb in front of her house and rang the bell. Amanda answered the door dressed in a striped halter-top and a pair of white shorts that showed off her long, bronze legs. Not an outfit someone wears when they stay home sick, Joe observed. His heart sped up just the same. Amanda's didn't. She looked more put out than ever.

"Joe . . ." she said, without putting any emotion behind his name.

The tone of her voice made it hard to breathe. Suddenly, Joe felt like there was no more air left in the world. Amanda was mad, but not in any way he had seen her before. This was different. She seemed almost . . . defeated. Like she'd given up. Joe didn't want to know what that implied. He stepped in and put his arms around her waist, afraid that if he let go he would lose her. She pulled away, and that made him feel even worse.

"Amanda, I'm sorry. It's not my fault. I got a flat and had to change it."

She looked over his shoulder at the car to make sure this wasn't a lie. "So you couldn't call me, then? Or answer any of my texts from yesterday? Or even call me to say goodnight, like we always do?"

Her tone changed. Now, it was assaultive.

"I lost my phone," Joe said in defense. "I didn't even know you texted me."

"Do you know how worried I was? You could have told me that you lost it, you know."

"How could I have done that?"

"I don't know. Your house phone, maybe? Someone else's cell?"

Joe looked down at his feet as he confessed that he didn't have her number memorized.

"You honestly don't know my number by now? You call it every day. I know yours."

"You're on speed-dial. I didn't think I had to memorize it."

Amanda huffed and folded her arms across her chest. Joe grabbed her around the waist again and pulled her close. She didn't try to break free this time, only turned her head away.

"Amanda, listen to me. I tried to find you in school today to tell you this. I even—"

"What about this morning?" she interrupted.

"This morning?

"What about picking me up this morning?"

"Oh. I was running late. Honestly. And I couldn't call you to tell you because I didn't have my phone, and since you don't have Facebook, I couldn't even write on your wall. I figured I'd just tell you when I saw you in school, but I never did." He paused, hoping she might say something that would indicate whether she had stayed home or not. When she didn't, he continued. "I even tried coming over straight after my workout, but that's when I got the flat. None of this is my fault. And to top it off, I don't even think it was an accident."

"What do you mean you don't think it was an accident?"

"The flat. I think somebody gave it to me."

"Why would someone give you a flat?" she said.

The minute she asked the question, she had an answer: *Because he lied to them, too.* It was that cruel voice again. If he had lied to her about the pizzeria, then he might have lied to other people about other things. She wanted to believe he *hadn't* lied to her—that there was a logical explanation—and wanted to ask just to be sure but didn't have the nerve. It had taken almost all of her will to avoid him during school for fear she might see him and break down, and it had taken the rest of her will not to break down right now. This was something that would have to go unanswered for the time being. She would have to believe him.

"Why would someone give me a flat?" he repeated. "How about because someone doesn't like me."

Amanda could only think of one person who didn't like Joe. "You think it was C.J. then?"

That had never crossed Joe's mind. He considered it for all of two seconds before dismissing it. "No. I think it was Bryce."

"*Bryce?* Your neighbor's boyfriend?"

Joe nodded. "Him. I didn't tell you this, but when I was replacing the zip-tie, I found a little slash in the hose. It looked like it had been made by a razor, like someone might have cut it while trying to get the tie off."

Amanda wondered what else he hadn't told her. She was just about to respond when what he said hit her: *I didn't tell you this, but when I was replacing the zip-tie, I found a little slash in the hose.*

I. Not *Luke and I*, but *I,* as in alone. As in the cruel voice had been right and he really had lied to her. Amanda felt her legs grow weak and would have fallen had Joe not been holding onto her.

"*Amanda!* Are you okay? What's wrong?"

Amanda paid no attention to the concern in his voice. As far as she knew, that was a lie, too. She struggled to keep her balance and hated herself a little for having to rely on Joe to stand.

"What's going on?" she finally managed to say. "Tell me, Joe. Tell me the truth."

"What are you talking about?"

"You've been acting weird lately, and I want to know why."

"*I've* been acting weird? What about *you*? I had a horrible day and you nearly jumped down my throat because of it. I lost my phone. I got a flat. And"—he was on a roll, so why not just come out with it?—"and to top it all off, I think you've been avoiding me."

Amanda didn't say anything.

"Well?" he pressed. "Were you in school today, or weren't you?"

Her silence was answer enough.

"I thought so. What's going on with us?"

Amanda wanted to ask him the same question but found that when she opened her mouth only air could come out.

Joe shook his head. “Forget it. Maybe I should go.”

From far away Amanda heard herself say, “Maybe you should.”

CHAPTER 11

The bus pulled away. Amanda watched that great yellow lumbering beast of transportation as it disappeared down her block along with the sound of the rowdy kids inside. It seemed like it had been ages since she had last taken it. Aside from yesterday, the count might have been up to something like four months, about the time she and Joe had started getting serious. He hadn't picked her up this morning—she hadn't expected him to—and she hadn't given him a chance to offer her a ride home this afternoon. She decided it would be best if they avoided each other again. She needed time to collect her thoughts, to figure out what was happening between them. Joe had lied to her. She needed to figure out why and what to do about it. She knew she might be overreacting—everybody in a relationship fights eventually—but that still didn't change the way she felt, and it didn't change the fact that if someone gets caught lying, it's usually because he or she has made a habit out of it.

Amanda reflected upon these things as she walked up her driveway, careful not to let them consume her thoughts. She knew if she let them, she would find herself in a depression. Because that's usually the way it happened, wasn't it? You let some guy into your life, you raised barriers until you were sure he's genuine, and the minute you dropped them, he attacked, crushing your heart. Joe hadn't done anything to break hers, exactly, and Amanda didn't think he would—*hoped* he wouldn't—but Joe had lied, and as stupid as it might be, there had to be a reason why.

She was about to take these thoughts and push them deep down where they could be forgotten, when she saw something sitting on the top of her mailbox. She knew what it was before she even reached it: the rectangular object was unmistakable, especially in its plastic case. She wondered how it had gotten there and decided that Joe must have dropped it while walking up to her house and someone had found it and placed it there hoping for the owner to find it. There was no other explanation. Since her mailbox was attached to the house, right next to the doorbell, it would be hard to miss something sitting on top of it.

But who had put Joe's phone there?

It was probably the mailman, who had found it walking up the lawn. And if not him, then someone else. That didn't matter. What mattered was that Joe's phone was back. She grabbed it before it could sit outside any longer and shoved it into her bag. She would give it to him tomorrow. By then she would have had enough time to think everything over. And by then, maybe they could sit down together and calmly talk about what was bothering them.

This might have worked had her curiosity not gotten the best of her. She made it all the way into the kitchen before the impulse struck. She tried ignoring it, but by the time she was in her room, Joe's phone was out and she was going through it.

If he had lied once he had probably lied before, and if he had, she wanted to find out what it was he had lied about. The first thing she did was go to his text message inbox. Her name was first with the most messages followed by Daniel, Timmy, Jacob, Emily, Andrew, and Mom. She half expected to find Luke there since Joe always talked to him, but figured he had either deleted their conversation or they only called each other. If it was the former and Joe did this with some of his other contacts, she suspected she wouldn't have much luck finding anything incriminating. Nevertheless, she pressed on, checking Emily's messages first. Since she was the only girl on there, Amanda supposed this was the best place to start. As she pulled up the texts, something her Honors

English teacher Mr. Stevenson had said came to mind: *Peek not through a keyhole lest ye be vexed.* Amanda knew that if she looked she might find something she'd be mad about, but she didn't care. She and Joe were in a relationship and she had a right to know if he was doing anything behind her back.

She scanned the first few messages until she realized that Emily was Joe's cousin. Now that she thought about it, she remembered him mentioning her once or twice before. Breathing a sigh of relief, she checked Timmy's texts. All he and Joe talked about was how much they hated Coach Heck and his special workouts. Amanda checked two other names before moving on to somebody named Daniel. She figured she'd find the same type of guy-talk as in the other conversations but was surprised when that wasn't the case. He and Joe talked about movies and common interests. It was weird, because reading it almost made Amanda feel like she was reading a conversation between Joe and herself. Joe asked Daniel the same types of questions and made the same types of comments, especially when Daniel said he liked something.

If she had closed the phone right then and there things might have happened differently, but she pressed on, determined to read every message until she discovered the reason for Joe's strange behavior. About a quarter of the way through, she did:

From: Daniel
I really liked the Harry Potter
movies. They were great.
March 15, 7:35pm

Oh cool. They were good but
the books are definitely better.
To: Daniel
Sent: March 15, 7:36pm

From: Daniel
Really?

March 15, 7:38pm

Yeah. The movies leave so much
out.
To: Daniel
Sent: March 15, 7:39pm

From: Daniel
I didn't know that. Maybe we can
watch the movies and you can tell
me what they left out ;)
March 15, 7:40pm

Amanda had to pause. Something was wrong. Guys didn't use the winky face while talking to one another. Not under these circum-stances. She went to the next text, and the next, feeling her heart beginning to thump faster.

Id like that. You can come to
my house.
To: Daniel
Sent: March 15, 7:40pm

From: Daniel
Are you sure that would be okay?
You don't think she would find
out, do you?
March 15, 7:42pm

Itd be fine. Shed never find out.
I have her wrapped around my
finger.
To: Daniel
Sent: March 15, 7:43pm

From: Daniel
Good. Because the last thing I would want is her interrupting something. You KNOW how I hate being interrupted ;)
March 15, 7:44pm

Trust me thats the last thing I would want. Ur too good to interrupt.
To: Daniel
Sent: March 15, 7:45pm

From: Daniel
You're better ;)
March 15, 7:45pm

Now Amanda's heart was beating so fast that it felt like it was trying to burst out of her chest. Her stomach was churning, and the back of her throat tasted like bile. She had to put the phone down and stagger over to her bed, burying her face into a pillow. This couldn't be happening. There had to be a logical explanation.

There is, that cold, cruel voice said. *He doesn't love you anymore.*

She hadn't wanted to listen to it before, but now she couldn't ignore it. Not after what she had seen, or the way Joe had tried to hide what he was doing by changing Whoever-the-hell's name to Daniel. Did he really think she wouldn't find out that Daniel was a girl? Did he really think she was that stupid?

No, she reasoned. He didn't. He probably hadn't expected to lose his phone. In fact, if he hadn't, then she probably wouldn't have ever figured it out. She would have just seen the name Daniel pop up every now and then and thought nothing of it. She would have never seen the conversation. And if she ever asked Joe who Daniel was, he would have lied to her. Easy.

What really upset Amanda the most was that she and Joe had basically had the same conversation when they first met, and again a few days ago after she agreed to finally watch the movies. Now he was having it with some whore. He even had the nerve to mention that the books were better than the movies. *She* had told *him* that! She could even go back to their conversation in her phone and find it, that's how recent it was! It made her blood boil! All of it! The flirting. The part about being wrapped around Joe's finger. The fact that Joe and the whore never mentioned Amanda's name, just referred to her by a disassociating pronoun. She wanted to kill Joe, cry, shout, and run away all at the same time. She contented herself by screaming into her pillow and kicking her feet instead. When her fit subsided, she rolled over and wiped the tears from her eyes. They were done. That was it. She wasn't going to let this go on any longer. She wasn't going to get hurt again. She knew she should have learned from her mistakes. She had even tried to push Joe away when he first came on to her, but he had persisted, and she thought there had been something different about him. Now she knew she was wrong. All guys were the same. Especially jocks. Every last one of them.

It took her some time to collect herself enough to go into her shed and find her bike. She wanted to end this right now. No waiting. Not even until her parents came home and she could ask them for a ride. Besides, this was her business, and she didn't want an audience. She'd just go over to Joe's, knock on his door, let him have it, and leave. She'd hop back on her bike and pedal away, putting as much distance between their lives as possible.

She didn't think it would take as long as it did. By car, whenever Joe picked her up, it took a little over fifteen minutes. By bike, it had taken her almost forty. She hated Joe even more for living so far away. She pulled onto his block, panting and out of breath. She braked a few houses down and took a sip out of the water bottle attached to the bike's bottom tube. The cool liquid (she had packed the bottle with ice cubes) slid effortlessly down her throat, and she tried to concentrate on the temperature to clear her mind. She needed to be focused for what she was about to do. The last thing she wanted was to let her anger cloud her thoughts. She had a very clear perception of what she was going to say and how she was going to say it, and she intended to say it all.

When she was ready, she coasted to his house. His car sat by the curb like it always did. That was a good sign. In her anger, she hadn't even taken into consideration that he might not be home. No need to worry about that now. The Altima parked next to the curb was his. She was sure of it. She had been in it enough times to know. Had even made him the little rope bracelet that hung from the rearview mirror.

Seeing it, she immediately wanted it back. She wanted everything back. Every single thing she had ever made or bought him. She wanted to collect it all, put it in a pile, and *burn* it. Maybe as the gifts vanished, consumed by the flames, so would her memory of Joe. It almost pained her to think like this, but if she really thought about it, all those fun times were lies. Each time he was with her, he was probably thinking about the other girl. Amanda wanted to find out who she was and claw her eyes out. However, taking back the bracelet would do for now.

She didn't think the Altima's door would open, but when she pulled the handle, it swung out. She didn't hesitate in the slightest. She reached inside and yanked the bracelet off, shifting the mirror in the process and nearly pulling it down. A devious thought gripped her. She could trash his car. That would teach him. He always kept it so neat and vacuumed, it would pain him to find the contents of his glove box and center console strewn about. She was psyching herself out to do exactly that when she saw the underwear lying on the floor. It was a lacy neon-pink thong, a color almost impossible to miss. Seeing it, Amanda felt like she had been sucker-punched all over again.

Joe sat in his room looking at the ceiling. He found that this was a great way to relax. He'd done it a bunch of times and needed to do it now more than ever, especially since spring tryouts were in two hours. Unlike most coaches, Coach Heck decided to hold tryouts at night. He did this for three reasons: The first was because he wanted the students to be well-rested and mentally prepared. The second was because studies had shown that the only healthy meal of the day students ever ate was dinner. And the third reason was—and this was just a guess on Joe's part—Coach Heck and Ms. LaBlanc, the economics teacher, had a thing for one another. There were rumors that their cars had been spotted at the local Motel 6. None of that mattered, anyway. What mattered was that tryouts were at seven. That meant Joe had a little over an hour to mentally prepare himself before he had to leave. He wanted to be calm and collected but was finding that it was a harder task than he had initially thought, all because of Amanda. He hadn't seen her all day and assumed she was avoiding him again. It might have been because he hadn't pick her up this morning—he wanted to give her some time to herself and let her cool off—but he didn't really believe that. He thought that if he had tried to give her a ride she would have turned it down, anyway. What it all came down to was that the two of them needed to have a heart-to-heart talk. Every relationship hits a rough patch, and it just so happened that they had hit theirs now. The only bad thing was it couldn't have happened at a worse time.

It took Joe half an hour before he could allow his shoulders to unbunch and his mind to relax. It was a great, tranquil feeling. It almost felt as if he were floating above his body, free, untethered from mundane anchors. He was just starting to wonder why he didn't do this more often, when the doorbell rang.

Bile kept trying to creep up her throat, and Amanda had to swallow to keep it down. This was almost too much to handle. One part of herself told her to turn around and leave—it wasn't too late—but another part told her to stand her ground. She had to look Joe in the eye and tell him it was over. What made her stay was the simple fact that if she didn't do it now, when she was angry and upset, she might never do it. She might begin to make up excuses and find herself stuck in another horrible relationship. She couldn't have that. Not again. She had to end this now before it went too far.

When the door opened, she dug her nails into the palms of her hands, reminding herself of all the pain she would have to endure if she stayed with Joe.

"Amanda!" Joe said, surprised. "What are you doing here?"

He poked his head out, looking up and down the street, trying to figure out how she had appeared on his step. That's when his eyes happened upon her bike.

"It can't be fixed," was all she said.

At first Joe didn't understand. Did she mean her bike? Had she gotten a flat on the way over? Bent one of the rims? He was just about to ask her if that's what she meant when she began to cry.

Understanding immediately followed.

"We're done, Joe. It's over," she said through a face full of tears. She held her hands in front of her body and twisted them nervously. Joe tried to take hold of them to calm her down, but she yanked them back when he reached out. "No!" she spat. "Don't touch me! Don't you ever touch me again! We're through!"

"B-b-but why?" he stuttered stupidly.

"Are you serious? You have the nerve to play dumb?"

"No. Honestly, Amanda, I have no idea why."

"You have no idea why I'm breaking up with you? Hurmm . . . let's think. Could it be because you *cheated on me?*"

Joe felt everything go numb. It took almost all of his strength to say what he said next: "I never cheated on you."

The look of hatred on Amanda's face was powerful enough to slay a dragon. She raised her hands in fists as if to hit him, then dropped them to her sides again, shaking like tiny jackhammers.

"*You liar!*" she screamed. "I can't believe you! I caught you red-handed and you can't even admit it! You disgust me!"

She dug her hand into her pocket, threw Joe's phone at him, turned around, and stormed down the steps, nearly tripping over herself in the process. When she got to the bottom, she said, "And don't you ever call me again!"

"Wait," Joe said, running after her. She ignored him, making her way down his driveway and mounting her bike. He reached out and grabbed her shoulder. "Amanda, wait! Let me explain—"

"*Don't touch me!*" she shrieked.

Joe jumped back, pulling his hand away as if he were afraid she might bite. "Amanda, please. Let's talk about this."

"There's nothing to talk about! We're done!"

Joe thought quickly. He couldn't let her go now. Not when she was this mad. He knew if he did, the result would be disastrous. He needed a chance to talk to her and calm her down, make her see reason. Suddenly he had a brainstorm. "Okay, fine, whatever you say. Let me give you a ride home then. You can put your bike in the backseat and—"

"Fuck you!" she shouted. "And fuck your precious car, too!"

Joe reached out for her again, but she slapped his hand away. She didn't give him a chance to reach out again. Before he could, she pushed down on the pedals and rolled into the street. Joe had a mind to go after her, get into his car and follow, pleading to her to understand, but then he remembered tryouts and cursed. If he missed them he wouldn't make the team. And even though at this point his relationship seemed like the most important thing in the world, there was still a rational part of his brain functioning enough to remind him that making the team was equally as important. Colleges looked at high school sports just as much as they looked at grades, and if he ever hoped to get that scholarship his mother relentlessly hammered him about, then he had to make the team. Besides, Amanda clearly didn't want him to chase after her. If he did, then he would make her madder than she already was, and he didn't want that. Maybe it was best to let her calm down first.

Torn between choices, feeling as if he wanted to pull all the hair out of his head, he watched her pedal down the block and turn the corner, vanishing from his sight, and possibly out of his life.

CHAPTER 12

Twenty minutes later Joe got into his car, where he found a pair of lacy pink underpants on the floor.

CHAPTER 13

Joe pulled into the school parking lot with time to spare. Unlike fall tryouts, there were other cars besides his. Joe guessed these belonged to those students who had early birthdays. It was funny: originally he thought he'd feel a bit of resentment when his classmates started driving to school. Now he pretty much didn't care. The novelty of being the only junior with a car had worn off. All he wanted to do was make the team so he could go over to Amanda's and get his girlfriend back. Maybe it was hanging out with adults like Luke, or maybe it was just the natural order of things; whatever it was, he felt like he was maturing and seeing things in a different light. His values were changing, and he was beginning to realize that some things were more important than others.

He got out of his car, trying to focus on the tryouts but finding it impossible. He kept thinking about Amanda. No matter what he did, he couldn't get her out of his mind. After she had left, he had tried to lie back down and re-enter that tranquil, almost trance-like state, yet each time he felt himself beginning to relax, he remembered the way she had screamed at him and he was wrenched back to reality. He thought about the hurt in her eyes, the tears dripping down her cheeks, and her trembling hands. He wanted to hold her and tell her everything would be all right, but knew he had to get through tryouts first.

As he walked toward the gymnasium, he watched as the rest of his classmates were dropped off, some by their parents, others by older brothers and sisters. He tried to look for someone among them who he talked to, but baseball was a lot different from basketball and not many of the same athletes played both sports. He had tried to convince Timmy to tryout, but Timmy had said that one season with Coach Heck was enough. Joe didn't blame him. He just wished C.J. thought the same way. Unfortunately, C.J. liked baseball just as much, if not more, than basketball. His height, like Joe's, gave him an advantage in both sports, and there was no way C.J. would miss tryouts. Especially after he had warned Joe not to show up.

After changing, Joe stretched, allowing his thoughts to drift to Amanda. Only half an hour had passed since they had broken up. How could he possibly perform well after she had dropped that bombshell on him? His body might be conditioned, but his mind was not. Not anymore. And to make matters worse, he had to worry about C.J. and his threat. He could imagine him saying something along the lines of—

"I thought I told you not to show up?"

Joe spun around. C.J was standing right behind him, dressed in mesh shorts and a cotton tee that had the sleeves cut off. By the ragged look of the fabric, Joe guessed he had done it himself, either by ripping it with his hands or by using his teeth. If it were the latter, it wouldn't have surprised Joe in the slightest.

"I don't want any trouble," Joe said. "I'm just here to try out, that's all. Same as you."

C.J. took a step forward so they were face to face. His eyes were a dark brown, as if colored by hate. "Well you should have thought of that before you made me fail my math test."

"I didn't make you fail anything," Joe said defensively. "You did that by yourself."

C.J.'s eyes narrowed. "Oh, so now you think you're funny, huh? Calling me stupid?"

"No. That's not what I meant at all." Joe didn't need this. Not now. He found himself hoping that Coach Heck would emerge from the locker-room and break up the confrontation. Instead, a crowd gathered, encouraging it, making *ooooo*ing sounds when C.J. pushed him.

"You think you're smarter than me? Is that it?" C.J. said, pushing him again.

Joe let his shoulder absorb the force, knowing that if he tried to resist, C.J. might throw a punch. If C.J. did, then he would have to throw one back, and that was the last thing he wanted. Deep down he still felt responsible for C.J.'s anger and didn't want to hurt him because of it. If he had just stayed friends with him in the first place then none of this would be happening. Although if he had stayed friends with him then—

"Huh? You think you're *better* than me?"

"Listen," Joe tried to reason, "I don't think I'm smarter or better than anyone." That was a lie—he knew by his test grade that he was smarter than C.J.—but what C.J. didn't know wouldn't hurt him.

"Yes, you do," C.J. said. "I can see it. The way you walk around, like you got a stick up your ass."

Joe used every bit of his willpower to ignore him. It was hard when C.J. kept pushing him, but he tried nonetheless, taking a step backward each time C.J. threw out his hand.

"That's right, a stick up your ass. How does that feel? Does it hurt?"

Another push. Another step.

"Or do you *enjoy* it?"

Now Joe felt the presence of hands on his back. He'd reached the border of the circle. It was apparent that the students making it weren't going to let him pass.

"Yeah, I bet you enjoy it," C.J. went on. "Just like that bitch of yours. I seem to remember she always walked with a stick up her ass, too. No, wait a minute. It was a dildo, wasn't it?"

Joe tried to ignore this last comment, but it was as if a switch had been flipped. The minute C.J. mentioned Amanda, Joe's cheeks began to flush red with anger.

C.J. noticed that he had struck a nerve and pursued it. "Oh, does that bother you? That your girlfriend has a dildo up her ass? Are you jealous she prefers it over the real thing?"

"You better shut up," Joe said, taking a step forward.

C.J. grinned his jester's grin. "Oh, yeah? What are you gonna do if I don't? You gonna send your bitch after me?"

Joe took another step forward. His hands were at his sides and they were trembling like Amanda's had—tiny jackhammers, powered by the same kind of fury. "Just shut up, C.J."

C.J. spotted them. "Oh, you wanna sign for me? Doet tawk abowt ma goalfwaind," he said, mocking a deaf person.

"Shut up, C.J. I mean it."

C.J. laughed, and along with him, everyone making the circle echoed that laughter. It was a horrible sound that resonated in the wide space of the gymnasium. Joe knew not to take it personally; the other kids just wanted to see a fight. They didn't care who they had to push in order to do it.

"I'm surprised you and that bitch are still together," C.J. went on, relentless as ever. "You're a jock and, well, she's got that dildo stuck up her ass. Aren't you tired of it blocking your path?"

That was it. Joe couldn't stand hearing C.J. talk about his girlfriend—his *ex*-girlfriend—like that any longer. Before he even realized what he was doing, he leaped forward and shoved C.J. as hard as he could. It took C.J. completely by surprise, and he stumbled backwards, tripping over his feet. The boys making up the circle let out a string of *oooooooooo*s as he fell to the floor.

Several of them were putting hands on C.J.'s shoulders, lifting him up, eager for him to get back into the ring. C.J. brushed them off, determined to get to his feet on his own. When he did, the circle-formers began chanting, "Fight! Fight! Fight!"

As if empowered by the incantation, Joe leaped forward for a second time and threw a punch. C.J. pulled his head back just in time and watched Joe's fist whiz by his face. He followed up by grabbing onto the back of Joe's shirt and pulling it over his head. Joe had seen C.J. fight before and knew if he didn't get his shirt off he was done for. Blinded, he reached up with both hands and pushed the fabric away from his head. It got caught on his ears, but with a wiggle, it came free. C.J.

stumbled backward again and Joe followed up by lifting his hands in front of his face like the fighters in the UFC. He'd never been in a fight before but had seen plenty, and knew if you didn't keep your hands up you were apt to get hit. When C.J. saw his stance, he smirked and said, "Who do you think you are? Matt Serra?"

Joe didn't answer. He kept his eyes locked on C.J.'s and sidestepped. When he felt he had an opening, he threw a punch. C.J. ducked it and followed up with one of his own. Joe ducked it as well, feeling the warm rush of air as it nearly grazed his skin. Since they were both tall, they had the same reach. That didn't seem to stop C.J.'s determination. Just as he played on the basketball court, he fought dirty. He threw Joe's shirt at him, blocking his vision, and then dove, arms outstretched, gripping Joe around the waist. Joe's cry of surprise was lost over raucous cheers as he and C.J. crashed to the floor, rolling around, each of them struggling to mount the other. Joe felt C.J.'s fists pounding on his back, and he tried to block these by putting his elbow back. Except instead of blocking a punch, he felt it push into something soft and heard C.J. scream.

He might have turned to follow up on this unexpected injury, but the next thing he knew, the high-pitched screech of a whistle split the cheers.

"What in the name of Mary and the rotten apple is going on in here?"

The boys forming the circle broke apart, pushing behind one another to get out of Coach Heck's way. He stood akimbo, looking like a mockery of Peter Pan with his legs spread and his fists pressed against his hips—a short, bald man with hairy arms that poked out of his Farmsville High School t-shirt. His head reflected the overhead fluorescents, and the cord of his whistle rocked back and forth on his neck like a pendulum.

"Well? Is anyone going to answer me, or do you think I can read minds?"

None of the boys answered. They just stood there, silent, looking at their shoes as if they were all bad puppies who had been scolded for wetting the carpet.

"Apparently all of you think I *can* read minds. Fine, let me show you my powers." He looked to the two boys getting up. Joe was the first to stand, followed by C.J., who cupped a hand over his right eye. From what Coach Heck could see, it was swelling up pretty bad. "Let's see . . . these two gentlemen got into a fight and the rest of you cheered them on. Is that right? Are my mental powers working correctly?"

Nobody said anything.

"Somebody say something, or everyone is going to do five laps around the perimeter of the school."

A short boy with long hair covering his eyes spoke up. "Joe threw the first punch."

Coach Heck looked at the boy in surprise. "*Panza* threw the first punch? Now why do I find that hard to believe?"

"No, he really did," two other boys confirmed.

"That's only because C.J. was—"

The minute Joe tried to defend himself C.J. interrupted him: "He's lying, he was the one to—"

Now everyone joined in, spilling the tale as they had seen it.

"Enough!" Coach Heck shouted. "Panza, Galeno, in my office. The rest of you, ten laps around the gymnasium and then the usual warm-up. For those of you who've never been on the team before it's—" He began to recite the exercises and then thought better, casting his eyes about the crowd, looking for someone dependable. "Martin, lead them through the warm-up when they're done with the laps. I'll be in my office with these two. If anybody—and I mean *anybody*—horses around they're immediately cut from the team—I mean they won't even *make* the team. Am I clear?"

The boys nodded. They got it, all right. Coach Heck was pissed. Don't piss him off any more.

"Good. Now go! What are you standing around for? Get those laps done!"

So much for acting mature, Joe thought as he stared at the motivational posters covering the walls of Coach Heck's office. One was of a young man with a beard resting an arm on his pickax as he looked out over the top of the world. The caption to the side read: CLIMBED MOUNT EVEREST BLIND. Another showed a teenage girl clutching a surfboard. Her left arm was missing. NEVER GIVE UP. Joe let his eyes wander over three more posters before coming to rest on Coach Heck. He sat on the other side of his desk, his hands steepled, his eyes unmoving. Joe immediately looked away. Sitting beside him, C.J. did the same. Finally, after what felt like a year of silence, Heck spoke.

"Okay, *gentlemen—*" He put special emphasis on the word, using it the way someone does when they mean the complete opposite. "—why don't you tell me in your own words what happened."

Without waiting for any further instruction, Joe and C.J. began blurting out their stories.

Heck raised a hand. "One at a time." He pointed to Joe. "You first, Panza."

C.J. grunted. Joe had to fight to repress a smile. He recounted the story from beginning to end, how C.J. had it out for him because he wouldn't let him cheat in math class, how he had mocked Amanda, and how they had fought because of it.

"Is this true?" Heck asked C.J. when Joe was done.

C.J. nodded. He knew better than to lie to the coach. The way he sat behind his desk, he looked like a judge, one with the power to decide the fate of whomever had the misfortune to sit before him.

Heck leaned back in his chair. "Okay, here's what we're going to do. Galeno, I'm going to give you detention for provoking the fight. You're also suspended for the first two games, providing you make the team. I'm going to talk to—who was your math teacher again?—right, Mr. Rugerdy—I'm going to have to inform him about your cheating. Whatever he decides to do for punishment will be in addition to mine."

C.J. started to groan but caught himself at the last second. He nodded, hating Joe more than ever.

Coach Heck turned to Joe now. "Panza, your punishment is a little bit harsher. Since you were the person to actually throw the first punch, I'm afraid I'm going to have to give you two detentions and ban you from trying out. Better luck next year."

Joe felt all the color drain from his face.

"Ban me?"

This couldn't be happening. Not now, not after Amanda had broken up with him. It felt like his whole world was crumbling. It was as if one bad thing was following another.

"That's just the teams I coach this spring," Coach Heck went on. "If you find yourself interested in any other sports, you're welcome to try out. Mr. Penchik's coaching . . ."

Joe felt his leg vibrate. He almost jumped. At first he had no idea what it could be, but then he realized it was his phone. Out of habit, he must have put it back into his pocket after changing into his shorts. He was amazed he hadn't broken it during the fight.

While Coach Heck talked, he slowly pulled it out and peered down.

Call from . . .
Amanda <3

Joe felt his body grow warm with anticipation. Amanda? What did she want? She was the last person he expected to be calling. But now that she was, he couldn't help but wonder if she was doing it so she can apologize. Maybe she thought about it and had decided her decision to end their relationship was a bit too impulsive. Each time the phone vibrated Joe was more certain of this, as if the vibrations were really Morse code trying to tell him just that.

He glanced up at Coach Heck, still in the middle of his speech, knowing that he should take this call. If he didn't, Amanda might think he was intentionally ignoring her, and if she thought that, then their relationship would be over for sure. Joe weighed his options—to answer or not to answer, that was the question—and decided that anything else Coach Heck could do right now couldn't be any worse than the punishment he had already received. He had already been banned from tryouts, so what was another detention anyway? Content with his decision, he accepted the call and put the phone to his ear.

Heck stopped talking, his mouth hanging open in disbelief. He had to blink to be sure his eyes weren't playing tricks on him. The student before him—the student he was *advising*—had pulled out a cell phone and taken a call. To add to the absurdity of the situation, when Heck tried to speak, the student put up a finger in a gesture for silence.

Joe ignored Coach Heck, turning away. He expected a lot of things—Amanda to be crying, to start yelling, to still be pissed, or possibly even sulking—but the last thing he expected was to hear her father's voice.

"Hello?" Mr. DeFallon said from the other end. "Is this Joe?"

Joe immediately regretted picking up the phone. He didn't need this. Now, on top of the third detention he'd probably just gotten himself, he was going to get screamed at by Amanda's father. She had no doubt told him what had happened. Why else would he be calling?

Joe had met Mr. DeFallon a bunch of times and knew he was the type of parent who looked out for his daughter. He had even questioned Joe about his intentions while Joe waited for Amanda to change one evening, so it didn't shock him that he would be calling now. He was nice but protective, and Joe cringed at the thought of being yelled at.

"Yes," Joe said a bit shakily. "This is Joe."

"Joe, this is Mr. DeFallon, Amanda's father . . ."

Something didn't sound right. Mr. DeFallon's voice was quick, somehow upset. As if he was struggling not to cry. It took Joe by surprise, and he kept silent, waiting for Amanda's father to speak.

Mr. DeFallon sobbed, got himself under control, and then continued. "I'm sorry, Joe. This is just really hard for me." He paused again. After what felt like an eternity, he finally said, "Amanda was hit by a car while she was on her bike. She's in the emergency room right now. It's touch and go."

PART 2

A FERVENT WISH

CHAPTER 14

She made it a point to ignore him. In fact, she made it a point to ignore everyone at the table.

He had seen her twice before—passing in the halls and walking to the buses—and each time she had been with the same girl: a short, chubby redhead with thick legs and a slightly bent nose covered in freckles.

It was the redhead Joe noticed first. She walked out of the hallway connecting the two cafeterias wearing a lime green shirt so bright that the cream wall next to her took on the color. Several people looked at her, and one or two catcalled. She ignored them, looking around the cafeteria. The way her eyes flitted from table to table, she looked more like an animal searching for food than a person.

C.J. groaned. "Here we go again."

If Joe remembered correctly, the redhead's name was Sarah and she was the girl who had introduced herself to C.J. after basketball tryouts. She had been trying out for cheerleading on the other side of the gym and hadn't made the team because of her spastic behavior. At least that's what she had told C.J. with a coquettish giggle. It probably wasn't the only reason, but definitely a major one because when she spotted Joe and C.J.'s table, she nearly tripped over a lunch tray someone had failed to toss into the garbage. Her friend who appeared behind her, however, was the complete opposite: taller and slender, moving with an innate grace only ballerinas could hope to achieve after years of practice. Had *she* tried out for cheerleading, she would have made the team no problem. She had auburn shoulder-length hair, green eyes, and lips a shade of pink that didn't require any gloss to shine.

It was this second girl that Joe was staring at as the two came over.

He was sitting at the table in the center of the west side cafeteria, the table reserved for all basketball players. It wasn't a privilege bestowed by the school faculty, but rather something understood by the students, one of the many unspoken rules of high school. Like how being an athlete gave you an extra point on the Hot Scale.

Joe was with three other teammates—a kid named Ian Richert, who looked like he could be the before picture in an acne commercial, another named Timothy Rogers, who was reading a sports magazine, and C.J.

Tim was reading an article on jump shots when C.J. groaned.

"What?" Tim asked, looking up. Then he saw Sarah. "Oh."

"Yeah, *oh*," C.J. said.

There was another unspoken rule: talking to a younger girl. It was excusable if they were eye candy but looked down upon if they weren't exactly attractive. And by the standards of the Hot Scale, Sarah was anything *but* attractive.

"Hey, C.J.," she said in what was supposed to be a seductive voice when she came over. It turned out to be more comical than anything, and Timmy snickered.

Sarah shot him a venomous look, and that seemed to do it. Ian erupted into laughter and buried his face into his sleeve.

Joe sat silently as this exchange went on, helpless to watch as the social hierarchy of high school produced another victim.

Sarah's friend huffed disapprovingly and tugged at her arm. "Come on, Sarah," she said. But Sarah didn't move. Her feet might as well have been encased in concrete. She just stood there, staring at C.J., determined to wait for him to respond.

Finally, and reluctantly, he did. "Hi, Sarah."

"You remembered my name!"

C.J. sighed. "Yeah."

Joe thought that if he listened close enough, he could hear a single unspoken word in that sigh: *unfortunately*. Sarah obviously interpreted it differently because she was absolutely beaming, her cheeks flushing.

"I'm staying after school today for extra help, and I was thinking that when it's over I might stop by the gym to watch you practice. Would you like that?"

Sarah's friend huffed again, folded her arms across her chest, and turned away. By now all eyes were on her. Sarah seemed to notice because she repeated herself. "C.J., would you like that?"

"Huh? No. Not really." He didn't put any force behind the words, just sort of let them fall out of his mouth. It was enough to cause Ian to erupt into another fit. He guffawed so hard that snot shot out of his nose. Before anyone could say anything, he clamped one hand to his face and plunged the other into his back pocket looking for a tissue. This spectacle was enough to cause the rest of the table to burst into laughter, Joe included. He laughed so hard that tears began to spill down his cheeks.

Sarah's smile drooped and her shoulders slumped. She was standing behind Ian and hadn't seen what happened. Sarah's friend also thought they were laughing at Sarah because she spun around, gave everyone a ruthless stare, and tugged at Sarah's arm again, this time succeeding at pulling her away from the table. Over her shoulder, she shouted, "Grow up!"

Joe watched through a kaleidoscope of tears as the most beautiful girl he had ever set eyes upon walked away.

When the laughing subsided, C.J. wiped his eyes. "Oh, God, that was priceless. Hey, Ian. Think you can do that every time an ugly girl tries to talk to me?"

"You guy are assholes, you know that?" Ian said, wiping his nose with the tissue. "Do I have any snot on my face?"

"You're beautiful," Timmy said. He made a puckering motion with his lips. "And not nearly as much of an asshole as this guy right here." He punched C.J. in the arm. "He might have gotten rid of the beast, but he also got rid of the beauty. Way to go, jerk."

"Who was she anyway?" Joe asked, trying not to sound too interested.

C.J. said, "Some freshman, probably. I've never seen her before. Tell you what, though—I wouldn't mind seeing her again."

Ian and Timmy voiced their approval. Silently, so did Joe.

Turns out he didn't have to wait long. He and C.J. saw her walking in the hall two periods later. Joe was talking about Coach Heck and his famous suicide drill when C.J. tapped his shoulder.

"Hey! Look who it is."

Sure enough, pushing through a jumble of students was Sarah's friend, clutching a book to her chest as she picked her way through the crowd. The second Joe saw her, he felt a warm sensation swell in his chest.

"Stuck up bitch, if you ask me," C.J. said. "All the hot ones are."

But Joe didn't think she was a bitch. It was true that he didn't know anything about her—hell, he didn't even know her name—but for whatever reason, call it wishful thinking, he refused to believe she was stuck up.

"I don't know," he said.

C.J. made a pssssh sound. "Oh, come on. You saw the way she acted at lunch. Wouldn't even look at any of us. *Us!* And we're on the *basketball* team. Tell me that's not stuck up?"

It was a good point. But then again, everyone has a reason for acting the way they do. "Maybe she was upset you made fun of her friend," Joe said.

"Nah, she was being a bitch the second Sarah dragged her over, remember? Plus, I didn't make fun of Sarah. Although that was still great, wasn't it? Did you see the look on her face?"

"Yeah. . . . Great . . ."

"Don't act like you didn't think it was funny; I saw you laughing."

"I was laughing at *Ian*," Joe said. Just the thought of laughing at Sarah made him feel dirty. He wasn't like the other kids on the team. He hated the way they treated people. If anyone was stuck up, it was them, and C.J. was a prime example.

"Uh huh, sure. Anyway, I know these things. She's stuck up. Just look at the way she's walking, like she's got a stick up her ass." He reconsidered. "Like she's got a *dildo* up her ass."

Joe narrowed his eyes and said, "You're just mad she wouldn't give you the time of day."

"Trust me, that girl wouldn't give *anyone* the time of day. I'll prove it. Go up and talk to her."

Joe stopped in his tracks. "Me?"

C.J stopped, too, and a kid bumped into him from behind. C.J. turned around, raised his fists, and jerked his head forward like a pigeon. The kid flinched and scurried away.

"Stupid freshman," he muttered. Then said to Joe: "Yeah, you, Romeo. Five dollars says she turns you down."

"I don't wanna bet." The truth was, Joe didn't want to talk to her. An interesting thing happened when he tried to talk to girls: he regressed in age. Suddenly he became a child looking up at a grown woman. Everything he said came out sounding pointless and stupid. Back in elementary school he'd had social behavioral issues and found it more satisfying to play by himself rather than in a group. The school psychologist sent a note home suggesting to his mother that she enroll him in a sports program so he wouldn't be as shy. It worked. Partially. Over the course of time he grew less timid and made friends, but talking to girls still presented a problem. They were the one obstacle he still couldn't overcome. And being on the basketball team didn't help any. In fact, it made things worse. Either by a lucky pairing of genes or a gift from God, Joe's physical features coupled in such a way that made him easy on the eyes. Add that with playing basketball for the school—especially since making Varsity—and the girls couldn't help but flock to him. For that reason, Joe made it a point to ignore their advances. And because of that, a curious phenomenon occurred: the more he turned them down, the more they wanted him. Surprisingly, turning down pretty girl after pretty girl got him the reputation of a player, even if none of them could claim they actually went out with him.

"Scared?" C.J. said. He tucked his fists into his armpits and flapped his elbows like a chicken. "Bock! Bock!"

Joe shoved him. "Shut up." He wanted to say *I don't see* you *talking to her,* but the thought of that frightened him more than ever. Next to him, C.J. was probably the second most desired kid on the team, and he wasn't afraid to talk to girls. Drawing up the image of C.J. talking to Sarah's friend made Joe's stomach turn. She was beautiful, seemed like she had morals, and deserved better than C.J. Which might have been the reason why Joe said what he said next:

"I'm not afraid."

C.J.'s lips peeled back in his jester's grin to show a set of teeth that would remain free of nicotine stains until his second year of college. "Oh, yeah? *Prove* it." He put his hand against the small of Joe's back and gave him a gentle push.

Reluctantly, Joe went. Almost as soon as he took his first step, it started to happen. He became aware of everything around him. Every footfall turned into a gunshot, every drawn breath a tornado. He walked in slow motion as if he were wading through Jell-O. The students around him seemed to drift by. He had to concentrate and push through the viscid air. His mouth dried up like a desert as he imagined himself talking to her. He licked his lips, and when he tried to speak, his voice came out long and drawn, the pitch deeper than he'd ever heard it before. For a moment, he wasn't even sure it was him who had spoken.

When she didn't respond he drew in a deep, swimming breath and spoke again. "Hey, I'm Joe . . ."

This time she acknowledged him. For a second she looked interested, her cheeks dimpling as she smiled, but then her eyes showed recognition and the glow in them disappeared. "Oh, it's you," she said. "Sir Laughs-A-Lot."

Joe frowned. "No—well yeah—I uh—I guess I was laughing—but—but not at your friend."

Her eyebrows rose. "No? Could have fooled me."

"Honestly. I wasn't." He shoved his hands into his pockets and restlessly played with the balls of lint he found inside. "This kid Ian—he sits at our table—he was sitting there when you came over—he uh—he . . ." He what? Blew snot out his nose? Was he really going to say that?

"What about him? Was he the one who made fun of my cousin?"

Joe blinked in surprise. "Your *cousin?*"

"Yes, Sarah's my cousin, and she's the sweetest girl I know. She didn't deserve to be treated the way she did."

"Ian didn't make fun of her—he—"

"Whatever. I honestly don't know what she sees in your friend C.J. I tried telling her she's wasting her time, but she's still too young to understand."

"Too young?"

"She's a freshman."

"And you're not?"

"No. I'm a junior. My dad and I moved here this summer."

That would at least explain why Joe had never seen her in any of his yearbooks. He was about to raise a different question when she asked it for him. "Why haven't you seen me in any of your classes? I'm in all Honors and AP. And just like Sarah's wasting her time talking to your friend, you're wasting yours talking to me. I don't date jocks. You're all the same."

They were now walking through the corridor that led to the gym, and when she said this, Joe felt a spike of pain shoot through his body.

"Jock? You—you think I'm a jock?"

She didn't have to open her mouth to answer. Her silence was enough.

"I'm not a jock," Joe said defiantly.

"I know your kind."

"But I'm not!"

"Then you're guilty by association." She paused in front of the locker-rooms. "If you want to do something nice then tell your friend to kindly tell my cousin she's too young for him, although I doubt someone like him has a nice bone in his body. Other than that, I have nothing more to say to you."

Joe drew in another deep breath, listening to the blood rush past his eardrums. He wanted to say something slick and witty, something that might make her change her mind, but all that came out was, "Can you tell me your name at least?"

"It's Amanda," she said. Then she disappeared into the locker-room, leaving Joe to watch the door close behind her.

CHAPTER 15

Just looking at her made Joe begin to feel warm all over again. He felt a sudden surge of adrenaline being near her. Her curves were breathtaking, and when he put a hand on her and ran it down her body, he felt his heart begin to race. A small fantasy of the future played in his head: driving her to the beach, to the mall, and basically anywhere else he could think of. He closed his eyes and silently prayed for her to be his.

"What do you think, Joe?" his father asked.

George Panza was standing back with his arms folded across his chest as he watched his son admire the car. The pose did little to improve his appearance—he was not the burly, barrel-chested man of fairy tales but meek and lanky with pale, stalky legs that stuck out of his shorts. An office worker if there ever was one. He wore a salt-and-pepper short-cropped beard, thick glasses that covered most of his face, and spoke quickly, yet almost in a whisper, as though he wanted to say everything he was thinking but didn't want to put any power behind his speech in case he got interrupted.

"It's awesome!" Joe said, breathing in the aroma of the Armor All on the tires. It really was. The car still held magical properties even if it was used. Like all first cars, it was an escape from the monotony of life, a social freedom. And by being a year older than the other juniors, he was granted this privilege alone.

When Joe was in first grade he'd contracted what the doctors believed to be chickenpox, but of course what did doctors know? It had actually turned out to be Impetigo, a common, but highly contagious rash that kept him out of school, forcing him to repeat the grade. The sickness wasn't all bad, however. Although he wasn't the tallest in his year—yet close—he was by far the oldest, and that always had its perks. He'd turned seventeen three weeks ago and a letter from the DMV had arrived shortly after containing that mythical piece of plastic that every teenager dreams of possessing. And it was that piece of plastic he was thinking of now as he stared at his father's boss's car.

"She's a good car," Mr. Lancaster said in his baritone voice. Unlike George, Mr. Lancaster was short, jocose, and almost as round as a ball. "Haven't had any problems with her yet. Of course, that's only because I make her sleep in the garage. Wish I could have said the same for my ex-wife." He bellowed laughter, elbowing a wincing George in the ribs. "But seriously, I haven't had a problem yet. Only thing is that fender bender I got inta the other week. It's just cosmetics though." He pointed out a set of scratches on the right side of the front bumper. "Might want ta fix that, but you don't have ta." He then gestured to the broken headlight. "You *need* ta fix that, though. Don't drive at night until you do. You'll get pulled over for sure."

"Yes, sir," Joe said.

Mr. Lancaster laughed again, a deep, throaty sound like a tugboat's horn. He turned to George and clapped him on the back so hard that the force nearly knocked his glasses off his face. "Your son's a riot, Panza! 'Sir.' Oh, that's rich." He turned back to Joe. "You don't have ta call me 'sir.' You don't work for me like your father. Call me Chaz."

"Yes, sir," Joe said again. Then immediately after: "I mean Chaz."

Mr. Lancaster nearly split his side. "If you call me 'sir' one more time, I'm going ta start calling you 'Little Joey,' like those kangaroos. Now come on, let me show you what she's got ta offer."

He waddled around to the driver's side door and slid in. The car rocked to one side like a ship at sea, and the shocks groaned in protest against his weight.

He pointed to the dash. "You got everything you could ever ask for. Heat, AC, CD, PCP"—he chuckled again at his quick wit—"radio, cruise control, and of course the speeeed-o-meter." The way he said this last made Joe want to crack a smile, but he held it back in case Mr. Lancaster wasn't trying to make a joke. He just nodded as he watched his dad's boss continue to point out the car's features like a game show host showing off a grand prize.

When Mr. Lancaster was done he said, "Hop in."

Joe looked back to his dad.

"Go on," George said in his meek, whispering voice. "See how it runs."

"You're not coming?"

George shook his head. "No, it would probably be best if I didn't. I have to write an email or two." He pulled out his iPhone and began tinkering away.

"That's what I like to hear, Panza," Mr. Lancaster shouted. "Always working. Good man. I want ta see ya on top of that McCammon account."

"Yes, sir."

"So what do you say, Little Joey? We taking this baby for a ride?"

Joe didn't waste any time. He ran around the front of the car, opened the passenger side door, and slid in. The leather felt hot and sticky against his skin, but he basked in the unpleasant sensation.

"Whooooweeeee!" Mr. Lancaster bawled when he shut his door. "Hot in here, isn't it?"

Joe guessed all cars got warm when they were sitting out in the sun for a few hours, even in November. Still, it wasn't unbearable. Mr. Lancaster seemed to think otherwise. His forehead was beaded with sweat and runners trickled down his sideburns.

"What do ya say we get the AC going?" He cranked the engine. It made a *whurr-whurr-whurr* sound, then spluttered to life. A moment later, cool air poured out of the vents. Mr. Lancaster aimed three at his face. Then he turned a knob so that the gentle breeze turned into a gale.

A moment later, he backed the car out of the driveway and into the street. They turned the corner and picked up speed, the red needle of the speedometer—or as Mr. Lancaster had called it, the *speeeed-o-meter*—creeping up to 30 and then 40. "That's nothing," he said, referring to the rubbing sound the car was making. Joe hadn't noticed it until Mr. Lancaster pointed it out, but now that he had, he couldn't ignore it. It sounded like a playing card clicking against the spokes of a bicycle wheel. "Only happens when you step on the gas," he explained. "It's the bumper rubbing against the tire. Wind blows it back. Damn fender bender loosened it up. Just gotta tighten a couple of bolts. I'd do it myself, but I don't have the time."

Joe thought the more plausible reason Mr. Lancaster hadn't tightened it was because he couldn't fit under the car.

"You could probably fix it yourself," Mr. Lancaster went on. "You seem like you're handy. And definitely athletic. Got a pretty good build for a kid. No wonder you made the basketball team. Bet you zip right through the defense."

"Sometimes," Joe said.

"Don't be modest. I can see that grin. Must have gotten your genes from your mother. Sure didn't get them from your father. Bet *he* never played basketball. Am I right?"

He was. The closest thing George Panza had ever played to a sport was chess. His bony frame and lack of muscle made a collision with a two-hundred-pound defenseman hazardous to his health.

Mr. Lancaster put on the blinker and pulled into a parking lot. Joe wasn't surprised to find that it belonged to a Dunkin' Donuts. "Here ya go." He handed Joe the keys. "I'm gonna run in for a second. Stomach's grumbling. When I come out, she's yours ta test drive."

With that, Mr. Lancaster opened the door and hoisted his body out of the car. It rocked wildly again, and then settled. Joe got out as well, and went around to the driver's side. Surprisingly, he didn't have to move the seat back for his long legs (it was already back as far as it could go due to Mr. Lancaster's prodigious stomach). He *did* have to adjust the mirrors, however, but that was an easy task. When he was finished, he sat behind the wheel looking out the windshield, imagining for the first time what it would be like to drive to the movies with a girl at his side, and not just any girl: Amanda, with her auburn hair blowing in the breeze.

He was still in this daydream when Mr. Lancaster knocked on the window. Joe snapped his eyes open and fumbled for the switch to unlock the door.

Mr. Lancaster plopped into the passenger seat, clutching a large white bag and extracting a powdered doughnut. "Police found another body, can you believe that?"

Joe looked at Mr. Lancaster in surprise. "Huh?"

"The Craig's List murderer. The police found another body. The clerk inside was talking about it. You *have* been following the news, haven't ya?"

Joe hadn't, but he'd still heard about the Craig's List murderer. For the past few months, that's all anyone could talk about. The police had discovered a bunch of bodies buried in the sand at the beach, each female, and each having apparently advertised their services as an "escort" on Craig's List. It was a little creepy at first to have the signs of a serial killer in your backyard, but when the police confirmed that the bodies had been buried there for over a year, the urgency quickly waned.

That is, until now.

"They found another?" Joe asked.

Mr. Lancaster nodded, taking a bite out of a second doughnut. "Yeap," he said through a mouth full of powdered sugar. "This one was buried recently, though. Must have just been murdered."

Joe didn't know what to say to this. He settled on, "Wow, that's nuts." Even though the bodies were discovered at a beach only a few miles away, it still felt like it was happening in another place, like it wasn't real. What felt real was the steering wheel under his hands and the leather pressing against his back.

"Yeap," Mr. Lancaster went on, "another escort. You know, I had my fair share of them back in the day. You don't need them though. You'll get plenty of pussy with this car."

Joe stared at him, shocked.

"Come on, I was your age once. Cars turn girls on. Lost my virginity in the back seat." When he saw Joe's eyes widen he quickly added, "Not this one, of course. An old car. Now start her up and give her a test run."

Joe didn't want to imagine his father's overweight boss losing his virginity in the back seat, didn't want to imagine him losing it at all. But as repulsive as it sounded, Mr. Lancaster was right. Cars turned girls on, and Joe secretly hoped that having a car would help his chances with Amanda.

What he didn't know, however, was that having a car would also lead him to make the worst decision of his life.

George Panza was standing on the gravel driveway, still typing on his iPhone, when his son pulled up with his boss and parked behind Mr. Lancaster's brand new Range Rover.

"How was it?" he asked.

"It's great," Joe said. "I love it."

"Perfect first car," Mr. Lancaster added as he pulled his bulk out of the passenger seat. "Don't want ta get something too new, and don't want ta get something too old, either. Know what I mean? The Altima here's perfect. So, what do ya say? You gonna buy it for the boy?"

George tucked his phone back into his pocket and pushed his glasses up the bridge of his nose. "Buy it? Gee I'm not sure. We only stopped by because you said we might be interested."

Mr. Lancaster waddled over to George and put a meaty arm around his shoulder. "Come on, Panza, your boy *is* interested. It's a smart buy. And I'm letting it go for a steal. Thousand dollars less than what I intend ta list it in the papers. What do you say?"

"I still don't know," George said. "With the McCammon account, I haven't found the time to talk to Maggie about another car yet."

Mr. Lancaster raised his hands, palms out. "Of course, of course. I wouldn't want ta pressure you into a decision. In fact, pressuring you is the last thing I would want ta do. How about I give Rogers the

McCammon account instead? That should take away some of the pressure at work and give ya a little more free time."

George blinked, the import of the words hitting him hard. "Give it to Rogers?" His voice was barely audible.

Mr. Lancaster grinned, the features of his face contorting to make him look sly and incredibly vulpine, like a fox. "Well, sure. If you can't find the time ta talk to your wife, then I'm obviously putting too much pressure on ya. I'll remedy that. No worries."

George cast a nervous glance at his son, but Joe was pacing around the car, looking it over dreamily, the way people do when they study a coveted item.

"Mr. Lancaster, I really need that account. Maggie's been wanting to go on a vacation for a while now and things between us haven't been as good as they used to be. I really need the commission to—"

"No, no, don't worry about it, Panza. Working's never worth the stress. Not good for your ticker." He made a show of thumping his chest. "How could I live with myself if I knew I was the cause of a coronary? Rogers is young and fresh and would be more than happy ta take on—"

"I'll buy the car," George said, defeated.

"What's that?"

"I'll buy the car."

Mr. Lancaster's grin broadened. "You will? Oh, that's excellent." He raised his voice. "Hey, Joe, did ya hear the good news? Your dad's buying you the car! She's all yours!"

Joe looked up at once, his face a mixture of surprise, elation, and skepticism, each emotion pulling equally in an opposite direction. "Are you serious?"

Mr. Lancaster nudged George, pushing him forward. "Go on. Tell him, Panza."

George swallowed. "It's—it's all yours, son. Just keep your grades up and don't get into trouble."

Joe beamed. He rushed over to his father, and for the first time in five years, embraced him in a hug. George hugged back, thankful that his son couldn't see the uneasy expression on his face.

CHAPTER 16

"You did what?" Margaret Panza shouted.

"I bought Joe a car."

"I heard what you said, George! I just can't believe you would go and do such a stupid thing like that! You didn't even consult me!"

They were in the kitchen, George with his back pressed up against the counter, feeling cornered, his wife standing in front of him with her arms planted on her wide hips. She wasn't by any definition fat—certainly nowhere in the ballpark of Mr. Lancaster—but she was stocky, and easily outweighed George by thirty pounds. The way she raised her voice and glared at him made him feel like he was back in elementary school being reprimanded for placing a wad of chewing gum under a desk.

"You *know* we're saving money for a vacation, and not just any vacation, our *marriage retreat.* Honestly, George. Am I the only one trying to keep this marriage together? How are we supposed to afford the trip now?"

George drew in breath and spoke in his quick, whispering voice. "Well, I was thinking, maybe if you didn't spend so much on shopping, we could—"

"I only buy what's on sale, George!"

"Yes, but you buy things you don't need. You—"

"I *do* need those things! Don't try to turn the tables! *You* were the irresponsible one who bought the car."

"Maggie, he let us have it at a steal. What was I supposed to do?"

"Umm . . . say *no*? Say you have to talk it over with your *wife?* Jesus, you could have told him *anything* but yes."

"But, Maggie, he's my boss."

"That sleazebag's only your boss during working hours. Bottom line, we needed that money and you spent it." She picked up a rolling pin, and for one moment George feared she was going to strike him with it, but then she slammed it down onto a ball of cookie dough and began rolling it flat, probably imagining it as her husband's head. "I swear, George, you make me so angry sometimes . . ."

George let her roll her frustrations out. When she looked like she had calmed down a bit he said, "We can afford the trip once I get the commission for the McCammon account. Plus, the car might bring Joe and me closer together. You can consider it an investment."

"*Investment.* That's horrible," Margaret said. "Do you hear the words coming out of your mouth? Not everything is banking. If you wanted to have a stronger relationship with your son, you should have invested your time more wisely instead of spending it at work or locked away in that damn room of yours."

"He hugged me when he found out he was getting the car."

"Great. Buy our son's love. That's a perfect example you're setting."

"It's not buying, it's—"

"I don't want to hear what you think it is. Where is he now?"

George sighed. "Out front. Washing the car."

She marched into the living room and peered out the window. Sure enough Joe was in the driveway, bent over the car with a sponge. Margaret didn't even need to look long before she spied the damage. "Christ, and it's been in an accident, too! This just keeps on getting better!"

George reached out, hesitated, and then put a reassuring hand on his wife's shoulder. "Maggie, it isn't as bad as it looks."

"Oh, it's not?" she said, rounding on him. "Buying your son a lemon isn't bad?"

George flinched, shrinking back. When he gathered up enough courage, he said, "It's not a lemon. Only a headlight's broken and the bumper's scratched. It runs fine. Joe test-drove it before I wrote out the check. Plus, it'll be good for him. Fixing it up will teach him discipline."

"So now you think our son needs discipline?"

George bit his tongue. "No, Maggie, that's not what I meant. He'll just appreciate it more if it needs some fixing up."

"You didn't even have it checked out by a mechanic, did you?"

"Well no, I—"

Margaret brushed past him, shaking her head in disgust. George didn't even bother to follow her. All he did was listen as she picked up the phone, dialed, and said, "Hello, Luke?"

Joe dipped the sponge into the bucket, watching as it absorbed the soapy water. The car hadn't been dirty, but he felt that since it now belonged to him he should wash it again. Almost as if he were baptizing it, washing away the original owner.

He thought about calling C.J. to tell him the incredible news, but in the end decided not to. It was better to let the car remain his little secret for now. Plus, he didn't really want to start showing it off until he could fix the broken headlight anyway.

He worked methodically, starting at the back and carefully working his way forward, soaping a fender, scrubbing a spot or two, then rinsing. When he got about halfway to the front, he stopped. The water in the bucket, which had once resembled the ocean at Key West, now looked more like the Great South Bay—brown and murky. He spilled it out, watching it trickle down the driveway like a dirty stream. As he was filling the bucket again, he saw the garage door to the house across the street open. A man with short hair wearing a white t-shirt stepped out, holding his four-year-old by the hand. Joe waved. Luke casually waved back.

Even though Luke had moved in two years ago, the only communication he and Joe had ever shared was the perfunctory neighborly wave.

Today, that changed.

Luke let his little girl lead him down the driveway but stopped when she came to the street. He hunkered down, wincing and grabbing his back, and whispered something in her ear. After they over-exaggeratingly looked both ways, they crossed.

"Hi, Joseph," the little girl said when she ran over.

"Hey, Kendra," Joe said. "Gimme five." He held his hand out and Kendra slapped it. When she did, Joe shook it, pretending that the slap hurt. "Wow, you're getting strong!"

Kendra giggled and ran around the car.

"Stay in the driveway, sweetie," Luke called out. For the first time, Joe realized that his neighbor bore a slight resemblance to Nicolas Cage. It was something about his narrow face and high cheekbones. Had he seen Luke up close before, he probably would have noticed this earlier.

"I see you got yourself a car there," Luke said.

Joe beamed, unable to help himself. "Yeah, my dad and I just picked it up today."

Luke looked it over. "Very nice, very nice. By the way, I don't think I've officially introduced myself. I'm Luke." He held out his hand.

Joe shook it. "I know. My mom always talks about you guys whenever she goes over and plays with Kendra."

"Your mom's very nice. If it wasn't for her, I think Crystal would go crazy staying home with Kendra all day." Luke paused, looking at the bucket Joe was filling. "What kind of soap are you using?"

"Huh?"

"To wash your car."

"Oh. I don't know. This stuff." Joe held up a clear bottle with blue liquid inside. "It was on the shelf."

Luke shook his head. "You should use Meguiar's. It's a thicker blend, and it's supposed to brighten the paint. I have some in the garage if you want it for next time."

"Cool. Thanks."

"Don't mention it."

Luke was about to say more when Kendra interrupted him. She was at the front of the car jumping up and down and pointing as she chanted "Broken! Broken!" in a high squeaky voice.

Luke drew in breath when he saw the headlight. "Oooh. I can help you fix that, if you want."

"You can?" Joe asked.

"Sure, I'm a mechanic."

"Really? I didn't know that."

"Now you do. I had to leave my job to have back surgery"—he lifted his shirt to show Joe the brace wrapped around his midsection—"so you'll probably see a lot more of me now. I have about thirty thousand dollars worth of tools sitting in the garage. It'd be a shame if they just sat there for the next two months. Feel free to come by if you need anything."

"I definitely will," Joe said. "Thanks."

"That's what neighbors are for. So, where's your mother hiding? She invited Kendra over to play with Snowball."

"She's in the house, I think. The door should be open."

"Thanks," Luke said, taking his daughter's hand. "Don't forget my offer."

"I won't."

When they vanished into the house, Joe dipped the sponge back into the soapy water. A breeze picked up, and for the first time while washing his car, he felt a chill.

CHAPTER 17

The gymnasium erupted into cheers. Rick Ridel, the point guard for the Farmsville Black Hawks, had just driven through the opposing team's defense and was approaching the basket. He looked left, faked right, and spun around, dribbling towards the hoop. Coach Heck screamed at him to watch his back for the love of God, there was a man on. Before anyone could stop him, however, Rick leaped into the air and scored with a lay-up. The crowd went wild.

"That's what I'm talking about!" Coach Heck shouted, spraying spit everywhere. He pulled the team in for a briefing, spoke quickly, and sent them out again. Joe and C.J would be in next, followed by three other boys. C.J. watched the game as he waited on the bench for the whistle. Joe scanned the bleachers instead.

The past two nights had been filled with thoughts of Amanda. As he lay in bed, he replayed his conversation with her and imagined it lasting longer, coming up with witty things to say to her responses. In his fantasy, she asked him what he liked to do when he wasn't playing basketball, and he told her that he liked to fish. To his surprise she also liked to fish, and they stood in the hall until the bell rang, talking about their biggest catches. Joe knew something this spontaneous would never happen in real life—he just wasn't smooth enough and couldn't think that fast under pressure—and he doubted that she liked to fish, but he *did* think that by having a premeditated conversation he could lower his risk of sounding stupid if they talked again. So for the rest of the night, until sleep closed his eyes, he envisioned their next conversation, coming up with a response to every possible thing she could say.

During school, he kept an eye out for her in hopes that he would have a chance to make that conversation real. He knew this was a cliché, but there was something about her that made her different from the other girls. Maybe it was her attitude, or the way she stuck up for her cousin. Whatever it was, it was enough to make Joe want to try talking to her again. He knew he'd never see her in any of his classes so he decided to spend a bit more time in the hall. He wasn't rewarded for his labors until the break between sixth and seventh period earlier today. By then, he was alone and walking to the science wing when he spotted her. She was also alone, and before Joe knew what he was doing, he was off, excusing himself through the crowd so he could get to her, the premeditated conversation and all her possible responses whizzing around in his head. He would have reached her, too, if he hadn't bumped into a freshman and knocked him down. By the time Joe helped him up, Amanda was gone.

That is, until now. He'd been searching the bleachers in hopes that he might find her. He knew it would be a long shot—she hated jocks, but there was a chance she'd be here to show her school spirit—and sure enough, there she was, about five tiers from the top and all the way over to the right, sitting next to her cousin, who, today, was wearing a pink neon shirt.

Joe had to blink to make sure she was really there. When she didn't vanish, he felt his chest swell with that incredible heat again. He dropped his head between his legs and sucked in air like Coach Heck had told him to do whenever he was feeling dizzy.

C.J. punched him in the side. "What's wrong with you?"

Joe sat up. "Look at the bleachers."

"At what? The fans? So what? They're always there."

"Just look. All the way to the right. A little down from the top. See the pink shirt?"

C.J. narrowed his eyes. "Christ. I don't believe it! She's stalking me!"

"Not her. Look who's sitting next to her."

C.J. looked again. "Ooh la la. The girl who got away. You like her or something?"

Joe didn't say anything. He was hoping C.J. would goad him into talking to her again. At least if he did then he wouldn't have to admit that he had what felt like a middle school crush.

When Joe didn't answer, C.J. said, "Hey, I asked if you liked her."

Joe mumbled something.

"What was that?"

"I said yes, okay?"

C.J. raised both hands, shooting them out toward the ceiling. "Hallelujah! I thought you might've been gay or something, turning down all those girls that hit on you. I was actually a little leery to change next to you today. Thought if I bent over you might've—"

Now it was Joe's turn to punch him. "Bite me."

"As long as you don't try to bite me back! But I guess since you're not queer, you wouldn't want a fine piece of ass like mine anyway." He leaned over as if he were going to fart and slapped his right buttock. "Who woulda thought you just had taste?" He looked at Amanda again. "She really is one of the hottest girls I've ever seen. You gonna try to talk to her again?"

Joe wanted to. He just needed to get up enough courage.

"Come on," C.J. said. "He who hesitates, masturbates, and man your right hand must be getting tired. Why don't you give it a rest and let someone else do it for a change?"

Joe punched him again.

"Go talk to her after the game. I wanna watch you strike out this time."

And that's when it hit him. He had struck out the last time he tried talking to her. It didn't matter if he practiced his conversational skills. The bottom line was that she didn't like him. No amount of talking would change that. Unless. . . . That was when Joe remembered what she had said: *If you want to do something nice then tell your friend to kindly tell my cousin she's too young for him, although I doubt someone like him has a nice bone in his body.* She might not have known it, but she had asked him to do her a favor, and if he made good on it then that was at least the first step in gaining her trust.

"Fine," Joe said. "I'll talk to her."

"Really? Even after she turned you down? Wow, who woulda thought that—"

"As long as you come with me."

C.J. raised his hands. "Na-uh. No way. I'm not going anywhere near Sarah. Last thing I need is that little redheaded troll following me around all year."

"Then I'm not going."

"Fine by me."

"Come on, C.J.," Joe pleaded. "I need you to apologize to Sarah and—"

"*Apologize?* For what?"

"For making fun of her, for leading her on, I don't care. I just need you to tell her you're sorry and—"

"Whoa, I never led her on, and I'm *not* telling her I'm sorry. If I do that she'll probably think I'll want to marry her or something. Freshmen are stupid, especially the girls. You say one nice thing to them and they fall head over heels for you. You should probably be thankful Sarah's friend turned you down. Saves you a hell of a headache."

"Her name's Amanda. And she's in our grade," Joe said.

"Really?"

"Yeah. And all I need you to do is tell Sarah that you're sorry, but you don't wanna go out with her."

"Wait, you want me to turn her down again?" C.J. grinned devilishly. "Okay, I'll go with you. This'll be amusing."

"But you have to do it nicely," Joe told him. "Tell her she's too young."

"Where's the fun in that?"

"Who cares? Just do it." Joe knew C.J. wouldn't unless there was a good enough reason, and Joe certainly wasn't about to tell him it was because he thought it would improve his chances with Amanda. Therefore he came up with: "Like you said, freshmen are stupid. If you make fun of her again she might think you're trying to flirt. Being nice and telling her the truth is the only way to get her off your back."

C.J. considered this. "I guess you're right. I mean, if she's still coming around after the way we all laughed at her, then she obviously needs me to spell it out."

"So you'll do it?"

"Yeah. What the hell. After all, it's a small price to pay to watch you strike out again."

"Gee, thanks."

"Hey, if we can't ask each other to turn down ugly girls then what are friends for?"

"Panza, Galeno! Are you two deaf?" Coach Heck shouted. His face was so red that the vein in his neck nearly exploded. *"Don't you hear me calling your goddamn names? Get in there!"*

Joe and C.J. looked at one another in surprise and nearly leaped off the bench. In less than three seconds they were lost amongst the players chasing the ball.

The buzzer rang and the fans in the bleachers supporting the Black Hawks broke out into a frenzy, screaming, hugging one another, holding up signs, laughing. The Black Hawks did the same on the court, slapping each other five and messing up their teammates' hair. Their first game had been close and Coach Heck would give them hell for it later, but they had won, and that's all that mattered. Between Joe and C.J., they had scored a total of fifty-seven points and found themselves at the center of the embrace.

When the group hug finally broke apart, Joe scanned the bleachers for Amanda. If he thought the claustrophobia of the hug was intense, it was nothing compared to the bleachers. Students, parents, and friends stood on what looked like an amusement park line from hell. It was worse than a school photo, people standing shoulder to shoulder, pushing and shoving to make their way down the bleachers. Amanda was nowhere in sight and neither was Sarah, which was saying a lot since she quite possibly had on the brightest shirt in the building.

Joe decided to wait until the crowd died down before trying to find her. While the rest of his team walked to the locker-room, he made his way over to the bench and sat down. There were a million thoughts buzzing around his head, and he needed a minute to sort them out. At the forefront was the conversation he hoped to have with Amanda. He kept replaying it, going over the responses to every possible thing she could say. He would start off by asking her if she had enjoyed the game and branch off from there, asking her what activities she enjoyed. If all went well, he would not only learn more about her, but she would learn more about him, too, and see that he wasn't the stereotypical jock. The only thing was, he had to find her first.

"What're you still doing out here?" C.J. said, walking up to Joe. "Thought you'd be in the locker-room by now staring at the guys' asses. Oh wait, I forgot you actually *do* like girls."

As annoyingly playful as C.J. could be, Joe could always count on him to break the tension. He hadn't realized how nervous he was until now. His shoulders felt like they were bunched up in knots, and he was clasping his hands so tight that they began to ache.

"I'm looking for Amanda," he said honestly.

"Wow, you really wanna give her an excuse to turn you down, don't you? You know you smell like Coach Heck's left armpit right now, right?"

Joe didn't hear him; he was too busy staring at a smudge of pink in the crowd. He followed it with his eyes until a tall, doofy-looking kid moved out of the way and Sarah appeared.

"There she is!" he said. "Come on. Time to make good on your promise." He shot up and grabbed C.J., pulling him toward the bleachers. "Remember, be nice."

"Yeah, yeah, yeah," C.J. muttered.

By the time they reached Sarah, she was standing with Amanda and another girl about four rows down from where they had been sitting. Sarah was the first to notice the two boys approaching. The mouth under her crooked nose turned up in a smile when she realized that one of them was C.J.

"Hayyy!" she said.

"Hey," C.J. said back, although without echoing any of her enthusiasm.

By now Amanda looked to see who Sarah was talking to. The second she noticed who it was she did what Joe thought of as that-cute-little-huff-thing and turned around to face the other girl, contorting her hands in front of her like she was doing origami with invisible paper.

Joe elbowed C.J. in the ribs.

"Oh, right. Sarah, can I talk to you?"

Sarah looked ecstatic. "Sure! What do you want to talk about?"

"Us."

Her smile swelled even more, but after what C.J. said next it completely deflated, like a balloon that had gotten a hole in it.

"There can't be any *us.* You're a very nice girl, but you're just too young. It wouldn't work. I'm sorry."

Sarah buried her face into her hands and sobbed hysterically. That was when she ran down the bleachers and bumped into a girl with glasses who, in turn, bumped into the boy one tier down, and so on, causing a domino effect. Without even waiting to see if they were okay, she pushed through the throng and was gone.

It took every ounce of strength for C.J. not to laugh. "That went pretty well. Don't ya think?" he said instead.

That was when Amanda spun around, her hands still knotted in front of her. "You made her cry and you have the nerve to make fun of her?"

C.J. either didn't hear or pretended not to because all he said was, "What's wrong with your hands?"

The question took Amanda by surprise. She looked down at them and then back up at C.J. "Nothing's wrong with them," she said harshly. "It's sign language. Julia's deaf." She gestured toward the girl behind her.

"And so was my little brother. Don't make fun. And don't try to change the subject."

"*Change* it? I wasn't even talking to you."

"Well, you made my cousin cry so now you *are* talking to me."

Joe didn't like the way this was going. He tried getting C.J.'s attention so he could tell him they needed to get to the locker-room, but Amanda had spurred C.J. on. He glared at her with the same eyes that made so many freshmen cower. "Listen, honey, I only came up here because Joe asked me to tell Sarah that I'd never go out with a troll like her. Okay? This has nothing to do with you."

"Troll?" Amanda screamed. Without any warning she leaped at C.J. the way a cougar does, coiling her legs and pushing off. She caught him in the chest, and he tumbled over. The crash they made when they hit the bleachers was so loud that everyone turned around.

Amanda swung her fists like the paddles of a windmill, letting them crash down on C.J.'s face. He put his hands up to block just in time and rolled. Since Amanda had her legs clinched around his waist, she rolled with him and they changed places. Now he was on top, straddling her. The students around them cheered, their shouts rising to a deafening roar when C.J. pinned her wrists back. He held them against the bleachers until the junior advisor, Mr. Banks, a tall African American man with a neck as thick as some of the freshmen's waists, rushed over and pulled them apart.

Joe could only watch in disbelief, knowing full well that any chance he might have had with Amanda was now long gone.

CHAPTER 18

There were no cars in the driveway, but Joe rang the bell anyway. He had asked his mother if she thought Luke would be home, and she had said that she thought he would. He told her how Luke had introduced himself a few days ago and how he had mentioned that he was a mechanic. He also told her how Luke had offered to help him fix the broken headlight.

"Really?" his mother said, hiding a coy smile. "That was very nice of him."

It *was* nice, Joe thought. He guessed that's what happened when you either didn't work or couldn't work . . . or when your mother made a phone call.

Footsteps approached the door, and Luke answered. He spoke Joe's full name, enunciating the two syllables heavily, something Joe would become used to: "*Joe-seph*, what can I do for you?"

After what felt like forever, the insurance on Joe's car had finally gone into effect, and he was ready to drive it to school. He just wanted to fix the headlight first.

"Hey, Luke. I was wondering—well, I cleaned my car. Vacuumed it and everything. But . . ."

"But you're afraid that when you drive it, the only thing people will notice is the broken headlight?"

Joe nodded. "Can you help me fix it?"

Luke looked at his watch. "Can you wait about an hour? Crystal's not home yet, and I can't leave Kendra alone."

"Yeah, sure, that'd be great. Thank you."

"I'll come by when I'm ready. The junkyards don't close for a few hours. We should have plenty of time."

"Junkyard?" Joe asked uncertainly.

"Sure." Luke pointed to Joe's car, parked against the curb. "That's an oh-eight, right?"

"Yeah."

"Let me make a few calls, and I'll see what I can do. I'll be over in about an hour."

Joe thanked him again and walked back across the street, feeling doubtful. Was Luke being serious when he mentioned the junkyard, or was that just his way of joking? Joe's car wasn't junk. It wasn't new, but it certainly wasn't old, either. He had cleaned it, and it looked rather nice. It didn't deserve to have a headlight from a car that had been in an accident. It would probably wind up being some cracked, foggy piece of crap, too. He wanted something new, clear, and shiny. Something to match the way the rest of the car looked. It figured: first C.J. had ruined any shot Joe had with Amanda, and now Luke was going to ruin any shot he had at making his car look nice. Combined, the two were a little too much to handle. When Joe got to his room he buried his face in his pillow feeling as if the world was against him.

Sometime later something wet pushed up against the back of his hand. Joe pulled it away, snapping his eyes open. When he saw Snowball, he patted his bed, still feeling a bit like a child who had let his emotions run away.

"Come on, boy. Up."

Snowball obeyed, leaping onto the bed and licking Joe's face.

"Thank you," Joe said. He put his arm around his dog and hugged him, feeling slightly better. He stroked Snowball's fur, wondering how he could fix things. Amanda, sadly, was a lost cause, but he could still tell Luke that he had changed his mind about needing his help. He was debating on what he could say when there was a knock at the front door.

Luke spoke the minute Joe opened it. "Joseph, you ready?"

Joe hesitated, unsure of what to do. He knew every minute that passed he was a minute closer to the junkyard. He thought about using an excuse or flat out lying that he couldn't go, but in the end he gave in. "Sure," he said hopelessly.

"Why do you look so glum?" Luke asked. "Come on, grab your keys."

"You want me to drive?"

"Of course! Show me what your car can do!"

The prospect of driving cheered Joe up. He'd sat behind the wheel countless times after getting the car, but he hadn't driven it since that time with Mr. Lancaster. Just the thought of pushing on the gas and hearing the rumble under the hood made him feel a little giddy.

"Okay, give me one minute."

He thought Luke would talk as he drove, commenting on his driving or even asking questions about the car, but all he did was sit silently in the passenger seat. Joe thought about asking him something to start a conversation, but when he saw the distant look in Luke's eyes, he didn't. Luke was so still and quiet that he looked like a wax figure. It was a little unnerving, and when it got too much to handle, Joe reached for the radio. Before he could turn it on, however, Luke said, "Slow down."

It was the last thing Joe would have expected him to say. Slow down? Was he serious? He was only going five miles over the speed limit. He checked his rearview mirror and the car behind him was nearly up his ass. Slow down? If he did that the guy would be more than up his ass, he'd be *in* it.

Luke said it again, this time more sternly, and Joe listened, taking his foot off the accelerator and letting the car drift. He watched as the needle on the speedometer—or *speeeed-o-meter* in Lancaster-eese—gradually dropped to thirty and then twenty-five. The car behind him honked. Luke responded by cocking his head to the side, the way a dog does when it hears something it doesn't understand. That was when Joe started to get nervous. Out of the two years that Luke had lived across the street, this was only their second encounter. What if he was a rapist? People you never expected hid the deepest, darkest secrets. What if he was crazy? Or what if the medication for his back surgery was fucking with his brain? Joe was a full three inches taller than Luke so if a struggle broke out Joe could easily overpower him, especially with the condition Luke's back was in. But when fear got the best of you, you didn't think logically.

The needle continued to drop.

Twenty-two.

Twenty.

Eighteen.

Joe glanced at Luke out of the corner of his eye, not daring to look at him full-on. He still had his head cocked. Joe stole another look in the rearview mirror. The car behind him was flashing its brights and honking religiously. Joe's nervous mind turned the sequence into a frantic S.O.S.

"Floor it," Luke said.

Joe raised his eyebrows. "Huh?"

"Floor it."

"But I thought you wanted me to slow down."

Don't argue with a lunatic, you idiot! his mind yelled.

"I did," Luke said. "Now, floor it."

Joe did, distancing himself from the jackass behind him. The needle on the speedometer began to rise again. When it crept past thirty-five, Luke told him to ease off the gas and keep the speed constant.

"Did you hear that?"

Joe hadn't heard anything except his heart pounding in his chest. In fact, he could still hear it now. He decided there was a perfectly good reason why he hadn't met Luke until a few days ago: God was protecting him. Only now, he must have done something to royally piss Him off because God had forced Luke into his life.

"Well, did you?" Luke pressed.

Joe shook his head. "Hear what?"

"That rubbing sound."

"The what? Oh!" Understanding dawned, and all the uneasiness drained away. "That's the bumper rubbing against the wheel," Joe said. "When you pick up speed it bends backwards."

"Pull over," was all Luke said.

When the jackass behind him sped past blasting his horn, Luke casually stuck up his middle finger. "Leave the engine running and pop the hood. You're going to have to lift it for me since I can't lift anything heavy."

Joe got out of the car and found the latch. He propped the hood open and took a step back. The engine compartment was as black as the inside of a fireplace. Grease, about a quarter of an inch thick, coated everything and anything inside. Joe was a little embarrassed to discover it looked like this. Luke didn't comment. He just stuck his hand into the running engine and fumbled around.

Joe immediately grew nervous. He forgot that no more than a minute ago he had been afraid of his neighbor. Now he was afraid *for* him.

"Hey—" he said, meaning to say something to the effect of *Are you sure that's a smart thing to do?* But before he could, the engine lifted up and roared with life.

Joe jumped back and cried out. Luke only looked at him and laughed.

"Did you hear it?" he asked.

Joe shook his head, trying to gather himself.

Luke thumbed some type of lever in the engine, and it lifted up again, roaring. This time Joe *did* hear something, or at least he thought he did. It sounded like the rubbing he'd heard a few minutes ago, except now it didn't sound like the bumper rubbing against the wheel at all. It sounded like it was coming from under the hood.

"Yeah," Joe said. "What is it?"

Luke thumbed the lever once more and then released it, pulling his hand out of the engine. He looked for all of two seconds before pointing out a tube sitting in front of the fan. "It's this," he said. "It's your radiator hose. When you step on the gas, the engine shifts and pushes it into your fan." He looked around the engine a little bit more and then said, "This car was in an accident."

"I know," Joe said. "Mr. Lancaster, my dad's boss, told me. A fender bender."

Luke pressed his lips together. "That might have been what broke the headlight and scratched the bumper, but it's not what shifted the engine compartment. Here, look . . ." He showed Joe how the strut on one side was uneven and how there was less of a space between the parts under that side of the hood.

"So, it was really in another accident?"

Luke nodded. "A pretty bad one, by the looks of it. Whoever fixed it up did a good job on the exterior bodywork, just didn't take the time to straighten out the frame."

"Son of a bitch," Joe grumbled. He now realized why his mother hated Mr. Lancaster so much.

"Don't worry about it," Luke said. "It doesn't look like it's affecting the performance. The rest of the car looks fine. I'll help you straighten it out a bit when we get back to the house, if you want. For now, let's go get your headlight."

The junkyard was exactly what its name implied: a pile of junk in a yard. Except the yard was huge, metal upon metal piled up high in great big mounds, and it was behind a store instead of a house. Joe parked in the lot and got out. Luke shielded his eyes from the sun and looked around like he was a captain at sea trying to find the distant horizon. He took in a deep breath of air—air that smelled like a combination of grease and motor oil—and let it out in satisfaction.

"Smells just like a garage," he said as he walked over to the building.

The bell above the door chimed and a broad-shouldered man behind the counter looked up. The blue jumpsuit he wore was stained so badly that it almost looked black. It matched the stains on his hands and forearms.

"How can I help you two?" he asked.

Luke walked up to the counter, reading the man's name off the little patch sewn onto his jumpsuit. "Frank, I'm looking for Mr. Hillstrom."

While Frank called into the back room, Joe busied himself by looking at the items on the shelves. Where he might have expected to find things carefully arranged and neatly packaged, he found radios, sun visors, mirrors, and other sorts of knickknacks strewn haphazardly about, each affixed with a circular orange sticker with a number written in the center. He picked up a foggy headlight. According to the price, it was thirty dollars. So that was what he would be spending. He frowned, wedged it carefully between two radios, and checked on Luke. He was tapping his fingers on the counter as he waited for Mr. Hillstrom. A moment later, a man wearing slacks and a button-down shirt walked out of the back office. He took one look at Luke and shouted, "Wow! Talk about the devil walking through the door! How the hell are ya, Luke? Heard you were going in for surgery!"

"Had it," Luke said. "I'm recovering now. Should be about two months before I'm back to work."

Mr. Hillstrom came around the counter and embraced Luke in a hug. Joe could tell from the delicate way he put his hands around Luke that he was afraid of hurting him.

"What about you? How's the yard?"

"Oh, you know. Same shit, different day."

They talked for what might have been five minutes, subjects that Joe realized would become the formalities of conversation after a certain age—how's the wife and kids, your health, and that last dying strive at an attempt to prolong the conversation: the weather—while Joe continued to pick through the litter on the shelf. Finally, he heard his name being called.

"Joseph, come over here for a minute. I'd like you to meet my friend, Mark. Mark, this is Joseph, my neighbor."

Mark/Mr. Hillstrom extended a hand. Joe noticed that it had no grease on it whatsoever. "Pleased to meet you. Any friend of Luke's is a friend of mine."

"Same here," said Joe, taking his hand.

"So what can I do for you, Luke? I'm sure you didn't just stroll in to bullshit with an old friend, not with your neighbor with you."

"I wouldn't mind it, but you're right. I'm looking for a headlight. I called ahead and one of your guys said he could order one for me."

"Sure," Mr. Hillstrom said. "Let me take a look and see if it came in." He walked over to a computer and started tapping away. "Two thousand and eight Altima, correct?"

"That's right," Joe said.

Mr. Hillstrom nodded. "Yup. Says here we have it. Hey, Frank! Come over here for a minute." The broad-shouldered man strode over. "Headlight for a two thousand and eight Altima. Should be with the batch of parts that just came in."

Frank disappeared. When he came back he was holding a cardboard box, which he handed to Joe. Joe opened it the way a child opens a Christmas present that he already knows is a sweater: slowly and without any joy. He prepared himself to put on a false smile when he saw the foggy headlight nestled inside. Except when he opened it, the headlight was new and clear.

"Is that it?" Mr. Hillstrom asked.

Joe had no idea which headlight fit what car so he showed Luke.

"That's the one," Luke said.

"Excellent. Let me ring you up." Mr. Hillstrom punched a few buttons on the cash register. If a used headlight was thirty dollars, Joe assumed a new one would be somewhere between fifty or sixty. He'd only brought forty with him. When the number 70 appeared on the screen, his heart dropped. It wasn't an incredible price, and he *had* just gotten his paycheck from his job at the sporting goods store the other day, but it was more than he'd intended to spend. He dipped his hand into his pocket, rubbing together the four ten dollar bills he'd brought with him, feeling a bit embarrassed. He was about to ask Luke if he could borrow some money when Mr. Hillstrom hit another button on the cash register. 70 disappeared and 30 took its place.

"Damage comes to thirty," he said.

Joe handed him the money, confused.

"Thanks, Mark," Luke said, "I appreciate it."

Mr. Hillstrom dismissed the gratitude. "Nonsense. You help me out when I come to you, why wouldn't I do the same when you come to me?"

"You're a good man, Mark."

Understanding dawned. "Yeah, thanks!" Joe said sincerely.

"Don't mention it, kid. Take care of that car. And, Luke, take care of that back. When you're all healed up, we'll start bowling again. Guys on my league are terrible."

"Sounds like a plan," Luke said. "If you're not doing anything during the week, maybe we can grab some drinks and watch the game."

"I'd like that," Mr. Hillstrom said, "but you know how it is with the wife and kids."

"Trust me," Luke said. "I know."

CHAPTER 19

It didn't take them long to fix the headlight; Luke had the knowledge and skill of a surgeon. Except where a surgeon dealt with blood, tissue, and organs, Luke dealt with oil, hoses, and metal. After loosening two screws, the broken headlight popped right out. Joe tossed it aside as Luke handed him the new one.

"It should slide right in and click into place," Luke told him. "Just make sure it goes in straight. Last thing you want to do is break the prongs on the new one."

Joe did as he was instructed. Luke didn't hover over his shoulder like he expected, the way an eager father might hover over a son doing homework. He just sat back, either staring off into the sky or at the slowly growing grass. Joe guessed that when you went from working ten-hour shifts to having two months off, your mind found itself wandering. He pushed the headlight a little harder and heard the click. "How's that?"

"Looks good," Luke said. "Now just put those two screws back in and you'll be in business."

After the headlight, they bent the frame. Luke poked around in his garage until he found a long metal rod used for breaking up concrete. He told Joe where to place it in the engine compartment and which way to pull. The job required a lot of effort, but it finally paid off. The frame shifted slightly; not enough to resemble the other side, but enough to notice a change, and after Luke secured the problematic hose with a zip-tie, it stopped rubbing against the fan.

About halfway through, Crystal gave Kendra two cans of Coke, which she struggled to bring out to them.

"Thanks, sweetie," Luke said, taking the drinks from his daughter. They stood on the driveway staring at the car: Luke and Kendra together, Joe off to the side wiping the grease off his fingers with a rag. He felt a sense of satisfaction knowing that he had been the one to do the work. Now that the headlight was replaced, the Altima really did look new. If it wasn't for the date on the registration, someone might have mistaken it for a car that had come off the lot this year.

"Do you think you can keep it between us that the car was in an accident?" Joe asked Luke when Kendra went back inside.

"You mean like a secret?"

"Yeah, if you don't mind. It's just that I think my mom's mad at my dad for buying the car. I heard them arguing today before breakfast. She was saying stuff about the scratches on the bumper and the broken headlight. If she found out it was in an accident she'd have a heart attack."

"I think that can be arranged. It doesn't look like it's going to give you too many problems."

"Thanks."

"Don't mention it. With the new headlight, it looks almost new."

"Almost?" Joe asked sarcastically.

"Almost." Luke disappeared into his garage. When he returned, he was holding a machine with a circular sponge attached to the end. He handed it to Joe. "There's still one more thing that needs to be taken care of." He put a hand against his back brace, wincing a bit as he bent in front of the bumper, and produced a little metal tin out of his pocket. Joe watched him open it and meticulously apply a thin coat of rubbing compound to the bumper the way an artist might flat wash a canvas. He did this until the scratches were covered. For the first time, Joe realized that Luke was missing the top part of his index finger. Where a normal finger would have ended in a nail after the third knuckle, Luke's ended in a stump. Joe remembered how Luke had plunged his hand into the engine on the side of the road and assumed he'd lost it while working on a car.

"What?" Luke asked.

Joe blinked. He hadn't realized he'd been staring. He thought about asking the question he wanted to, but then saw that Luke's back brace was exposed and asked a safer one instead: "How'd you hurt your back?"

Luke felt for the brace, found that his shirt had ridden up, and pulled it back down. "Too much heavy lifting. Strained it when I tried to lift an engine block as a teenager and then it just got worse over time. I never really took care of it. Guess I'm prone to injury." He held up his hand, showing Joe the missing part of his finger. "See?"

So much for trying to be discreet.

Joe tried to act as if he hadn't noticed it earlier. "Ouch! How'd that happen?"

"Got it caught in a band saw," Luke said simply. "I put one in the basement when we first moved in, and I was a little careless. Sucked the sleeve of my shirt right in. The blade spins so fast it'll nip anything off in the blink of an eye, no hesitation."

"Wow," was all Joe could say.

It seemed a satisfactory reply because it closed the subject. "Ever buff?" Luke asked him.

Joe hadn't.

"It's easy. All you have to do is keep the buffer moving. I like to go in circular motions, other people like going from side to side. The important thing to remember is not to press too hard or leave it in the same spot for too long—that'll burn the paint. Want to give it a shot?"

Joe shrugged. Why not? Luke hadn't steered him wrong yet, and the idea of using the buffer excited him. Holding it, he felt a sense of power. This was *his* car, *his* ride, and *he* was the one doing the work on it.

"Nice and easy," Luke reminded him when Joe turned the buffer on and bent down in front of the car. It produced a gentle hum, and the sponge started spinning. Joe moved it forward until it made contact with the bumper. Immediately the rubbing compound Luke had applied began to disappear and an almost fruity smell filled the air. Sure enough, the scratches came out. It was like he was a magician and this was his magic wand. With each pass, another scratch disappeared. *Presto! Abracadabra! Poof!* He stopped every few seconds to let Luke apply more rubbing compound, and when they finished, only one scratch remained, one so thin you could barely tell it was there unless you were looking for it.

"Wow, that's incredible!" Joe said.

"The magic of detailing a car. I have some wax inside if you want to give it a fresh coat. Should make it shine pretty nice."

Joe didn't need to think about it. "Yeah, that'd be great. I really want it to shine tomorrow."

"Trying to impress a girl at school?"

Joe put the buffer down. He hadn't thought about Amanda since the game, had actually made a conscious effort to forget that she even existed. Now that Luke brought up the subject, however, it made him wonder. Would having a car impress her? Luke had worked wonders helping him with his car problems, so maybe he could do the same for his girl problems, too.

"There *is* a girl," Joe said carefully. "But I don't think she's interested."

"Why's that?" Luke asked.

"Because she flat out turned me down."

"You? That's hard to believe. You're tall, handsome, and athletic."

"Thanks, but that's my problem. She said she doesn't date jocks and that I'd only be wasting my time talking to her."

"Ouch, that's pretty harsh."

"Tell me about it."

"What's her name?"

"Amanda. She's skinny, has reddish-brown hair, green eyes, and these cute little dimples when she smiles." Just thinking about her and knowing that he'd never get a chance to be with her made a lump rise in Joe's throat.

"She sounds very pretty." (*She's beautiful,* Joe wanted to say.) "Is she right, though?"

"About me wasting my time?"

"About you being a jock."

"No!"

"Then why does she think you are?"

Joe picked a pebble up off the driveway, studying it. "I don't know. I guess it's because I play basketball. All sports players get that reputation. And most of the guys that I hang out with on the team really are jocks."

"I see," said Luke. "You ever hear the expression 'you are what you eat'?"

"Yeah . . . ?"

"Same goes for who you hang out with. If you see someone hanging out with a bunch of kids in a gang, you're going to assume that person's also in the gang. Your friends reflect your personality. How you choose them is a big indicator for others on the type of person you are."

Joe tossed the pebble. "Yeah . . . you're probably right."

"Do you want some advice?"

"Sure."

"You're a good kid, and I can tell by the way you treat your car that you'd treat a girl right, so you have two choices. You can either move on to someone different, or you could find out something that interests this Amanda and talk to her about it. Give her a chance to get to know the real you."

It was good advice. The only thing was, what would he talk to her about? He knew nothing about her, and C.J. had made the only girl who did cry. He therefore couldn't ask Sarah what Amanda's interests were. He doubted if Sarah would even say two words to him on the sheer grounds that she knew he and C.J. were friends.

"And most importantly," Luke added. "Be confident. Girls admire confidence."

Joe thought about this. Luke had to be right. He was married to Crystal, and Crystal was quite attractive. Not even having a child had marred her figure. Luke might bear a slight resemblance to Nicolas Cage, but Joe didn't think Nicolas Cage was all that handsome for a guy. Therefore, there had to have been something else that had attracted Crystal.

"Confidence . . ." Joe said, tasting the word.

"Confidence," Luke echoed. "Don't be cocky, be confident. Girls can tell the difference. Find something she's interested in. Talk to her about it. Then, ask her if she wants a ride home. Tell her it'll be a good opportunity for you guys to continue the conversation."

"Thanks," Joe said. "I'll give it a shot."

"Do more than that. Be positive. Make it happen."

"Luke help you with your car?" Margaret asked Joe when he came in for dinner.

The kitchen smelled of chicken, and sure enough, on each of the three plates set at the table, was a large chicken cutlet. Around them were three pots: one with potatoes, another with beans, and a third with a mixture of questionable vegetables that Joe would not be eating tonight, or any other night his mother decided to make them.

"Yup, we fixed the headlight and buffed out the scratches on the bumper." He left out the part about bending the frame back. "Came out pretty good."

" 'Well,' " his mother corrected.

"Right. Well."

"Go wash up for dinner. And tell your father to get off that damn computer and join us if he wants to eat."

Joe passed his father's home office on the way to the bathroom and peeked in. Sure enough, his father was there, sitting in what might just be the modern pose of Rodin's "The Thinker." He was leaning forward, his elbow propped on the surface of the desk, his thumb and forefinger absentmindedly stroking his beard, and his eyes set in such concentration that they appeared to almost disappear behind the lenses of his glasses.

His other hand, instead of hanging over his knee, caressed the computer mouse as he restlessly tapped the scroll wheel.

"Dad, dinner's ready."

George looked up from the computer. "Huh, what?" He cocked his head left, then right—the reflection of the chess game on the screen jumping in his glasses—before he found his son. "Oh, right, right," he said in his soft, but fast, whispering voice. "I'll be down in a minute."

For a second, Joe thought his father looked like someone who was lost. And maybe he was. It had been a full five years since he had last shared a bed with Joe's mother. As far as Joe knew, it wasn't any argument that had prompted George to start sleeping on the pull-out couch, but a bad back. He had claimed that he needed a softer mattress and Margaret a firmer one. But Joe wasn't sure how much of that he believed. Now that he was older, he was beginning to see that maybe the precarious balance of their marriage had something to do with it. Joe thought his mother looked for problems. She wasn't happy unless she had something to be unhappy about, as odd as that sounded. Perhaps that's why his father carefully retreated to his home office whenever he wasn't required to be in the room. Maybe this was the only place he could go to escape, where he felt safe and couldn't be yelled at.

Joe stared at his father for a little longer—George once more focusing on the computer, not even aware that his son was still standing in the doorway—then made his way to the bathroom.

At the dinner table, he spooned some potatoes on his plate. Margaret asked him more questions about the car. The conversation stopped when George joined them halfway through the meal.

It wasn't long before Joe turned on the television and tuned it to the sports channel to drown out the silence.

Joe lay in bed, staring at the ceiling, Luke's advice guiding his thoughts. Luke had told him to talk to Amanda about something that interested her, and Joe kept replaying the two times they'd talked, hoping to discover what that something might be. He couldn't come up with anything. Already the memory was turning into a choppy 16mm film, the volume growing hazy, as if it were something that had happened years ago. Eventually, only a silent moving picture would remain: Amanda sitting majestically on the bleachers, twisting her hands as she . . .

Joe sat up. Amanda had been twisting her hands. He remembered because he had thought it looked odd. Odd, until she had said . . .

He tortured his mind to recall the conversation. Finally, he was rewarded for his efforts. C.J. had asked her what was wrong with her hands, and she had replied, *Nothing's wrong with them. It's sign language. Julia's deaf, and so was my little brother.*

Sign language, Joe mused. He pulled his laptop over and did a Google search. He found a YouTube member that taught basic signs.

Using Amanda as motivation, he began to practice.

CHAPTER 20

Joe didn't know Amanda's class schedule, but he did know that she walked the east wing between second and third period and the west wing between sixth and seventh. He had hoped that he might run into her during one of these breaks. As it turned out, luck was not on his side. And since it was a Friday, he would have to wait until Monday to try again while his mind taunted him all weekend, convincing him that she would meet a nice guy while she was out. The horrible thing about that was it was entirely possible. How long did he think a beautiful girl like Amanda would stay single? If he hadn't known she had just moved here, he would have already assumed she had a boyfriend. Time was not on his side. Each day that passed was another day that somebody else, somebody who she didn't consider a jock, might ask her out.

These were the bothersome thoughts that ran through Joe's mind as he and C.J. walked to math class. He had picked C.J. up first thing in the morning, driving with the windows down and relishing the way the warm breeze blew his hair back. For the first time, he felt like he was in control of his life. When he had gotten to C.J.'s house, C.J. flung his bag into the back, put on a pair of sunglasses, and reclined his seat. He remained in this position until he saw a group of sophomores on their bikes and undid his seatbelt, pushing himself halfway out the window.

"Hey, you turds!" he yelled. "Mommy let you ride your tricycles to school today?" He gave them the finger and laughed like a jester. Joe thought about rolling up the window but in the end decided not to.

He immediately regretted this decision.

He thought C.J. was going into his backpack for a book, but when C.J. pulled out a brown paper bag, he decided that C.J. wanted a snack instead. He confirmed this when C.J. produced a container of applesauce and carefully peeled back the aluminum foil cover. Joe was about to tell him not to spill any inside the car, but C.J. didn't eat it. He threw it. Without warning, as Joe passed a second group of kids, C.J. pushed himself out the window again and hurled the container of applesauce. It cleaved the air like a bullet, juice dripping like contrail, and struck a blonde girl wearing a halter top upside the head. She shrieked and staggered sideways, clutching her ear as if she had been shot. Her feet tangled, and she fell over into a flower garden. Joe only had a second or two to watch her fall and her friends rush to her aid, but during that time he saw her once-cheerful expression divide and transform into fear and surprise. He also saw that the whole side of her face had been caked with apple puree.

"Oh man!" C.J. said when he pulled himself back into the car. "Did you see that? I nailed her right in the head! Bam! Bitch went down!" He punched Joe in the arm. "Did you see?"

Joe felt sick to his stomach. He saw, all right, but wished he hadn't. And to make matters worse, C.J. was smiling. He wore that same smile throughout the day as he bragged to girls that Joe had a car and had driven him to school. He even had it on now, but not for the same reason.

The bell was about to ring, and the hallway was practically empty. The only people occupying it besides Joe and C.J. were a group of freshmen. Three of them stood around a short, fat kid with curly hair, his books scattered everywhere.

"Hit him again, Steve," one of the kids said.

The one who must have been Steve pulled his foot back and let it fly forward like he was kicking a soccer ball. "How do you like that, fatass?

Right in your jelly rolls!"

The kid on the floor moaned, clutching his stomach.

C.J. pointed to the freshman. "Look, they're putting on a show for us."

The second Joe saw the fight, he grew serious. "We should stop them."

C.J. shook his head. "Fuck that, we'll be late for class. I'm already on Mr. Rugerdy's shit list."

"We can't just let them beat him up," Joe argued.

"Who's this 'we'? You got a mouse in your pocket?"

"Come on, he needs our help. I can't do this myself."

"Not a chance." And without waiting for Joe to respond, C.J. walked away.

Joe felt his anger boil. He'd deal with C.J. later. For now he rushed over to the fat kid, shouting "Hey! Leave him alone!" to the kids around him. When they saw Joe coming, they ran off, snickering.

"Are you all right?" Joe asked, bending down.

The kid moaned again, rolling over. He paused with his knees and palms on the floor, his chest shuddering as he struggled to catch his breath. At last he said, "Yeah—I'll—I'll be all right. Thank you."

"What's your name?"

"Peter," he said, turning his head to look at Joe. "Peter Rubin." He had big brown eyes, a doe's eyes, swimming with tears. They were filled with knowledge but also with melancholy—a serf who knows his role in the class system.

"Peter, you have to tell someone what happened. Do you know who those kids were? Do you want me to come with you to the office?"

"No!" Peter said with such force that Joe could hear the fear in it. Then softer: "No, please don't say anything."

"Why? They just beat you up."

"Because they'll—you just don't understand. Getting them in trouble will only make it worse. I'm fine, really."

The late bell rang, but Joe ignored it. He studied Peter instead. Aside from the tears running down his cheeks and his disheveled hair, he didn't look that bad. Joe had never been fat, and guessed that the extra weight cushioned the blows.

"Are you sure?" he asked.

"I'm positive," Peter said, getting to his feet. He gathered his books and put them in a pile. "Can I trust you?"

The question caught Joe off guard. Of course the kid could trust him, but was that the right thing to do? He thought that in this type of situation the right thing would be to tell a teacher, despite what the kid wanted. Yet, when he saw the way Peter looked at him, pleading with those doe's eyes of his, he couldn't say no.

"Yes . . ." he said reluctantly. "You can trust me."

"Thank you," said Peter. He picked up his books and scurried off, leaving Joe to stand in the empty hallway.

Except it wasn't empty. Someone behind him asked, "Is he going to be all right?"

Joe turned to find Amanda standing there holding her books to her chest, her face full of worry. Without thinking, Joe flashed her one of the basic signs he learned: the "okay" sign.

"You know sign language?" she asked, a bit surprised.

By now, Joe had memorized all the basic signs and the first few letters of the alphabet. "A little," he confessed. "I'm still trying to learn."

"Oh. Well that was really nice of you. Helping that kid. You could have just ignored him like your friend."

"How long were you watching?"

"Long enough to tell that I might have been wrong about you. I'm sorry about the way I acted before."

Joe didn't know what to say to that. He felt a familiar warmth surge in his chest, and his heart begin to race, but he ignored these things when he spied one of Peter's books lying on the floor.

"I guess he forgot one," he said, picking it up.

Amanda looked at the cover. It was a J.K. Rowling paperback. "*Harry Potter and the Half-Blood Prince.* That's a really good book."

"I only saw the movie," Joe said distractedly. He put the book in his backpack on the off-chance he ran into Peter again.

"I've never seen it," Amanda said. "Was it good?"

Joe looked up. "Yeah, it was, actually. I can't believe you haven't seen it."

"I haven't seen any of them."

"Really? I'm not even into fantasy, and I've seen all of them. I thought they were great."

"I don't really like to watch the movies after I read the book. I guess I'm weird like that."

"Nah. Believe it or not, my cousin's the same way. She doesn't want them to ruin it for her. "

"Exactly. You have an idea how the characters should be in your head and most of the time they're completely different in the movies."

"Yeah. Although, I heard they did a pretty good job with the *Harry Potters*. Since we're on the topic of movies, do you have a favorite?"

"*Tomb Raider.* When I was little I used to imagine I was Lara Croft running around shooting bad guys." She giggled. Each note of laughter sent a pleasant chill racing up Joe's spine. "I really liked *A Silent Dilemma*, too, because the main character's deaf and has to—"

"And has to sign," Joe finished.

"Yup."

"How long have you known sign language?"

"About ten years. My family started learning right after we found out my brother was deaf."

Joe was about to respond when he remembered what she had said to C.J. back at the game: *Julia's deaf and so was my little brother.*

Was, as in the past tense. Did that mean he'd gotten his hearing fixed, or . . .

She must have sensed Joe's uneasiness because she said, "You don't have to feel bad when I talk about him. I hate how everyone always tries to change the subject. He was sick and in a lot of pain most of his life, but I think it's worse to pretend that he didn't exist. Do you know what I mean?"

That confirmed it, but surprisingly Amanda's logic, and the casual way she talked about her late brother, made Joe feel a little easier about the subject.

"I do," he said. "I feel the same way."

"I'm glad. I hate it when that awkward pause ruins the conversation."

Joe didn't let that happen. "Did it take you long to learn sign language?"

"Not really. I was young, and they say you pick things up a lot easier then."

"Yeah, that must be true because I'm having a lot of trouble now. I can't seem to get the letter *P* right." He tried twisting his hand, but got a cramp and had to massage it instead.

Amanda giggled again. This time her cheeks dimpled, and he stared at the cute little indentations, wishing they didn't have to disappear. "You have to relax," she said. "Here, like this."

Joe copied her and found that his hand didn't cramp as easily when he did it her way. He also realized that he was having a full-on conversation with the girl of his dreams and wasn't faltering or stumbling around for things to talk about. He guessed this was because the conversation had been so sudden, so unexpected, that he hadn't had time to plan anything to say. Try too hard, and you got yourself worked up. Be yourself, and it came naturally. He remembered Luke's advice. This was proof. Only it had come at the wrong time. The bell had rung over a minute ago and they were both late for class. Fearing that the conversation would have to come to an end, he broke topic and asked, "Do you usually take the bus home?"

Amanda eyed him suspiciously. "Yeah, why?"

"I have my car with me and was wondering if you'd maybe want a ride later." When he saw that she was hesitant, he added, "It'd give us a chance to continue our conversation. We're kinda late for class right now."

Amanda furrowed her brow in thought. After a moment she said, "Umm . . . sure. Why not?"

"Really?"

"Yeah."

Joe tried not to act too surprised. He also tried not to act too happy, either, although both emotions were swelling. "Okay, cool. I'll meet you by the parking lot after ninth. How's that sound?"

"Sounds good," Amanda said. "See you then." She smiled and made her way down the hall, leaving him to watch her auburn hair sway back and forth over her shoulders as she walked.

"Where the hell were you?" C.J. asked when Joe strolled into class five minutes late. "Taking a shit?"

Joe didn't answer, just sat at his desk with a big grin on his face.

"What are you so happy about? Was your shit that good?"

Joe didn't pay him any attention. It wasn't because he was annoyed with him—he had forgotten that he was, and even if he remembered, it would have been impossible to let anything upset him now—it was because he was replaying the conversation he'd had with Amanda. She had said yes. Yes! In less than an hour, he would be driving her home. Just him and her and . . . and that was when he realized C.J. expected a ride home, too. As it turned out, something *could* upset him after all.

"*Hellooo?* I'm talking to you. Earth to Joe."

He couldn't let C.J. ride with them—he'd ruin everything. There was no telling what he'd do. What if he threw something out the window again, or decided to fart the alphabet? Amanda already hated C.J., and Joe didn't need C.J. doing anything stupid to ruin his chance at making a good impression.

"C.J.," he whispered.

"Oh, so *now* you're talking to me?"

"Sorry. Listen, do you mind if I don't give you a ride home today?"

"*What?*" C.J. shrieked. "Dude, what the fuck?"

Joe winced and looked up to see if Mr. Rugerdy had heard them talking. He hadn't.

"Lower your voice."

"No," C.J. said. "Why won't you drive me home?"

"I can't tell you right now. Is it okay? You can take the bus, right?"

"No, I can't take the bus. I already told Melissa Pandolfo we'd give her a ride home. She was gonna show me her new underwear."

"Come on, C.J. I wouldn't change plans if it wasn't for something important."

"What could be more important than driving your best friend to a girl's house so he can get laid? Tell me, 'cause I honestly wanna know."

Joe took a deep breath. "Okay, remember that girl Amanda? Sarah's cousin? Well I'm giving her a ride home."

"What? Her? That bitch got me detention!"

Joe looked up at Mr. Rugerdy again. "Lower your voice."

"Why? Afraid you'll get detention for talking in class? Hell, you can have the seat next to me. I start mine on Monday. Maybe it'll give you a chance to experience what I have to go through for a full week. Do you know how pissed Coach Heck was when he found out?"

"That was your fault you got detention."

"How was it my fault? That crazy girl tackled me, and now you wanna give her a ride home? That's fucked up. Bros before hoes."

"You called her cousin a troll," Joe pointed out.

"And with good reason. You've seen what Sarah looks like."

Joe sighed. "Listen, I'm giving Amanda a ride home. I want a chance to get to know her better."

"If she hadn't gone psycho on me, I'd wanna get to know her better, too. She's hot, I'll give you that. But there are easier ways to get laid."

"That's not what I'm talking about."

"Yeah, okay . . ."

"Honestly, I don't wanna rush anything. She seems really nice. She's gonna teach me sign language."

"You wanna learn sign language?" C.J. said. "Here." He gave Joe the finger. "That's for choosing her over me. Girls like her exist for one thing and one thing only: fucking. You *fuck* them, and when you're done, you fuck them *over*. Get it?"

Joe got it, all right. He got that if he hung around C.J. any longer people would start to think he had the same philosophy. Luke had been right: people viewed you the way they viewed your friends. Amanda had already proved this true.

CHAPTER 21

Luke answered his door on the second ring.

"Joseph. What's up?" He had a towel draped over his shoulder and his shirt was splattered with water.

"Sorry," Joe said. "Are you busy?"

"Nah, I was just doing some chores around the house. Washing the dishes right now. I needed something to do. Sitting around all day gets boring pretty fast."

Joe bet it would. As an active person, he couldn't imagine being forced to do nothing. He'd probably wind up going crazy after the first day and wondered how Luke had lasted this long with Crystal always at work and Kendra at school.

"How's your car?" Luke asked him. "The headlight holding up?"

"Yeah," Joe said. "It's great. I waxed it and everything."

"Really? Let's take a look."

Joe's car sat at the side of the curb, its newly waxed surface reflecting the sun. Luke studied it after he changed.

"Was this your first time waxing?"

Joe frowned. "You can tell, huh? I tried to follow the directions on the can as best I could."

"No," Luke said. "I only ask because it looks great. This was really your first time?"

"Yeah," Joe said brightening. "You really think it looks okay?"

"*Okay?* You should be getting paid to detail cars! First buffing the scratches out of the bumper, and now this? You're a natural."

"Thanks."

"I bet a lot of people complimented you when you drove it to school."

Joe couldn't hide his smile. Amanda had done just that when she saw it. She had told him that he had "a really nice car." He didn't waste any time telling Luke. "Remember that girl I told you about the other day? Amanda?"

"The one that you said wasn't into you?"

"Yeah, her. She complimented me on it."

Luke raised an eyebrow. "Did she now?"

"She did. I took your advice and talked to her today."

"And how did that go?"

"Surprisingly well. We're actually going out tonight to play mini golf."

Luke clapped Joe on the shoulder. "See? All you had to do was be confident."

"You were right," Joe said. "She's into sign language. She used to have a deaf brother, so we started talking about signing, and one thing lead to another. I gave her a ride home, and on the way we passed this indoor mini golf place and she seemed excited about it, so I asked her if she wanted to go."

"That's great," said Luke. "I'm sure you guys will have a good time."

"Thanks. I hope so. My mom doesn't seem too fond of the idea of me going out on a date, though."

"You told her?"

"Kinda had to. She asked why it took me so long to get back from school. When she found out I drove a girl home, she said, 'You're wasting your time. You shouldn't get involved with girls. Not until you're done with school. They're a distraction.' "

Luke had to laugh. "All mothers think like that. They think the girls are going to steal their sons away from them."

"Yeah, you're probably right. Anyway, I hope I don't do anything stupid to screw it up tonight."

"You won't. Just be yourself and you'll do fine." After a pause, Luke asked, "Was that why you rang my bell?"

"Oh! No, there's a problem with my CD player." Joe opened the car's door and started the engine. When the CD player powered up, he pressed the eject button. It made a *whirring* sound, as if the motor was turning and trying to spit out the disc, but nothing happened. "It's stuck."

Luke came around to the passenger side and gently lowered himself into the seat. Like Joe, he pressed the eject button only to receive the same response. He scratched his chin. "How old is the CD player?"

Joe answered honestly. "I don't know. It came with the car when we bought it. Mr. Lancaster, my dad's boss, had it put in. Do you think I need a new one?"

Luke looked at it again, this time bringing his face closer. "Do you care if the CD gets damaged?"

"Not really. I can just burn another."

"Okay, give me a minute. I have an idea." Luke went into his garage, and when he returned, he was holding a pair of needle-nosed pliers, which he inserted into the disc slot. He rummaged around until he had a firm grip on the CD. Then he pulled. With some effort, it came out. "Here you go."

"Do you think that fixed it?"

"One way to find out. Put it back in."

Joe looked hesitant.

"It's the only way to be sure. If it gets stuck again then you know there's something wrong with the player."

Joe stuck the CD in. The player gobbled it up like a hungry mouth. When he pressed the eject button, it spit it right back out.

"Guess you don't need a new player after all. If it gets stuck again, let me know. By the way, the charge on your battery's a little low."

"Charge?"

Luke pointed to the gauge on Joe's dash. "Might want to keep an eye on that. You can charge it by running the engine without the lights."

"What'll happen if it gets too low?"

Luke turned the key. "That," he said simply when the engine died. "You'll need to jump it to get it started again. You have cables?"

Joe shrugged. "I don't know. I don't think so."

"Hold on." Luke pulled himself out of the car and returned to the garage. He came back holding a yellow contraption with two electrical cords ending in alligator clips.

"What's that?"

"It's a portable jumper. It's better than cables. Just attach these two clips to the battery terminals—red to red and black to black—and turn the jumper on. When you try to start your car, it should give it enough juice for the engine to turn over."

"And you're giving me this?" Joe asked, shocked.

"Sure, it's an extra one. The guys at work bought it for me, but Crystal and I already have one."

"Wow, thanks!" Joe took the contraption and put it in his trunk.

"Don't mention it. You have to charge it before you can use it, though. It's been sitting for a while. Little good it'll do you if it doesn't have any juice in it."

"Right. Thanks again." He paused for a second, then asked, "Hey, Luke. What's your cell number? You know, in case I have a car problem and have to call you."

Luke started to give it.

"Hold on," Joe said. "My cell's in the house." He thought for a second and then pulled the box the headlight had come in out of the trunk. "Write it on this."

"You still have this thing?" Luke asked.

"I've been too lazy to throw it away," Joe said, a little embarrassed. The truth was, he didn't feel right getting rid of it. It was sentimental to him. It represented the first car project he had ever worked on. Having Luke put his number on it would almost be like getting an autograph, a way to remember the man who had taught him the fundamentals of being a mechanic.

"You have a pen?"

Joe pulled his backpack out of the back seat and found one. "Here."

Luke wrote down his number, and Joe put the box back in the trunk.

They talked until their shadows lengthened and the sun began to drop out of the sky.

"You cheated."

"I did not!"

"Yes, you did! I saw you kick the ball in when I wasn't looking!"

Joe couldn't keep a straight face any longer. "All right, you caught me," he joked. "I just didn't wanna look bad in front of you." He pulled his ball out of the hole and walked over to the next green. Amanda followed.

He had picked her up a little after eight and driven straight to the mini golf place. Like earlier today at school, Joe found that he didn't have to try too hard to talk to her. Whatever he said just seemed to flow, the words effortlessly pouring out of his mouth like the steady surge of a stream. Once he found a topic that both of them were interested in, nature took its course. They talked about movies, sign language, pets, family, and finally school.

Now Joe asked her which classes she was taking, and she told him.

"I just hope they'll help me get into a good school with a nursing program," she added.

Joe admired her determination.

"What about you?"

"I'm not sure," Joe said. "I like playing basketball, but I'm smart enough to know it's not gonna turn into a career, unlike a few kids on the team." Joe didn't tell her that C.J. was one of them. "It's sad, really. They're gonna have a rude wakeup call when they go to college and realize that everyone's just as good, if not better than them."

"That's a depressing thought," Amanda said. She put her ball down on the green and putted.

"It might be, but it's a rational one. If I make it to the NBA, great. I certainly wouldn't complain. But I wouldn't wanna gamble my future on a long shot. I'd rather try to get into a good college and have a backup plan."

He put his ball in the same place and putted. It rolled down a twisting corridor of bricks, up a small incline, between two snarling gargoyles, past Amanda's ball, over a patch of bumps, and dropped into the hole. He stared in disbelief. "Hey, look at that."

"See," Amanda said. "Sometimes you do make the long shots."

At the end, they tallied their score. They tied.

"So much for the loser buying Red Mango," Joe said.

"I wasn't going to let you pay either way," she said coquettishly.

It took him a moment to process that. "Hey!"

Amanda giggled. Joe wished he could record her laugh so he could play it over and over again when she wasn't there.

After they handed in their putters, they made their way back to the car. Joe opened the door for Amanda, and she thanked him. He slid in behind the wheel and cranked the engine. Only . . . it didn't start. He looked down at the battery gauge and felt like kicking himself. In his haste to get ready for the date, he had forgotten to run his car with the lights off like Luke had told him to. He had also forgotten to put the jumper back in his trunk after he'd taken it out to charge it. He peeked over at Amanda to see if she had noticed anything was wrong. She hadn't; she was checking her phone. Joe tried to hide the troubled expression on his face, in case she should look over, and tightened his grip on the ignition key.

Please, oh please, he prayed, leaning forward and looking up at the headliner. He closed his eyes, bit his lower lip, and cranked the engine. He knew if it didn't start, the perfect flow of the evening would be ruined. Already, he felt his confidence melting away like an ice cube on a hot surface.

Thankfully, the engine turned over, as it had every other time. He sank back into his seat, relieved.

"Are you all right?" Amanda asked.

Joe jumped. "Huh? Oh yeah, I'm fine. You ready for that Red Mango?"

"Yup. Let's go."

Joe dropped the gearshift into drive and exited the parking lot. They made it two miles before Joe's headlights started to flicker. At first he thought there was something wrong with the streetlights, but when he paused at a stop sign, he realized that his car was the object that had been transformed into a strobe light. That was only the start of his troubles. As he continued to drive, he watched each light on his dash blink out like a star that's reached the end of its life. Soon, all he was left with was a black backdrop swallowing the needle of the speedometer in an ominous shadow. That's when the engine died and he lost power steering. Amanda felt the rumble cease and looked over at Joe with concern.

"What happened? Is everything all right?"

"The car died," he said, trying to conceal his apprehension. He didn't do that good of a job. The minute he felt the steering tighten, he panicked, grabbing the wheel with all his might and heaving it, one hand over the other, so that the car slowly turned. With its remaining speed, he guided it to the side of the road.

"What do you mean 'the car died'?" Amanda asked when they came to a stop.

"I mean it just died. I don't know."

"Can't you start it again?"

It was a good question. Could he? It had worked the first time. Joe turned the key, hoping that he would be rewarded with the blissful purr of the engine. He closed his eyes again, repeating the same ritual as before. It didn't help. He got nothing. Not even the rapid clicks of the starter motor.

"It didn't work," he said.

"What are we going to do?" It was obvious that Amanda was panicking. The healthy glow had faded from her skin, and her hands were twisting uncontrollably in her lap. Even though Joe had only learned the rudiments of sign language, he understood enough about body language to know that if a deaf person tried to read her hands they'd find the task impossible. She kept looking out the windows—first Joe's, then hers—to make sure they were still alone. They were in an industrial neighborhood composed of abandoned buildings left over from one of the wars. Joe remembered his father telling him that they used to manufacture airplanes here. He had opted to take this winding back route because he thought it would prolong the ride. He wanted as much time with Amanda as possible. As it turned out, he was getting more than he had bargained for.

The big buildings rose up on both sides of the car, looming over it, almost frowning with faces of open windows and broken glass. Dark gray clouds floated by, occasionally blotting out the moon.

Amanda made sure the doors were locked.

Joe thought about his options. If there had been houses nearby he could have walked over to one and asked for help, but with the nearest one being over a mile away, he didn't think that was plausible. He could do it, but he didn't think Amanda would go with him. More so, he didn't think she would stay in the car alone.

"I'm not sure what to do," he said honestly. "This has never happened before."

"What about your parents? Can you call them? Get them to pick us up?"

Joe considered the option. "No," he decided. "My mom will flip out. She'll yell at my dad for not getting the car checked by a mechanic before he bought it. They have enough problems as it is. I don't need this to make it worse."

"Then what about my parents? I could call them." Amanda was almost begging.

"No, please, just let me think for a minute." Joe didn't want to burden her, especially not on their first date. He grabbed the steering wheel for support. The moment he touched it, his phone began to vibrate. *It's my parents,* he thought. Somehow, they knew something was wrong. They sensed it in that odd way parents often sense things. He pulled his phone out of his pocket and looked at the screen:

Call from . . .
C.J.

"Is it your parents?" Amanda asked hopefully.

Joe looked from the screen to her, debating if he should answer the call. He could ask C.J. for help—C.J. could get his older brother to come and give him a jump—but he knew what C.J. and Amanda thought of each other and knew having C.J. around would only make things worse.

"No," he lied. "Wrong number." He silenced the call and put the phone back in his pocket.

This was turning into a night from hell. The date had started off so well, and now it was crumbling. He didn't think Amanda would want to talk to him any more after this. If only he had remembered to run his engine or put the stupid jumper back in the car, he wouldn't be in this predicament.

Almost instantaneously, as though his mind was playing a word association game, he thought of Luke. He could come and help. Joe knew Luke wouldn't tell his parents that the car had died.

"I have an idea," Joe said, brightening. "But I have to go into the trunk."

Amanda flashed him a worried look. Her gaze darted from one window to the other. "You're going to get out of the car? Here? Wasn't this where one of the bodies was found?"

"Bodies?"

"The Craig's List murderer. Not all the bodies were found at the beach."

Now that Joe thought about it, she was right. He did remember something on the news about one of the bodies being found in the abandoned industrial area. The police had put up sawhorses, blocking off the road, until they had investigated the area as thoroughly as they could. But that had been months ago. Surely the killer couldn't be here now.

"Don't worry," Joe reassured her. "I'll be fine." As he stepped out of the car, he added *I hope* under his breath.

The night was cool and crisp. Fallen leaves littered the ground and crumbled under his feet. As he made his way to the back of the car, he couldn't help but find himself looking around. He had never been on this road at night. During the day it looked so much bigger, so much *friendlier.* Now, in the dark, it looked ominous, more closed in, as if the buildings were slowly creeping up on him. There were streetlights every twenty feet or so, but like the buildings, their power had been shut off long ago. The only light he had to go by was the light of the moon, which was a round opalescent shape in the sky.

He heard a noise off to the side and spun around to see the outline of a small animal scurrying under a bush.

Only a raccoon, he told himself. *Get a grip. Amanda's counting on you.* He peered through the rear window and saw her staring at him, her green eyes wide with concern. He put on a false smile and opened the trunk. The faster he got out of here, the better.

His mind raced. What if the Craig's List murderer really was still here? What if this was his hideout? What if he just so happened to be waiting for two unlucky kids to come along? Joe had heard what the murderer had done to the bodies and forced himself to push these dreadful thoughts out of his head.

He hadn't noticed during the day, but the light in the trunk didn't work. "Figures," he mumbled. He was going to get maimed and murdered out here all because his father's boss was too cheap to replace a ninety-nine cent bulb. He took out his cell phone, opened it, and used the screen's backlight so he could see. It filled the trunk with a milky iridescence. He moved his hand back and forth, trying to find the headlight box. He had been planning to get Luke's number off of it—he hadn't had time earlier to store it in his phone—so he could call him, but stopped when the light fell upon a rectangular object he didn't recognize. Then all at once, he did. It was the jumper Luke had given him.

"How the hell—?" He stopped himself, deciding that he shouldn't question miracles. It was there, and that was enough. He pushed the tester button on its side, and a little green light illuminated, indicating that it had a full charge. He pulled it out at once, abandoning his original plan.

"I'm gonna try to jump the car," he told Amanda when he came around to the door and hit the hood release. "If it works, we should be out of here in no time."

"You can do that?" she asked.

"Yeah."

She watched through the window as he lifted the hood and did something with the cables. Joe was thankful she didn't have a clear view because he had no idea what he was doing. Luke had given him instructions—he remembered his words: *Red to red, black to black*, something about the battery terminals—but he had no idea what battery terminals were. He searched around with his cell until he found a square object with what looked like two silver nipples sticking up out of the top. There were two thick cables attached to them: one red and one black.

This must be it, he said to himself. He proceeded to connect the jumper's alligator clips to the silver nipples. When he tried to clamp the first one to the red terminal, he accidentally touched part of the car's frame also. Like a firework, a huge spark erupted, lighting up the night. He cried out and jumped back, throwing the clip. He saw the car shake and for one horrible moment thought of Frankenstein's monster, imagining he had summoned the car to life. Then he realized it was shaking because Amanda was shifting so she could poke her head out.

"Joe, is everything okay?"

"Yeah," he said, trying to keep his voice from trembling too much. "No problem."

She glanced at the buildings, at Joe, and then cautiously got out.

Great, Joe thought, *now I get to make a fool out of myself in front of her.*

"You didn't wanna stay in the car?" he asked.

She shook her head. "I don't like it in there alone." She reconsidered.

"I don't like it out here either, but at least there's safety in numbers, right?"

Joe hoped so. He approached the engine again. The jumper cable was lying on the engine block like a sleeping snake. Any second it might stir awake and strike. He handed Amanda his cell. "Here," he said. "Can you hold this and light the engine for me?"

She took the phone and positioned it so he could see the terminals again. Slowly, he reached out for the cable, his eyes playing tricks in the muted light. It looked like it was writhing, trying to coil and escape his grip. He swallowed hard, pushing his fear away, and grabbed it. He then opened the clip at the end and once more tried to attach it to the terminal. This time he didn't touch the frame and there were no sparks. Satisfied, he attached the second clip to the second terminal. When he was done, he paused to remember what to do next. As he studied the jumper, he couldn't help but notice Amanda staring at him with what might be wonder. She brought the light closer, but never took her eyes off him.

Don't mess up, don't mess up, Joe coached himself. He found the dial on the jumper that Luke had told him about and turned it to the *ON* position.

"There," he said, backing away.

"That's it?" Amanda asked.

"That's it." At least he hoped that was it. Amanda handed him his phone, and he led her back inside, where he slid in behind the wheel. He forced a smile and turned the key. *Please* . . . he prayed, crossing his fingers. As if God had heard his prayer, or the great Zeus residing in the jumper machine had decided to cast a lightning bolt through the cables, the engine turned over.

Joe didn't even realize he'd been closing his eyes until he opened them. When he did, he noticed that the dash was lit and the interior lights were on.

"It worked!" Amanda exclaimed. It was impossible to miss the relief in her voice.

That was when the most unexpected thing happened. Without any thought, without any warning, Amanda leaned in and kissed him. For a moment, Joe didn't realize what was happening. Then he felt her warm lips against his and kissed her back. Awkwardly, he brought his hand up and placed it on her waist. She placed hers on the side of his face. And together, in the car and under the eerie buildings with the broken faces, they created their own light and purged the darkness from the night.

PART 3

DARK AS MIDNIGHT

CHAPTER 22

Joe got to the hospital in record time. The minute Amanda's father had said she was hurt, Joe ran out of Coach Heck's office, rushed to his car, and pressed the gas pedal all the way to the floor, completely unaware that he was endangering himself as well as every other motorist on the road. If told, he wouldn't have cared anyway. He wouldn't have even slowed if that old joke had come true and the Pope was actually crossing the road. All he cared about was getting to Amanda.

As he weaved in and out of traffic, he couldn't help but remember Amanda telling him that while her little brother had been alive, her mother's biggest fear was that he would get hit by a car while riding his bike. Now her biggest fear had come true, except it had happened to the child who should have heard the car coming. Joe couldn't help but feel like this was his fault. If he hadn't lied to her, she wouldn't have gotten upset and ridden her bike to his house. Guilt ran through his veins, a much thicker blend than blood. Combined with the panic he felt, it was nearly fatal. In front of him, an old Ford Escape switched lanes. He didn't see it until the last second, and swerved. The Altima nearly flipped over but just managed to stay on the road. Joe sucked in air as if he had been holding his breath.

He parked in the first empty spot he found and sprinted to the hospital's entrance. The words ST. MARTIN'S HOSPITAL marked the front of the tall brick building. The lobby inside was clustered with people, some celebrating life, some mourning death, and the majority hovering somewhere in that purgatory in between. Joe pushed past them without giving them a second glance and rushed over to a counter, behind which sat a slightly overweight woman.

"Excuse me," Joe said, gasping. "Can you—"

Without averting her eyes from her magazine, the woman held up a finger. It was long and slender, the nail coated with shiny red polish.

Joe couldn't wait. "Please," he begged. "Can you—"

The woman raised her eyes, ready to give the same terse response she gave to everyone else. However, she must have seen something in Joe's face—maybe fear, panic, or both—because she immediately grew compassionate. She dropped her magazine and stood up.

"Are you hurt?" she asked.

"No," Joe said. "My girlfriend was hit by a car, and she's in the emergency room, and I have no idea where it is." He spoke so fast that his words nearly blended together.

"Oh!" she said at once. "The emergency room is on the other side of the hospital." She leaned over her counter, bumping aside some of the gift shop items she was selling, and pointed down a corridor. "The fastest way to get there would be to go down this hall, exit through that first set of doors, go across the parking lot, and go back in through the doors under the big red cross. There should be a sign that says TRIAGE. Do you understand?"

"Yes," Joe said. He was already running down the hall. "Thank you!"

The outside air was a blessing against his face. Even though he'd only spent less than a minute in the hospital, the air inside had already begun to feel thick, stuffy, and had nearly robbed him of his breath. His head had begun to spin. Now, as he ran, he thankfully felt it clearing.

His footfalls accompanied him as he ran toward the cross the lady had described. It was big, red, and affixed to the façade of the building. Just above it, the sun shone the last bit of its light as it prepared to rest for another night.

No more than a few seconds later, Joe burst through the doors, looking around. Several people sitting in chairs looked up at him. He ignored them all, continuing his search until he found two people standing off to the side with their arms wrapped around each other: a mother and a father, both looking lost in their anxiousness. They probably wouldn't have noticed Joe's entry if he had come in sounding a bullhorn.

He ran over to them, bumping his hip against a chair on the way and ignoring the pain. Mr. DeFallon noticed him first.

"Joe," he said, and that was all. No *Thank you for coming.* No *She's improving.* Just *Joe.*

Hearing his name in that inflectionless tone scared Joe more than ever.

Mrs. DeFallon saw the worried look on his face and opened her arms, holding them out for him the way a mother does to a child. Joe instinctively came forward, allowing her to wrap them around him. And when she did, he began to cry.

"We still haven't heard anything new, but we're praying," Mr. DeFallon said. He was a tall man—although not as tall as Joe—with wide shoulders and jet-black hair. Because of the sports coat and slacks he wore, anyone could tell he had rushed to the hospital straight from work. He put a hand on Joe's shoulder. "By God, we're praying."

Joe nodded. He felt like saying something reassuring but didn't have the words. It was apparent that neither of them knew about the breakup, and Joe wondered how they would react when Amanda told them it was over.

You mean if *she tells them,* a cruel voice inside Joe's head said. *Who says she's even going to make it?*

He pushed the horrible thought away. She *would* make it. She *had* to. He couldn't stand to think of life without her.

CHAPTER 23

Sometime later—it might have been an hour, it might have been twenty minutes—the doctor, dressed in a long white coat with a stethoscope poking out of one pocket, stepped into the waiting room, looking around. When she spotted the DeFallons, she walked over. She was an Indian woman with jet-black hair whose face bore the indications of someone who frowned a lot, her skin deeply lined on her forehead and around her mouth.

"Mr. and Mrs. DeFallon?" she asked.

"Yes," Amanda's father said. "That's us."

"I'm Doctor Masood."

Joe saw the stethoscope sticking out of her pocket and absurdly thought of the thing sailors looked out of when they were in a submarine. He almost giggled, the fear of what had happened to Amanda making him delirious.

"Please," Mrs. DeFallon said. "Is she okay?"

Dr. Masood dropped her head, and Joe felt his heart plummet. It was as if he had tried looking over a steep ledge and accidentally slipped. He was falling now, unsure when the splat would occur, but certain it would be soon.

"She's stable," Dr. Masood said. She had only dropped her head to check her clipboard.

Her words shot through Joe like a bolt of energy.

"She's okay?" he asked.

"She's stable," Dr. Masood repeated. "Her injuries are extensive, but not fatal. She's suffered fractures to the jaw, arm, and hand. Her jaw will need to be wired shut. I wish we could take less evasive action, but it was weak from the previous fracture and fractured along the temporomandibular joint again. Wiring it shut is the only option. In addition to that, she'll need her arm placed in a cast. There also seems to be some swelling of the brain."

"What's that mean?" Mrs. DeFallon asked, alarmed.

Dr. Masood calmly said, "It means that she's in a coma." She quickly added: "But she is extremely lucky. It doesn't look as if there will be any traumatic brain injury. We tried a procedure where we induced hyperventilation to constrict the blood vessels and relieve pressure, and it seems to be working."

Mrs. DeFallon gasped.

"Why is my daughter in a coma?" Mr. DeFallon asked brusquely.

"The brain is made up of three major parts," Dr. Masood said simply. "The cerebrum, the cerebellum, and the brain stem. The brain stem controls breathing, blood pressure, sleep cycles, and consciousness. In addition to these parts, there's a large mass of neurons beneath the cerebrum called the thalamus. It's believed that consciousness depends on the constant transmission of chemical signals from the brainstem and the thalamus to the cerebrum.

"If a person suffers severe head trauma—like your daughter when she hit her head, for example—the impact can cause the brain to move back and forth inside the skull, tearing nerve fibers, causing swelling. This swelling presses down on blood vessels, blocking the flow of blood and, along with it, oxygen to the brain.

"This is why Amanda is unconscious. Typically a tube is surgically placed inside the skull to drain the excess fluid causing the pressure, but as I've said, we opted for a less—how can I put this—a less *dramatic* procedure."

"Oh God." Mrs. DeFallon sobbed. She pulled over her husband and buried her head into the spot between his neck and shoulder. "Our baby!" she cried. "Our baby! She's going to be a vegetable!"

"Will she—" Mr. DeFallon stopped himself, needing a moment to utter the impossible idea. "Will she be a vegetable?"

This was almost too much for Joe to handle. He couldn't imagine what it would be like to have Amanda sitting next to him unable to understand what he was saying, unable to react to his touch. He felt like running back outside into the waning daylight and away from the hospital, the breakup, and the horrible thoughts his mind was conjuring. What made him stay was what Dr. Masood said next.

"It's important for you to remember that the body is very good at healing itself. As a defense mechanism during head trauma, the body essentially puts the brain into hibernation. This reduces the amount of blood and oxygen flow it needs, and helps protect against tissue damage. Where a coma should always be considered serious, it is expected in this situation."

"You didn't answer my question," Mr. DeFallon said.

"I'm sorry, but it's impossible to tell at this point. The sooner she comes out of the coma, the better."

Amanda's mother sobbed again.

"When can we see her?" Mr. DeFallon asked.

"She'll be moved into the Intensive Care Unit within the hour. I'll inform you when that happens."

When Doctor Masood walked away, Joe hugged Amanda's family again. The three of them stood off to the far side of the waiting room forming a circle with their bodies, reaching out with their minds for a miracle.

CHAPTER 24

The Intensive Care Unit was open, bright, cold, and sterile. Joe had only been in a hospital three times—once when he was born, a second time when he had split his chin open on a picnic table, and a third when he'd visited his cousin after she had her appendix out—but he remembered enough from his latter visit to know that the ICU was much different from the usual recovery rooms. Instead of there being one or two beds, the room was filled with fifteen, all lined up against the wall, with beeping monitors flanking every one of them. And instead of one nurse, there were a bunch of them, scurrying back and forth in a flurry of activity. It almost made Joe feel like he had stumbled into a mad scientist's laboratory.

Almost all of the beds were filled. The first one had an elderly woman stretched out on the mattress with so many machines connected to her that she looked like the bionic woman. On the second was a man, naked to the waist, with square patches of gauze taped to his chest. Across from him sat a police officer. Joe moved his eyes past the other beds until he recognized a shock of auburn hair resting against a pillow. His heart jumped at once, and he pulled ahead of the DeFallons, feeling a force draw him forward as if he and Amanda were magnets.

He approached her bed in what felt like a dream. All at once, he didn't feel like he was in his body, but outside it, watching as he looked at his girlfriend . . . *ex*-girlfriend. He just couldn't get that out of his head. He wanted her to wake up so they could get back together, couldn't understand why she wasn't waking up now. He had been expecting the worst—her beautiful hair shaven, her face scraped and covered in bandages, her body a twisted wreck—but the only signs of injury were the few scratches on her cheeks and forehead and the cast on her arm. She looked like someone who might be resting after a long day of school, not someone who was in a coma. He stared down at her and felt a tear slip out of his eye and run down his cheek. He reached for Amanda's hand and then hesitated, looking up.

"Go ahead," Dr. Masood said. "You can touch her."

Joe did, feeling the warm, slender hand rest motionless in his, a hand that had so often reacted to his touch by drawing circles on his flesh or squeezing back. He couldn't bear the thought that her hand might never move again. He closed his eyes as another tear raced after the first.

Like the bionic woman in the first bed, there were a bunch of machines connected to Amanda, although not nearly as many. The most prominent of them had a thin, clear tube sprouting out of its side and running under her nose. Joe knew from movies that this was the tube supplying her oxygen. He also knew that if her injuries had been worse and she'd had trouble breathing, she would have had a larger one connected to her throat (he thought the procedure was called a traykeyottome, or something like that, but wasn't too sure). There were several other tubes connected to transparent bags that hung from metal coat racks. These ran into her arms, feeding her with liquid, electrolytes, and who knew what else. A few even poked out from under the sheets, and he was thankful that they were covered and left their destinations to the imagination.

Mrs. DeFallon stepped beside Joe and touched Amanda's cheek. Amanda didn't react. Mrs. DeFallon began to cry again. Mr. DeFallon looked away when he saw all the tubes running out of his daughter. For the next hour they all stood around Amanda's bed in silence, holding her hand, caressing her head, and shedding tears.

The days seemed to slip by, one after another. There was no time. Each hour morphed into the next without notice, as if the short, thick hand moved around the clock as fast as the long, thin one. For the first two days, nobody left Amanda's side. On the third, Mr. DeFallon went back to work. On the fourth, so did Amanda's mother.

During that time, a short nurse with freckles came into the room to reposition Amanda. When Joe asked her what she was doing, she explained that patients in comas often got bedsores and that moving their bodies prevented this. Joe asked her if he could move her instead, but the nurse only gave him a wan look and said that she'd rather he didn't. Joe didn't think that was fair but decided not to push his luck—Dr. Masood let him stay after visiting hours, and that was enough.

Over the course of that first week, Amanda had lots of visitors. A bunch of Amanda's relatives stopped by, crying on shoulders and giving their blessings. Joe's parents stopped by, too, dropping off flowers and giving their condolences to Mr. and Mrs. DeFallon, even if Margaret wasn't particularly partial to the idea of her son "getting involved with a girl." It was the first time they had met, and although they would have preferred to make acquaintances under better circumstances, they made the best of it. Even Sarah paid a visit, wearing a yellow neon shirt that nearly lit up the room. That was on the day of Amanda and Joe's four month anniversary. Joe had decorated her bed with little cut-out paper hearts and rose petals and had placed a stuffed bear clutching a heart-shaped pillow under Amanda's arm, even though he knew she had no idea it was there. He had also gotten her a necklace, but when he saw that all her other jewelry had been removed, he decided to hold onto it until she woke up. He kept reassuring himself that she would. He had to stay positive, and Sarah agreed with him.

"Just keep your head up. Amanda's counting on you to stay strong."

"I know," Joe told her. "But it's just so hard sometimes. Especially now."

"Yeah," Sarah said. "I don't blame you. Look what you did, though. This looks beautiful. I'm sure if she were awake, she would be thrilled."

"My original plan would have been better. I think she would have enjoyed that a lot more."

It was true that his original plan was much better. What girlfriend wouldn't love having her cousin take her out to go shopping while her boyfriend snuck inside her house and decorated her room for a romantic stay-at-home picnic/massage? Sarah didn't think it would be appropriate to tell Joe that Amanda would have enjoyed anything over lying in a bed, unconscious, so she said, "Maybe, but this is sweeter, under the circumstances."

"I guess so," he said. "Anyway, thank you for sneaking around with me and helping plan out the other idea. Maybe I can use it for our five- or six-month." After he said it, he felt a lump in his throat as he remembered that Amanda had broken up with him. He couldn't get their last fight out of his head, and couldn't help but embrace the feeling of self-loathing. He was convinced that it was his fault Amanda had broken up with him. She had been pissed ever since he had lied to her about being in the pizzeria when he had really been planning out their anniversary. She must have found out he hadn't gotten pizza that day, or maybe she or somebody else had seen Sarah in his car and hadn't recognized her. That must have been what she meant when she had said she caught him red-handed.

No, his mind told him. *It was the underwear. She was talking about the underwear.*

That made more sense. The bracelet she had made him for his rearview mirror was missing. Therefore Joe reasoned that she must have taken it back and seen the underwear lying on the floor. It certainly wasn't hard to miss. Any girlfriend who found a pair of underwear in her boyfriend's car would have suspected the worst. But since it obviously didn't belong to Amanda, and Joe had never seen it before, its presence raised more questions than answers.

Where the hell had it come from? Whose was it? How did it get there? His mind was running wild with speculation. Was it C.J. trying to get back at him? Or worse . . . did this have something to do with Bryce?

Joe refused to accept this last. He hated to think of the implications if it was true.

"Just stay strong," Sarah said, patting Joe's arm and interrupting his train of thought. "Amanda will get through this, and when she does, she'll be glad for all the love she has."

Joe tried to conceal his uneasy thoughts as best he could. "You're right," he said. "You're a good person. Amanda should be thankful to have you as a cousin."

"And she should be thankful to have you as a boyfriend."

Joe became aware of the lump in his throat again. He hoped that when Amanda awoke what Sarah said would be true.

CHAPTER 25

Joe missed a full week of school staying at the hospital. Finally, after much persuasion, he went back but didn't learn much. He just sat at his desk in a daze staring through the blackboard and whatever was written on it, thinking about nothing but Amanda and wondering if she had woken up. Yet each time he went to the hospital after school, he found her as he had left her: lying in bed, motionless, the tubes feeding her, the machines beeping by her side.

Every now and again she twitched. The first time she did this Joe jumped up, calling for the nurses. However, when they arrived, they told him that this was normal and that people in comas often twitched or moved involuntarily. That was probably why Joe ignored it when Amanda twitched on a Tuesday afternoon three weeks later.

He was sitting in the chair beside her bed, resting his head on her arm. By now the days were slipping by so fast that he had lost track of time. The only way he could really be sure of the duration of her stay was to check the calendar. He rarely slept anymore, and when he did, especially at home or at school, his dreams were haunted by the knowledge that he unwittingly had a hand in her horrible condition. He often awoke in cold sweats, gasping, sometimes moaning. The only time he got a peaceful rest was when he was with Amanda. He didn't know why this was—

maybe her presence chased away his inner demons, or maybe it was something more—but when he was with her he didn't dream at all, and after all the nightmares, that was simply beyond pleasant.

When he leaned his head against her arm he passed out, his body thankful for the chance to rest.

He didn't get to rest long. After about twenty minutes, Amanda twitched. Joe didn't feel her. When she twitched a second time, he parted his eyelids. He felt her hand move under his but didn't pay it much attention, just settled back down, waiting to drift back off to sleep. Except this time Amanda didn't just twitch. She *moved.* Her hand rotated and grabbed Joe's wrist. Joe sat up in terror, not remembering where he was for a moment. When his vision cleared and understanding followed, he realized that Amanda's head, which normally faced the ceiling, was turned toward him, her eyes staring into his own.

"Amanda?" he asked, not believing what he was seeing.

He had to be dreaming. There was no way she could be awake. Things like this didn't happen. People didn't just come out of comas and start smiling. But he didn't dream when he was with her. And if that was true, then that had to mean—

Amanda mumbled something, and even though it was impossible to make out what she said, Joe could tell that her weak voice was filled with confusion. She tightened her grip on his wrist but only a little, peering into his face with beseeching eyes.

"Amanda, you're awake!" he nearly shouted. He stood up calling "Hey! Hey, is anyone here?" but was only greeted by the sound of beeping machines.

Amanda mumbled something again, her eyes growing wide with fear as she realized that something was wrong and she couldn't open her mouth.

"Don't try to move," Joe told her. "Just stay right here, okay? I have to go get someone."

She mumbled again.

"Amanda, I'll be right back. Just don't move, okay?"

And with that he took off, running down the length of the ICU, past the beds, and pushing through the doors at the end of the room. They fluttered open like the doors at a saloon, and he stepped out into the hallway like a cowboy stepping out into the street, ready to draw on the villain. He only had his voice as a weapon, and he used it to scream, not at a villain but at a hero. He called for a doctor, a nurse, anybody. Two people stopped what they were doing at once—an orderly and a doctor—and rushed with him back into the Intensive Care Unit. Joe led them to Amanda's bed, but when he got there, he was not prepared for what he found. Like always, Amanda was unconscious, her head resting on the thin white pillow, the machines around her beeping.

"But she was awake!" Joe cried. "I swear! She was mumbling and everything!"

The orderly frowned. "I'm sorry," he said.

The doctor cast him a reprimanding look and then turned to Joe. "Are you sure she was awake?"

Joe stared at him as if he had five heads. "Yes. I'm positive. At first I thought I was dreaming, but unless this is a dream right now then she was awake."

The doctor nodded. "Then that's a wonderful sign."

"But she's not awake now."

"I wouldn't expect her to be. Recovery from a coma is gradual. Patients may only be alert for a few minutes the first day, but gradually stay awake longer each time after. You say this is the first time she's woken up?"

"Yes," Joe said.

"Then this is excellent news. I'll page her doctor for you, and you can tell her everything that happened. She'll want to examine her."

Sure enough, over the next week, Amanda awoke more and more, staying up longer each subsequent time until she fully emerged from the coma. On her first full day awake she started to speak. She had learned by now that her jaw had been wired shut and had to find another way to communicate. The nurse brought her a pad and a pen, and she used these to correspond with the hospital staff, but she found it annoying when she wanted to say anything longer than a short sentence. She was slow at writing. Her right hand was in a cast, and of course, that was the one she used. Her left was slow and stupid and didn't know how to make words. She nearly gave up because of it. Until, in a bout of frustration, she got the idea to use sign language.

CHAPTER 26

The bed felt soft under Joe's buttocks as he sat next to Amanda, getting as close to her as possible. He could tell by the way she reacted that she was happy to see him. There was no anger left over from the nasty breakup. She had either forgotten all about it or regretted it entirely.

"How are you feeling?" he asked her.

Amanda scrawled something down on the pad. It took her a long time. When she was finally finished, Joe looked at it. He had to puzzle out the sloppy words, but after a minute he was able to read *Better, now that you're here.*

He smiled. "I've always been here." Amanda tried to return the smile but winced. "Does it really hurt that bad?" he asked, and gave the pad back. She scribbled something else.

Kinda.

He thought for a second, and then asked, "What happened?"

Amanda's brows knitted together, as if she was wondering the same thing. Then, all at once, her eyes widened, the way one's does when they remember something startling. She tried mumbling a few words without success. Joe could tell that by the way she fought to articulate her thoughts it was important. She motioned for the pad again, and when Joe handed it to her, she attacked it with the pen, writing in a fury. When she reached the end of the page she huffed in disgust, tore the sheet away, and continued on to the next one.

Joe picked up the first sheet and tried reading it without much luck. In her haste to get everything down, the letters became illegible. They had been hard to puzzle out before, but now they were impossible.

"Hold on. Amanda, I can't read this." He held out the note for her to see. She looked at it for only a second before going back to what she was writing. The pad, resting on her leg, slipped and fell off the bed. She huffed again and tried mumbling, wincing against the pain.

"Don't try to talk," Joe told her. He picked up the pad, flipped to a clean sheet, and gave it back to her. "Here. Just write slower. There's no need to rush. We're not going anywhere."

But he could tell by the speed with which she wrote that she thought there was most certainly a need to rush. When she reached the bottom of the sheet, Joe tried reading it. The penmanship was slightly better this time—he could make out a few words like "the," "car," and . . . was that "knife"?—but the note as a whole was still impossible to comprehend. When he told Amanda this, she slammed her hand down on her leg.

That's when she got the idea to sign. Since she didn't have two hands, she had to sign each letter individually. Joe had to ask her to stop and go through the letters of the alphabet so he could remember. Amanda looked annoyed, but she did as he asked. When she finished, she began signing again. Now, the words came together with ease.

The underwear were the first two.

Followed by: *in the car.*

Joe didn't need any more to know what she was talking about. "The underwear in the car. . . . Amanda, I have no idea where they came from. Honestly. I never cheated on you. I lied, yes, over the phone, but that was because I was with Sarah. She was helping me plan a surprise for our four-month anniversary, and I didn't want you to find out. I swear."

The look she gave him just then was a combination of relief, gratitude, and delight, but it vanished just as quickly as it had appeared, and she continued signing: *Your phone. Texting conversation. Daniel.*

Joe thought for a second, puzzled, and then remembered. He'd come across the conversation in his phone when he was going through his messages a few weeks ago. He didn't remember what it said exactly—he had deleted it since—but knew that it had been odd and that he hadn't taken part in it. More so, he had no idea who Daniel was.

"What about it?" he asked, curious as to how this had anything to do with the underwear.

She signed one word, five letters. As she got closer and closer to finishing it Joe's jaw slowly unhinged.

"Bryce?" he asked in shock. "What about him?" But he already knew. And what she said next confirmed it:

He tried to break us up. And then he tried to kill me.

CHAPTER 27

Joe stared with rapt attention as Amanda signed without pause for the next half hour. She told him how she had left his house after breaking up with him, decided to come back, and saw Bryce tampering with his car. Then she told him how he had chased her. It was so vivid in her memory that it felt like she was reliving it:

The pain is almost too much for her to bear. She feels like stopping, leaning her bike against a tree, curling up into a ball, and dying. Who knew how deeply you could fall in love with someone after four months? And who knew how much it could hurt when it comes to an end?

She fights her emotions and pedals the next few blocks, trying to hold back her sobs. She doesn't do such a good job. Tears leak down her cheeks and turn the world into a shimmering mess. That's when she looks down and sees something glistening on her finger. After a moment, she realizes it's the ring Joe got her when he asked her out. It's catching the light of the sun and throwing it into her eyes. Looking at it, she instantly feels disgusted. How can she bear to let it touch her skin? She stops, twists it off—not even caring about the pain she summons when it gets stuck on her knuckle—and prepares to throw it away when she gets a better idea. Why throw it onto some guy's lawn when she can throw it in Joe's face instead? Like she had thrown his phone. It would be a childish thing to do—especially after already leaving—but strangely the thought makes the suffering slightly better to handle.

Yes. She thinks she'll do just that.

When she reaches his street, however, she stops. Bryce is outside, bending over Joe's car, holding something in his hand that catches the sun the same way her ring did. For one bizarre moment she thinks Bryce has a ring like hers, then she sees that the thing in his hand is a knife.

She utters a harsh gasp and clamps her hand to her mouth, hoping that Bryce doesn't hear it. It doesn't seem like he does. He just goes on staring at Joe's tire the way a surgeon might stare at a body as he debates where to make the first incision.

Amanda doesn't waste any time. She turns around and pedals as fast as she can, determined to put as much distance between herself and Bryce as possible. Suddenly, she couldn't care less about Joe's ring. In fact, she doesn't even know where it is anymore (in her haste to leave, she must have dropped it). All she can think about now is Bryce, and the hungry way he stared at her when she met him for the first time. The last thing she wants is those lecherous eyes falling upon her again.

She pumps the pedals hard, climbing a small hill and coasting down the other side. With each second that passes, she gets farther away. With each yard, she realizes that she needs to call Joe. Even if they just broke up, he has a right to know what Bryce is about to do. It's funny, if she thinks about it: Joe suspected Bryce the whole time, and she never believed him. She does now, and she thinks about pulling over to the sidewalk to call him, but the thought of stopping unsettles her. She needs to keep going. For that reason, she reaches for her cell when she coasts down the next hill. To her horror, it's not in her pocket. In her preoccupation, she must have forgotten to take it with her.

She reaches for her water bottle instead, her mouth feeling like it has turned into a desert. As she's sipping the cool liquid, she becomes aware of an approaching car. It's behind her, and she can't see it, but by the way its engine grows louder, she knows it's getting closer. Almost too *close. When she finally chances a look back, she nearly screams. It's the white Mercedes, the silver emblem glistening in the sun only a foot away from her back tire. In her panic she envisions it as the crosshair mounted on a World War II fighter plane. And it's aimed right at her. To confirm this, Bryce spreads his lips in an eerie smile.*

Amanda screams for a second time and drops the water bottle. It crashes to the pavement rushing by beneath her tires and bursts open, spraying water everywhere. She pays it no attention. Her focus is on surviving. She grabs the handlebars tighter than ever and stands up, pistoning her legs up and down like machinery. For a moment she begins to pull ahead, but by slightly adding pressure to the accelerator, Bryce pulls up beside her. He looks over, his smile widening, and raises his hand, tipping it slowly back and forth in a salute.

If Amanda's hands weren't clutching the bars for dear life, she might have given him the finger just then. What she does instead is shout.

"Leave me alone!" she shrieks.

Bryce responds by slightly turning the wheel. For a moment Amanda doesn't know what this will accomplish, then she sees that the Mercedes is coming closer and closer, the side of its door almost touching the end of her handlebars.

"Stop!" she cries. "What are you doing?"

Bryce's smile widens even more. It's so wide that it looks like his cheeks might rip.

There are houses on either side of them, but soon they will be approaching the stretch of road bordered by vacant lots and high tension wires. Amanda knows that if she is going to save herself it has to be now. She looks around, hoping to find somebody outside mowing their lawn, washing their car, walking their dog, anything for Christ's sake, but it's too late and the houses have already passed by. She and Bryce might as well be the only people alive. She can shout until her throat goes sore, but in the end it won't help her any.

She has to think. There has to be something she can do. Bryce is swerving the car back and forth, laughing maniacally. Any second, he might decide to ram into her.

He's playing with me, *she realizes with a sickening intensity.* The way a cat plays with a mouse before it kills it.

She doesn't want to be Bryce's mouse any longer. A number of things she can do flashes through her mind, but she rejects them all. If she stops, Bryce will stop. If she tries to go faster, Bryce will go faster. She can't even turn down another road because there aren't any more, just a straight shot. Therefore, she reaches out and grabs onto Bryce's door.

Bryce looks at her in surprise. "What do you think you're doing?" He doesn't ask in anger or fear, but amusement. The way a clever parent might ask an inquisitive child who's trying to climb out of his playpen.

Amanda stares coldly into his eyes. In truth she doesn't know what she's doing, has no fucking idea, only hopes that by grabbing onto his car he won't be able to run her off the road.

But that's exactly what he does. Bryce smiles one last time, waves, then fumbles around for something on his door. Suddenly, the passenger side window begins to roll up. Amanda cries out in surprise, forced to let go, and nearly swerves off the road herself. She hasn't noticed it, but by grabbing onto the Mercedes she has picked up speed. Much more than she would have liked. If her bike had a speedometer—or speeeed-o-meter—*she would realize that she's heading down the road at a little over forty miles per hour. The trees by her side whoosh past, first one, then another. The sound of the Mercedes's engine bounces off them, making her think of a tiger growling. Bryce slams his foot on the accelerator, and it roars. She cries out again, but it's for the last time.*

Before she knows what's happening, Bryce swerves, there's a loud sound like a gunshot, and then she's weightless.

Amanda twisted her hand into the final letter and then put it down, feeling it begin to ache. She couldn't believe how many details she had recalled for something she hadn't even remembered until a moment ago.

Joe still couldn't say anything. He was in shock. The zip-tie, the flat tire, the underwear, and now Amanda's near-death experience—Bryce was responsible for all of them. But why? What had Joe done to make Bryce do such horrible things? And then he suddenly knew, clear as ever. He had spied on Bryce. And Bryce had caught him. It was as simple as that. His phone had been pressed against his ear, and Bryce had probably assumed that Joe was talking to Luke. Who else would ask for Bryce's license plate number but an ex-husband? And if that were true, then that meant Luke was in serious trouble. Because, as Joe was finding out, Bryce was ruthless and didn't stop for anything.

CHAPTER 28

Nothing felt the same anymore. Every little thing—not making the baseball team, fighting with C.J., the detention that had since doubled for his skipping school—seemed inconsequential compared to this. This was real, when everything else seemed fake, as if they were things he'd seen in a movie that were slowly fading from his memory. Like a fashion trend, they were out and Bryce was in. He filled Joe's head with horrible thoughts as Joe drove home, giving him goose bumps.

He had stayed with Amanda for a full hour after she stopped signing. At first he didn't talk, but as the shock of what he had learned wore off, he began to come around. He told Amanda not to worry, that he would take care of everything, even though he had no idea what to do. She recommended the obvious—calling the police—but he wasn't sure if that was the best idea. What if Amanda couldn't prove what Bryce did and they let him go? He would become as vindictive as ever. Joe told her this, and she told him that she trusted his decision but to do something because she was scared. That angered Joe more than anything. He could see the fear in her emerald green eyes—eyes that once sparkled with hope and affection—and wanted to kill Bryce for it. What right did Bryce have to take that away from her? What right did he have to attack her?

Oh, he had plenty of right, that cruel voice in Joe's head had whispered.

Now that Joe thought about it, he decided that the voice was right. That is to say, at least in Bryce's mind. Amanda had seen certain things, certain *incriminating* things, and therefore needed to be silenced. If you knew too much, you had to be taken care of. First Joe, by cutting the zip-tie and giving him a flat. Then Amanda, by hitting her on her bike. Who next? Luke? Joe's parents? And to what end? Death? Joe's skin rippled at the thought. He knew he couldn't wait for that to happen. Bryce was upping the ante each time, and soon he would be all in. Joe was left with no other option but to attack Bryce before he attacked him. The best defense is a strong offense, as Coach Heck was wont to say. Joe thought long and hard and finally decided that Amanda was right. He had to tell someone: first his parents and then the police. It was a gamble, but one he had to take.

As he turned onto his block, his eyes immediately went to Crystal's house, looking for the white Mercedes. He had a feeling that if he looked close enough he would be able to find a circular dent on Bryce's passenger side door, proving he had hit into Amanda's bike in order to run her off the road. This wouldn't exactly be evidence, but it would sure support the story he planned on telling the police. The only thing was, Bryce's car wasn't there.

He's getting it detailed, the cruel voice told him. *He's getting rid of the dent.*

Joe scolded himself for letting his imagination run away again. Bryce was just out, either at work or at the store. But strangely, when he tried to tell himself this, he found that he didn't believe it. As he was learning, Bryce was cunning, and the thought of him going to a body shop didn't surprise Joe at all.

He parked and got out. The first thing he noticed was that his house was abnormally dark. He'd left the hospital when the sun was setting—having to shield his eyes as he drove—and when he reached his block it had dipped just under the horizon, bleeding the last of its dying rays into a crimson sunset. His mother usually put the light on over the stove at this time. Except when he walked in, he found that it was off, the kitchen bathed in shadows. Had it burned out? Had she forgotten to turn it on? That made him wonder something else: were his parents even home? He couldn't seem to remember if their cars had been outside or if the little light in the garage—the one that turned on when the door opened—had been lit. Suddenly, this seemed very important to know.

He felt the presence of someone else in the house and called out "I'm home" as he set his keys on the kitchen counter. He almost expected Bryce to answer. When he didn't—when *nobody* did—he made his way through the other rooms.

Like the kitchen, the other rooms were dark and neglected. He had to blindly pick his way through furniture that would have otherwise been visible during the day. It seemed that the dying light from outside was fading at an alarming rate, as if time were speeding up the way it had seemed to do at the hospital.

When he reached the staircase, the house was almost pitch-black. He would have wondered where his parents were had there not been a single light seeping out into the hallway from one of the upstairs rooms.

"Mom? Dad?" he tried calling again.

Nothing.

Bryce was so prominent in his thoughts that he almost felt some-one breathing down his neck. His mind dredged up terrible fantasies: the Craig's List murderer at large, his mother and father lying on the floor, marinating in a pool of blood; his father hanging in the closet by one of his ties; his mother strapped to the bed with her wrists slit, slowly dying as the fluid of life drained from her body . . .

Joe shook his head, purging these horrible images. None of them had happened. The Craig's List murderer only went after prostitutes, and Bryce was mad, yes, possibly even crazy, but Joe's parents hadn't done anything. There would be no reason for Bryce to—

Kill them? The cruel voice reappeared. *Why not? Once a killer, always a killer. What's two more? Or three? Or four? Hell, why not try to get everybody? Collect them all!*

But Bryce was no killer. He'd come close with Amanda, but maybe that had been an accident. He sure hadn't tried to do anything remotely close to that to Joe. The worst he'd done was give him a flat tire and try to break him and Amanda up.

Joe felt slightly better as he reasoned this out. He was now at the bottom of the stairs. Yet, no matter how hard he tried to reassure himself, he found that he could not begin the climb to the top. It was as if there was still something there that he was afraid of: a monster, or even more horrible, the truth.

Quit being a baby, he told himself. *Go!*

Slowly, like a hesitant climber ascending Everest, he put his hand on the banister. Equally slowly, he raised his foot and placed it on the first stair. About halfway to the top he heard a noise coming from the room with the light on. It sounded like a drawer being closed. He kept climbing. Now that he was closer, he was able to discern a faint murmuring. When he finally reached the landing, he stopped, cocking an ear. The murmuring was louder. An argument. A male's voice, servile and clipped, and a female's, slightly louder and domineering: his parents.

He moved down the hall and pushed open the door at the end.

His parents moved back and forth across the room with mechanical slowness, carrying clothes and placing them into suitcases on the bed.

"Mom? Dad?"

"Huh?" his father said in his familiar whispering tone. He stopped what he was doing and looked around. When he spotted Joe standing in the doorway, he said, "Oh. Hi, Joe," and resumed his task.

His mother made a livelier show of affection, setting down the clothes and walking over to him. She planted a kiss on his forehead and asked him how Amanda was doing.

"She's getting better," Joe said. He might have said more, but he could tell that something was bothering her. He wanted to ask what it was but could only manage: "Why are you guys packing?"

"We're going on our marriage retreat," she answered. "Remember?"

Joe tried to, but with all that had happened in the past month, he honestly couldn't.

"Your what?"

"Our marriage retreat. I've definitely told you. We've been planning a vacation for a while now. Your father's cheap boss finally gave him the proper commission for one of his accounts, so we booked it."

Now that Joe thought about it, he remembered his parents saying something about leaving for a vacation. He guessed that his father's plan of having Mr. Lancaster over for dinner had actually worked, even if his mother hated to admit it. That just went to show you that the way to a man's heart really was through his stomach (especially a man whose stomach accounted for ninety-five percent of his body mass). But if that was the case, and they *were* going on vacation, then why was there so much more tension between them than usual? They had been arguing when Joe had come in, avoiding each other's eyes as they packed. They had their problems, sure, but wasn't the whole purpose of this trip to rekindle the dying flame of their marriage?

Joe didn't know. He just watched the way his father methodically rolled up his clothes and placed them in his suitcase, arranging them so they took up as little space as possible. His mother had done the complete opposite. One look at her Burberry suitcase told him that she had unceremoniously tossed her clothes in, not caring if a shirt or a pair of shorts hung over the side. The two of them were polar opposites. How they had lasted together this long was a mystery.

Margaret saw the glazed look in her son's eyes. "Joe?"

Joe blinked. He had been drifting. "Oh, right. *That* trip." He looked at the suitcases again, then back to his mother. She wore the same dour expression, not at all like her normal self. "Is everything all right?" Joe finally asked. "Why's it so dark in the house?"

"It's dark already?"

George pushed aside the blinds, looking out. He mumbled something and let them go, turning them into a pendulum.

Margaret said, "I guess we lost track of time. There's been a lot on our minds."

Joe could have laughed at that. What did they possibly have on their minds that could compete with what he had on his?

She must have seen the question on his face because she said, "Joe, come here. Sit down." Without waiting, she put her arm on Joe's shoulder and led him over to the bed. When he was seated, she took in a deep breath. Surprisingly, Joe could see that she was fighting to hold back tears. Finally she said, "Snowball ran away while you were at the hospital."

Joe stood up at once. *"What?"*

He hadn't noticed earlier because of everything on his mind, but now that he thought about it, Snowball hadn't greeted him on the way in. Usually the moment he stuck his keys in the door, Snowball popped his fluffy head out from between the window blinds, the way the bird does in a cuckoo clock. Tonight, that hadn't happened.

Margaret hung her head. Her voice was softer than ever, filled with sympathy. "I let him out this afternoon, and when I went to bring him in, he wasn't there."

"What do you mean he wasn't there?" Joe asked. Just the thought of his dog alone in the world was almost too much to bear. Not now. Not on top of everything else.

"Just what I said. He wasn't there." She paused, biting her lip. After the grief passed she added, a bit accusingly, "When I went to look for him I found the gate open. Apparently *someone* forgot to lock it this morning after he let the oil man in."

Without warning George whirled around, the clothes in his arms nearly spraying about the room. "Dammit, Margaret. I already told you. I locked the gate after he left." He didn't shout, but spoke in his whispering tone, although a bit coarser than usual. His glasses came askew, and his body shook. It was the closest Joe had ever seen him come to yelling.

Margaret leaped at the opportunity to shift her weight. Unlike George, she *did* yell, raising her voice like a champion. *"Then who did it, George? Answer me that! Because I know I sure didn't!"*

George mumbled something, pushed his glasses up the bridge of his nose, and continued packing. Margaret shook her head. "Honestly, why can't men ever own up to their mistakes? Don't you be like that, Joe. You'll never get married if that's the case." She reconsidered. "Not if the woman's smart."

George mumbled something again, then fell silent.

After a while Joe asked, "What's going to happen to Snowball? Did you call anyone? Put out signs?"

Margaret nodded. "I did just that. I called all the neighbors and went around putting up flyers. Nobody's seen him, but if they do, they'll call us immediately. I even listed a reward."

George snapped his head around at this last. A reward was obviously news to him. Joe could tell by his intent stare that he was itching to ask his wife what she thought they could afford. Knowing her, it would be some outrageous amount. *The more I put, the sooner we'll get Snowball back,* would undoubtedly be her logic. He wanted to ask but was afraid at the same time. Fear seemed to outweigh curiosity because he kept silent.

"Okay," Joe said at last. "I'll try to drive around and see if I can find him."

Margaret put her hand back on his shoulder. "I'm sorry, Joe. This really happened at a horrible time."

You're telling me, he thought.

"Are you okay? You look a little pale."

"Yeah, I'm fine," he lied. Then: "Actually, no. There's something I need to talk to you about. The both of you." He tried to think of the best way to bring it up, and then decided to plunge. "Mom, Dad. Someone tried to kill Amanda."

CHAPTER 29

Margaret stared at her son, unblinking, as if she was trying to figure out if he was joking. His face was set, serious, his eyes focused and his pupils wide. It didn't look like he was.

"What?" George asked in surprise. He had been rolling up a shirt, but stopped and set it aside. "What did you say?"

"I said, someone tried to kill Amanda."

"At the hospital?"

"No, on her bike. It wasn't an accident. It was on purpose."

"How do you know?" Margaret asked, skeptically.

"Because she told me!"

"How? Isn't her jaw wired shut?"

"It is, but she knows sign language. Plus, the nurse gave her a pen and she wrote some of it down." He immediately wished he'd taken what she'd written so he could have something to show his parents.

"She told you through sign language?" his mother asked in surprise. "*You* know sign language?"

"She used to have a deaf brother. She taught me the alphabet, enough for me to be able to understand her, okay? You have to believe me!"

"Calm down," Margaret said.

"Does Amanda know who did it?" George asked, concerned.

"Yes!" Joe nearly shouted. "It was Bryce! From across the street! *He* did it!" He had shouted almost loud enough for Bryce to hear. But he realized he didn't care. The secret was out, and he was on a roll. "He tried killing her because she saw him about to slash my tires! He didn't want any witnesses!"

Now it was Margaret's turn to shout. *"What? Why on earth would Bryce do such a thing?"*

"Because he's evil!" Joe shouted back. "He's pissed because he caught me spying on him. Luke called and asked if I could get his plate number, and Bryce caught me while I was looking with a pair of binoculars. Then he cut my zip-tie and gave me a flat tire."

George looked confused. "Zip-tie? Flat tire?"

"Is that why you were riding around with that spare for a while?" Margaret asked.

"You saw him do this?" George interrupted, his voice returning to his calm whisper.

"Not exactly . . ." Joe said. "But you have to believe me!" He felt his blood boiling.

Margaret's eyebrows came together. "I think I know what's going on here . . ."

Finally! Joe thought.

". . . and I don't appreciate it one bit. That girl really has some nerve, making up lies like that."

Joe looked at his mother, unable to believe his ears.

"I can understand that she had an accident, but to blame our neighbor? That's ridiculous. I always knew there was something off about her. Guess it runs in the family."

"Mom, her brother was deaf! He didn't have mental problems!"

"And to lie right to your face," she went on, barely hearing a word Joe said. "That's just not right. I told you to stay away from her. Don't you see what she's doing? She's trying to make herself seem needy so you can pamper her. She's trying to take advantage of you."

Joe was fuming now. This wasn't at all how he hoped his parents would react. He had hoped they would shout in surprise and rage and make a huge commotion. Well, maybe not so much his father but definitely his mother. In fact, he had *expected* her to. But now she was shouting for the wrong reason.

"I'm sorry, Joe," Margaret said, "but Bryce wouldn't do that. You've been under a lot of stress lately. I think you've been spending too much time with that girl. Your school even called and said that your grades are slipping. Maybe we should take you to see someone so you can deal with all this pressure."

"See someone?" Joe and George cried at the same time. There was anger in both of their voices, but for entirely different reasons: George because he knew how expensive psychiatrists could be, and Joe because . . . well . . . it was obvious.

"I don't need to see a stupid doctor!" he shouted. "I need you to believe me!"

"Lower your voice, Joe," George said. "He's right, Maggie. He doesn't need to see a doctor. He's fine. Under the circumstances, it's normal for him to be upset."

"Because of that girl, yes. I understand that, George. But did you hear what he said about Bryce? He's looking for someone to blame all his bad luck on. That's not normal . . . or healthy. I'm scheduling him an appointment with a psychiatrist as soon as we get back."

George grunted and turned away, packing his last shirt and zipping up his suitcase.

"Don't ignore me, George. This is your son, too. You can't put a dollar sign on his mental health."

George rounded on her, his glasses once more slipping from his nose. "No, but you can put a dollar sign on a mortgage, and there is! If you keep throwing away money like this"—he pointed to the Burberry suitcases—"like it grows on trees, then we're not going to have any left to pay the bills!"

"Honestly, I can't believe you. For someone who's supposed to be so smart, you're really stupid sometimes. I buy *necessary* items, and *only* when they're on sale, unlike that car your boss swindled you for."

George grunted again, picked up his suitcase, and put it on the floor.

Joe ignored the comment, looking at the bags. "You're not still leaving, are you?"

"Yes," George said. "Our flight's tomorrow afternoon."

"Are you serious? Didn't you hear anything I said? Bryce tried to kill Amanda! If you leave, he might try to kill me next! We have to call the police! We have to get him arrested!"

"You see?" Margaret shouted. "That's exactly what I'm talking about! That's not healthy!"

George grabbed the sides of his head as if he were trying to keep his brain from leaking out of his ears. "We're not canceling the trip," he said through clenched teeth. "And Joe's not going to a doctor."

"Well, at least we agree on one thing: there's no way we're canceling this trip. The tickets are non-refundable, and who knows when your cheap-ass boss will keep his word again and give you your full commission. As for the psychiatrist, George, I'm calling first thing tomorrow morning."

They continued to argue back and forth while Joe watched. He knew by the way his father quarreled instead of retreating to his office that he was at a bursting point. Joe didn't want to be around when that finally happened. More so, Joe realized that he would get nowhere with his parents. They were set on leaving, and they were stubborn. They wouldn't believe him about Bryce no matter what he said because he was younger and therefore inferior. They didn't realize that he was seventeen and almost an adult and capable of rational thought. Which is why he decided to let them think they had won. He would just wait until they left tomorrow and call the police himself. What they didn't know wouldn't hurt them, and if they weren't there, they couldn't stop him.

"Mom . . ." When he got no answer, he raised his voice. "Mom!"

His mother and father turned around.

"You're right. Both of you. I *am* under a lot of stress. Maybe Bryce didn't do those things. I don't know. I'm just tired, I guess. I'm going to bed."

"You see?" Margaret said, triumphantly. "He admits that he's under pressure. I'm calling, George, and that's that."

Joe walked out. As he made his way down the hall he heard his father telling his mother to hold off on calling a psychiatrist, that he had a better idea.

The next day began bright and sunny, light shining through Joe's blinds, illuminating the room, as though it were foreshadowing optimism.

Joe awoke about half an hour before his parents left, the sound of the suitcases clapping against the stairs pulling him out of sleep. He tossed and turned and then finally got up, wiping at his eyes and squinting against the brightness of the day.

The lower level of his house was full of activity: his mother going in and out of the door loading the car, his father checking to make sure he had his passport, tickets, and hadn't forgotten anything important. Joe gave them both a wide berth, not wanting to engage in conversation, and disappeared into the kitchen. A few minutes and they would be out of his hair for a full week.

He poured himself a bowl of cereal, and as he was eating, George stepped into the room, moving with the quick, almost spasmodic jerks of a weasel hunting its prey. He double-checked to see if he had packed all the right vitamins, and when he noticed that Joe was at the table, he pulled up a chair.

"Morning," he said.

Joe echoed the word through a mouth full of Frosted Cheerios.

There was something different about his father today. He carried himself a little higher, and there was a hint of a smile on his face. Joe wondered if it was because his long-awaited dream of visiting Italy was finally about to come true.

"You know how you were confused about Bryce last night?" he asked.

Joe nodded, chewing. How could he forget? It made him wonder why his father would even ask such a thing. And then it hit him: it was because his father believed, just hadn't wanted to say anything in front of

Margaret. Joe didn't know how to react. One parent believing him was better than none, even if it was his father.

"Well," George continued. "I went ahead and solved that little mystery for you."

That confused Joe. "What do you mean?"

"I called Bryce and told him what you thought."

Joe had the spoon halfway to his mouth. Now he dropped it into the bowl with a splash. *"You did what?"* he shouted, standing up.

"I spoke to Bryce and told him how you thought he was mad at you for 'spying' on him. He actually thought it was funny. He feels bad that you're upset and wants to set your mind at ease."

"Are you kidding me? Did you really do something that stupid?"

The half-hidden smile immediately vanished from George's face, and his shoulders slumped. "Joe, I—"

"Dad, I can't believe you! How could you do that?"

"Joe, I was only trying to help. It was either that or therapy, and I know you wouldn't want—"

"I'd rather go to therapy than let Bryce know I told you what he did! I can't believe this!"

"Joe—"

But Joe was already out the room. He ran up the stairs and slammed his door loud enough to shake the house.

His parents came up to his room and knocked twenty minutes later. Joe refused them entry.

"Joe, are you okay?" Margaret asked.

"I'm fine," Joe lied.

"Then open the door."

"No, I don't want to."

"Come on, Joe," George insisted. "Open the door."

That was a laugh. Joe didn't want to come out. He couldn't believe how utterly stupid parents could be sometimes. His father had basically signed his death warrant and handed it to his killer.

"We're not leaving until you come out," Margaret said.

Joe didn't believe her. She might be playing the concerned parent now, but when the time came and the whistle blew, she would punch her timecard and deal with it another day.

"Joe, please?" Margaret begged.

"No," Joe said. "I'm just upset, that's all. I wanna be alone."

He heard his mother and father bicker over something after that. He didn't need supersonic hearing to know that it had to do with the psychiatrist and his father's brilliant phone call.

Finally, after one last persistent attempt to get Joe to open the door, they left, telling him to be safe and that they would email him the moment they could find a computer. Joe wished them a good trip from the other side of the door, even though by this point he couldn't care less, and watched as their car pulled out of the driveway. When it was out of sight, he picked up his cell and dialed three numbers.

"911, what is your emergency?"

Joe told the dispatcher his problem. After listening for nearly five minutes, she got his address and told him she would send over a police officer. Joe thanked her and ended the call. The nearest police station was over half an hour away. There was a chance they might contact one of the officers at the fire house (it was closer, and there was always one or two officers hanging out there), and if that was the case then he had about ten minutes. Either way, he had some time to kill. He thought about turning on the TV or checking out Facebook, but in the end he decided to flop onto his bed and text Amanda.

He rapped quickly on the keys and hit the send button, launching his message toward that great satellite in the sky that all Verizon customers prayed to. A few minutes later he got an answer:

From: Amanda <3
Good morning :)
April 30, 11:07am

He smiled, fascinated that she could brighten his day just by adding a little happy face at the end of her message.

How are you feeling?
To: Amanda <3
Sent: April 30, 11:07am

From: Amanda <3
Better, thanks for asking.
April 30, 11:07am

Np. Ur gonna feel even better after I tell you this . . .
To: Amanda <3
Sent: April 30, 11:08am

From: Amanda <3
What?
April 30, 11:09am

I thought long and hard and decided that the best thing to do was to call the police. Their sending over an officer right now. Were gonna get that piece of shit thrown behind bars.
To: Amanda <3
Sent: April 30, 11:09am

From: Amanda <3
I thought you said that wasn't the best idea? What happens if I can't prove he did it? It's my word against his, isn't it?
April 30, 11:10am

> Thats just a chance were gonna
> have to take. The longer we wait
> the more time he has to try
> something like this again.
> To: Amanda <3
> Sent: April 30, 11:12am
>
> From: Amanda <3
> Yeah . . . I guess you're right.
> April 30, 11:12am
>
> Itll be okay. I promise.
> To: Amanda <3
> Sent: April 30, 11:14am

Through the open window came the sound of a car driving down the block. From the way the engine grew quieter, Joe thought it was slowing down. He scooted off the bed and looked outside. Sure enough, he was right: a white and blue police car had pulled into his driveway. Before the officer could get out, Joe was out of his room and down the stairs, thinking about how he was going to return the favor and brighten up Amanda's day. After all, what could be sweeter than revenge?

He sent her one last text—

> Cops here. Gotta go. Love you.
> To: Amanda <3
> Sent: April 30, 11:16am

—and then opened the door.

Joe could tell by the height of the officer's belt buckle that he was tall. The ironed and creased pants of his uniform seemed almost endless, starting just above the polished black shoes and ascending toward the sky. Joe followed their progress with his eyes, coming to the shiny buckle, then playing hopscotch with the buttons on the officer's shirt. He stopped when he came upon the collar. Instead of the ends being blank, there were two gold bars stitched into the fabric. Joe knew enough of the police ranking system to know that this stood for captain.

He sighed in relief, feeling as if someone finally understood the gravity of the situation. And this cop—excuse me, captain—looked pretty brawny. If anyone was going to talk to Bryce, Joe was glad it was this guy, because anyone else wouldn't be intimidating enough.

"Somebody here call the police?" the captain asked.

Joe froze, feeling his mind whirling. He knew that voice. Until this point he had been so transfixed by the captain's size that he hadn't even looked at his face. Now he did, and what he saw made his legs feel like they had turned into rubber.

CHAPTER 30

The shock shot through his body like a charge of electricity, paralyzing every muscle along the way. It struck Joe so hard that he could barely stand and had to clutch the door frame to keep from falling. In addition to this, he felt all the blood drain from his face. If he'd had a mirror he would have seen that he looked like a vampire: skin as white as canvas. Distantly, he felt his cell vibrate in his pocket, but it might as well have been a million miles away. He was wilting and withering like a dying plant, words of the past echoing in his head: *I'm a captain for the police department. Been on the force for twenty-eight years now.*

"What's the matter, Joe?" Bryce said. "You don't look happy to see me."

A spasm raked Joe's body, and he gripped the doorframe even tighter. Now he knew what it felt like to stare death in the face. He tried to speak, but once again, when he found himself in a situation he didn't know how to handle, all that would come out was air. This didn't seem to bother Bryce in the slightest. He stood there patient as ever, waiting for Joe to collect himself. It took a full two minutes. At last Joe managed: "Why are *you* here?"

"I'm here because you made me come," Bryce said. "You told your father about me." He raised his finger in front of Joe's face and rocked it slowly back and forth the way a school teacher does when scolding a child. "That wasn't smart. You know this only works if you keep everything between us, don't you?"

Again, Joe had no words.

"I heard your call come in at the station and knew I had to handle it personally. To tell you the truth, since your father called me, I've been expecting it. And now, here we are."

Of course. Joe felt like hitting his father. If he hadn't called Bryce, he might have had a chance going to the police. Now all hope was lost. Bryce would intervene the moment he set foot in the station or dialed the number. He didn't know what else to do, so he asked the one question he had to have the answer to: "Was it you? The zip-tie, the flat tire, the underwear. Was it you?"

"Yes," Bryce said. "It was me. Everything except the tire. That was just a little bad luck on your part. I *was* going to slash your tire, but that's when your girlfriend caught me, and I had to take care of her instead."

A torrential surge of anger rushed through Joe's body like water escaping a dam. He could hear his heart thudding in his ears, almost deafening, blocking out the sound of everything else. He hated Bryce more than ever right now, and it took all his willpower to restrain himself from doing something unbelievably stupid, like attacking.

"You're not going to get away with this," he hissed.

Bryce laughed as though this was the funniest joke he'd ever heard. "Joe, I already have. I've been getting away with it for years. There's nothing you can do to stop me. And if you try, I'll kill that little girlfriend of yours."

Joe hated himself for admitting it, but Bryce was right. There was nothing he could do. He felt his throat start to close as he thought about Amanda lying in the hospital with her jaw wired shut and those tubes in her arm. It nearly made him sick to his stomach knowing that her pain would never be avenged. "Fine," he said. "You win. I won't go to the police again or tell anyone else about this as long as you promise to leave us alone. Deal?"

Bryce raised his hand to his chin, stroking it, thinking. "No," he said at last. "No deal." And leaving those last words to hover in the air, he turned around and strode back to the police car.

Joe stood dumbstruck. He waited for Bryce to pull out before he locked the door and crumbled to the ground. Then he drew his knees to his chest, dropped his face into his hands, and cried. He had never felt so defeated in all his life. Just as Amanda had needed his comfort when she was in pain, he needed hers now. He pulled out his phone to call her, but on the screen, waiting for him, was the text he received while answering the door and hadn't had time to view:

From: Amanda <3
Good luck, baby!
April 30, 11:18am

He stared at it for a long time before closing his phone. Luck. That was exactly what he was going to need. And a lot of it.

CHAPTER 31

Joe sat there without moving for a long time, letting his hitching chest press against his thighs as he cried. He felt like a child again, unable to control his emotions. All he wanted to do was wake up from the horrible dream which had become his life.

After a time, he managed to pull himself to his feet. He showered and forced himself to eat something. Then he turned on the television, not really aware of how long he sat in front of it. He didn't watch anything, just let the voices fill the room so he wouldn't feel so alone.

He debated whether or not to text Amanda back—she had texted him twice since Bryce left—but didn't know what to say to her. He felt lost, and still loathed himself for even suggesting that he and Bryce call it a draw after what Bryce had done to her. More so, he had to wrestle with his brain for a way out of the horrible predicament in which he found himself. He remembered the motivational posters on the walls of Coach Heck's office. If a blind man could climb Everest and a girl who had her arm bitten off by a shark could continue to surf, even though it probably scared the absolute shit out of her, he could find a way out. He just had to think.

Since he couldn't go to the police, and his parents were in another country, he thought about telling Luke. But that option lasted no more than a few seconds. By this point in their relationship, Bryce was sleeping at Crystal's house, and that meant that he was also sleeping under the same roof as Luke's daughter. Luke knew this, and if he heard what Joe had to tell him, Joe didn't think Luke would hesitate in the slightest to hurt Bryce. And if that happened, Luke would either get himself killed or sent to jail, and then he would be no help at all. In the best case scenario, Luke would go to Crystal and tell her everything, but then she'd just think he was a jealous, raving lunatic. No, Joe couldn't have that. He had to think carefully. Bryce had all the aces up his sleeve, but Joe thought he could still form a pretty good hand. All he had to do was draw the right cards.

He ran through his options countless times, coming up with nothing. It seemed that all hope was lost. That is . . . until he took a step back. Someone had to tell Crystal the truth about Bryce, this was true. Except it couldn't be Luke. It had to be him, Joe. He was on neutral ground and had the best chance of getting her to see how evil Bryce was. Joe could even take her to the hospital so she could talk to Amanda. Once she heard the true story, she would have to end things with Bryce. And once she did, he could try going to the police again. They might not listen to a teenager, but they would certainly listen to the woman Bryce was living with. Joe didn't think it would be all that hard to get her on his side after she saw what her boyfriend had done to Amanda.

By the time he came up with this plan his stomach was grumbling again, and he realized that a few more hours had passed. Not wanting to waste a minute more, he downed a quick glass of milk and looked out the window. Crystal's car was in the driveway. The spot where Bryce usually parked was empty. Good. Very good. Joe was out the door in an instant. He had to do this, and he had to do this fast, before Bryce came back.

As he walked down the driveway a bit of the past came back to him, and he couldn't help but remember when Luke had first told him the horrible news about his divorce:

CHAPTER 32

Joe walks down the driveway, breathing in the warming air. He can barely see his breath when he exhales and knows this is a good sign. Spring will be here before he knows it. Already most of the snow has melted. All that is left are the remains of the piles the plows have built up while clearing the streets. What has once been huge mountains are now tiny brown mounds no more than a foot high.

Joe walks past one of these as he approaches his car, twisting his face at the murky pile of slush. He's glad spring is on its way so he won't have to deal with them anymore or scrape the ice off his windshield while he waits for his car to warm up. He can just hop in and drive, like he does now. He checks his mirrors and pulls out, ready to make his way down the block, when he catches a glimpse of Luke sitting on the bumper of his car and smoking a cigarette.

Like C.J., he and Luke had gone their separate ways, but not for the same reasons. It was easy to stay in touch during the fall with Luke being off from work—it seemed as if every time Joe went outside, Luke was there, sitting in a lawn chair, watching Kendra ride her bike back and forth in front of the house—but when winter came, it made things harder. Luke no longer hung out outside, and by then his back had healed, and he had gone back to work. The only times they spoke were when Luke called him to ask how his car was doing and if he needed help with anything. Joe always answered the calls eagerly and chatted until the conversation dried out. But, like everything else, nothing lasted forever. When they ran out of things to talk about, and nothing broke on Joe's car, those calls tapered off.

Joe told himself he'd call Luke just to shoot the breeze, but each time he thought about picking up the phone, he got sidetracked by one thing or another. That's why when he sees Luke outside, he knows he should use the opportunity to catch up.

He stops the car and rolls down his window. "Hey, Luke," he says teasingly, "I didn't know you smoked."

The man sitting on the bumper looks up, and for a second Joe thinks he has just suffered a case of mistaken identity. This man looks much older than Luke, his face deeply lined, the hair at his temples beginning to gray. He gets up and begins to walk toward the street. As he pitches his cigarette, Joe can't help but notice that he is missing part of his index finger.

Holy shit, *Joe says to himself.* It is Luke. *He wants to ask him what the hell has happened, but knows it would be rude. What is more, he hopes the shock doesn't show on his face and ask the question for him.*

"Joseph," Luke says in his favorite two-syllable gambit. He approaches the car and offers his hand.

Joe shakes it. "I haven't seen ya around lately."

"That's because I haven't lived here in about two months."

Time stops for a second. Joe has to rewind to be sure he has heard right. Luke sees the look on his face and confirms the news.

"Crystal and I are getting a divorce."

Joe's mouth drops. "What? Are you serious?"

"Scout's honor."

As if to confirm this, Luke rests his hands on the car's door. Even though it is the end of winter, he still has the tan line where his ring used to be, as if it has been burned into his skin from years of wearing it.

"Oh God, Luke. I'm so sorry."

"Don't be. I'm not. In fact, it's probably for the best."

Joe is at a loss for words. He isn't good at these types of situations. In fact, he isn't good at most adult situations. Luke was the only adult he'd found that he could actually carry on a conversation with. Now, it seems like he has been robbed of this pleasure.

Finally he manages to ask, "Are you okay?"

Luke laughs, arching his back and looking up at the sky. It sounds eerie in the still air. "Am I okay? I've never been better. I asked a woman out the other day. She called up to have her car inspected, and she sounded attractive, so I asked her if she would like to have coffee, and she agreed."

Joe doesn't think Luke is okay, not by the looks of things, and certainly not after hearing that little anecdote. If anything, it confirms the complete opposite.

"Cool," Joe hears himself say, but his voice sounds distant, not his own. For a moment, he is outside himself, watching the conversation take place. It makes him think of his parents. If the impossible can happen to what appeared to be a happily married couple, it can certainly happen to a couple in a dysfunctional relationship like theirs. His parents were already exhibiting the telltale signs of divorce: constant arguing, separate sleeping arrangements, and avoidance to name a few. It would be only a matter of time before they followed suit and walked down the same road as Luke and Crystal.

"Just do me a favor," Luke asks. "Don't tell anyone about all this. I'm sure they'll find out in time, but for now keep it between us, okay?"

"Sure," Joe says. "Yeah, I can do that."

"Thanks. So are you still seeing that girl? What was her name? Amanda?"

"Yeah. Amanda. I'm on my way to her house now."

"How's that going?"

"Good."

"Good to hear. Make sure things stay that way between you two. Be faithful to each other. Nothing destroys a relationship more than a lack of trust."

Joe feels himself nodding.

"How's your car? Is it still holding up?"

"It's good," he says.

"Very good. You can still call me if you have any problems with it. I'm not living here, but I do have an apartment not too far away. We can always work on it there."

"Thanks."

"Don't mention it. I wouldn't want your car to suffer because of something that happened beyond your control."

Joe hasn't realized until now, but Luke is trying to prolong the conversation. He wonders if Luke has talked to anyone else about the divorce. If he hasn't, this might be his way of reaching out, asking for help without really asking. If that's the case, Joe doesn't know what he's supposed to do.

He tries to think of something and hears himself asking the question before he even realizes it: "What are you doing Thursday? Would you wanna watch a movie? I can bring one by."

For the first time since seeing him today, Luke looks happy, grateful even. His eyes twinkle, the lines around his mouth soften, and for a second he doesn't look as old anymore.

"I'd like that," he says. "I'd like that very much."

CHAPTER 33

Joe paused at the foot of the driveway, letting the memory fade from his mind. It made him realize that if Crystal and Luke had stayed together, he would have never found himself in this horrible predicament. Because of that, he grimaced, hating Crystal a little. He crossed the street, however, knowing that he'd have to swallow his anger if he wanted her help. This was not the time to hold grudges. He already held one against Bryce, and that was enough.

By the time he reached her door, he had replaced the look of contempt with a neutral expression. It wasn't the greatest of faces, but it was the best he could come up with considering the way he felt: his heart was pounding, his skin was wet and clammy, and the palms of his hands were nearly dripping with perspiration. It was now or never, he told himself, and he only had one shot. If he couldn't get her to go along with his plan then he would be helplessly lost.

He drew in breath, trying to steady himself, and felt his head swim. When it cleared, he reached out with a trembling finger and rang the doorbell. The chimes sounded inside, and Crystal's footsteps approached the door after what felt like an eternity. When it began to open, Joe bit down on his lower lip, preparing himself for what he was about to say.

PART 4

WATCHES CAN NEVER TICK BACKWARDS, ONLY THE MEMORY

CHAPTER 34

"Joseph," Luke said, opening the door the rest of the way and letting him in. "Thanks again for babysitting Kendra tonight. It means a lot to Crystal and me." He called over his shoulder, "Crystal, they're here!"

"Oh, no problem," Joe said, stepping into the house. He waited for Amanda to step in behind him, and when she did, he introduced her. "Luke, this is Amanda. Amanda, Luke."

Luke stuck out his hand. "So this is the beautiful Amanda I've been hearing so much about?"

Joe blushed. Amanda giggled. She took Luke's hand and shook it. Joe saw that by the way she hesitated she had noticed the tip of his missing finger. Luke didn't seem to care.

"Nice to meet you," she said.

Without any warning, Kendra came barreling around the corner and crashed into Joe's leg, wrapping her arms around it in a bear hug.

"And this little whirlwind," Luke said, prying his daughter off Joe, "is Kendra."

"She's beautiful," Amanda said. Even dressed for bed Kendra exuded a bit of radiance, the type of radiance only a child could give off. With her red feetie pajamas and long golden hair, she looked like a miniature version of Little Red Riding Hood.

Kendra took a step back when she noticed Amanda. "Who's that?" she asked.

"That's my good friend Amanda," Joe said. "She's really nice. She's gonna hang out with us tonight. Is that okay?"

"Hi," Amanda said, bending down. "I like your pajamas. They're really pretty."

Kendra shied away, hiding behind her father.

"Don't mind her," Luke said. "She's being a little actress."

Amanda didn't look dissuaded. "Do you want to show me your toys, Kendra? Maybe we can play with some of them."

Kendra poked her head out and shook it vehemently.

"She'll come around," Luke said. "Just give her time."

"So what movie are you guys seeing?" Joe asked.

"That new one with Brad Pitt. I forgot the name. It starts at eight thirty so we should have plenty of time for dinner first." Luke looked at the empty hallway. "Providing Crystal stops taking forever to get ready."

"Women," Joe joked.

Amanda playfully hit him.

Soon enough Crystal emerged, putting on her earrings. When she noticed her husband standing with Joe and Amanda, she stopped short. "Oh," she said. "I didn't hear you guys come in. Luke, why didn't you tell me they were here?"

Luke rolled his eyes.

Crystal came over and kissed Joe on the cheek. "Thanks again for watching Kendra. This is the first time we've been able to go out since Luke had his surgery."

"It's no problem," Joe said.

"And this must be Amelia."

"Amanda," Joe said.

"I'm sorry. Amanda." Crystal held out her dainty hand and greeted Amanda. "You ready?" she asked Luke.

Luke confirmed that he was.

"Okay, you three have fun," Crystal said. "There's a list of emergency numbers on the fridge, along with my cell and the other neighbors'. And not to mention your parents are across the street, Joe, so there shouldn't be any problems. Plus, Kendra is well-behaved. Aren't you, honey?"

Kendra ignored her.

"Just be sure to have her in bed by nine, latest. Don't let her smile or that sad puppy dog face she does persuade you otherwise."

"She's very good at it," Luke admitted.

"We'll make sure she's sound asleep by nine," Joe reassured them.

Luke pried his daughter off his leg and kissed her goodbye. Crystal did the same. They gave her a brief pep-talk and sent her into the den to play with her dolls.

"Have fun tonight," Joe said.

"Thank you," said Crystal. "That's the plan."

As they walked out, Luke added: "Don't get into too much trouble while we're gone." He winked at Joe and then shut the door behind him.

After successfully jumping the car and dropping Amanda off after mini golfing, Joe had charged the battery like Luke told him to and then called to tell him how the car had died. He also told him how the jumper had saved the day.

"That's what it's for," Luke said. He asked if the battery charge was still low, and when Joe said that it was, Luke concluded that he needed a new alternator.

"Alternator? Is that expensive?"

"It is if you bring the car someplace to have it done. But if we do it, we can replace it for the price of the part."

"And how much is that?"

"About a hundred and fifty."

Joe sucked in breath. After paying for gas and his first insurance installment, he was beginning to realize how expensive having a car was.

"If you bring it to a mechanic," Luke reasoned, "it would cost you anywhere from three fifty to five."

Joe realized that he would have to part with a large chunk of money either way. "Would you help me put the part in if I gave you the money?" he asked.

"Of course," Luke said. "I've helped you with your car this far, why would I stop now?"

Three days later they installed the new alternator. The procedure took an hour and fifteen minutes, mostly because of where it was located and the fact that Joe had to do the work himself. Luke stood nearby giving him instructions, knowing that bending over the engine would be death for his back. Nevertheless, they got the job done.

"That should do it," Luke said. He motioned for Joe to start the car. When he did, it purred to life, all the interior lights glowing steadily without pulsing like a strobe.

Joe slumped back in the driver's seat in relief. "Thank you so much. If there's ever anything I can do to pay you back, let me know."

"Actually . . . there is." Luke told him how he and Crystal planned on going to the movies and needed someone to watch Kendra.

"That's all?" Joe said. "Sure, I'll watch her." He didn't think that was a fair trade—Luke spending all this time helping him with his car in exchange for a few hours of babysitting—but he wasn't going to argue.

"You can even invite Amanda over if you want," Luke told him.

"Really? She can come?"

"Sure, you guys only went on one date so far. Consider this the second. Plus, girls love children. If there's one thing I've learned, it's that girls are suckers for guys who like kids. If you think she was into you before, she'll really be into you after this."

"Thanks. I'll see if she wants to."

"Just one thing. Don't do anything while Kendra's awake, if you know what I mean . . ."

Joe felt abashed that Luke would think he'd do such a thing. After all that he had done for him, he'd never disrespect his neighbor like that.

"I know how kids move a lot faster than they did when I was younger," Luke continued. "So just wait until you're sure Kendra's asleep. And make sure you're in the den where you're far enough from her room so she won't hear anything."

If life had a rewind button, Joe would have surely pressed it now. He looked at Luke, sure his ears were playing tricks on him, but when he saw the twinkle in Luke's eyes, he knew he'd heard right.

"This is a perfect opportunity for you two to be alone, and I'm not going to ruin it by telling you that you can't enjoy each other. The stairs creak, so if Kendra wakes up for any reason you'll hear her coming. And you'll hear the garage door open when Crystal and I come home. That should give you anywhere from half a minute to a minute to make yourselves decent in either scenario."

All Joe could do was stare. Luke grinned and said, "You're welcome."

"You sure you're up for this?" Joe asked Amanda after Luke and Crystal left.

"Of course! I love kids. It'll be fun."

"Just making sure." He didn't dare tell Amanda that he had never babysat before and therefore had no idea what he was doing. It was also the first time he had been inside Luke's house, and as he and Amanda made their way to the den, he found himself looking over the decor the way an explorer might examine the features of a newly-discovered cave. The main level was a mirror image of his house—living room, kitchen, den—except the walls were painted a creamy white and the floors were hardwood. Same with the stairs. Now he understood why Luke said they would creak.

They found Kendra in the den playing with her dolls and a large wooden castle right out of a fairytale. The castle didn't look like something that was sold in any store. It looked custom-made with tall wooden spires, little windows, and a drawbridge that actually worked. It stood as tall as Kendra and at least twice as wide. The scrollwork on the gables was so intricate that it appeared as if tiny masons had done the work. She positioned a doll with long golden hair on top of one of the towers and a prince by the drawbridge at the bottom. There was something oddly familiar about that arrangement, but Joe hadn't read a fairytale since he was a kid and couldn't make the connection.

"Is that Rapunzel?" Amanda asked Kendra.

Kendra answered by releasing the doll and letting it fall, squashing the prince. Without waiting to see if he was okay, she dove into the space between the couch and the wall.

"What are you doing, Kendra?" Joe asked. "Come out of there."

She didn't answer, only tried to burrow deeper into her hidey hole.

Joe walked over and tried tickling her. She screamed, and Joe jumped back. That made Amanda laugh. "Thought you said you were good with kids," she asked sarcastically.

"She usually loves me," Joe said. He knew the night would be a disaster if Kendra kept running from them and had to think of something fast. The way she was hiding gave him an idea. "Hey, Kendra? Wanna play a game? How about hide-and-seek?"

"Hey, that sounds fun," Amanda said.

That seemed to do it. Kendra popped her head out from behind the couch.

"You wanna play?" Joe asked.

Kendra nodded and then stabbed a finger at Amanda. "Only if *she* counts."

"How about it?" Joe asked. "Wanna count?"

Amanda shrugged. "Why not? You two better watch it, though. I was hide-and-seek champion when I was younger."

Joe expected Kendra to ask *Were you really?* with astonished eyes, but all she said was, "You better not cheat!"

"That's not nice, Ken. Amanda wouldn't cheat." Joe turned to her. "Would you?"

Amanda shook her head and raised a hand. "Scout's honor."

Kendra clearly wasn't persuaded because she began dictating the rules of the game, putting specific emphasis on the fact that once you chose a spot to hide you had to stay in that spot until you were found.

After she had rattled off about a thousand and a half other regulations, she grabbed Joe's hand and ran off while Amanda counted. She dragged Joe into the living room and told him to hide behind the couch. Joe did so obediently, watching as Kendra squeezed herself under a chair. As they hid, they listened to Amanda finish the countdown: "Three, two, one. Ready or not, here I come!"

They heard her check the den first and then move into the dining room. When her footsteps grew louder, Joe knew she had entered the living room. He peeked out to watch her look in the closet and a few other places before moving on to the kitchen. Before he could dip his head back down, he saw Kendra scurry out from under the chair and tiptoe over to the closet Amanda had just checked.

That little cheater, he said to himself.

When Kendra closed the door behind her, Joe crept out of his hiding place and moved stealthily toward the kitchen.

"Hey! Aren't you supposed to be hiding?" Amanda said when she saw him.

Joe put a finger to his lips. "Not too loud, Kendra'll hear you."

"So she's still out there, huh? And are you here to help me find her?"

"Let me put it this way: If I don't help you, you'll never find her."

"Oh come on, I'm not *that* bad."

"It's not about being bad."

"Pleeease. You're forgetting who you're talking to. I'm a former champion, remember?"

"I think this little one's a champion, too. Ever hear the expression 'Cheat, cheat, be hard to beat'?"

Amanda looked confused.

"She's cheating," he said plainly. "She's in the closet."

"The one I just checked?"

"The one you just checked."

Amanda frowned. "She really doesn't like me, does she?"

"I guess not. I can't explain why. She usually loves everyone." Joe thought for a second. "Maybe she's jealous."

"Of *me*?"

"You know how kids are. Maybe she has a crush on me or something. It would make sense. You're beautiful, so she definitely has a reason to be jealous."

Amanda's eyes widened, and in the light her green irises seemed almost to shimmer like emeralds. "You really think I'm beautiful?"

"I do," Joe said truthfully. He kissed her, feeling her soft lips against his, and wishing they could remain there for the rest of the night. When he finally pulled away, he said, "I think I have an idea how you can get Kendra to like you."

"Do you now?"

He explained and then crept back to his hiding place. A second later, Amanda came into the room and "found" him. Together they "searched" the house, being sure to let Kendra overhear Amanda telling Joe how great a hider she thought Kendra was and how there should be a new hide-and-seek champion. After pretending to search for ten minutes, Amanda asked in a hushed voice, "Should I *really* find her now?"

"No," Joe whispered back. "If you do, then it'll ruin everything because she's not supposed to be hiding in the closet. She has to come out on her own when we're not watching."

"Gotcha," Amanda said. Then louder: "Joe, I can't find Kendra anywhere. I think she wins. Want to wait with me in the den until she comes out?"

"Sure," Joe said just as loud. He took Amanda by the hand, and together they walked into the den.

Kendra found Joe and Amanda on the couch as she came strolling in with a look of satisfaction on her face. The minute Amanda saw her, she stood up and exclaimed in mock surprise, "Where were you hiding? I couldn't find you anywhere!"

"I'm not telling," Kendra said teasingly.

"You shouldn't," said Amanda. "That was a really good spot."

"Yeah, Kendra," Joe added, "that was probably the best spot ever. You really are a great hide-and-seek player."

Kendra smiled smugly, an expression that said *as if there was any doubt.* "You really couldn't find me, could you?" she said to Amanda.

"I couldn't. I searched everywhere. I found Joe, but no matter where I looked I couldn't find you."

Kendra giggled and grabbed Amanda's hand. "Come on, I wanna show you my playroom." She dragged her over to the door leading to the basement, and as she did, Amanda gave Joe a wink. Joe winked back.

For houses that had similar floor plans, their basements were very different. Joe was surprised at how small Luke's was. It was finished, like his, but it only stretched about fifteen feet until the floor encountered a wall. Joe's stretched all the way under the house. If his father had wanted to, he could have placed both a pool table and a ping pong table down there. Luke could only fit one. As it turned out, the space was filled with Kendra's toys. He found her and Amanda sitting in a pile of blocks and board games playing with dolls, Kendra sprawled out on her stomach, Amanda with her legs neatly tucked under her. She looked up when Joe came down.

"Want to play dolls with us?"

"Not particularly," Joe said.

"Please, Joseph!" Kendra begged. "You can be the boy doll and Amanda and me can be the girl dolls and you can choose which one of us you wanna marry."

Joe sensed trouble in that game and opted for something safer. "How about you show me around your playroom instead?"

Kendra shot up. In an instant she turned into the world's greatest tour guide, showing Joe where she kept certain toys, pointing out a fort she had built with blocks.

"What's behind here?" Joe asked when they came to a door.

"That's my daddy's workshop." Kendra reached up for the knob and turned it.

"Are you allowed to go in there?" Amanda asked.

"Uh huh. He let's me go in here all the time and watch him. Come and see." She took Amanda's hand again and pulled her inside.

The space beyond the door was pitch-black, the hungry darkness swallowing the light from the playroom. Joe wondered why Kendra wasn't scared. He had assumed all kids her age were scared of the dark. When she flipped the light switch, he understood why. Luke had left his mark everywhere. Just like his father had his home office to retreat to, Luke had his workshop. It was even bigger than the play room, ending in a concrete wall covered in a pegboard. Hanging on it was every tool imaginable: screwdrivers, pliers, clippers, hammers, chisels, drills, handsaws. You name it, and it was there. They were displayed the way a hunter might display his guns. The adjacent wall had a little counter built in front of it, except instead of appliances or a sink, it was occupied by portable grinders, sanders, and electric saws. Another saw stood alone in the center of the room, dominating the floor. It was as tall as Joe and had a long steal blade as sharp as a sword. Joe got a chill just looking at it.

"That's my daddy's rubber band saw," Kendra said when she saw Joe looking at it.

Joe had taken a shop class last year and understood that she meant a band saw, a heavy-duty piece of machinery that rotated a blade in the shape of a rubber band around two pulleys. Because of the way it was constructed, the blade spun so fast that it devoured any piece of wood put in front of it. Or, as Luke had told him, part of his finger.

Sitting next to this monolithic beast was what looked to be an unfinished project. Joe leaned over to inspect it. The way some of the pieces were already joined together it almost looked like a house, except huge, almost as big as Kendra. He made the connection immediately. Luke hadn't paid anyone to build the wooden castle upstairs. He'd built it himself. Had Kendra not shown him this room he would have never guessed that Luke was into woodworking, and by the looks of it, very good at it, too.

"Wow," Amanda said when she saw the unfinished project. "That's going to be a doll house, isn't it?"

"Yup!" Kendra said proudly. "My daddy's building it for me. He builds me lots of things."

Something vibrated in Joe's pocket, and as Amanda marveled over Luke's work-in-progress, Joe pulled out his cell. C.J. again. He'd called twice today, and Joe had let both calls go to voicemail. He did the same for this one. It was funny: when he was with Amanda, he didn't feel bad at all about his decision to no longer talk to C.J.

Soon enough, Joe and Amanda found themselves back in the playroom, marveling over Kendra's sticker collection. She brought out books upon books and they passed the remainder of the evening flipping the pages and telling stories, Kendra taking turns to sit on both of their laps. When it finally came time to put her to bed, the tears broke out. Joe and Amanda tried everything to stop the waterworks, but in the end they had to promise to read her a bedtime story. When Kendra finally dozed off, they crept silently down the stairs and flopped onto the couch in the den.

"That was a handful," Joe said.

"A handful," Amanda agreed, "but fun."

"Yeah. It was kind of fun, wasn't it?"

Amanda answered by pressing her lips against Joe's for the second time that night.

And then the third.

They almost didn't hear the garage door opening forty minutes later.

CHAPTER 35

"What the hell was that? That was shameful! Higher! Higher!"

Coach Heck screamed at the top of his lungs, his face red, the vein on his neck bulging and looking like it was about to pop. Joe stood on line with the rest of the team, practicing layups. At the whistle, Coach Heck tossed Ian Richert the ball. Ian took off immediately, catching it midair and dribbling down the court. He weaved in and out of the cones and jumped when he came to the basket.

"Keep your knee up, dammit! You need protection!"

The line shifted.

Joe watched the coach blow his whistle and toss Timothy Rogers the ball next.

"Been busy lately?"

Joe turned around. C.J. had moved up in the line. Joe had made it a point to keep at least three people between them at all times, not wanting to talk. But when he heard C.J.'s voice, he realized his plan hadn't worked out too well.

"Yeah, kinda," Joe said. He talked fast, trying to pretend to focus on the drill. If he did, then maybe C.J. would get the hint and stop talking.

He didn't. "What's with you, man? You didn't even say hi to me today."

"Nothing's with me," Joe said. "I've just been busy, you know how it is."

"No, I *don't* know how it is. You don't give me rides anymore. You barely even talk to me in class."

On the court, Timmy got scolded for missing the basket. Joe watched him walk shamefaced to the end of the line.

"Well?" C.J. prompted.

Joe tried to play dumb. "Well, what?"

"Ever since you and that bitch started dating, you've changed."

"Bitch?"

"You know who I'm talking about. Miss Prissy."

"Hey, Amanda's not a bitch."

"Po-tay-toe, po-tot-toe. Say it however you want, she's still a bitch. Before she came along we used to go everywhere together, and now you're ignoring me. Don't think I'm too stupid to make the connection."

Joe had initially hoped he would be. Now he was glad that C.J. realized what was happening. It was C.J.'s stupidity that had prompted Joe's actions in the first place. If C.J. had been a nicer person, things might have been different. But he wasn't. He threw applesauce out car windows, threatened underclassmen, and thrived on others' misfortune. Joe couldn't believe he'd ever been friends with C.J. in the first place. They were opposites. Contrasting elements. Fire and ice. Good and evil. And all it took were two new people in Joe's life to get him to realize this.

"I don't like what she's doing to you," C.J. continued. "She's changing you."

No, Joe wanted to say. *She's just made me realize a few things.* What he said was, "Maybe *you* need to be the one to change."

C.J. raised his eyebrows. "What the hell's *that* supposed to mean?"

Joe took a deep breath. "It means that I think it would be better if we didn't hang out so much anymore."

"Am I really hearing this? You don't wanna be friends with me? *Me?* Charles Galeno the second? The person who carried you almost all the way through high school?"

"C.J., I—"

"No. I see how it is. If that's the way you want it to be, fine." He poked a finger at Joe's chest. "Just remember this: If we're not friends, we're enemies."

"C.J.—"

"Enemies!"

Coach Heck threw the ball. Joe reached out to grab it, but C.J. intercepted. He dribbled down the court, weaving in and out of the cones, and didn't look back once.

CHAPTER 36

Joe searched for the doorbell on the side of the house. When he couldn't find it, he pulled out his cell and called Luke. He had followed his directions and found the block without a problem, but all the houses on it looked alike, and he could have walked up the wrong driveway.

Luke picked up on the third ring. "Joseph."

"Hey, Luke. I'm here, but I'm not sure if I got the right house."

"It's number 231."

Joe walked around to the front of the house, looking for a number. He couldn't find it. He tried looking for Luke's car, but couldn't find that, either. When he told Luke this, Luke said, "Oh, right. I should have told you, the landlord lets me park in the garage. He's got an extra space. You're at the right house, though. I see you in the driveway."

Joe looked up and saw a figure looking out one of the upstairs windows.

Not too long after, the door on the side of the house opened and Luke stepped out. "What's up?"

"Not much," Joe said. "I brought the movie." He handed it to Luke.

"*The Ledge.* That's supposed to be good."

"I heard it was," Joe said, not having the heart to tell Luke he'd already seen it.

"All right, let's put this bad boy on. Come on up and I'll give you the grand tour." He led Joe up a narrow staircase to the apartment. It was smaller than Joe had expected: only two rooms, a bath, and a little nook for the kitchen. The ceiling sloped so that if Luke stood up in the wrong place, he would bump his head. It didn't take Joe long to realize that they were in a finished attic. He wondered if Luke could hear water hitting the roof when it rained. The larger of the two rooms had two pieces of furniture in it: a futon and a television stand. On it were two framed pictures. One of Kendra and another of Kendra and Luke. Joe noticed Crystal was not present in either.

Joe said, "Nice place you got here."

"It's a bachelor pad. Nothing fancy, just a living room and a bedroom. The landlord's pretty reasonable. Doesn't bother me when I play my music or watch the TV too loud. He's got a kid about your age, maybe a little younger, who does the same thing, so whatever noise he makes usually drowns mine out."

Luke was making it out to be like he had it pretty good, but Joe thought he'd gotten the raw end of the deal. While he was living here in this matchbox apartment, Crystal was living in the house with Kendra. Joe wanted to ask Luke why it hadn't been the other way around, but knew prying for information was disrespectful. He asked Luke about his job instead. Luke told him, and then asked about Amanda.

"She's good," Joe said. "We just celebrated our two month not too long ago."

The second he said this he wished he could cram the words back into his mouth. He knew anniversaries and love would be a touchy topic right now and saw by the look on Luke's face that he had been right.

"Congratulations," Luke said, a little halfheartedly. He rubbed his naked ring finger. "She seems like a good girl. Just make sure it stays that way. Never give her any reason to get bored with the relationship."

It was the closest Joe would ever come to knowing what had happened. "I won't," he said.

Luke nodded. "Good. Want to watch the movie now?"

~ ~ ~

When it was over, Luke walked Joe down the narrow staircase. He paused at the stoop and pulled out a pack of cigarettes.

"Still smoking?" Joe said, remembering how he'd seen Luke smoking the day he learned of the divorce.

"It's an old habit," Luke said. "I just started again. Crystal always hated it, but who's going to stop me now that she's not around?"

Joe didn't answer, didn't think Luke really wanted him to. He just watched as Luke blew smoke into the air.

After a while Luke said, "Listen, Joseph, I want to thank you for coming over tonight."

Joe tried to wave away the gratitude. "You don't have to thank me. I wanted to watch that movie for a while now."

Luke nodded, seeming to think this over. "Well, thank you anyway."

They stood in silence looking at one another, neither sure what to say. Joe was glad he could help Luke feel a bit better. Thought he might even make his visits a weekly thing.

At last, Luke said, "Can you find your way back out?"

Joe thought of the directions sitting on the passenger seat. "Yeah, I think I can manage it."

"Good. Don't be a stranger. Stop by any time."

"I will," Joe said. But he never did.

CHAPTER 37

The next day before dinner, Joe's mother told him an interesting piece of news she'd learned through the grapevine. He came into the kitchen with Snowball at his heels to grab a snack when Margaret spoke up. At first Joe thought she would reprimand him for spoiling his dinner, but when she put a hand on his shoulder, he knew it was something a little more serious.

"I know how you and Luke have been spending a lot of time together lately . . ."

He didn't know what to make of the comment. A disturbing thought made its way into his head: Luke had had an accident. This was how people usually broke the bad news. They touched you in a comforting way, and reminded you that you were close to that person. A horrible way to do it, but a way nonetheless.

". . . and it might be hard to hear what I'm about to tell you . . ." Margaret continued.

Joe froze, feeling his skin prickle. Snowball sensed his discomfort and started licking his hand.

". . . but it turns out he doesn't live across the street anymore."

Joe relaxed. That was it? Hell, he'd known that for almost three weeks already. He guessed news didn't get around as fast as he thought it did. He remembered the promise he'd made with Luke about keeping it a secret and therefore pretended to be surprised. "Really?" he said, hoping he put enough shock and misery into his voice.

Margaret frowned, rubbing his shoulder.

"I'm sorry. It turns out they're getting a divorce. I just found out this afternoon. Harriet was next-door taking in the groceries when she saw a man with a white Mercedes park in Crystal's driveway. He got out and went inside the house. It looked like he had a key."

Joe could imagine the old woman pulling the bags of food out of her trunk and hunkering down while she spied on the neighbors.

"She called Crystal about two hours later and asked who the man was. That's when Crystal told her that she and Luke had split up and that she was seeing someone new."

As Margaret was telling Joe this, George slipped into the kitchen. He made it a point to do it as silently as possible, but the creaking of the refrigerator door announced his presence, and Snowball ran over to him.

Margaret spotted him at once. "Hey, George, did you hear what I said? Crystal and Luke are getting a divorce."

George poked his head out from behind the door, and in his fast whisper said, "Huh, what?"

"Our neighbors across the street. They're getting a divorce."

George stood up, holding a carton of orange juice and pushing his glasses up the bridge of his nose. "Oh, really? That's terrible."

"Yeah. Guess they couldn't put up with each other."

"I wasn't aware they were having problems."

"You're not aware of a lot of things," Margaret muttered.

"Huh?"

"I said you wouldn't know your own mouth if it bit you in the ass."

Without answering, George put the orange juice back and slumped out of the kitchen, Snowball trailing after him.

CHAPTER 38

Ever since Margaret learned of Luke and Crystal's separation, she found herself parting the blinds and peering out the windows in hopes of catching a glimpse of the illusive boyfriend. She did this more frequently as the days drew on. It might have been the fact that Harriet had seen him before she had, or it might have been genuine curiosity. Whichever it was, she needed to see him with her own eyes.

She and Harriet were in constant contact, both on the lookout for Bryce, or as they began calling him: *Mr. Right.* Harriet had told Margaret that he was tall and brawny like that guy on the paper towel package, yet older and different.

"Different?" Margaret had asked. "What do you mean *different?*"

"I can't really explain it," Harriet answered. "Just different."

"Different how?"

"Well . . . his hair's darker. But other than that, I can't really say."

Margaret thought she couldn't say because she didn't know. She'd probably only caught a fleeting glimpse of him, and since she knew she was the only neighbor on the block to do such a thing, she was acting like she wore the crown now and was the queen of gossip. Margaret couldn't let her do that. The crown was rightfully hers. Nobody had a right to take it away. Harriet might have lived on the block longer, but

Margaret knew more people, was more social, and made it a point to stick her nose in everyone else's business. It was hard work, and therefore she deserved it. She wouldn't let a little thing like being in the right place at the right time inaugurate a new queen. She had to step her game up. Harriet might have talked to Crystal about her current situation, but Margaret would do more. Seeing the boyfriend wasn't enough. She had to *talk* to him, find out something nobody else knew and spread the word, reminding them who the *true* queen was.

She debated on whether or not to call Crystal and make an excuse to invite herself over, but it turned out she didn't have to. The next day, when she was backing out of the driveway, ready to go to the mall with a pile of coupons, a car honked at her and scurried past. She couldn't believe it. The asshole had to get by that quickly? She had a mind to honk back, but when she saw that the car was white, and that it had turned into Crystal's driveway, she paused, unable to believe her good fortune.

The Mercedes's door opened, and the illusive Mr. Right stepped out. Margaret had to rub her eyes. Harriet was correct. He *was* like the guy on the paper towel package, except a little older. He wore a long-sleeved button-down, dark jeans, and shoes the color of his hair, which she thought was black and matted back with some type of gel. She might have been surer had he not been moving away so fast.

That was when Margaret realized she was going to lose her opportunity. Not knowing what else to do, she honked. He stopped in his tracks, looking around. When Margaret honked again, he trained his vision on the SUV in the street. Even from a distance Margaret could tell that his eyes were cold, blue, and staring at her with an intensity that sent a chill racing up her spine. Her instincts told her that she had made a mistake honking at him and that she should immediately drive away before it was too late, but her self-importance took over and she held her ground.

"Hi, I'm Margaret," she said, rolling down the window and introducing herself. "I live across the street."

He continued to stare at her, giving her a look as if to say *I see that, you moron.* What he said, however, was the complete opposite: "Nice to meet you. I'm Bryce." As he approached the SUV, Margaret noticed that he was slightly older than she had originally thought. The little wrinkles at the corners of his eyes and the way his skin was beginning to loosen around his neck put him at about forty-five, fifty oldest—George's age. Since Luke was only thirty-six, two years older than Crystal, Margaret never would have guessed that she would go for someone as old as Bryce. She took one look at the car he'd pulled up in and the shiny watch on his wrist and decided Crystal had done it because Bryce was established. Why lie? Even at George's age, he was more handsome and defined. So, it was for looks also. Margaret immediately felt a twang of jealousy.

She felt her body grow warm like it had done when she was a teenager. She floundered for something to say and came up with: "Your car's been in the driveway a lot recently, and I just thought I should finally introduce myself."

"Of course," Bryce said. "I'm happy to make your acquaintance. Crystal's already told me so much about you."

Margaret found herself blushing. "She has?"

"Sure. She tells me how good you are with Kendra and how you always invite her over to play with your dog. What's his name again? Snowbird?"

"Snowball," Margaret said, blushing even more.

"And what type of dog is Snowball?"

"A Labradoodle. He's a mixed breed. Half Labrador, half Poodle. They're loyal, hypoallergenic, and very good with children. Most dogs—"

"They must be good with children if he's that good with Kendra," Bryce said, cutting her off.

"He's a sweetheart. You and Crystal should come over sometime so you can meet him."

"I'd like that. If you'll excuse me, though, Crystal's rearranging the bedroom and asked me to help."

"Of course," Margaret said. "I'm sorry for keeping you."

"Not at all. Like I said, it was a pleasure making your acquaintance."

Margaret waved goodbye, watching Bryce walk back up the driveway.

Now that she had met the illusive boyfriend, she had more than what she needed to keep her crown. She had what might amount to a school-girl crush, as well.

CHAPTER 39

Margaret and George bumped heads more frequently these days. It might have been due to the fact that they had been forced to spend more time in the house together because of winter, or it might have been something completely different. Whatever it was, the arguing had intensified. It started out with small things—"Did you take out the garbage, George?" "Did you put a red sock in with the whites, George?"—and progressed to Margaret hounding him about spending all his time in his home office and never spending any with his son. When George finally announced that Mr. Lancaster would be coming over for dinner, the shit really hit the fan.

"What?" Margaret said. "You're kidding me, George. This is a joke, right?"

"Maggie, it's just for one night. Be civil."

"Civil? You want me to be civil to that fleabag boss of yours?"

"He's my boss, Maggie. I need to get on his good side. There's this new account the office is about to handle, and if I want to get it, I have to stand out above the other employees."

"You already stand out! You're six three and as skinny as a rail!"

"Maggie . . ."

"Why do you want to suck up to that ball with legs, anyway? He screwed you with the McCammon account. You said he would give you a ten percent commission, and he only gave you five. Because of him, we couldn't go on our marriage retreat!"

"He had to cut back and filter the other five percent into the company," George said, telling her this as much as he was telling himself.

"I don't like that man," Margaret continued adamantly. "He's cheap, and he's crooked. Just look at the car he sold you."

"What's wrong with Joe's car?"

"What's wrong with it? What *hasn't* been wrong with it? There was the broken headlight and the scratches on the bumper, to name a few, and if I had to guess by the amount of time Joe spent with Luke during the fall, there's been a lot more wrong with it than that. Did you know that I found a battery jumper in the garage a few months back? Neither of us owns one, so I assumed it was Joe's and put it in his trunk. You don't have to be a genius to figure out Luke gave it to him because he was afraid Joe's car would die. I'm just thankful I called Luke when you first bought that lemon. He's really looked out for Joe. Unlike you. That was a perfect opportunity to bond with your son, and you missed it."

"So now we're arguing about Joe?"

"If we were arguing about Joe you'd be telling me it was natural for him to be spending all of his time with that girl instead of on his homework, like he should. And I'd remind you how I've told him time and time again how I feel about him getting involved with someone at his age. But that's neither here nor there. This discussion is about your boss. Bottom line is he's crooked, and instead of inviting him over for dinner, you should spend the time with your son. Take him to the park. Get him away from that girl. Shoot some hoops. You don't even have to be good, for crying out loud, just walk up to the damned basket and drop the ball in."

George regarded her through his glasses, the thick lenses making his eyes look twice as big; big enough for her to see that she had struck a nerve. He thought about what his wife had said. He also remembered how she had told him that he always let people walk all over him. She had been right. He *did* let people walk all over him. Especially her. He decided to change that, and what not a more perfect time than the present?

He pushed his glasses up, straightened his back, and said, "Mr. Lancaster's coming over for dinner tomorrow, and that's final." At first he felt nervous, fearing that Margaret would lash out at him, but when he saw the surprised look on her face, he felt a rush of adrenaline. He also felt like he'd grown an additional two inches. He liked the sensation, and before it could go away, he walked out of the kitchen, feeling as if he'd won not a battle but a war.

Margaret just blinked, unable to believe what had just happened. Fine, if George wanted to be that way then two could play at that game. She went over to the phone and began dialing.

Joe was about to go over Amanda's house when his mother stopped him.

"Where are you going?" she asked.

"Amanda's. Why?"

Margaret frowned. It was clear she didn't like that answer one bit. "Your father didn't tell you, did he? He's having his boss over for dinner."

"And that means I have to stay?"

"Yes," Margaret said. "I want this to be a nice family dinner. I've invited a few other guests over as well."

"Like who?"

"Harriet and Nathaniel for one . . . and Crystal and Bryce."

The last two names hit Joe hard. Bryce? Who the hell was Bryce? Every time he'd heard Crystal's name in the past, it had been paired up with Luke. Now there was somebody new?

"Who's Bryce?" he heard himself ask.

Margaret didn't miss a beat. "Bryce is Crystal's new boyfriend. He's a very nice man. I've had the pleasure of meeting him. If you stay for dinner you can meet him, too."

"But I *don't* want to meet him!" Joe said it a bit harsher than he'd intended. He watched as his mother's eyes opened wide in surprise and her brow came together as she prepared to say something back. "Sorry," Joe quickly said, lowering his voice, "but I don't wanna meet him."

Margaret frowned. "I know he's not Luke, but he's coming over just the same, and it would mean a lot to me if you could stay. Make a good impression and show him that we don't have a dysfunctional family."

You mean more dysfunctional than we already are? Joe wanted to say. "Why did you have to wait until last minute to tell me, though?"

Margaret didn't hear him. Having said what she needed to say, she was already off, walking into the kitchen to prepare the food.

Joe slumped onto the couch, pulled out his cell, and sent a text:

> Hey bad news my moms making
> me stay home for dinner. Im gonna
> be a bit later then I thought.
> To: Amanda <3
> Sent: March 6, 5:46pm

He draped an arm over his face while he waited for Amanda to reply. A moment later his phone vibrated.

> From: Amanda <3
> : (Really? Grrrr. Okay. I'll see
> you when you get here then.
> March 6, 5:50pm

He thought about typing something back but didn't. He closed his phone and closed his eyes, wondering if Luke knew that Crystal had already moved on and was seeing somebody new. He thought of something Luke had told him—*Nothing destroys a relationship more than a lack of trust*—and supposed that he already knew. Might have even known sooner than he was supposed to.

~ ~ ~

The sound of the doorbell woke Joe from a sleep he hadn't even known he'd fallen into. He rubbed his eyes and looked at the clock on his phone: 6:30. Over half an hour had passed.

"Is anybody going to get that?" Margaret shouted from the kitchen. By the intensity of her voice, it sounded like she was fighting to make last-minute preparations.

Joe got groggily to his feet. He knew his father would be locked away in his home office, so he said "I'll get it," wondering who would be on the other side of the door first. It turned out to be Harriet and Nathaniel Flanagan. Joe knew them as the older couple from next-door, who, to this day, still gave him little baskets for Easter. Nathaniel was dressed in brown slacks and a tweed jacket, his silver hair gleaming in the fading light. He pulled a wrinkled hand out of his pocket and presented it to Joe.

"Ah, Joseph. Good to see you tonight."

For a moment, Joe was reminded of Luke and the way he always called him by his full name. It wasn't the same—there was something off about the inflection when Nathaniel said it. Joe shook his neighbor's hand nevertheless, wishing Luke and Crystal were still together so he could have someone to talk to.

"Where's your mother?" Harriet asked when Joe had shown her and Nathaniel in.

"I think she's in the kitchen," Joe said.

The moment he said it, Margaret appeared, brandishing a smile. She ran over and greeted the neighbors with hugs and kisses. Joe took their coats and put them in the closet. A moment later, the doorbell rang again.

Great, Joe thought. *No surprise who it's gonna be this time.*

Even though he'd never met Bryce, he hated the man because he had taken Luke's place. And yet . . . he almost looked forward to opening the door. Call it simple curiosity, like the way a scientist might want to study a slide of a particularly virulent disease under a microscope. He'd seen Bryce's car but never Bryce and found himself wondering what the man looked like. In his head he drew up the image of someone tall, like him but broader and more handsome than Luke. Yet when he opened the door, the person who stood before him was short, pasty, and as round as a ball.

"Mr. Lancaster," Joe said with a hint of disappointment.

"Little Joey!" Mr. Lancaster bellowed in his bombastic voice. "I thought I told ya ta call me Chaz? Ya gotta stop watching television. Rots your brain. How are ya? How's the car?"

"It's really good," Joe said, remembering all the work he had to put into it.

"Good to hear, Little Joey, good to hear. Where's your father? Is he—?"

"Hello, Mr. Lancaster," Margaret said, hiding a scowl. She had come out of the kitchen and was now holding a plate of hors d'oeuvres out to Harriet and Nathaniel.

George appeared at the top of the stairs, frowning when he saw that his wife had invited the neighbors over. It was just like her to do something like that in spite of his standing up to her earlier. Not wanting to have an argument now, he forced himself to shrug it off and descend the stairs. "Mr. Lancaster, I'm glad you could make—"

Mr. Lancaster ignored George in favor of the hors d'oeuvres. He made for the shiny tray, hypnotized. Margaret held it out to him, hoping that the little treats would clog his airway if he ate too many. "Why look at these!" he exclaimed. "They look like miniature cakes." Without saying anything more, he swallowed one in a single bite. Then, to Joe's disbelief, he reached out for another, and another. Joe watched him shovel the treats into his gullet, fascinated, disgusted. Margaret only looked on with a smirk, eagerly awaiting her dark fantasy to come true. If there was any question why Mr. Lancaster had never married again, this was surely the answer: nobody would ever stay with him long enough—he'd eat the bride before she could say, "I do."

When he was done, he wiped his mouth delicately with a napkin and belched, the sound echoing off the walls. Harriet and Nathaniel exchanged looks.

"Ya know," Mr. Lancaster said. "In England that's considered a compliment!" He paused and then bellowed laughter.

Margaret didn't say anything, just glared. George saw the mingled look of hate and disgust on his wife's face and contented himself that karma was acting in his favor. "I'm glad you could make it, Mr. Lancaster," he said. By now George was at the bottom of the stairs, his hand outstretched.

Mr. Lancaster clapped him on the back instead. "Thanks again for having me over, Panza. How'd ya know dinner was my favorite meal of the day?"

By the looks of it, any *meal is probably your favorite,* Joe thought.

The bell rang again as Margaret reluctantly introduced the neighbors to Mr. Lancaster. This time, Joe opened the door to find Crystal and Bryce on the stoop. Joe's eyes happened on Crystal but only for a moment. Once they paid their cursory glance, they moved on to the subject of his curiosity. Bryce was a lot older than he'd expected—almost as old as his own father—but tall, broad-shouldered, handsome, and distinguished. He still couldn't believe Crystal and Luke had separated and she had replaced him with this stranger.

"Hi, Joe," Crystal said after an awkward moment of silence.

Joe tried to make his mouth work. For a second, it seemed as if he'd forgotten how to talk. Then, slowly, he learned to form words again. "Hi . . ." he said.

They stood looking at one another, Crystal obviously waiting for Joe to invite her and Bryce in. When he didn't, and the uncomfortable moment seemed to draw out, she said, "Joe, this is Bryce. Bryce, this is Joe, Margaret and George's son."

Joe felt his hand automatically reaching out. He wanted to yell at his brain to stop, to tell his body to yank it back, that this was the enemy, this was the man Crystal had left Luke for, but before he could stop himself, he found his hand enclosed in Bryce's.

"Nice to meet you, Joe," Bryce said. "I've heard a lot about you."

Joe had to blink. "You have?"

Bryce flashed a smile showing a set of teeth too straight not to have been filed. "Sure. Crystal's told me that you're a nice young man and a star athlete in your school. How many sports do you play again? Four?"

"Three," Joe corrected.

"Three? That's a lot. I give you plenty of credit. I did two myself back in the day. And Crystal tells me you have a beautiful girlfriend. How do you find the time for everything?"

"I don't know," Joe heard himself say.

Bryce showed his teeth again. "Well, you obviously manage your time efficiently. Anyway, it was a pleasure to meet you. I hope we can become friends."

As he and Crystal stepped into the house, Joe couldn't help but think that that was an odd thing to say. Wanted to be friends? What did he expect, to shoot hoops with him one day? Joe would never do that, and thought that Luke would be proud of him for being so loyal.

Margaret found her way over and inserted herself into the conversation. "I'm so happy the two of you could make it."

"Thank you for inviting us," Crystal said.

"We wouldn't miss it," Bryce said. "I was just telling Crystal how I couldn't wait to meet the rest of your family." He gestured toward Joe. "You have a very well-mannered son."

Margaret put her other hand on Joe's arm. "Why, thank you. You hear that, Joe? You made a good impression." She stepped back to give her guests room to take off their coats. "Speaking of children, where's Kendra?"

"With her father," Crystal replied.

Right away Joe picked up on the fact that Crystal hadn't mentioned Luke by name, as if by using the anonymous term she was slowly erasing him from her life. It made Joe boil with anger. He looked at Crystal and Bryce again, and at the way they stood next to each other, side by side, both with stupid grins on their faces, the type he might have recognized on his own face the first time he hung out with Amanda. It made him sick.

"Oh, that's too bad," Margaret said. "I love little Kendra." She glanced toward the den, where she had set up a bunch of toys. "You'll bring her over soon though, right?"

"Of course."

From outside, Snowball barked at the guests.

"Is that Snowball?" Bryce asked.

"That's the ball of fluff," Margaret confirmed. "I'd let him in, but he'll jump all over everyone."

"Nonsense," said Bryce. "Bring him in. I promised you I'd meet him, didn't I? How can I come all this way and not meet the famous Snowball?"

All this way, Joe huffed. Like it was really so much effort to walk a few feet across the street.

"If you insist," Margaret said. "Joe, will you let Snowball in while I introduce everyone?"

Joe said, "Sure," happy to have an excuse to walk away.

While Margaret introduced Crystal and Bryce to everyone else—especially Harriet, smirking happily as she did so—Joe made his way to the back door. He bent down and stroked Snowball's fluffy fur. Snowball jumped up on him, licking his face. "You don't really wanna go in there, do you, boy? Just a bunch of boring old people. And that guy. . . . I don't like him."

Snowball barked.

"I know, you liked Luke better. So did I."

Snowball confirmed this by rushing past Joe into the house.

A white ball of fluff came barreling around the corner and leaped into the center of the crowd. Crystal gasped and jumped back, Bryce cocked his head to the side inquisitively, and Mr. Lancaster bellowed laughter, slapping George on the back while he said, "Panza, is that a dog or a sheep?"

Margaret was at Snowball's collar at once, holding him steady. "I'm sorry," she said. "He gets a little excited with visitors. You can pet him if you want."

It took Mr. Lancaster some effort to bend over due to his prodigious stomach, but when he did, scratching behind Snowball's ears, he was rewarded by a thumping tail, a dog's non-vocal way of saying *Thank you, that feels good, keep going.*

Bryce leaned in to do the same. When he did, Snowball's pink ribbon of a tongue shot out and licked Bryce's hand.

Traitor, Joe thought.

Bryce turned to Crystal. "He likes me."

Crystal's eyes widened.

Mr. Lancaster bellowed laughter, filling the room with its baritone sound. "Likes you a little too much, don't ya think?"

Bryce knitted his eyebrows together in confusion but then raised them when he looked back at Snowball. The dog had one of his rear legs raised and a yellow arc of liquid was spurting out from somewhere in between, as if he had turned himself into a fountain. The stream struck Bryce's leg, saturating it.

Bryce leaped back.

"Oh my God," Margaret said, her face burning with embarrassment. She tightened her grip on Snowball's collar and hauled him out of the room. "Joe!" she yelled. "Joe, take him outside!"

Joe snickered as he took hold of Snowball. *Good dog,* he thought.

"I am *so* sorry," Margaret said. She grabbed Bryce by the arm and pulled him into the kitchen. "Here, let me clean that up for you."

Ten minutes later, the group found themselves in the living room, where Margaret passed out glasses and George poured wine.

Almost as soon as they sat on the couch, Mr. Lancaster took control of the conversation. "This is a fine set of neighbors you've got here, Panza."

"They are," George agreed. "We really got lucky when we moved into this—"

"So tell me," Mr. Lancaster said, "what do you all do?"

"Harriet and I are retired." Nathaniel patted his wife's leg with a wrinkled hand. "But I used to work in the steel industry. I was a factory worker."

"Factory worker, huh? I like that. Honest hard work." Mr. Lancaster trained his gaze on Bryce. "How about you?"

"I'm a captain for the police department," Bryce said. "Been on the force for twenty-eight years now."

At the mention of this, Crystal couldn't help but square her shoulders and grin a little haughtily. Margaret picked up the body language for what it was at once: pride.

"Police, huh? Wish I could say the same about honest work, but then I'd be lying." Mr. Lancaster slapped his leg—causing the fat on his thigh to ripple under the fabric of his pants—and roared with laughter. He looked around the room for approval. "Am I right?"

All he got were silent stares.

"Oh come on, people. How many times have ya gotten a ticket when ya didn't deserve one? Why, every time I get pulled over I get a ticket for not wearing my seatbelt."

Bryce looked genuinely interested. "Really? Even though you were wearing it?"

Mr. Lancaster snorted so loud it sounded like a bark. "Wear it? Let me tell ya something, if I could get that thing around me I'd be singing 'Hallelujah' ta sweet holy Jesus and His twelve disciples." He snorted again. "Wear it. That's a good one."

Joe sat on the other side of the couch. He snuck a peek at his phone. 6:51. The night was dragging. At this rate he might die of boredom before he got to Amanda's.

"How about you?" Bryce asked Mr. Lancaster. "What do you do?"

"I run an accounting firm in the city. C.V.C. Innovations." He leaned over to extract his wallet from his backside, and for one horrifying moment he almost tipped over the section of the couch on which he sat. It rocked up onto two of its tiny peg legs and then settled down again when he shifted his bulk back. "Holy Christmas!" he shouted. "What are ya trying ta do, Panza, murder me? I'll tell ya, setting booby traps for your boss isn't the way to a promotion!" He held his business card between two pudgy fingers and handed it to Bryce. "You can keep that," he said. "Nearly cost me my goddamn life getting it for ya."

Bryce studied the card and then tucked it into his own wallet.

"What type of clients does your company represent?" Nathaniel asked.

"A little of this, a little of that," Mr. Lancaster said. "Businesses, mainly. Investors. Sometimes wealthy celebrities."

"That sounds very interesting," Harriet said. Joe didn't think it sounded interesting at all. "Do you have any famous clients?"

Mr. Lancaster tapped his nose with a pudgy finger.

"And what about you two?" Bryce asked George and Margaret. "What do our wonderful hosts do?"

"Well Margaret doesn't—"

"I'm a homemaker, George!" Margaret said with such vehemence that George recoiled, nearly spilling his wine. "Don't you dare say I sit home all day and eat bonbons, because I don't. I take care of the house. You'd know how hard a job that was if you'd try it."

"Right," George said apologetically. "Margaret is a homemaker, and I—"

"Oh, nobody wants ta hear what you do, Panza. They just heard it. He works for me," Mr. Lancaster explained to everyone, "and I just told you what I do. No use repeating ourselves, is there? First Panza tries ta kill me with his booby-trapped couch, and now he's trying ta kill me with boredom. Hey, Bryce, can I call for an investigation? I think there might be grounds to arrest this guy! Cruel and unusual punishment!"

George lowered his head, looking as if the only investigation that was going on was his inspection for crumbs on the carpet.

Joe's phone vibrated. He looked at it, thankful for the blessed interruption.

> From: Amanda <3
> How's dinner going?
> March 6, 6:59pm

Joe typed back.

Kill me now. We havent even
sat down yet. Although when
we do I think itll go pretty fast.
My dads boss will make sure of that.
To: Amanda <3
Sent: March 6, 7:00pm

From: Amanda <3
He's that bored?
March 6, 7:02pm

Hes that fat.
To: Amanda <3
Sent: March 6, 7:02pm

From: Amanda <3
Lmao!!! You're terrible!
March 6, 7:03pm

Joe tucked his phone back into his pocket, waiting for the next round of boring questions. He'd been at family and business-type dinners before and knew it was only a matter of time before the conversation drifted his way, inquiring about school and sports. He assumed it was a safety net that adults used when they didn't have anything else to talk about. He usually didn't mind it. Tonight, he did. He knew the ones asking the questions would be Crystal and Bryce. He'd already promised himself he'd be terse with Bryce and ignore Crystal if they decided to talk to him again, and he intended to keep his promise. As it turned out, he didn't have to—the spotlight tonight seemed to be trained on Bryce.

"So, Bryce," Harriet said with a flirting smile, "tell us how you and Crystal met."

Bryce patted Crystal's thigh. "Would you like to tell them?"

"Sure," she said. "It's actually a funny story. I was driving back from my mother's with Luke when I got pulled over."

"Don't tell me it was Bryce," Margaret said.

Bryce hid a guilty smile. "Yup. I don't usually pull people over, but I was on my way to the station and couldn't help but notice how fast this one here was driving."

"Hey, I wasn't driving *that* fast," Crystal joked.

"If you say so. But you *did* cut me off."

"I was having an argument. Give me a break."

Bryce chuckled. "Go on."

"Anyway, this one here pulled me over. I thought he was flirting with me while he was getting my information. Luke seemed to think so, too, because he got all quiet and we argued about it later. At the time, though, I couldn't help but admire Bryce's boldness. He seemed to know exactly what he wanted."

"Still do," Bryce chimed in, grabbing Crystal's hand.

Crystal squeezed back. "We didn't bump into each other again until after Luke and I split up"—Joe noticed that Crystal gave Bryce a sly look as she said this—"but after we did, we went out on a few dates, and now here we are."

"That's a wonderful story," Harriet said. "So Nicholas Sparks."

"Agreed," said Nathaniel.

Mr. Lancaster mimed sticking a finger down his throat. "Come on, if I wanted ta hear a love story I woulda watched a soap opera. Tell us something exciting."

"How about it?" said Margaret. "Do you have any stories working on the force?"

"Tell them the one you told me the other day," Crystal said.

Bryce put his glass down and folded his leg over the other. "If you insist." He licked his lips and turned toward the others. "This story takes place about twenty or so years ago in Brooklyn. I was still an officer back then, and my partner and I were on tour when we decided to stop for some coffee."

"You mean doughnuts," Mr. Lancaster interrupted, barking laughter.

"Actually, that's a common misconception," Bryce said. "With long shifts—especially nights and early mornings—police officers need caffeine to stay awake. It just so happens that Dunkin' Donuts is twenty-four hours and has the best coffee. A cop might indulge in a doughnut or two, but it's really the coffee they're after."

"Whatever flips your switch," Mr. Lancaster said. "If it was me personally, I'd go for the doughnuts."

You would, Joe thought.

"Anyway, we were on line when somebody decided to rob the store," Bryce continued. "Since it was five thirty in the afternoon and everyone was getting off work, it was pretty crowded. My partner Anthony and I couldn't even tell it was being robbed until the crowd gasped and the perp ran right past us. He was in such a rush that he steps on my foot, and I swear to you when he looked up and saw whose foot he stepped on, he turned ghost-white.

"Without missing a beat he takes off, running down the block. I run after him, zigzagging between civilians, while Anthony calls it in.

" 'Stop!' I yell. 'Stop!' But they never do. He just ran. I chased him for five blocks before he turned down an alley. A brick wall about six or seven feet high separated it from the other side. And standing in front of it with his gun drawn was the perp."

"Oh God." Harriet inhaled deeply and put her hand to her mouth.

"Weren't you scared?" Margaret asked.

"I might have been," Bryce admitted, "but my adrenaline was pumping, and all I wanted to do was catch this guy. I knew if I didn't collar him soon he'd be on the street the next day doing the same thing, being a danger to society."

"What did you do?" Nathaniel asked.

"Well, I could tell that he was scared. His hand twitched. My gun was already out—the second I had spotted his I whipped it out—and I was sure to hold it steadily by my side, knowing that if I raised mine he'd do the same.

" 'We don't have to do this,' I told him. 'Just put your gun down and nobody will get hurt.' "

"Did he listen?" George asked. He'd been sitting fairly silent, waiting to hear what happened next, but the suspense was overwhelming.

"Just wait," Crystal told him. "You won't believe this."

"He *didn't* listen," Bryce said. "In fact, I thought he was going to do the complete opposite and shoot. But he didn't do that either. He just turns and runs. There were a few garbage cans in front of the wall, and he leaps onto one and boosts himself over it. When he disappeared onto the other side, there was a gunshot. I hit the ground, trying to figure out what to do. I couldn't run back, mind you, because that would have left my rear exposed, so I took off instead, sprinting toward the wall as though his shot was the sound of a starter's pistol.

"I thought I'd hear footsteps on the other side, him running away, but all I heard was silence.

"I pressed myself against the wall, straining my ears, listening to see if I could hear his breathing. I found myself wondering where Anthony was. Had he called for backup? Was he on his way? Had he driven around the block and collared the perp on the other side?

"When I couldn't wait any longer, I peeked over the wall. You'll never guess what I found. To my surprise, the perp was sprawled out on the ground, his right arm twisted behind his back, and a bullet wound in his head."

Harriet gasped. "You're kidding!"

"Nope!" Crystal exclaimed.

"In his haste to get over the wall, he must have slipped and fell and shot himself. I climbed over to check his pulse, but he was already dead. About a minute later, right as I was about to radio Anthony, Anthony pulled up in front of the alley."

"Wow!" Harriet said. "I can't believe that!"

"Me neither. That's incredible," Margaret said.

Mr. Lancaster leaned forward, his stomach resting on his thighs, clapping his hands. "Bravo," he said. "Bravo. I agree with Mrs. Panza. That *was* an incredible story. There's only one thing I don't understand."

"What's that?" Bryce asked.

"Where was Detective Crockett when all this was going on? This was an episode of Miami Vice, right?" He bawled laugher, slapping his knee again and causing the fat on his leg to ripple once more. His face got so red from lack of oxygen that Joe thought the man might have a heart attack right in front of him. When he got control of himself, he looked around at his audience. "Oh come on, Panza," he said when nobody laughed, "you gotta admit, that was funny."

George produced a chuckle. It was dry and sounded about as real as a bad impression.

Joe's phone vibrated again, and he looked at it:

From: Amanda <3
Want to watch a movie
when you come over?
March 6, 7:16pm

Joe typed back.

Sure. But first I want to steal
a time machine so I can go back
and warn myself about this
EXCITING dinner party
To: Amanda <3
Sent: March 6, 7:17pm

From: Amanda <3
Still haven't eaten yet?
March 6, 7:18pm

Not even close. My neighbors
are swapping stories about their
jobs and my dads boss is trying to
crack jokes.
To: Amanda <3
Sent: March 6, 7:18pm

From: Amanda <3
The fat one?
March 6, 7:19pm

Yes the fat one.
To: Amanda <3
Sent: March 6, 7:19pm

From: Amanda <3
Well good for him. Laughing's good exercise.
March 6, 7:20pm

Anythings good exercise for him.
To: Amanda <3
Sent: March 6, 7:20pm

From: Amanda <3
Oh stop. Just hang in there. I'm worth the wait ;)
March 6, 7:21pm

I know you are <3
To: Amanda <3
Sent: March 6, 7:21pm

While Joe and Amanda texted, the adults continued their conversation, moving from the topic of jobs and job-related stories to recent events. As it turned out, they were job-related anyway. At least for Bryce. His department had been dealing with the Craig's List murders for some time now. Bryce didn't give any information the media hadn't, but said, with a bout of confidence, that the police were on the killer's trail.

" 'On the killer's trail'? What the hell's that supposed to mean?" Mr. Lancaster bellowed. "Do ya know who it is, or don't ya?"

"It's not that simple," Bryce told him.

"Simple? You wanna know simple?" He held out his pudgy hands, shaking each one in turn. "This is my left and this is my right. And I can say that with a bit more certainty than some of those cops on the case."

"Are you implying that—"

"That they can't tell their dicks from a corndog?" (Harriet gasped.) "Absolutely. And if that's the case, how do you expect them to catch a criminal as sick as this guy?"

Margaret stared at Mr. Lancaster with burning eyes. "I'm sure Bryce's men are doing the best job possible," she said in as derisive a tone as she could muster.

"I'm sure they are," Mr. Lancaster agreed. "But my point is, do you think it's good enough?"

Crystal gave Bryce a worried look. He just patted her thigh and said, "If that's how you feel, then what would you propose we do?"

"Do? Hell, I don't know. Call in the military, organize a mob, just do something. I'm sick of this guy taking up the front page every time a new body's found."

They bickered a little longer, Joe drowning out the conversation by busying himself with his cell, until this wonderful topic was concluded and Margaret ushered everyone into the dining room, where she served lasagna and a roast. Joe gratefully took his seat, counting down the minutes until he could flee from this torture. Mr. Lancaster didn't miss a beat. He devoured the lasagna in a way that would have made Garfield proud. The process of shoveling food into his mouth didn't seem to dissuade him from speech, either. At each interval between bites he resumed conversation, spraying food everywhere as he put in his two cents and supplied a healthy dose of sarcasm. Every attempt at a joke went sour, but he made up for this by clapping George on the back, since he had the misfortune to sit next to his boss.

After dinner, the Panzas showed their guests to the door. Mr. Lancaster told George that he'd had a wonderful time and that he'd love to come over again. Margaret shot George a look so stern that he instantly developed the ability to read her mind: *If you do any such thing, Luke and Crystal won't be the only couple on this block to file for divorce.*

Harriet and Nathaniel thanked the Panzas, and so did Crystal and Bryce.

"You have a beautiful house," Bryce said as he pulled on his coat.

The exuberant smile Margaret gave him made her look almost five years younger. "You really think so?"

"I do."

"I can tell why you like this one," Margaret said to Crystal. "He knows all the right things to say." And even though George was standing right next to her, or quite possibly *because* of it, she added: "Better watch it or I might try to steal him away."

George hung his head, undoubtedly counting the seconds until he could vanish into his home office.

"He does say a good thing or two," Crystal agreed, playfully elbowing Bryce in his side. "That's why I keep him around."

Bryce nudged her back and then shook hands with George and Joe. "Thank you again for having us. It was a pleasure to meet you, George."

George mumbled the same.

"And it was a pleasure to meet you as well, Joe. Maybe next time we can shoot some hoops."

Margaret put an arm around her son's waist. "You hear that, Joe? You can show him a thing or two on the court. How's that sound?"

Joe tried mumbling something along the lines of *Sure* in the same halfhearted tone as his father but was surprised to find that the idea of shooting hoops actually excited him.

As he drove to Amanda's, he couldn't help but feel as if he'd betrayed Luke by having dinner with the enemy.

CHAPTER 40

Joe got a phone call two weeks later. He was lying on his bed debating if he should go to the track and get into shape for spring tryouts when the phone rang. He could tell who it was without even looking at the caller ID: the way the caller spoke his name, enunciating each syllable, was as identifying as a fingerprint.

"Joseph. I need to ask you for a favor. Can you look out your window for me?"

PART 5

REVENGE

CHAPTER 41

Joe heard Crystal's footsteps approaching and bit down on his lower lip, preparing himself for what he was about to say when she opened the door. Except, instead of seeing her slim figure, he was greeted by another: this one bigger, blockier . . . and familiar.

Just like when he had answered the door for the police man, Joe's heart dropped.

"Expecting someone else?" Bryce asked him, the sides of his lips curling into a menacing smile.

Joe felt his world tip. This was the last thing he needed. It seemed that Bryce was everywhere, and at all the wrong moments.

When Joe didn't answer, Bryce said, "If you're looking for Crystal, you just missed her. She took Kendra to her grandmother's."

For some reason, Joe couldn't understand that. His brain was whirling so frantically that it wouldn't allow him to process the information. How had Crystal taken Kendra to her grandmother's if her car was still in the driveway? And then it hit him. The answer was so plain and simple it was almost ridiculous: Crystal had taken Bryce's car. That was why it wasn't in the driveway. He wondered if Bryce had goaded her into taking it so this very confrontation could take place. He was about to ask and then decided on a better question instead, a question he should have asked much earlier:

"Why? Why are you doing this?"

Bryce chuckled. It was an unsettling sound, like marbles clacking together. "Why am I doing this? Hurmm . . . let me think. You know what? I have a better idea. You seem like a smart boy. Let me see if *you* can figure it out."

Joe said the only thing he could think of. "Because I was spying on you."

"Very good. That's part of it, yes."

"What's the other part?"

"Nothing that you need to concern yourself with. The less you know, the better."

"Listen," Joe said. "I'm sorry. I'm sorry if I spied on you and pissed you off. I'm sorry if I got involved with anything I shouldn't have. And I'm sorry for . . . for whatever you want me to be sorry for, okay? Just please . . . please leave me and Amanda alone. That's all I want. And I promise I won't tell anybody about any of this. Can you do that?"

Bryce didn't need to think this over. "No," he said. "I can't."

"Why not?" Joe whined. His voice rose, becoming thin and reedy, and he felt tears welling in his eyes. He had reached his breaking point and was about to crumble.

"Because you're acting like a child," Bryce said. "That's why. Plus, I'm having too much fun."

"Fun?" Joe asked, barely able to speak above a whisper now.

"Yes. Fun. You and your nosy neighbor—your nosy *ex*-neighbor, I should say, now that I took his place—couldn't mind your own business. Now, I'm teaching you a lesson because of it. You need to have a conscience, Joe. And I'm yours now. Just call me Jiminy Cricket. When I'm through with you, you'll never consider poking your nose into another man's life again."

That meant that Bryce wasn't done with him yet. He had already tampered with Joe's car, tried to destroy his relationship, and put Amanda in the hospital. Who knew what he would do next? Bryce might hurt, maim, or murder everyone in Joe's life *except* Joe—so he would be forced to watch them suffer—and Joe couldn't think of a worse punishment. He just thanked God that his parents were over a thousand miles away and Amanda was safe and sound in the hospital. But that wouldn't last forever. His parents would come home, and Amanda would recover. And when that happened, Bryce would strike again. All of this was like the hands of a clock. They might tick away as time went on, but eventually, they always came back to the point from which they had started. What Joe needed to do was pull out the batteries before that could happen.

"Yup," Bryce repeated in a dreamy voice. "Just call me Jiminy Cricket."

Joe had no idea who that was and had no intention of asking. As he was finding out, talking with Bryce was useless. Some people you could reason with, and others you couldn't.

Because he's crazy, the cruel voice said. *You can't reason with him because he's crazy.*

For once, Joe thought the cruel voice was right: Bryce *was* crazy. And that meant that there was no telling what he would do next.

CHAPTER 42

Bryce watched Joe walk down the driveway, downcast and dejected. It didn't surprise him in the slightest. In fact, it made his smile widen. Teenagers were all the same, male or female. They all whined when they didn't get their way. And that whining was music to Bryce's ears. It was a melody that rivaled Mozart's greatest symphonies, and he could listen to its soothing tune for hours on end. More so, their tears were his elixir of life. Tears of pain worked well, but tears of fear worked best, and that was the type of tears he'd seen welling in Joe's eyes. The same he'd seen in Amanda's as he ran her off the road. And the same he'd seen in the eyes of all the other—

He stopped, knowing what would happen if he allowed his mind to drift there. Not wanting to just yet, he forced himself to think about how easy it had been to trap Joe instead.

Bryce knew his license plate had been run just as someone might know they were low on gas: a little light went on, except this one inside his head. When you were a police officer—hell, a *captain*—you knew what went on in your precinct. He even knew that Joe had been talking to Luke the minute he met him. After years of police training, he knew how to read a person. It was in their eyes. They were the windows to the soul, revealing secrets with each twitch, flicker, or twinkle. He'd seen that flicker in Joe's eyes and had known exactly what it meant. He had known just how to get back at him, too: aim for the heart. It was the weakest organ, especially in a love-struck teenager. And it had been so easy to fuck with his girlfriend's mind, it was almost child's play. He'd gotten the idea when he saw Joe standing outside with another girl. What could be more perfect than a little relationship drama? And then fortune had shined, almost as if it were a gift from above: the girl dropped her Snapple bottle and it shattered, and in their preoccupation, as they cleaned it up, Joe left his cell phone behind. Bryce knew he had to seize the opportunity. It wasn't hard to save his own cell number under the name *Daniel*, and it was almost fun to text himself from Joe's phone and have a fake conversation. All he had to do was read some of Joe's old messages so he could mimic the way he talked.

Bryce had learned early on that the mind was a curious thing. It latched onto the idea it feared the most and blew it up, feeding the absurdity, making it real. He knew all couples secretly feared that their significant other would cheat on them. All he had to do was give Amanda a reason to suspect that Joe might do the same, and her mind would do the rest, confirming it. He just had to place Joe's phone on her mailbox so she could find the fake conversation, and he could sit back and watch the show.

Of course there was always the chance that she would be a good girlfriend and not invade Joe's privacy and go through it, but that hadn't bothered Bryce. That's what the underwear had been for. He had felt his prick rising while the lacy fabric rubbed against his hand as he picked the lock on Joe's car. He just had to plant it someplace visible, and pretending to be a concerned schoolmate, text Amanda, informing her that Joe was going behind her back and to look in his car. It turned out he didn't have to do that. She had already gone through his phone and thought the worst, had even looked in Joe's car without having been told to and had seen the underwear. Everything would have been perfect had that little bitch not caught him about to slash Joe's tire after she'd left. Bryce had wanted the unhappy couple to stew in their misfortune, wonder how they could ever function without the other, but nothing ever went according to plan. There were always a few setbacks, and in those times, you had to improvise. It's what had kept Bryce on his feet after all these years. For that reason, he went after Amanda. Had to. She had left him no other choice. And after he ran her off the road, he'd gotten out and stared down at her unconscious body, wishing that she was still awake so he could see the fear in her eyes. Since she wasn't, and since he didn't have the time to wait around for her to wake up, he snapped a quick photo instead and licked the blood off the side of her face.

Once again his mind drifted, and this time he allowed it to go where he hadn't allowed it to earlier.

There was a bookcase in the living room that Crystal used for knickknacks—vases, picture frames, photo albums, candles—but since Bryce moved in, he had claimed the top two shelves for a collection of Tom Clancy hardcovers. He liked Clancy for three reasons: his novels were engaging, they were either about the police or the military, and they were long. *Really* long. It was for this last reason, especially, that he liked them.

He stood in front of the bookcase looking up at the titles. His eyes shifted until they came upon *The Bear and the Dragon.* He pulled it out—almost needing to go on his tiptoes to do so—and brought it down. It wasn't as heavy as Clancy's other books, even if it was his longest, and this was because it was Bryce's favorite. He opened the cover, barely able to contain his excitement. Inside, resting in the hollowed out section of its pages, was a small album of photos. Bryce took it out, cradling it in his hands like a child. Had Crystal liked to read, he would have had to think of a safer place to hide it, but Crystal barely read the recipes when she cooked. Plus she was much shorter than he was and would never waste the energy to pull over a chair so she could reach something as unsatisfying as a book.

Bryce opened the album to the first photo. It was a picture of a woman in her mid-twenties, pale, with her eyes closed, and purplish bruises making a necklace around her throat. Bryce remembered her in perfect detail (the photos always helped him to remember). He flipped the page.

There was another girl, her head resting against the concrete as if it were a pillow, her blue eyes staring distantly at something she'd never be able to see, her mouth slightly parted, a small river of blood dripping out the side. On the next page was a redhead in a bathing suit and a multitude of scrapes and gashes crisscrossing her chest, as if she had fallen through a bunch of rose bushes. Bryce never raped the people he took photos of—the thought disgusted him—he just wanted to watch them suffer before he killed them, see the fear in their eyes. He flipped through the pages—some guys, mostly girls—remembering his past. The ones toward the back he'd met off Craig's List. It seemed that ever since that little website had popped up, his life had gotten so much easier. No more waiting for the perfect opportunity or searching to find the ideal victim. He had convenience at his fingertips. All he had to do was peruse the site for girls advertising themselves as "escorts." He knew they wouldn't be afraid to meet a stranger, and they weren't missed until he could get rid of the body.

Bryce paused when he came upon the photo of a teenage boy. With his dark hair and brown eyes, he almost looked like his childhood friend Charlie. And just thinking about Charlie, and what had happened on that day so many years ago, sent a warm spike shooting through his nether regions.

He had been on his bike, pedaling down the street. Charlie told him they were going to the park because he heard some kid had caught a fish, cut their line, and hung it from a tree, where it had dried up and birds had pecked its eyes out—a must-see for any thirteen-year-old.

The trip to the park would have taken close to an hour, but Charlie and Bryce knew a shortcut. It was a winding trail that cut through the woods. They had taken it that day. Not because it would save time but because it gave them a rush. When riding through a trail with shrubs threatening to close in and block the path, you could pretend that you were in a forest running away from Indians. The boys played this game each time, pedaling faster and faster, seeing who could get past the bushes first before the Indians jumped out. At least that's what they had told each other, never fully wanting to admit that the trail actually scared them.

On this particular day, Charlie was in the lead, his legs pumping mechanically. It had rained the night before, and Bryce watched as his friend steered around the puddles as if they were booby-traps. The boys were about halfway in when it happened. Charlie looked back to check on Bryce's progress. When he did, his front tire found one of the puddles. Instead of there being earth beneath the water, there was a hole about six inches deep and eight across. It swallowed Charlie's tire like a hungry mouth and pitched him over the handlebars. Bryce watched in disbelief as his friend soared through the air and shot out his hands to ward off an oncoming tree. His efforts didn't help much. He struck it hard enough to make most of the pine needles fall down in a green flurry, and he collapsed to the muddy ground beneath it in a twisted mess.

Fearing that his friend might have been terribly injured, Bryce squeezed his brakes as hard as he could. He let his bike fall into the mud and rushed over to where Charlie lay curled up in the fetal position, writhing in pain and moaning like a zombie. He had his left arm clutched against his chest, the bone punched through the skin, dribbling blood down his arm.

"Ahhh, Bri. Ahhh, get help!" Charlie cried.

Bryce turned to rush back and do just that, but stopped. He felt odd. It wasn't how you felt before you threw up: that stomach-churning, gut-wrenching sensation. This felt different, almost *warm*, and it wasn't in his stomach either, it was *behind* it, if that made any sense. Curious, he looked at Charlie again. The minute he saw the red liquid dripping down his arm like syrup, the feeling returned, intensifying. It took a full minute for him to realize that it was actually a pleasant sensation, one that grew as Charlie's face contorted in discomfort.

Bryce stared down at his friend, fascinated.

"Bri! Ahhh! What are you doing? Go! Get help!"

That snapped Bryce out of it. He grabbed his bike and rode back to Charlie's house faster than he thought possible, so fast that no Indians, imaginative or not, would ever be able to catch him.

Later that day, he sat up in his bed with the television on. He had led Charlie's mother back to the trail, and she had carried him out and brought him to the emergency room. There, they had set the bone and put on a cast. At least that's what Charlie had told Bryce over the phone. Injuries were almost funny that way. When they were happening all you could think about was the immense pain, and then after you could laugh about it.

Bryce was wondering if Charlie would let him sign his cast—wouldn't it be funny if he tricked him and drew a penis on it instead?—when "Scooby Doo, Where Are You?" cut to a commercial of two women riding bicycles. Watching the way their tight bodies propelled those pieces of metal down the street sent a warm spike shooting between Bryce's legs.

He rubbed himself, then reached under his bed and pulled out the *Playboy* magazine Charlie had given him for his birthday. He flipped through the pages until he came upon a particularly pleasant photo of a blonde with huge knockers. Except, when he tried to pleasure himself, nothing happened. He tried a different photo only to get the same result. He stroked harder and faster, but the effort was lost. He attributed it to the fact that the magazine was old and he'd seen the photos one too many times. He was just beginning to wonder if Charlie had stolen a new one out of his brother's closet when Charlie's face popped into his head, looking as it had after he'd fallen off his bike: his forehead smeared with mud, his eyes slit closed, and his teeth clenched together in pain. He remembered the look in explicit detail and almost heard the moans coming out of Charlie's mouth again.

All of a sudden, Bryce's body tensed up and his head jerked forward, something very pleasurable happening below.

For the next few days, he suffered from the constant fear that he was a homosexual. To his relief, what happened a week later proved otherwise. He was sitting in school when Becky Matheson, a girl in his math class, made fun of him. She twisted around in her seat and said, "What are you, a shit mummy?" Bryce looked at her in utter bemusement. Then she pointed, and he saw with horror what she meant. When he went to the bathroom, a piece of toilet paper had gotten stuck to his shoe, and now it trailed out like a mummy's wrapping. Rachel Barone turned around, too, and started chanting: "Shit mummy! Shit mummy!" Pretty soon, the whole classroom joined in. Bryce felt his face growing red, his anger boiling, and he pictured Charlie again writhing in pain on the muddy floor. Except he replaced his face with Becky's. Then Rachel's. Then both of them tangled together in a pile of pain. And, to his surprise, he felt that warm spike shoot through his lower region again. That was when he discovered that he wasn't a homosexual after all. Sex actually played no part in how he felt. It was pain, and the fear in the eyes of the person suffering from it. All he had to do was envision them that way and his prick throbbed.

This troubled him to no end. He spent years praying that he could be normal. Had even joined the police force as a way to try to turn over a new leaf and forget his dark fetishes. But in the end, after trying so long to repress it, he had snapped, realizing that this was not an abnormality but a gift that he should embrace.

Like he did now.

He flipped to the last page of the photo album, where a teenage girl with auburn hair lay unconscious by the side of the road. Her eyes were closed, but he knew they were a bright emerald green. Thinking about the fear he'd seen in them before he drove her off the road made his pants stiffen even more.

With the delicate care of a nurse extracting a splinter, he reached between the two transparent sheets of plastic that held Amanda's picture and slid it out. He paused, debated, and then flipped back through the book and pulled out four more. He placed each of these on a table, one next to the other, as if he were laying out all the cards in a game of Texas Hold 'Em at once. He then ran a hand over each, as if he could feel the faces.

When he came to Amanda's, he unzipped his fly, remembering the moment of her injury in explicit detail.

CHAPTER 43

Joe walked down Luke's old driveway feeling defeated. He couldn't believe his horrible luck. Bryce had caught him for the second time trying to get him in trouble, and he had been there as if he had been expecting him. How the hell had he known? It was almost as if he was reading Joe's mind, and that unsettled Joe to no end. Just the thought of having Bryce in his head made him want to scream. He hated the man more than ever and desperately yearned for revenge for what he had done to Amanda. Yet it didn't seem as if that was possible because Bryce had all the bases covered.

Not all, a voice suddenly said.

Joe stopped, halfway up his own driveway. It wasn't the cruel voice, but another: the voice of reason. It hadn't spoken in so long that Joe almost didn't recognize it. But now that he did, he thought about what it said. It was true that Bryce made it seem like he had all the bases covered, but that wasn't exactly the case. There was one he had forgotten to put a man on. And that was home plate.

"Luke . . ." Joe whispered to himself.

Because who else was closer to home than Luke? He had always been there when Joe needed him, and he would be there now. Joe hadn't wanted to call him earlier because he was afraid of dragging another person into this horrible mess, but if he thought about it, Luke had been the one to drag *him* into it in the first place. Therefore, Luke owed him. Besides, Joe had no one else to turn to, and Luke had told him to call if he ever needed anything. Well, he needed something now, and he was going to take Luke up on his offer. Hell, that's what neighbors were for, right?

CHAPTER 44

Particles of light converged into a blue and white glowing orb as Nicolas Cage assembled a ball of energy behind his back and prepared to throw it at the man with the cane. To his surprise, the man held him in check, and then propelled him backward with a whoosh, as if he were a baseball that had been smacked right out of the park. He struck the ground and rolled, catching hold of a gate before he could fly away. He barely had time to collect himself. With a wave of his cane, the man summoned the statue of a bull to life. It twisted its massive bronze head in Cage's direction and charged, snarling and thumping its horns on the ground.

Luke sat on the couch with a bag of Doritos resting on his lap as he watched Cage dive aside and flee for his life. Luke pulled a chip out, studied it, and then shoved it into his mouth, listening to it crunch inside his head. On the screen, David, the sorcerer's apprentice, pulled up in a car and wrenched the cane out of the bad man's hand with a bolt of lightning. It was a cute movie, and Luke couldn't help but think of Joe as he watched it. The way Nicolas Cage took on David as his apprentice reminded Luke of how he had taken Joe on, showing him how to fix his car. It pained him to think that their relationship had ended as abruptly as it did. He guessed that's what happened with teenagers. They had short attention spans, and if you weren't constantly in their lives, you slowly faded from them. He reasoned that Amanda took up most of Joe's time as well. He didn't blame Joe for it, though. He had once been a teenager himself and done the same thing. He just wished they could have spent a little more time together, that's all.

Now that his visitation rights only allowed him to see Kendra twice a week, he had nothing to do when he didn't see her but work and watch old movies on Netflix. Watching them always reminded him of the time Joe had brought over that DVD. He had enjoyed Joe's company a whole lot more than the movie and wished it hadn't been a one-time thing. It seemed that after Luke's life had crashed, Joe had been the only light at the end of the tunnel, and now that that light was fading, it was getting harder and harder to see.

He was thinking about this as he reached into the bag to pull out another chip. His fingers found the point of one and were about to close around it when his cell rang. It danced to the ringtone and nearly vibrated off the television stand.

Luke took one look at the caller ID and smiled. Maybe things would turn out for the better after all.

"Joseph!"

"Hey, Luke. How are you?"

"I'm all right. Watching a movie. Yourself?"

"I'm good."

Although, for some reason, Luke didn't think he *was* good. There was something in his voice that hinted otherwise, as though something were upsetting him.

"Are you sure?" Luke asked.

There was a pause on the other end. Then: "Actually . . . no."

Here we go, Luke thought. He pressed the phone against his ear, ready to listen and give advice if he could. He thought he might know what it was about, too. Joe and Amanda had probably had their first fight. Or maybe they had even broken up and Joe was looking for some comfort, someone to talk to who had been through it all before. If that was the case then Luke would do the best he could to console him, but as he had found out firsthand, there was nothing to heal those bottomless wounds except time.

Joe took a deep breath then said, "I've been having some problems lately."

Luke kept quiet, waiting for Joe to continue.

"Remember the hose you helped me zip-tie?"

"Sure," Luke said, a little relieved. Car problems were a whole lot simpler. "How's that holding up?"

"It's fine now, but the zip-tie broke over a month ago. Actually, it didn't break. Someone cut it. And then someone sabotaged my relationship with Amanda. They found my phone and made it look like I was trying to hide a conversation with a girl. And then they put a pair of girls' underwear in my car and Amanda found it and broke up with me."

Luke sat up straighter. "Are you serious? Someone broke you two up?"

"Yeah, but we're back together now. I just don't know what to do about the person who broke us up."

"You actually know who did it?"

"Yes."

"Was it that kid C.J. you told me about?"

"Not exactly. . . . It's somebody you know, though."

"Come on, Joe. You're not going to make me guess, are you?"

There was a long silence. Then: "No, I guess not."

After another pause Luke said, "Well . . . ?"

"It was Bryce."

Luke drew his eyebrows together, trying to put a face to the name. "Bryce . . . ? Bryce . . . ?"

"Tall, almost as tall as me, but older, older than you, dark brown hair, almost black, blue eyes, wide shoulders. Looks like the guy on the paper towel package."

"I'm sorry, I—"

"Your ex-wife's *boyfriend*."

Very slowly, Luke lowered the phone from his ear, staring distantly at the wall. He felt his chest growing tighter. He heard someone calling his name, but it sounded far away, as if he were in a dream and the person was trying to wake him. His eyes followed the sound and they came to rest on the phone. He raised it with a numb hand and pressed it back against his ear.

"Hello? Luke? Are you there?"

"Yeah . . . I'm here."

"Luke, you have to help me. He tried to kill Amanda. She saw him about to slash my tire, and he ran her bike off the road while she was trying to get away. She's in the hospital."

"*What?* Are you serious? Is she okay?"

"Her jaw's wired shut, and she's got a cast on her arm, but other than that she's fine. She came out of her coma the other day."

"Coma? Why didn't you call me?"

Joe hesitated. "I . . . I didn't wanna get you involved. Bryce is sneaky. I tried to handle it myself by going to the police, but he *is* the police. He's a captain and monitors everything. He even knew when I called them. And instead of sending over a regular police officer, *he* came. I didn't wanna tell you because I was afraid you would try to hurt him or something."

"Try? I'm not going to *try*. I *am* going to hurt him. He vandalized your property, almost killed your girlfriend, and is sleeping in a room that's a few feet away from my daughter's. You think I'm going to just sit here until he decides to hurt Kendra next? Or touch her? Or . . . worse?"

"You can't," Joe begged. "It won't work. You'll get arrested, and if that happens, who will I have to go to? You're my only hope. You have to help me. Promise that you'll help me."

Luke thought about this. The ache and misery in Joe's voice made his plea all the more meaningful. "Okay," he finally agreed. "I'll do it your way. What's the plan?"

"To be honest . . . I don't know. I'm going to see Amanda now. I'll call you as soon as I get to the hospital, and we'll figure something out."

"Okay. I'll wait for your call."

"Thank you, Luke. I really appreciate this."

"No problem. Drive safe."

"I will."

Luke hung up, instinctively grabbing his keys. He was about to leave when he remembered his promise. He couldn't go after Bryce. But that didn't mean he was going to sit around and wait for him to destroy Joe's life. He had to do something. He thought long and hard before the idea hit. It might not work, but he could try to talk to Crystal. She probably wouldn't believe anything he told her, for obvious reasons, but if she heard the same story from Joe *and* Amanda then she might. And that at least was a step in the right direction.

His old house was fifteen minutes away. If he didn't hit any traffic, he could get there before Joe even got to the hospital. He was making good time as it was. It seemed that the roads were emptier than usual, as though the motorists knew the gravity of his situation and cleared them especially for him. He looked down at his speedometer, saw that he was only going forty, and pushed it up to fifty.

It was the first Sunday of the month, and if Crystal still held true to her traditions, she would be taking Kendra to get her hair cut. He pressed on the gas a little harder and the speedometer inched up to fifty-five.

He was on the service road now, about to reach an intersection, when the light turned yellow.

"Bastard," he grumbled, reluctantly stepping on the brake. He looked at his watch. 1:15. Crystal usually left around 1:30. He still had time, and if he gunned it when the light turned green, the way a driver does off the line at a drag strip, he'd make it. Except in order to gun it off the line, you had to stop first, and he hadn't done that. He pressed on the brake harder, but the car just continued to coast.

The light changed from yellow to red, and Luke panicked, slamming on the pedal like he was trying to squash a cockroach. It pushed all the way in until it struck the carpet.

The car kept going.

Luke cursed, his eyes darting around the dashboard, trying to fall upon something that would help him stop. He couldn't find anything. He tried to pump the brake again, but it hadn't come up from the last time he'd pressed it in. Up ahead a Chevrolet whisked through the intersection, followed by a red Mustang. Luke laid his hand on the horn. The sound blared, but for all the good it did it might as well have been broken.

"Get out of the way!" he tried shouting. He tried jerking the wheel back and forth to lose speed, but that didn't help either. His car was determined not to stop. He couldn't even hope to crash into the back of a car waiting for the light—he was the first in the line-up. Therefore, he did the only thing he could think of and yanked his wheel all the way to the left. The side of his car slammed into the guard rail, producing a scintillating shower of sparks, spraying light as friction took its hold and reduced his speed.

It's working! Oh dear God, it's working!

Relief swam over him. Then, as quick as it had come, it was gone. The guardrail ended, and he went sailing through the intersection, heading straight for an old brown Cadillac Brougham.

CHAPTER 45

The days seemed to pass with excruciating slowness, each one bleeding into the next as though there was no point to delineate the change except her sleeping. Just the sight of the other patients made her heart ache, forcing her to remember where she was. The man with the gunshot wounds was the worst of all. He moaned throughout the quiet hours of the night, keeping Amanda from sleeping. And when she finally managed to doze off, the moans crept into her dreams, becoming the lamentations of mummies and zombies.

When she awoke she was haunted by a different kind of terror, perhaps the worst kind of all: her memories. Joe had left his basketball jersey on the back of the chair next to her bed, and because of the way it was thrown over the backrest, the big white 24 was visible. It stood out in stark contrast against the maroon fabric of the jersey and was observable in every reflective surface. The cool metal post holding Amanda's IV flipped the numbers so they read 42. And when Amanda saw this, she was instantly jerked backward in time.

She knew by the excessive makeup she wore and the tight fabric hugging her lustful curves that she was back in her old school. Eyes belonging to the students leaning against the lockers followed her while she strutted down the hall like it was a catwalk. She ignored the less popular—turning her nose up at them like they had an infectious disease—and smiled at the others, her cheeks not yet knowing how to dimple, her hoop earrings dangling like Christmas ornaments. When she came to the burly senior with the golden locks, she stopped, putting her arms around his neck. He wore a yellow jersey with the number 42 emblazoned on the back and the school's patch on the sleeve above his bulging bicep. And when she tilted her face up to his, he kissed her. She remembered thinking that she was the luckiest freshman in the world to have gotten an older boy on the football team. Even luckier to have been invited to one of their parties. She still couldn't believe that Tony had asked her out while she had been waving those pompoms in a fury at the last game.

The day played out, and Amanda watched through the eyes of her past as she went from class to class, flipped her hair, and laughed at those less fortunate. She cringed at her every action, disgusted that she had ever behaved in such a way.

She watched as she got home from school, showered, reapplied her makeup, and put on even tighter jeans and a shirt that exposed her midriff. When her cell rang, she looked out the window. Down in the street, sitting in the driver's seat of a brand new convertible, was Tony, waving for her to come out. She did, almost tripping down the stairs in her excitement and shouting a halfhearted goodbye to her parents.

The party was like nothing she had ever seen before. There were upperclassmen everywhere playing beer pong, holding red cups, drinking, smoking, shouting, laughing, stumbling, using a permanent marker to draw on the face of a kid who had passed out on the couch. She held onto Tony's thick arm as he led her through the house, feeling as if she was on top of the world.

Music was blasting from speakers, spilling over speech with power chords and rap lyrics, combining to form a dissonance that was oddly appealing. It filled the rooms and imbued the ears of drunken teens. As Tony greeted friends, Amanda looked around, aware that she was the only freshman at the party. It made her swell with pride. She caught several boys looking at her, and she tossed her hair, feeling giddier than ever.

After a while, Tony brought her upstairs. It was quieter up there, with only a few teens hanging out on the staircase and even fewer in the hall. He led her past them to a closed door. He knocked twice, making the door shudder in its frame, his fist having the power to cause thunder. When nobody answered, he turned the knob.

"Here," he said, ushering her in. It was a large room decorated in the fashion of someone's parents. Probably the kid's who owned the house, Amanda thought. She walked in and sat on the bed, knowing what was coming next. She was a little nervous and a bit tipsy from the alcohol Tony had given her, but mostly she felt the anticipated excitement of the young and inexperienced. She knew older kids did more than just make out, and she was ready to take the next step so she could brag about it later.

Tony closed the door behind him, locked it, and strode over to the bed. Through Amanda's blurred vision, he appeared to almost swim through the air. He sat next to her, making a depression in the mattress, causing Amanda to fall into his arms. He didn't waste any time; he started kissing her. At first Amanda kissed him back, letting her hands explore his well-developed body—his swelling chest, tight abs, hard biceps—finding ecstasy through her fingertips, but when he grabbed her ass, she paused.

"Tony," she said.

Tony either didn't notice or didn't care. He continued to probe her body, moving his hands up to her breasts.

"Tony," she said again, this time a little louder.

He responded by squeezing. It felt good for a second, and she thought about giving in to the pleasures that awaited, but then he squeezed a bit too hard.

She sucked in breath and pushed him away. *"Tony!!!"*

He stopped, looking at her stupidly, like a child who has been scolded and doesn't know why.

"What?" he asked.

"I don't know about this."

"Don't know about what?"

"This . . ." Amanda said, motioning at herself and then at him. "What we're about to do."

Tony grinned and pulled a condom out of his pocket. "Don't worry about it. I brought protection. You'll be fine."

"No," Amanda said. "I . . . I . . ." She didn't want to say it. Didn't want him to think she was some stupid, innocent freshman. But she wasn't ready. She realized this now. And she had to tell him. "I've never done anything like this before," she confessed.

She waited for him to frown, yell, get up and walk away, but he didn't do any of these things. He just sat there, staring at her with hungry eyes, a throbbing bulge in his pants. "That's all right," he said. "I've done it enough for the both of us. I'll show you." And without giving her a chance to say anything more, he pulled off his shirt and was on top of her, pushing his lips against hers and moving his hands all over her body. She tried to squirm and roll away, but he took it as if she were playing hard to get. He grabbed her shirt—a shirt that she had spent three hours picking out at the mall for tonight's occasion—and she heard it tear with heart-rending clarity. Then his fingers were fumbling clumsily at the clasp of her bra.

"Stop! Tony! *I said stop!*"

His nails dug into her skin as she struggled, and as she tried to get away, she felt blood trickle down her back.

He tossed her bra unceremoniously across the room, where it landed on a lampshade, and moved his attention to her pants.

Amanda sat up in the hospital bed, rubbing her jaw, feeling the pain of it echo the pain of that very night. She had tried everything in her power to stop him—had begged, had pleaded, had even prayed—but he had been suffused with a ravenous lust. He ripped off her pants, exposing the leopard-print thong beneath, and then tried ripping that off, too. Amanda did the only thing she could think of. She kicked him in the face as hard as she could. Had her aim been a bit better things might have turned out differently. As it was, she struck him in the forehead, and instead of breaking his nose, she only angered him. He yelled out in vehement rage and grabbed her leg. He pulled her toward him, and as she screamed and flailed, he drove his powerful fist into the side of her face. Amanda heard a loud *Crunch!* resonate somewhere within her skull, and then felt a burst of pain shortly after. She tried to open her mouth to scream as Tony tore her thong off, but found to her surprise that her jaw no longer worked. She struggled with her body, fighting to open her mouth so she could scream for help, for somebody, for *anybody* to get this monster off her, but whatever sounds she made were drowned out by the thunderous music pouring out of the speakers downstairs. And if she listened close enough, she thought she could make out the bass riff to Akon's "I Wanna Fuck You" coming through the floor.

That was when a pain even greater than that of her broken jaw detonated, only this one between her legs. And it kept exploding, repeating like a jackhammer, joined by a horrible burning sensation. Amanda tried to scream but didn't have the strength. Only had enough to watch the sweat bead on Tony's forehead as his face contorted into a hideous mask of pleasure. And finally, before she blessedly passed out, she heard him mumble, "Stupid bitch. Don't false advertise if you're not gonna be easy."

Amanda leaned her head back on the pillow, pushing the memory and the pain in her jaw away. Those were not things she wanted with her right now. She wanted Joe, his kindness, and the life they were going to lead together. She closed her eyes, waiting for him to visit.

CHAPTER 46

Joe turned on the radio, trying to let the music calm him down but, the second he did, the lead singer of some heavy metal band screamed at him like a banshee. He recoiled as if he had been stung, jerking the steering wheel. The car beside him swerved at the last possible second to avoid a collision, and the driver honked his horn and flipped Joe the bird in one fluid motion. Joe honked back, and with shaking hands, reached out to lower the volume of the radio.

Nice one, Bryce. Mess with my radio, too. Mess with my whole goddamn life, why don't you?

He was worked up. The last thing he needed was something else to make him agitated. He was almost at the hospital, and therefore one step closer to having to make a decision on what to do about Bryce, and that disturbed him even more. He was just glad he'd called Luke—having an adult on his and Amanda's side made him feel a bit safer. The was only one problem: there was no guarantee that Luke could help. If anything, Joe might have just dragged another person into this horrible mess.

CHAPTER 47

The driver of the Cadillac, an old man with gray hair and bushy eyebrows, saw some asshole in a Ford Taurus about to blow the red light and honked his horn. When the Taurus didn't stop, he slammed on his brakes. Unlike the Taurus, the Cadillac screeched to a stop.

Luke heaved his steering wheel to the right. The Taurus responded immediately, but the Cadillac was so long that Luke clipped the back bumper, tearing off one of the long cat-like taillights in a spray of metal and plastic. The impact sent the Taurus into a spin, Luke cursing as he held onto the wheel. He rotated once, twice—fearing every second that he might flip over—and finally came to rest on the side of the road about a hundred yards from the intersection.

He sat with his face pressed against the steering wheel, his chest heaving like the bellows in a blacksmith's shop. His life hadn't flashed before his eyes like everyone said it did when a near death experience occurred. That didn't bother him, though. He didn't really want to relive the last few months of it anyway. Behind him, he could hear horns honking as angry motorists shouted for the old man in the Cadillac to stop blocking the intersection. But that was distant, barely audible over the pounding of his heart, which had seemed to relocate to his throat.

Luke released a shuddering breath and raised his head, patting his body with his hands to make sure he was still in one piece. His examination told him that he was, not even a scratch, just a bruised ego. He should have thought to slam the car into a lower gear or run into the guard rail earlier.

Oh well, you couldn't change the past, he decided, and pulled out his cell. An operator picked up, asking him what his emergency was. He told her he'd just had an accident and gave his name, the location, and the approximate time it had happened. When she told him a police officer would be along in a few minutes, he hung up and called a tow truck. After that, he tried getting out of his car.

The Taurus's door opened about six inches before it struck a bush.

"Great," Luke said sarcastically. He climbed over the center console, thanking God he wasn't injured, and opened the passenger-side door. This one wasn't blocked, and he stepped out, sucking in the warm spring air as if he'd never smelled it before.

He reasoned he had a good ten to fifteen minutes before the police arrived and decided that instead of talking to the old man in the Cadillac—who, by the looks of it, was getting harangued for stopping traffic—he would diagnose his car. It wasn't every day that your brakes failed, and like the cat, he was as curious as ever to find out why.

He got to his hands and knees, feeling the dry stalks of grass crumple under his palms, and looked under the Taurus. It was dark and full of shadows. That didn't bother him. He had a flashlight in the glove compartment. When he opened it, he found something he didn't expect to find. There, resting on top of the long body of the flashlight, was a lacy pair of women's underwear. He pulled it out, feeling the texture of the pink fabric against the pads of his fingers, then cast it away in disgust when he saw the bloodstain.

What kind of a sick prank is this? he wanted to know. He tried to think who would do such a thing, when his eyes happened upon the underwear again. Something was wrong. The bloodstain was on the *outside* of the elastic waistband and nowhere else. Then, unbidden, a voice spoke in his head: *And then they put a pair of girls' underwear in my car.*

It was Joe's voice, and he was talking about . . .

Luke froze, unable to accept the implications.

Finally, hands trembling, he pulled out his cell and made one last call.

CHAPTER 48

The light turned green, but an old lady with a bent back and what looked like blue hair crossed in front of Joe's car.

"Come on! Come on!" Joe said impatiently.

The car behind his honked. The old lady didn't pay the noise any attention—that is, if she heard it at all; she looked old enough to be deaf—and continued her slow, shambling walk across the street.

Joe watched her, feeling his impatience grow. Every minute that passed was another minute that Bryce could strike again. Bryce had told Joe that he wouldn't leave him alone, that he was having too much fun, and Joe didn't want to find out what Bryce would do to amuse himself next. Joe had to get to the hospital so he could talk to Amanda and figure out a way to end things with that horrible monster once and for all.

The light turned yellow, and immediately the honking intensified, turning the quiet street into an echoing cacophony. Now the old lady looked around as though she'd heard something. She stopped, cupped her hand to her ear, and turned toward the sound. Joe could see that she was squinting as well, trying to make out the shapes before her.

Feeling bad for doing so, Joe honked his horn like the other motorists. The old lady's eyes widened. She raised a hand in apology and continued walking at a snail's pace. The second she was out of Joe's way, he scooted through the intersection.

He pulled into the hospital's lot five minutes later, the big cross on the roof catching the sun and shining like a beacon. He pulled into what had become his customary spot in the back and began walking toward the building. Just as he got to the doors, his phone vibrated.

Luke's voice shook on the other end. He told Joe that he'd been in an accident and needed Joe to come get him.

"*Accident?* Are you all right?"

"I'm fine," Luke said.

But Joe didn't think he was fine. He sounded worked up, unsettled, and even though those were common emotions to go along with being in an accident, Joe thought something else might be causing them.

"Are you sure?" Joe asked.

Luke said, "Yes. I'm sure . . . this time. Next time, I might not be so lucky. Come and get me. There's a lot we have to talk about when you get here. Don't drive fast, whatever you do. And please make sure your brakes are working first."

Joe hung up, confused. He ran back to his car like a track star. He was out of the lot within a minute and cruising down the road a second later.

CHAPTER 49

Luke ended the call, watching the beam of his flashlight play on the severed brake lines under the car. They looked like something a dog had chewed through, brake fluid dripping everywhere. Just seeing them this way made Luke uneasy. He'd seen too many movies to know what it implied.

After clicking off the flashlight and putting his phone away, he used the end of a stick to pick up the bloody underwear. He had no idea whose body it had come off, but knew he had to get rid of it before the police came.

He looked around for someplace to dispose of it—a storm drain or the bottom of a trash can would be best—but he was on the side of the service road, and the only things around were shrubs and bushes. Deciding that he couldn't find any place better, he shoved the underwear into the biggest bush he could find, using the stick to press it deep into its center.

The moment he turned around, two squad cars pulled up, an officer in each. The first to get out was a middle-aged man with a moustache and a shock of scraggly brown hair. The second was younger, at least four inches shorter, and bald with glasses. It was this latter officer that approached Luke first.

"Were you just taking a leak?" he asked in an irate tone.

Luke looked at him, confused.

The officer pointed. "That bush right there, when we pulled up. Were you just taking a leak in it?"

Understanding dawned. With his back turned, it must have looked like Luke was relieving himself. Knowing that he couldn't tell the officer what he was really doing, Luke said, "Yes, I was. I'm sorry."

"Sorry's not good enough, buddy. That's indecent exposure, a punishable offense." The officer whipped out his citation book.

"Come on, Sal," the second officer said, "cut the guy a break; he was just in an accident."

"How do you know he wasn't the one who caused it?" Sal asked. "What if he had one too many and that's why he had to piss so bad?"

"I *did* cause it," Luke said simply. "But that's not why. Someone cut—"

"You see!" Sal said, triumphing. "He admitted it! Make him blow! See if he's not tanked!"

Luke looked to the taller, more sympathetic officer, whose shiny badge bore the name DONALDSON in tall silver letters. He said, "Officer, I haven't been drinking. Someone cut my brake lines. That's why I couldn't stop." He thought for a second, and then added: "I was the one who called in the accident. Why would I do that if I knew I'd get arrested when you showed up?"

Donaldson's eyebrows rose. "Back up. You say someone cut your brake lines?"

"Yes. Someone tried to kill me. They almost killed my neighbor's girlfriend, and now they cut my brake lines."

Sal turned to Donaldson and puffed air out his lips. "Right, and I'm the Jolly Green Giant. This guy has an accident and all of a sudden somebody's trying to kill him."

"Excuse me?" Luke said, his anger beginning to show. "Are you calling me a liar?"

Sal rounded on him. "Not to your face, no—I can't do that—but I *do* think you're letting your imagination run away with you."

"Sal . . ." Donaldson cautioned. The tired tone of his voice indicated that this exchange wasn't something new.

Sal paid his fellow officer no attention. He just looked at Luke and said, "Everyone thinks they're the goddamn center of the world. Well, I got news for you, buddy. You're not. *I'm* not. Hell, *nobody* is. We're just pawns in a game the big guy is playing. Okay? Just pawns. Nobody cut your brake lines. They just got old and broke."

"Got old?" Luke said, unable to believe what he was hearing. "It's a two thousand and ten, for Christ's sake! I've been working on cars my whole life, and brake lines don't just break like that. Mine were cut! You want to be arrogant because of your little Napoleon complex, fine, but Jesus, do your job!"

Sal's never-ending forehead flushed red, and he took a step forward. "Are you calling me *short?*"

Donaldson put out a hand and restrained him. "Hold on, Sal." He turned to Luke. "You said someone tried to kill your neighbor's girlfriend, right? Let's do this the right way and look into it. How many days ago did you file the complaint?"

Luke blinked, caught off guard. "Complaint?"

"You *did* file a complaint, didn't you?"

"Well, no, I didn't. I—"

"See!" Sal said. "Just another pawn seeking attention."

"I didn't *file* anything," Luke said angrily, "because I just found out about it today. I don't know if my neighbor did, either. I think he was too scared to."

"Likely story."

Luke grabbed his hair and mimed pulling it out. "Oh my God! I don't believe this! Why are you making everything so difficult? Just look under my car! Look at the brake lines and tell me they didn't cut themselves!" He turned to Donaldson, pleading. "Can you do that? You're the more sensible officer here. Just one look and you'll see that I'm not out of my mind, okay?"

Sal put both hands on his hips, standing defiant. Donaldson looked from him to Luke then said, "Yes, I suppose I can do that."

Luke breathed a sigh of relief. "Thank God."

Donaldson pulled out his flashlight, but before he could turn it on, a car pulled over behind his cruiser. Sal didn't waste any time. With his hands still on his hips, he stalked over to the car, shouting, "Hey, didn't you see those cones back there, buddy? Intersection's closed! You can't—"

The driver rolled down his tinted window.

Sal stopped in his tracks. "Oh, Captain!" he said, his demeanor immediately changing. "I'm sorry, I didn't know it was you."

"It's okay," Bryce said, stepping out of the Mercedes. He was dressed in a pair of dark blue jeans and a button-down shirt. "I was just passing by, and I saw the road block. Thought I'd see if everything was okay."

"Yeah, everything's fine," Sal said. "Just routine." He jerked his thumb over his shoulder, and in a low voice, added: "This guy's a nut, though. Thinks he crashed because someone 'cut' his brake lines."

Bryce grinned, showing the top row of his filed teeth. "The public's full of nuts, isn't it?"

"Sure is, Captain."

"Well, let's see if we can't calm this nut down, then."

Bryce walked over to where Donaldson knelt, readying himself to look under the Taurus. Before he could, Bryce said, "Officer Donaldson," in an authoritative tone.

Donaldson looked up. When he saw who had called his name, he got to his feet. "Captain! How are you?"

"Can't complain. It looks like I'm doing a bit better than this guy here." He turned to Luke, looking him over. "You got away lucky," he said, extending his hand. "I'm Captain Zapalski."

"You don't know the half of it," Luke said. "I'm Luke Suriano." He shook the captain's hand, looking him over as well. He was at least fifteen years older, and tall, with wide shoulders. If it hadn't been for his dark hair, he might have looked like the guy on the paper towel pa—

Suddenly Luke found it hard to breathe. The captain looked like the guy on the paper towel package. Tall and brawny but with dark hair and cold blue eyes. As in the exact way Joe had described Bryce. Luke snapped his head around and looked at the car the captain was driving. A white Mercedes. He happened upon the plate, and his heart plunged. They were the same numbers Joe had read to him over the phone what felt like half a lifetime ago. Seeing them, he remembered that his friend who had run the plates told him that the car belonged to a police captain.

Bryce saw the look on Luke's face, and the corners of his lips curled. "Pleased to meet you, Luke."

Luke pulled his hand back as he felt the captain's grip tighten. "You're Bryce . . ." he said.

"Yes, I'm Captain Bryce Zapalski," Bryce said simply.

"It was you . . ."

"Excuse me?"

"*You* did it . . ." Luke said, suddenly angry. "*You* cut my brake lines, and *you* tried to kill Amanda! You son of a bitch!" He lunged. If Sal and Donaldson hadn't been fast enough, Luke might have hit Bryce. As it was, the two officers caught him mid-punch and twisted his arm behind his back. Luke cried out in pain.

It was music to Bryce's ears.

"What's wrong with you?" Donaldson shouted, his previously composed demeanor melting away in the presence of danger. "Don't you know who that is? That's a *captain!* You assault him—or anyone in uniform, for that matter—and you go away! Do not pass go! Do not collect two hundred dollars! Straight to jail! Do you understand me?"

"Told you he was crazy!" Sal said joyfully, almost cackling. "Crazy as a priest in a pet shop!"

"I know who you are!" Luke roared, still thrashing and trying to break free. "You tried to kill her, you bastard! And now you tried to kill me!"

Donaldson twisted Luke's arm harder, and the pain skyrocketed. It felt like it was going to twist out of the socket.

"I'm going to give you one last warning," Donaldson said simply. "If you resist or try to assault my captain again, I'm going to have to put my steel bracelets around your wrists and take you down to the station. Do you understand?"

Luke nodded. He understood, all right. He understood that that's exactly what Bryce wanted. He therefore restrained himself, refusing to give Bryce the satisfaction. Donaldson loosened his grip, and instead of attacking, Luke calmly said, "Officer, this is the man who cut my brake lines and attacked my neighbor's girlfriend. He also vandalized my neighbor's property and tried to slash his tires."

There was silence for a moment, a rustling in the nearby bushes, then, almost as if on cue, the three men of authority burst into laughter.

"*I* cut your brake lines?" Bryce said, amused. "How could I have done that, sir? I've never even met you."

"Bullshit! You did it, and you know—"

"Watch your mouth!" Sal barked.

Luke continued a bit more cautiously. "Officers, he—" And that's when it hit him. Luke *had* met Bryce before, once, almost a year ago. Staring into those cold blue eyes brought the memory back. He had been with Crystal, coming home from her mother's, when suddenly blue and red lights started flashing in the rearview mirror. Crystal was behind the wheel and had pulled over to the side of the road.

"I told you you were going too fast," Luke had told her.

Crystal just sneered, keeping her mouth shut to avoid another argument. They seemed to be occurring more frequently, always starting out as a disagreement and then erupting into a full-blown shouting match, like a small flame that suddenly bursts into a conflagration.

Crystal drew in a deep breath and rolled down the window. On the other side of it was the same face Luke saw before him now.

"Excuse me, ma'am," Bryce had said, "but do you know . . . how fast you were going?" His voice went from direct and in control to faraway and dreamy, the way it does when its owner finds himself in the presence of a beautiful woman. Luke had seen the look in those cold blue eyes and recognized it as the look he himself had given Crystal the first time he saw her.

"You . . ." Luke said now, his voice laced with hatred. "You planned this, didn't you? You broke us up!"

"What's he talking about, Captain?" Donaldson asked. "Should we bring him in?"

Bryce chuckled. "No, there's no need for that. He's just mad his wife left him."

"How do you know his wife left him?" Sal asked.

"Because," Bryce said, "I'm sleeping with her now."

Luke lunged forward again. Donaldson had to use all his strength to restrain him. Bryce didn't seem to care. He just tipped his head back and laughed. Sal laughed, too, cackling wildly like a hyena, as if this was the funniest thing he'd ever heard.

"That's it!" Donaldson said. "I tried to be reasonable! Come with me!"

Luke felt something cold and hard bite down on his wrists, and the next second there was pain. The rustling in the bushes sounded again. Luke ignored it, preoccupied by more urgent matters.

"No, no," Bryce said, waving a dismissive hand. "There's no need for that. He's just upset. It's perfectly understandable. I didn't recognize him at first, but now I do. My girlfriend showed me some old pictures, and he was in a few of them." He said this last staring directly at Luke, making sure to say the word "girlfriend" with a hint of derision.

"What do you want us to do with him then?" Donaldson asked.

Bryce thought about it, but it seemed like he already had the answer. A sly smile crossed his face. Without pause, he asked, "Mr. Suriano, do you have any narcotics in the car?"

Luke stared in disbelief. "Narcotics?"

"Yes, Mr. Suriano, narcotics. As in drugs?"

"No, I don't."

Bryce's smile widened, showing more of those filed teeth than ever. "Then you wouldn't mind if we checked your car, would you? Perhaps your glove compartment?"

"Of course not. Check it if you want, but you won't find anythi—" And that's when it hit him: the glove compartment. Bryce knew what his officers would find in there if they checked. And Luke knew, too. If he hadn't already disposed of the bloody underwear, he would have had a lot of explaining to do. Joe had been right: Bryce was mischievous and cunning. He'd first tried to kill Luke then had come along to check on his progress. And, it just so happened, he even had a backup plan if that didn't work.

Sal didn't waste any time. He was already moving forward with the determination of a bloodhound—head dipped down, shoulders squared, nostrils flaring—picking through the contents of the glove compartment. He found a flashlight, Luke's insurance card, the Taurus's user manual, and a few scattered items of little importance: rubber bands, paperclips, pennies, etc. But that was all.

"Nothing, Captain," Sal called over his shoulder. It was impossible to miss the disappointment in his voice.

Bryce wrinkled his brow and turned a cold stare on Luke. There were two words in that stare: *Well played.* Luke avoided the look as if it might turn him to stone. In avoiding it, he glanced at the bush in which he'd hidden the underwear.

Bryce curiously watched this display. He didn't need to think twice—this was textbook psychology. The guilty always gave away their secrets with their eyes: the slimy bastard had taken the underwear out of the car and stuffed it into the bush.

"Tell you what," Bryce said to Sal, "why don't you check that bush over there for the hell of it."

Sal raised his eyebrows. Because of his bald head, they looked like two pieces of driftwood floating in an ocean of flesh. "Why the bush?" And then it hit him. That was the bush into which Luke had been "relieving himself" when he and Donaldson had pulled up. Sal smiled deviously. "Yes, Captain. Right away."

Luke watched in fear as the officer's bald head disappeared into the bush. Luke tried to move forward to stop him, knowing what would happen when the officer found the underwear, but he was still being restrained.

Sal pushed branch after branch aside, first checking inside the bush and then under it. Finally, he pulled his head out. "Nothing, Captain."

A great weight lifted itself off Luke's chest. He didn't understand it. Had Sal not found the underwear? Or had he found it, but ignored it because he was searching for narcotics? Whichever it was, Luke didn't care.

Bryce did, though. He stared at Luke with eyes full of hate. "Nothing?" he asked.

"Nothing," Sal repeated.

Bryce moved forward to check the bush himself, sure that's where Luke had hidden the underwear. As he pushed the branches aside, a rustling sounded again and something furry with a long copper-colored tail and a pointed face darted out.

Luke was the only one to notice that it had something pink clutched in its mouth.

CHAPTER 50

"Keys?"

"Huh?" Luke shook his head, clearing his thoughts. He had been rubbing his wrists where the cold metal of the handcuffs left impressions on his skin.

"I said I need the keys," the tow truck man repeated. He was a short, fat man in a tank top with hairy forearms.

"Oh, right, here you go," Luke said, as he handed his keys over. He had been so deep in thought since the police left that he was barely aware of what was happening now. He still couldn't believe how they had acted, taking Bryce's side on everything. Joe was right: Bryce had the police in his pocket. He couldn't go to them. Not for this, or anything else, for that matter. That is, unless he and Joe had evidence. And all they had right now was one person's word against another's.

The sound of tires rolling on asphalt found Luke's ears, and he turned around. Just like the white Mercedes had pulled over to the side of the road, so did another car. Luke recognized it immediately.

"Joseph," he said thankfully, when Joe flung the door open and rushed out.

"Luke, are you okay? What happened?"

"I got into an accident." He cast a corner-of-the-eye glance at the tow truck man.

Joe instinctively understood that he would have to wait until they were alone before he got any answers.

They waited for five minutes, talking about sports and the weather, while the tow truck man finished his job.

"Well . . . ?" Joe pressed when they were in Joe's car, driving back. "Are you gonna tell me, or what?"

Luke drew in a breath of air and let it out slowly. "Okay," he said, and he told Joe about the brake lines being cut, his miraculous plunge through the intersection, and the bloody underwear.

When Luke mentioned this last, Joe nearly lost control of the wheel. *"Underwear?"*

"Watch the road!" Luke reproved.

"Sorry," Joe said, getting a hold of it again. "But underwear?"

"Yes, like the ones you told me about. Except there was blood on these, and I think Bryce put them in my glove compartment to set me up."

"Set you up how?"

"Maybe he wanted the police to think I raped someone or hurt them. I don't know. I don't want to think about it. All I know is that you were right, and we have to find a way to stop all this."

"Yeah, but how?"

Luke thought, the silence stretching. Finally he said, "I wish I knew . . ."

Joe wished he knew, too. Without thinking, he put on his blinker and turned at the light.

"Where are you going?" Luke asked.

"Huh? Oh, sorry. I forgot. I was going back to my house. Let me turn around."

"No," Luke said. "Keep going." He remembered where he had intended to go before the accident. "Maybe I can talk some sense into Crystal. Maybe the both of us can."

Joe told him how he'd tried to do just that, but Bryce had answered the door instead.

"It can't hurt to try again."

It could, Joe thought, sickly. If Bryce got involved, it could hurt a lot.

"You ready?" Luke asked when Joe parked in his usual spot in front of his house.

That was a funny question, Joe thought. He didn't think he would ever be ready. It was like pulling off a Band-Aid: you were never ready because you knew about the pain it would cause. But you had to get it off eventually, so you pulled it off quick. That's what Joe had to do now. He had to do this quick before he thought about it too much and chickened out.

Bryce's car wasn't in the driveway—and that was a plus—but that didn't mean Crystal would believe them. She would most likely think it was a hair-brained scheme Luke had concocted to win her back. Nevertheless, they had to try.

"I'm ready," Joe said, resigning himself to the fact that they had no other options left.

Luke led the way. He walked up the familiar driveway, feeling a bit empty. This house, where he had begun a life and a family, was nothing in comparison to the matchbook apartment in which he lived now. There had been love and laughter, celebrations and birthdays, in this house. And Bryce had ruined all of that. He had stepped between Luke and Crystal, and like a crowbar, had pried them apart. Now, it was Luke's turn to pry him and Crystal apart.

Out of instinct, he reached into his pocket to pull out his keys. When he remembered that he had given them to the tow truck man and that Crystal might not appreciate the intrusion, he rang the bell.

"Is she home?"

Luke shrugged. "Either she is and doesn't want to answer, or she isn't."

Joe decided to figure out which by walking over to the garage doors and peering in through the crescent-shaped windows at the top. It was dark inside, but enough light spilled through for him to make out that the garage was empty.

"No car," he told Luke.

"Then she isn't home. We can always wait, if you want."

That would work, providing Bryce didn't come back during that time. If he did, he would ruin everything. They needed Crystal alone. Needed time to break into her mind and convince her that everything she thought was sunshine and rainbows was really darkness and thunderclouds.

"I guess," Joe said. "We can go back to my house in the meantime. Watch TV or something." In truth, he didn't think he would be able to watch anything—he was so worked up that whatever pictures or sounds the television produced would be lost on him. Then again, they did need something to do, and it would be a distraction while they waited.

What he didn't know was that they would get just that.

He walked up his own driveway but stopped short about halfway.

"What's wrong?" Luke asked.

Joe stood still, his eyes locked on the ground. "Blood," he said in a strangled voice.

Sure enough, there were tiny splotches of blood on the brickwork, starting from where Joe stood and leading up the driveway, like the breadcrumbs Hansel and Gretel had put down so they could find their way out of the forest. Except Luke had a feeling that this trail didn't lead whoever followed it *out* of the forest—it led them *in*, and into a much darker version of the life they were living.

He wanted to tell Joe to ignore it, to turn around, get back in his car, and drive away. But he knew Joe couldn't do that, just as much as he knew he couldn't.

"Joseph . . ." he said, but Joe was already following the trail. Luke quickened his pace to catch up, holding his aching back. "Joseph, maybe you shouldn't."

Joe didn't answer. The splotches led around to the side gate, increasing in size. The gate was locked, but Joe hopped it easily. Luke had a bit of trouble, getting stuck at the top.

"Joseph!" he called out. "Wait!" He had a sinking feeling in the pit of his stomach that it was a trap, that Bryce had laid the blood on purpose and wanted Joe to follow it. "Joseph, stop!" But Joe was already on the other side, turning down the brick path.

A second later, a blood-curdling scream rent the air.

CHAPTER 51

Joe felt his legs weaken and spill his body to the ground. He fell on his knees hard enough to leave bruises, but he didn't feel any pain. He didn't even hear Luke shouting after him as he struggled to get over the gate. All he could do was stare in disbelief, uttering choked, mournful cries.

Before him, resting on top of the patio table, was his dog Snowball. His eyes were cloudy, glazed over. His mouth was open in an eternal yawn, his tongue lolling out. And staked through the side of his body, pinning him to the table like a butterfly to a pegboard, was the shaft of the table's umbrella. His fur, once white, was stained a dark crimson, almost black from all the blood that had spilled out of the wound. It saturated the table, making it look like a child had tried to finger paint but had been careless and spilled the bucket. For some reason, Joe could hear the sound of the blood dripping to the floor with maddening clarity, as if the volume on life had been turned all the way up.

"Joseph! Joseph! What— Oh, Christ!"

Luke stopped short. The next second he was turning away, vomiting.

Joe advanced as if in a dream, inching closer and closer to the companion that used to sleep at the foot of his bed. Unable to believe what he was seeing, he reached out and laid a trembling hand on Snowball's side. The second he did, Snowball twitched, his legs quivering. His eyes cleared and focused on Joe long enough for a mournful whine to escape his mouth. His pink ribbon of a tongue shot out and licked Joe's arm. It felt dry, like sandpaper. Snowball tried to lift his head, but the effort was too much. He wagged his tail lazily instead, like the flopping fin of a dying fish. Then he was still.

It felt like hours before Joe could summon himself to move again. Luke waited patiently, wiping his mouth with the bottom of his shirt. Through a shimmer of tears, Joe found other injuries on Snowball's body. There was a cut on his ear, one on his snout, and another on his tail, each one deeper than the last. Had the umbrella not been thrust through his body, it might have looked like he'd been mauled by a rabid beast. But Joe knew better.

His first emotions were grief and sadness, but they faded quickly, overcome by rage and hostility. A tear trickled down his cheek, but it nearly evaporated; his face was burning up. He felt like he was suffused with the fires of hell. Bryce was going to pay for what he did. He was going to pay dearly. Luke tried to put a comforting hand on Joe's shoulder, but Joe shrugged it off, stalking around the side of the house. He hopped the gate like a machine, barely even giving it a glance (for one crazy moment, Luke thought he was going to burst right through it). Then he was on the other side, making his way across the street and up Crystal's driveway. He wanted to do something to get Bryce back. His mind was percolating with fury, his pupils dilating, his heart rate increasing, the airways in his lungs expanding. He was left with a primitive urge to fight and picked up the first object he could lay his hands on. If he couldn't break Bryce's face at that moment, then he was going to break something else. He chambered the rock behind his ear and stepped forward, preparing to launch it. He planned to throw it through the large bay window at the front of Crystal's house the way a pitcher might send a fastball rocketing over home plate. Before he could, however, someone grabbed his hand.

"That won't solve anything," a sympathetic voice said. It belonged to Luke. Joe looked at him with the mad eyes of someone who comprehends nothing. "Put it down," Luke tried to reason. "Bryce doesn't even own the house. Crystal does."

Slowly, Joe let Luke take the rock out of his hand. Luke tossed it aside. "There," he said. "Now let's go back to—"

That was as far as he got, because the next moment a white Mercedes pulled into the driveway, stopping just before the bumper made contact with Luke's leg.

Joe's eyes narrowed as the driver got out.

"Well, well, well. Looks like I have some visitors," Bryce said. There was an insane smile on his face. "It's the two troublemakers, together at last."

There was no need to think, no need to even hesitate. Joe lunged. Luke grabbed him at the last instant and hauled him back.

"What's the matter?" Bryce taunted. "Upset about something?"

"You bastard!" Joe shouted. *"You fucking asshole! You killed him! You killed my dog!"*

Bryce looked up and down the block, then childishly pressed a finger against his lips. "Shhhhh. You should keep your voice down. You're going to upset the neighbors."

"Fuck you!" Joe spat. "I'll kill you!"

"You know, you're lucky you have someone holding you back. It's just a pity he couldn't hold onto his wife the same way. Guess she realized he wasn't worth that much as a husband and had to find a *real* man."

Now it was Luke's turn to fume. His face turned beet red, as if someone had ignited a flare in his head. Bryce saw the look of hate in his eyes and knew what was about to come next. "My, my, how quickly one forgets," he said, ticking his index finger back and forth. "Don't you remember what happened the last time you tried to hit me? Those cops would love for an excuse to come after you. Come on, give it to them. Finish the job. Hit me." He thrust out his chin, giving Luke a target. "Hit me, and let's see how much help you'll be to the boy behind bars."

Luke restrained himself, hearing the words from a few hours before echo in his head: *What's wrong with you? Don't you know who that is? That's a* captain! *You assault him—or anyone in uniform, for that matter—and you go away! Do not pass go! Do not collect two hundred dollars! Straight to jail! Do you understand me?*

As much as Luke hated to admit it, Bryce was right. He *wouldn't* be much help to Joe behind bars.

"Forget it," he said, defeated. "Let's go."

Joe answered by thrusting forward again. Luke, caught off guard, was barely able to restrain him.

"Joseph, forget it! It's not worth it!"

"He's right, Joseph," Bryce mocked. "It's *not* worth it. Now, why don't the both of you go home and think about what you did to deserve this."

Without giving Bryce the satisfaction of seeing how much his words angered him, Luke turned away and did just that.

CHAPTER 52

"I hate him!" Joe shouted. He was seething, his head so hot that if he were a teakettle he would have begun to whistle. "I hate him, and I wanna kill him!"

"I know," Luke said. "I do, too. But that's exactly what he wants. He wants us to come after him. We can't give him what he wants."

Joe paced around the living room. During one of his revolutions, he had knocked a throw-pillow off the couch. Now he punted it. It sailed across the room and struck a lamp, toppling it off the table. There was a tiny explosion as it crashed to the floor and the bulb shattered. "Great!" Joe said sarcastically. "Just great! What else can go wrong?"

"Calm down," Luke said.

"Calm down? He messed with my car, he hurt Amanda, and now he killed my dog! How the hell am I supposed to calm down?"

"Listen, I know this—"

"And look who's talking! You nearly tried to tackle him when he started talking about Crystal!"

Luke ran both hands through his hair. "Okay, you're right," he admitted. "I almost did. It's hard not to listen to your instincts. But hear me out . . . I know this is going to sound horrible, but maybe what he did to Snowball is a blessing in disguise."

Joe nearly erupted. *"What?* How can you say that?" He pointed outside to the black leaf bag he and Luke had put Snowball's body in. "My dog's dead! And he's never coming back!"

"Just listen. You have to think positive. Before that, we had no proof that Bryce did anything. Just your word and Amanda's against his. Now, maybe we have something. He didn't attack Snowball in your backyard—that's obvious. If he did, then there wouldn't have been any blood on your driveway. And he certainly didn't do it there, where everyone could have seen him. Which leaves only one other place he could have done it: Crystal's house. If we find evidence that he attacked Snowball there, then we'll finally have the proof we need. Maybe not enough to put him away, but it'll be a start. It's like dominoes: if we get the first one pushed over, it'll knock into the next and the next, and eventually they'll all fall."

It sounded like a reasonable plan. There was only one problem: Bryce was cunning, and Joe didn't think he'd let himself get caught.

Unbidden, a snatch of conversation he'd had with Bryce came back to him: *I've been getting away with it for years. And there's nothing you can do to stop me.* For the first time since Bryce had said that, Joe finally understood what he meant: Bryce had actually done these things before, maybe once, maybe twice, maybe a dozen times. It was a nauseating realization.

Think positive, Joe coached himself. *Think positive.*

Maybe the fact that Bryce had gotten away with it before was a blessing in disguise, too. People got cocky over time, and when that happened, they usually let their guard slip. Joe prayed that this would be the case in their situation.

"But we can't do this just the two of us," Luke continued. "We have to search the house when Bryce is out. We need lookouts and scouts. We can't have him coming home and finding us snooping through his things. That would be disastrous."

"What if Crystal's home?" Joe asked.

"That's probably the second best scenario. If that happens then we'll tell her everything, just like we planned to today. But if she isn't, then we have to sneak in. I can keep a lookout from your house—that'd be the best place for me because of my back—but we need at least two people to search. We have to be in and out of there as quickly as possible."

"Who can we get, though?" Joe asked. "Amanda's still in the hospital, and she's the only one who knows about Bryce. I told my parents, but they didn't believe me. Besides, they're on vacation."

Luke thought about this. "Are you sure you don't know anyone that could help? One of your friends, maybe?"

Who did Joe know that could help? He might be able to ask Timothy Rogers, but he wasn't sure if he wanted to drag him into this. It would be dangerous, and Timothy wasn't that adventurous. Once Joe told him the plan, he might back out. He needed someone daring, audacious, and bold. Someone who wasn't afraid of danger. Someone who had a little bit of a mean streak in them.

Joe smacked the front of his head with his palm. "Think," he said. "Think." And then it came. The answer was so simple, he almost laughed.

The cafeteria the next day was in an uproar as usual: students shouting to one another across the room, some teasing, others laughing, some playing songs on their phones and iPods when the lunch monitors weren't watching. Joe ignored all these things, having eyes and ears for only one person. He scanned the tables, looking for him, but he wasn't there.

Joe could have called him the night before, but figured it would be better to talk in person. At least in person you couldn't get hung up on, which after everything that had happened, would have been a very strong possibility.

Joe browsed the tables once more and came up with the same result. He was just about to search the east side cafeteria—even though he knew it would be pointless because athletes didn't sit on that side—when he caught sight of C.J. walking in from outside.

Joe drew in breath, psyching himself up for what he was about to do next. He hadn't spoken a word to C.J. since the fight. Hadn't even made eye contact. The black ring around C.J.'s eye was almost gone, but that didn't mean he forgave Joe, even if he had nobody to blame for it but himself. Which was precisely why Joe needed him to help. He needed to fight fire with fire, evil against evil. And if C.J. wasn't a perfect adversary for Bryce, he didn't know who else was.

He stood by the vending machines, watching as C.J. took a seat next to Bobby Wiseman, this year's starting pitcher, Eddie Munch, the first baseman, and two girls he recognized from the cheerleading squad.

It was now or never. He drew in another deep breath, let it out, and walked over.

C.J. saw him approaching the table and gave him the death stare. "What do *you* want?"

"To talk to you," Joe said.

"Fat chance. I've got nothing to say to you."

Joe tried another approach. "I'm sorry, okay? I didn't mean to hit you. You were talking about Amanda, and I just lost control. I—"

"You think *you* did this?" C.J. said, standing up and pointing to his eye. Beside him, Bobby and Eddie pushed their chairs back and stood, too. The chairs squeaked on the cafeteria floor and everyone looked their way, hoping to see some excitement. "Let's get this straight," C.J. said, jabbing his finger in Joe's face. "*You* didn't do this. *I* did it. Your elbow just got in the way when I tried to head-butt you, that's all."

Joe looked from Bobby to Eddie, then to the girls. The latter wore the eager look of spectators, the former of gladiators, their hands opening and closing at their sides, warming up for action.

"Okay, *you* did it," Joe said to C.J. "Whatever. It doesn't matter. I need to talk to you. You're the only one who can help."

"Help? You want me to *help* you?" He grabbed Joe by the shirt and started walking forwards, pushing Joe backwards, more for the sake of distancing himself from his teammates than anything else. As he did, he whispered harshly, "You should have thought of that before you decided to drop me for that bitch. You're dead to me now. Do you hear me?

Dead. Which is exactly what you wanted." He let Joe go and gave him one final shove. "I hope you're happy."

By now the students were cheering, hoping for either C.J. or Joe to swing at one another. The lunch monitors were on their way over. "*Please*," Joe said. "You probably know that Amanda's in the hospital. But what you don't know is that my neighbor's new boyfriend tried to kill her. You're the only one that can help. I was wrong to stop talking to you. I'm sorry."

C.J. ignored the hand that fell on his shoulder and the stern voice that asked him if there was a problem. He just stared at Joe, unblinking. "Are you serious?"

"Yes," Joe said. "I wouldn't make something like this up. I need your help."

"I said is there a problem?" the voice repeated. It belonged to Mr. Banks, the junior advisor.

"No," Joe said. "There's no problem." He looked to C.J. with pleading eyes. "Is there?"

C.J. thought long and hard. Then he said, "No. No problem." He turned to Mr. Banks. "We're friends."

CHAPTER 53

They sat in Joe's living room after school going over the plan. The atmosphere was grave, especially after Joe showed C.J. what Bryce had done to Snowball. The dog's mangled body was the exclamation point at the end of the menacing paragraph Joe had narrated, describing everything Bryce had done up until this point. The gravity of the situation wasn't lost upon Luke either, who sat across from the two boys like a general in an army. He leaned over a piece of paper on the table between them, his face set in concentration. He had spent all day preparing and wanted to account for every possible contingency.

"Let's go over this one more time," he said. "I'm going to be here." He pointed to a crudely-drawn bush beside the big rectangle that was labeled JOE'S HOUSE. "I'll have perfect visibility from here. If I see anyone coming—Crystal, Bryce, *anyone*—I'll let you know on the walkie-talkie. Got it?"

"Got it," C.J. said. He held up the walkie-talkie Luke had bought while they were in school. "Channel thirty-seven, right?"

Luke nodded. "Channel thirty-seven. And keep it on all the time. Last thing we need is miscommunication."

C.J. turned his on and found that it was already tuned to the appropriate channel. Luke picked his up and did the same. "Testing,

testing. One, two, three. Over."

The walkie-talkie in C.J.'s hand sparked to life. At first there was a burst of static, then shortly after, Luke's voice followed, clear as a bell.

"These things are rated for up to five miles," Luke told them. "So there should be no excuse for going out of range."

"Why channel thirty-seven?" Joe asked.

"Because we're communicating over radio frequency. It's a public domain. Anyone could tune in to our channel. Most people with walkie-talkies usually stick to the lower frequencies. Last thing we want is company blocking one of our transmissions."

C.J. thumbed the button on the side. "Makes sense," he said. There was another burst of static, this one from the Luke's walkie-talkie, and C.J.'s voice echoed his words.

"Say 'over' after you end the transmission," Luke told him. "This way I know when you're done talking so I don't talk over you. I'll do the same."

"Okay." C.J. tried it again, this time saying "over" when he was done.

"Perfect," Luke said. Then he asked, "What's the procedure if, for whatever reason, somebody else decides to share our channel?"

Without hesitation, C.J. said, "We switch to channel thirty-six."

"Excellent. I think we're getting the hang of this. Okay, now let's go back to the plan. You two are going to enter here." He tapped the second large rectangle on the piece of paper, this one labeled CRYSTAL'S HOUSE. On it he had drawn three doors: the front door, the sliding glass door in the den, and the backdoor in the kitchen. It was this last that he was pointing to. He tapped it again, then reached into his pocket and tossed Joe the keys he had gotten back from the tow truck man. "It's the big square one."

"Got it," Joe said. He located the key, then shoved the key ring into his pocket. "Is that all?"

"For getting in? Yes. That's not the hard part. The hard part will be finding the evidence. I think it would be best if you two split up. C.J., you might want to check the backyard while Joe checks inside the house. Joe, I recommend that you search the basement. There's a door at the end of

Kendra's playroom that leads into my workshop. It would have been a perfect place for Bryce to . . . you know."

Joe nodded. He knew. And he knew about the workshop, too, from the day he and Amanda had babysat Kendra.

"Try to look for anything incriminating. Bloodstains. Dirty knives. Etcetera. You get the point. And when you do . . ."

Joe held up the disposable camera.

"Exactly. Snap a picture of it. We need evidence. We can show Crystal, the police, and whoever else." Luke spoke with a hint of excitement in his voice, especially the part about showing Crystal. Joe had a feeling that deep down Luke hoped he and Crystal might get back together after all of this. Joe had hopes, too. He hoped that he and C.J. would find what they needed to make Bryce's life as miserable as he had made theirs.

"Wait," C.J. said. "I've got a question."

Luke raised his eyebrows.

"There's no alarm, right?"

"There is, but Crystal and I never used it."

"What if she decides to use it now?"

That was a good question. Luke had a good answer to go along with it: "Then it'll go off when you open the door."

Joe felt his skin crawl. The last thing he wanted to do was get arrested. If he was in jail, there was no telling what fun Bryce might have with him. Bryce probably knew all the guards, even some prisoners. Hell, he might even make a deal with them: a cigarette to whoever could beat Joe up first. Two for making him their . . .

Joe shook the unpleasant thought out of his head. "Okay, so what if she turned it on and it goes off when I open the door? What happens then?"

"Then you run," Luke said simply. "By the time the police get there, you'll be long gone. And if any of the neighbors see you, just tell them you heard the alarm, saw someone back there, and went to investigate. They'll never think you were the person that set it off."

Joe didn't like the uncertainty in the plan. There were too many variables. Luke hadn't lived in the house with Crystal for over four months. During that span of time many things could have changed without his knowledge, and Joe didn't want to be the one to have to find out what they were. Yet, if he wanted to get Bryce back, there was no other way.

"Okay," C.J. said. "When do we do this?"

Luke strode over to the window, poked a finger between the blinds, and pushed them aside. The white Mercedes stared back at him from Crystal's driveway. "As soon as Bryce leaves."

For the next two hours they took turns looking out the window and playing cards. Each time they looked, however, Bryce's car was still there. It was like watching a pot of water trying to boil: the more they looked, the more certain they became that nothing would happen. C.J. fumed over this, complaining that Coach Heck would never let him miss another day of practice.

"Why don't we just do it now?" he asked. "Joe can ring the doorbell and distract Bryce while I sneak around back."

Luke shook his head. "I like your determination, but it would be too dangerous. There's no telling what Bryce will do if he caught you."

C.J. snorted. "I ain't afraid of him."

"But *I* am," Luke said. "Crazy people are like wild animals—they might snap at any moment."

"He's right," Joe told C.J. "Bryce is crazy. Look what he did so far. There's no telling what he could do next. He might even shoot you and claim self-defense. He knows the laws, and he knows how to go around them."

C.J. shook his head in disgust but didn't argue. "So we just sit here then?"

"That's all we can do," Luke said. "Sit around and wait."

That's exactly what they did. They played eight more hands of Texas Hold 'Em, one game of Rummy, and were getting ready to play Go-Fish when C.J. exclaimed, "It's him! Hey, he's leaving!"

Sure enough, a figure emerged from the garage, walking toward the white Mercedes. By the height, the width of his shoulders, and his dark hair, Joe could tell that it was Bryce. He walked around to the back of the car and opened the trunk.

"What's he doing?" C.J. asked.

Joe shrugged.

"Looks like he's going to put something in there," Luke said.

Bryce walked back into the garage. When he stepped out again he was dragging a long bag. It looked heavy and awkward, bulging at the seams. Bryce had to reposition it twice as he shuffled over to the car and struggled to lift it into the trunk.

"What do you think that is?" Joe asked.

C.J. said, "It's a duffel bag. You know, those bags they give you in the army to put your shit in."

"Yeah, but what do you think is *in* it?"

"I don't care what's in it," Luke interrupted. "We can't let this distract us. We have a job to do."

"Yeah, it's getting late," C.J. said. "Let's do this already."

Luke looked at his watch. He was surprised to discover that it was almost four. Immediately, a disconcerted feeling wove its way into the fabric of his being. "Kendra's bus never came. She should have been home by now. Same with Crystal."

Joe thought about this. If he remembered correctly, the bus came every day at 3:35, dropping Kendra off in front of the house. Every day *but* today. "Maybe Crystal picked her up from school," he suggested.

Luke bit his lower lip, trying to accept this. After a minute, he said, "Yeah, you're probably right. After all, Bryce has been here the whole time, so he hasn't had anything to do with it. If that's the case, then we'd better do this fast before they come home."

"I'm down," C.J. said. "Let's do it."

Joe paused for the slightest of seconds, pulling his phone out of his pocket. "One minute. Let me text Amanda real quick." They waited for him. When he sent the message through the intricate system of satellites and antennas, he closed his phone. "Okay, let's go."

CHAPTER 54

Bryce took off the gloves with extreme caution, making sure that none of the blood got on his hands. When he was finished, he took off the garbage bag he had turned into a make-shift poncho and wrapped the gloves in it. Then he placed those items in a Ziploc bag, which he then tucked into the empty duffel bag as he walked back to his car. It was parked on the side of the street, and as he got in, he surreptitiously leaned over and tossed the duffel bag into a storm drain.

There, he thought. *Out of sight, out of mind.*

He was pleased to find that even though the years were creeping up on him, they hadn't affected the way he worked. He had originally assumed that by now he'd have to slow things down, or regretfully, stop, but the past few days only proved that time had not robbed him of his talents. If anything it had honed them, made them keener, and he was glad to get a chance to unwind after pretending to be so nice to Crystal's annoying neighbors.

He started the car and pulled out onto the road, heading toward the hospital. The little bitch was next. He knew she had broken her jaw and couldn't talk—Crystal had learned that little piece of information from Margaret the Gossip Queen and had passed it along to him. He also knew that injuries healed and her silence wouldn't last forever. . . . That is, unless he intervened. And he planned to. Oh God, how he planned to. He couldn't wait to see Joe's face after he killed the object of his affection. Kids were stupid. By now, Joe probably assumed he'd spend the rest of his life with her. What a tragic surprise it would be when he found out that wouldn't be true! He'd cry, throw a tantrum, curse the almighty Himself, and Bryce would be there to watch it all, drinking the sweet nectar of his emotions.

He got to the hospital fifteen minutes later, pulling into the big lot out front. He was dressed casually and was as cool as the inside of a freezer; nobody would suspect his true intentions. Those he passed in the corridors would just assume he was a concerned father, uncle, or brother visiting a loved one. He checked his face in the mirror to make sure it held this appearance. It was almost there. He pitched his eyebrows a bit more, turned out his lower lip, and when he was happy with what he saw, he stepped out of the car.

The halls were filled with men and women walking around in green pants and white jackets—orderlies and doctors. They all glanced at Bryce, but dismissed him as another customary face they immediately forgot. So far, everything was going according to plan. All he had to do was walk into the ICU (another beautiful piece of information gleaned by gossip), kill the bitch quickly and silently, and slip out.

Out of sight, out of mind.

The directory said the ICU was on the third floor. He rode the elevator up, checking his watch to even further his image as a concerned relative, and found the sign for the ICU when he got out. It was at the end of the corridor. He walked towards it, passing doors on his left, each with a little gold-plated number at the center. They triggered something in his memory, and the world slowly dissolved, revealing another from his past. In this one he was walking by similar doors, except these were crudely painted dark green, the color of rotting garbage. And it smelled like garbage, too. The trash littering the hallway probably had a lot to do with it. Behind him, his partner Anthony stepped on a Dunkin' Donuts cup, crushing it beneath his boot.

"Shit," he said. "This place is disgusting."

Bryce nodded, happy to be leaving the shitty apartment complex. If it hadn't been for the domestic disturbance call, they wouldn't have even had to come. They would have been cruising around in air-conditioning, passing the time bullshitting, swapping stories, and staring at the long-legged bimbos crossing the street. But no, the diseased public had to have disputes and drag others in to solve their problems.

"Coffee?" Anthony suggested.

"What?"

Anthony kicked the cup towards him. "Coffee. You want to get some?"

It sounded like a good idea. It was almost five, and he needed a pick-me-up, something to carry him through the rest of his tour. "Sure," he said.

If there was one good thing about being a cop, it was that you didn't have to obey traffic laws. They turned on their lights and double-parked in front of the first Dunkin' Donuts they came to. The line was long, and as they waited, the crowd gasped. It was a collective gasp, the sort you don't hear in a crowded Brooklyn store unless it's being robbed. Sure enough, the crowd parted and a man wearing a ski mask emerged. Since he was looking over his shoulder, assuming the gun in his hand was a talisman that would clear the way before him, he bumped into Bryce and stepped on his foot.

"Watch it, asshole!" the robber shouted. He turned to see what type of moron would block an armed man's retreat. "Can't you see that I—"

He froze, first looking at Bryce's uniform and then at his face.

Bryce glared, his eyebrows coming together, marking his displeasure. He had just polished his boots this morning, and now some contaminated sewer rat had stepped on them. His blood boiled, and he began to sweat rage.

The robber, unable to miss the malevolent look, let out a gasp and pushed his way out the door as quickly as he could. Bryce didn't give him a chance to escape. He put on a burst of speed and zigzagged through the conglomeration of mouth-breathers that lined the busy sidewalk.

After about six blocks, the robber turned down an alley. Bryce turned down it, too. What he saw made him smile maliciously. About midway was a six- or seven-foot-high wall made of brick. And standing in front of it, his head frantically, darting back and forth like a frightened animal looking for a way to escape, was the robber.

"End of the line, fucker!" Bryce shouted. His chest was heaving. It wasn't at all an unpleasant sensation. It actually felt kind of good. His adrenalin was pumping, and he was enjoying it, much more than he had enjoyed killing small animals and watching them suffer. This was a person, someone real, like his childhood friend Charlie who had broken his arm on the bike path. Except, unlike his friend, this was someone who he didn't know and could hurt without suffering any legal repercussions. In fact, he could downright kill the man and just claim he had shot him in self-defense. The idea turned him on more than ever. He had been yearning to kill a person for some time now. The idea intoxicated him. He waited to see if Anthony would pop into the alley behind him. When he didn't, he pulled out his gun.

The robber took one look at the death-dealing device, saw Bryce's intention, and scurried onto the top of a trash can, using it to boost himself over the wall.

Bryce didn't let him get very far. He was on the can a second later, bounding over the wall after him. He caught the robber on the other side and shoved him back-first against the wall, pressing the barrel of his gun deep into the robber's neck.

"Thought you could just step on my foot and get away with it, didn't you? Didn't you?"

The robber cringed.

"Well you can't!" Bryce shouted, spraying saliva everywhere like a mad dog. *"You have to take responsibly for your actions!"*

The robber closed his eyes. He jerked them back open when Bryce cocked his gun. He knew he didn't have much time. This crazy cop had short-circuited and was going to shoot him. He felt his own gun hanging limply in his trembling hand and tightened his grip on it. Then, ever so slowly, he raised it.

Bryce caught the movement.

"And just what the fuck do you think you're going to do with that? Shoot me?"

The robber didn't say anything. He just continued to raise the gun. Bryce helped him. He grabbed the barrel and pulled it into his chest, placing it right above his heart.

"Go on, shoot," Bryce said, staring coldly into the robber's eyes. He felt the weight of the barrel pressing against the fabric of his uniform, and excitement leapt within. "If you're going to carry a gun, you'd better be prepared to use it."

The robber swallowed, hard. He had never killed anybody. Never even shot a gun before. Hell, he was just a homeless man trying to feed himself. He had thought that when he found the gun in the sewer he had found the key that unlocked the golden door to opportunity. As it turned out, it only unlocked the black door to trouble.

"Shoot," Bryce repeated. He lowered his own gun and re-holstered it. Now the only gun out was the one pressed against his chest. "Show me what kind of man you are. If you pass the test, you live."

This was not supposed to happen. The robber was a robber, not a killer. He was only supposed to go into the Dunkin' Donuts, get the money, and get the hell out. He saw the crazy look in Bryce's eyes and knew if he didn't shoot the cop, he was going to die. For that reason, he summoned all his will, and with a trembling finger, pulled the trigger.

Nothing happened.

Bryce wrenched the gun out of the robber's hand. He didn't stop there—he grabbed the robber's arm, spun him around, and twisted it behind his back. There was a sickening crunch, and the robber screamed. Then, Bryce had the gun pressed against the robber's neck again.

"You failed," he whispered into his ear. There was a click—"By the way, it works better without the safety on"—then an explosion.

The shot echoed in the close confines of the alley, but Bryce barely heard it—he was too busy coming in his pants.

~ ~ ~

The doors to the ICU were wide enough to accommodate the size of a gurney. When Bryce approached them, he noticed that they were automatic and opened for the orderly walking in front of him. This mundane observation allowed the past to slip from his mind. That day, long gone but not forgotten, had been the glorious day that started his killing streak, and it had opened doors to a state of emotion more intense than he ever could have fathomed. In the time since, he had basked in that emotion again and again, savoring each occasion as though it were a delicacy. Now he was going to indulge again. That is . . . until he saw what awaited him in the room.

The ICU was a flurry of activity. Nurses bustled back and forth stabilizing patients, administering medication, checking vital signs, and God knew what else. They worked with the unaffected air of guardian angels. The sheer size of the room caught Bryce off guard, too. There were at least fifteen beds, each with retractable curtains at their sides to give the impression of separate rooms. And sitting on a chair across from the second bed was a familiar-looking man in a police uniform. All at once, Bryce's plan of looking like a concerned visitor crashed and burned like a plane without engines.

The man in the uniform looked up from his magazine. "Captain?"

Bryce racked his brain for the man's name. Wessen? Westering? Something like that. And then he caught sight of his badge.

"Westing," he said. "How are you?"

Westing stood up, looking as surprised as Bryce did. "Good, sir. What are you doing here? Is everything all right?"

"Can I help you?"

An extremely overweight nurse stepped out from behind one of the curtains. She stood defiantly with a clipboard in one hand and the other pressed against a pudgy hip. The way she stood, she almost looked like a troll barring passage of a bridge.

Bryce gritted his teeth, looking for a way out. He couldn't have any connections to the girl. His eyes darted about the room, quickly and efficiently, and came to rest on the man with the bullet wounds in the second bed. He remembered issuing an order for an officer to watch over the injured drug dealer, and couldn't believe his good fortune that he was still here.

"No," he lied, as casually as ever. "Police activity." He pulled out his wallet and showed the nurse his badge. "I came to talk to the officer."

The overweight nurse's eyes widened. She dropped her defiant behavior and became the inquiring Mary of so many civilians. "Is it about the guy who got shot?"

Bryce shook his head in mock apology. "Sorry. It's confidential."

The nurse frowned. "I figured. Your buddy wouldn't tell me, either. Well, carry on."

"Is everything all right?" Westing asked again when she left.

"Everything's fine. I was just passing by on my way to the market and thought I'd check in. Anything?"

Westing shook his head. "No, he's still out cold. No telling when he'll wake up. Anyway, until he does, we won't have any information on that drug lord, Ruther's, whereabouts."

Bryce nodded, appearing to be interested. What he was really doing was searching the room for the little bitch. She had to be in here somewhere.

"Comas are tricky things," Westing went on. "They can either last days or years. Doctor said the girl in the last bed came out of hers after a month. Wonder if we'll be that lucky."

Bryce's ears twitched. Girl? Coma? He peeked over Westing's shoulder and down the length of the room, but the curtains around the last bed were pulled closed. He thought for a second then asked, "How long have you been on?"

Westing checked his watch. "About five hours. Been on since eleven this morning."

"Why don't you take a break? There's a McDonalds down the road. Go get yourself a burger."

Westing's eyebrows went up. "Really?"

"Sure." Bryce looked to the curtains again. "I've got some time to kill. I'll take your post, just leave the magazine."

Westing thanked Bryce about three times for his generosity and then left. When he did, Bryce sat in his chair and picked up his magazine. Several of the nurses looked his way but dismissed him after a glance.

Out of sight, out of mind. Soon, he would blend into the scenery and they would forget all about him. And when they did, he would strike like a snake hiding in the grass.

He got his opportunity thirteen minutes later. All but five nurses left the ICU, and those that stayed disappeared behind closed curtains, tending to their patients. It would be easy now. All he had to do was sneak over to the little bitch's bed, press a pillow against her face until she stopped struggling, and then slip behind the curtains when the machines started screaming. There would be so much commotion going on that he could easily disappear and reappear in the chair as effortlessly as a magician might pull a rabbit out of a hat. The real trick would be to keep from smiling when Joe came in, bawling his eyes out. But that was a trick he would have a little time to practice for.

When he was sure that nobody was coming, he got to his hands and knees and looked under the curtains. He could tell by their ankles that the nurses were busy with their patients, and he tiptoed over to the last bed.

Sure enough, the bitch was behind the curtain. And she was asleep. He couldn't have paid for a better opportunity. Her arm was in a cast and there was metal wire fastening her jaw shut—it caught the light and gleamed through her parted lips—but the cuts on her face had healed, bearing fresh and unmarked skin, making her look beautiful again. Almost saint-like. As if *she* was an angel, not the nurses. Well, he wouldn't deprive her of the chance to become a real angel. He snatched up the pillow that rested on the chair next to her bed—the chair Joe had probably sat in day and night while she lay unconscious—and held it poised over her head. Before he could press it down, however, something vibrated, catching him off guard. It was as if she knew through her sleep that she was in danger and had set off an alarm. But that was ridiculous, and Bryce confirmed this when he saw that her cell phone, resting on the little tray next to her bed, had lighted up and received a text.

Do it! the voice in Bryce's head demanded. *Do it now!*

The little bitch stirred and mumbled something in her sleep. Bryce bit his lower lip. He knew it would be a great risk, but now that she was waking up, he wanted to—almost *needed* to—see the fear in her eyes before he smothered the life out of her.

She stirred again, then fell back into the land that brought dreams. Bryce almost woke her up himself but stopped when he looked at the phone and caught sight of who the text was from:

Joe <3

Curious, he put the pillow down and picked up the phone.

From: Joe <3
Were gonna search the house
now. Hopefully we can find
something to put this bastard
away. Wish me luck!
May 9, 3:58 pm

Bryce didn't like the sound of that. He scrolled through the previous messages and confirmed his suspicion. The little asshole was going to search Crystal's house and try to find signs that he had butchered the dog. Well, good luck to him. He wouldn't find any. Bryce was a pro at this type of work and had meticulously cleaned up after himself. Even Crime Scene would have trouble finding any evidence. Then he thought of the incriminating photographs. What if Joe was an avid reader, and while searching Crystal's house, got bored and decided to peruse Bryce's shelf and pull down his favorite Tom Clancy book? Bryce knew that would probably never happen, yet he couldn't help but worry. Criminals always got busted for the little treasures they kept lying around. He had initially wondered why they did such stupid things in the first place, but when he started doing it himself, he knew. It was because memory was not permanent. Often, with time, it faded, failing to recall specific details that had once been so clear. Sometimes you needed an object to help recall those details, something that had been there during the time of the event. Or, in Bryce's case, a photograph, which could preserve a snapshot of the mind better than anything else. It was permanent, concrete, and it was worth a thousand words. And, in this case, it was the incriminating evidence Joe was looking for.

Bryce cursed under his breath. He felt like smashing the phone into a million pieces. But no, he couldn't. It would make too much noise. Therefore he settled on killing the little bitch. He would teach Joe what happened when you fucked with someone like him. Like the bull, you got the horns.

He picked up the pillow again and held it over Amanda's face, this time ready to drive it down with all his force. Yet, as he prepared himself to do this, a little voice spoke inside his head. A niggling voice. A *cruel* voice.

He's going to find the photographs.

Bryce ignored it. He squeezed the pillow in his hands, his fingers digging into the soft fabric.

He's going to find them and get you sent to prison. There's nothing worse for a law enforcement official than going to jail.

Bryce shook his head, trying to free himself of the voice. He'd heard stories of what happened to cops when they went to jail. He didn't want to think about that now.

You're wasting time. Each minute you stand here is another minute Joe has to search Crystal's house. Another minute he has to get closer to those photographs.

Slowly, Bryce put the pillow down. The voice was right: he was wasting time. It would take at least four minutes to smother the little bitch, and those four minutes were precious when you took into account how long the drive back to the house would take.

Bryce couldn't chance Joe finding the photographs. He had to leave. He could kill the little bitch another day. She wasn't going anywhere.

CHAPTER 55

On the front lawns of other blocks, children capered in the rays of sun, chasing one another, staining their knees. In the streets, older boys in their teens played basketball, sweating, bickering about scores and fouls. But on Joe's block, all remained still and silent in the shadows of clouds. Somewhere, off in the distance, a dog barked, and the branches of trees swayed in the breeze, but that was all.

Joe was the first across the street, ducking his head and holding it in the crook of his arm as if he were protecting it from falling debris. C.J. followed shortly after, mimicking his actions. Luke winced as he watched this shameful display from behind the bush on the side of Joe's house. A second later, C.J.'s radio crackled.

"What are you guys doing?" Luke's voice demanded. "Don't make it obvious you're doing something illegal! Just walk casually! Over."

He had nobody to blame for their performance but himself. He had gone over every facet of the plan in intricate detail except the approach. He just thanked God there was nobody outside to watch them bumble around.

There was a crackle from his radio, and then C.J.'s voice came out: "Sorry. Guess we got caught up in the moment."

"Say 'over' when you stop talking," Luke said. "Over."

"Sorry," C.J. said. He waved in apology from across the street. "I forgot. Over."

Luke put a hand to his head. This mission was doomed for failure.

The backyard was as Joe remembered it. There was a large deck extending off the back of the house, furnished with a table, a few chairs, and a barbecue. There was also a swing set, a sandbox in the shape of a turtle, and a small wooden house that Luke had built for Kendra. Joe remembered Kendra playing in it on the few occasions he had been in the backyard. And off in the corner, where the two sides of the fence joined together, was a large steel shed. It was this last that Joe told C.J. to search while he opened the back door.

"Why do *I* have to search the shed?" C.J. wanted to know.

"Because," Joe said. "I have the keys. Therefore, I need to open the door. Just look the shed over, okay? If there's blood in it or on any of the tools, yell for me. If not, come in the house and help me search. I'll leave the door unlocked."

C.J. wouldn't have it; he wasn't here for grunt work. "How about you give me the keys, and *you* search the shed."

Joe sighed. He felt like he was talking to a child. "Because you have the walkie-talkie, okay? It's either one or the other. Just do it. I don't wanna argue."

The walkie-talkie crackled. Luke's voice asked, "Are you guys in yet? Over."

C.J. thumbed the button. "Not yet. James Bond over here won't get off his high horse." He lowered the walkie-talkie, then remembering, quickly raised it and added: "Over."

It crackled again. "Well quit horsing around. You two have a job to do. We don't have all day! Over."

Joe gave C.J. a look as if to say *see, I told you so*, and C.J. finally gave in. While he walked toward the shed, Joe pulled out the key ring Luke had given him. He found the big square key and shoved it into the top lock.

It slid in effortlessly, as if it were oiled. But when he tried to turn it, he encountered all the resistance in the world. Puzzled, he tried shaking it and jiggling it back and forth. No matter what he did, he couldn't get it to open the lock. He tried every key on the key ring only to get the same result.

"Why aren't you inside yet?" someone asked from behind.

Joe spun around to find C.J. standing with his hands defiantly on his hips.

"The keys don't work," Joe said in frustration. "Why aren't you in the shed?"

"There was nothing in there. And what do you mean they don't work?"

"Just what I said. They don't work. You try."

He exchanged the keys for the walkie-talkie and radioed Luke.

"Luke, it's Joe. The keys don't work. Over."

A crackle. "They don't work? Over?"

"No. Over."

"I was afraid of that. Crystal must have changed the locks. Over"

C.J. frowned, pulling away from the door. There was annoyance written all over his face. "Changed the locks? What the hell does that mean?"

"It means we can't get in with the keys."

"Well who said we needed keys anyway?" He tossed them back to Joe and walked to the edge of the deck. Then he bent down and picked something up. "This will do the job," he said, hefting a rock.

Joe grabbed C.J.'s wrist, the way Luke had grabbed his. "No! Don't break anything."

The walkie-talkie crackled again. "There's got to be another way in," Luke said. "Just don't do anything stupid. Last thing we need is a broken window or something."

Joe eyed C.J. harshly, and C.J. tossed the rock aside in disappointment.

Luke thought for a second, then inspiration struck. When he spoke again, he sounded excited. "Look at the second floor."

Joe and C.J. did.

"Look at the windows. Second from the back. Is it open at all? Over."

It *was* open, about two inches.

"That's the bathroom window. Crystal always used to leave it open. Guess she still does. It shouldn't be locked. You guys have to climb up onto the roof and go in through there."

"Through there?" Joe looked up at the steep pitch of the roof. "How the hell are we supposed to get up there?" he asked C.J.

As if he had heard Joe's question, Luke added, "There should be a barbecue on the deck. Just push it up against the house and climb on top of it. You guys are tall. It'll give you enough height to grab onto the conduit—that's the little steel pipe—on the side of the second story. Use it to pull yourselves onto the roof, and then walk over to the window. I locked myself out once and had to get in the same way. Over."

Joe looked around. He saw the conduit Luke was talking about.

"I still think the rock would have been easier," C.J. grumbled.

Joe ignored him and pushed the barbecue over. When it was in place, he said to Luke, "Okay, we're gonna give it a try. Over."

"Good luck," Luke said. "Radio me when you're in. Over and out for now."

Joe handed the radio back to C.J., and he clipped it to the waistband of his pants. It took him all of two seconds to boost himself onto the roof, where he sat crouching, looking down at Joe. "You coming?"

Joe shook his head. He was athletic, yes, and climbing onto the barbecue wouldn't pose a problem, but climbing onto the roof would because he was afraid of heights. "You're already up there. Can't you just go in and open the back door for me?"

C.J. didn't need to think this over. "Not a chance."

"What? Why?"

"Because you made me check the shed, and that was a boring, shit-ass job. And maybe because I'm still a little pissed at you for ending our friendship so easily."

Joe stared up at him, stunned. "Are you serious? I said I was sorry, didn't I? Now just go in and open the door."

C.J. shook his head again. He looked like an owl the way he was perched up there. Joe almost expected him to start hooting.

"C.J., I'm not kidding around. Open the door for me."

"I'll give you a hand up," C.J. said. "But I'm not opening the door."

Joe's eyebrows came together. He almost wished C.J. hadn't tossed the rock away. If it was close, he might just throw it at him and try to knock him down. "Fine!" he said when he saw that C.J. was going to be difficult. "Give me a hand."

He climbed onto the barbecue, and with C.J.'s help, shakily got onto the roof.

"There now," C.J. mocked. "That wasn't so bad, was it?"

Joe ignored him. Very carefully, he sidestepped to the open window, grabbing onto it for dear life when he reached it.

The walkie-talkie crackled. "Don't just stand there!" Luke shouted. "Hurry up and get in! Everyone can see you!"

Joe looked across the street and over to his house. The moment he did, he wished he hadn't. From this high up the world below seemed to tip and spin, and he nearly sunk to his knees. What made him stay up was Amanda. He needed to stay strong for her.

Across the street, Luke, looking at least four times smaller, popped out from behind the bush and heatedly waved his arm to the side, indicating that Joe should go in as quickly as possible. Joe didn't waste any time—he wanted to get off the roof more than ever.

He shoved his hands into the gap of the open window and heaved it upward. For one terrible moment he expected to hear the blare of an alarm. When none sounded, he fed himself through the window and flopped onto the bathroom floor, thankful to have solid ground under his feet again.

C.J. followed shortly after.

"We're in," C.J. said.

"I see that," Luke said. "And say 'over'! Over."

"Oh, yeah. Right. Sorry. Over."

"Now, search the house. I'll keep you posted from out here. Over and out."

The upstairs yielded no results, even though they split up to cover more ground. They checked the bedrooms, the bathroom, the closets—especially the ones they found Bryce's things in—only to come up short.

"That was a waste," C.J. said, when they'd finished. It was obvious he was expecting to stumble into a scene out of a horror movie: empty room, walls splattered with blood, organs in jars, etc.

Joe wasn't about to tell him that if they found anything it would most likely be an errant drop of blood that had gone overlooked, because if he told C.J. this, he was afraid C.J. might become disinterested. So what he said was, "Keep searching. There might be something downstairs or in the basement." He added: "Remember, if you see anything bloody, anything at all, even a drop or two, call me over. It may lead to more."

C.J. nodded, and they continued their search. Joe wasn't sure how much time had elapsed—working against the clock had an odd mind-numbing effect—but what he *was* sure of was that they hadn't come upon anything. It seemed that whatever Bryce was—killer, psycho, asshole—he wasn't careless. If he had splattered blood, he had cleaned it up without a trace.

"This is stupid," C.J. finally said when they had moved into the living room. "We're not gonna find anything."

Joe was starting to believe he was right but refused to admit it. "No, we're already in the house. We have to keep looking."

C.J. grunted. "We're just wasting time. He might come back any minute. You should just break something and be done with it. Get your revenge for what he did."

The idea sounded appetizing, but Joe couldn't. This wasn't Bryce's house. More importantly, he didn't want Bryce to know he had snuck in. And what not a better way to advertise his presence than a broken chair or a smashed—

"*C.J., no!*"

C.J. had picked up a small porcelain vase off the shelf and raised it high above his head, preparing to smash it to smithereens. "I thought you'd say something like that," he said with a grin on his face. "Well, if you're too pussy to do it, then I will."

"No!" Joe shouted, leaping forward and grabbing C.J.'s arms. "Don't be stupid!"

The walkie-talkie on C.J.'s waistband crackled. "How's it going in there?" Luke asked. "Over."

The boys ignored the disembodied voice, locked in a struggle. C.J. was determined to see some destruction. If he couldn't stumble upon anything Bryce had done, then he would make sure Bryce stumbled upon something *he* had.

"Put it down!" Joe yelled as he tried to wrestle the vase free.

"No!" C.J. tried turning and twisting around, anything to make Joe let go. "Just—let—me—break it!"

Joe held on with all his might. He tried stepping on C.J.'s toes to distract him, but C.J. moved them out of the way.

"C.J.—I'm serious—put it—down!"

"Never!" C.J. growled. "Let me—break it!"

"C.J.? Joe?" Luke said. "Are you guys there? Over?"

C.J. pulled the vase toward him, but Joe pulled it right back. The way they struggled, they looked like two men stranded on a desert island fighting over the last coconut.

"Give it!"

"No!"

"Give it!"

"No!"

"Joe? C.J.? Hello? Guys? Can you hear me?"

They were too equally matched. Neither of them would relinquish their grip. They might have stayed locked in this stalemate until the world ended if Joe had not tripped. He felt his balance wavering and let go of the vase, shooting his hands out to catch himself as he fell.

It was too late. His shoulder struck something, and he heard a crash. Except it wasn't the sound of him hitting the bookcase or the sound of the books tumbling down that he heard. It was the sound of the vase bursting into a million little pieces on the hardwood floor.

He got to his feet, staring at the porcelain fragments. C.J. was standing over them with a satisfied smile on his face.

"You idiot!" Joe roared. "Look what you did!"

C.J. kicked disinterestedly at one of the pieces, making it spin like a top. Like a child who has broken his toy, he was already bored again. "So what? From what you've told me, this asshole deserves it. Come on. Let's find something else to break. Maybe we can steal some money, too. Make it look like he got robbed."

Joe was fuming now. "I already told you! This isn't his house! It's—"

That's when his foot encountered something. It wasn't the mess that cut his words short, or the presence of the overturned book, it was what was spilling *out* of the book. Speechless, he bent down to pick up the Tom Clancy novel. As he lifted it, a crude photo album fell out of a hollow carved into the pages. It wasn't one of those nice albums with an engraved cover that someone might use for their cherished family memories. In fact, it didn't have a cover at all. It was just a bunch of plastic sleeves with pictures in them being held together by wire. Yet, by the way it had been carefully hidden, Joe could tell it held cherished memories nonetheless.

"Joe? C.J.? Answer me! Are you guys all right? Did something happen?"

By now C.J. had seen the album, too, and he reached down, absentmindedly thumbing the button on the walkie-talkie. "Yeah," he said. "We're fine." There was no emotion in his voice. It was all consumed by what he saw in that first photograph: a pale woman in her mid-twenties with purplish bruises surrounding her throat.

Joe flipped the page to another girl with vacant eyes, then another, this one a redhead in a bathing suit.

Page after page.

Death after death.

Joe flipped through the photos with numb fingers, unable to believe what he was seeing. The walkie-talkie crackled again, but both he and C.J. barely heard it.

There must have been about twenty-eight photos in total, all showing similar scenes. Interspersed here and there among them were empty spots where a select few had been removed from their plastic sleeves.

There was no way for Joe to know that Amanda's picture was among one of the ones missing.

Joe closed the album, his fingers trembling over the plastic. "Tell Luke," he said weakly. "You have to tell him what we found."

C.J. thumbed the button on the walkie-talkie. "We found it," was all he said.

"Found what?" Luke asked a second later. "A knife? Blood? Over."

It took C.J. almost a full minute to collect himself and respond. "We might as well have. It's a photo album. . . . One with pictures of dead people. At least I think they're dead—"

"They have to be," Joe said distractedly.

"—they're just lying there with their eyes closed, blood all over them."

He held the button for a second longer, not speaking, and then released it. He waited for Luke to respond. When he didn't, he thumbed it again and added, "This is really fucked up. I think he killed them. I think he killed them and took their pictures so he could look at them later. You were right: this guy's crazy."

C.J. released the button. The moment he did, Luke's voice poured out of the speaker, already in mid-sentence: "*—right now! Over!*" It didn't take C.J. long to realize that this was because he had forgotten to say "over." He had never officially ended his transmission. Therefore, Luke had gotten tired of waiting and started his.

"Sorry," C.J. said. "I didn't get all of that. Say it again?" And this time he was sure to add: "Over."

There was a crackle, and then a high, reedy voice chanted, "One, two, three. Ready or not, here I come!"

C.J. jerked backward and pulled the walkie-talkie away from his ear.

"What the hell was that?" Joe asked.

C.J. shrugged. "Beats the hell out of me. It sounded like a kid, didn't it? Maybe the frequency got crossed?" And that's when he remembered Luke telling them about the possibility of a third party sharing their channel. He thumbed the button and said, "Luke, I'm switching channels."

Without waiting for a reply, he pressed a button on the walkie-talkie and tuned it to channel 36. Unlike the last channel, this one had no other parties on it. It didn't even have Luke. He thought about changing back to 37 and telling that little kid he'd kick his ass if he didn't get off, when there was a crackle, and Luke's voice came out of the speaker, worked up, laced with panic. It sewed all his words together into one long repetitive chain: "*GetoutGetoutGet—*"

Before he could finish, a car door slammed somewhere outside.

Joe snapped his head toward the sound. Through the window he could make out the white Mercedes in the driveway, smoke rising from its engine like a breathing dragon.

His stomach plunged.

CHAPTER 56

Luke's walkie-talkie crackled, and C.J.'s voice came out. He only said three words, but they were the most beautiful three words Luke had ever heard: "We found it." Luke felt relief rush over his body like cool water after a hot day working out in the sun.

"Found what?" he asked, just to be sure. "A knife? Blood? Over."

There was a second's pause, and then: "We might as well have. It's a photo album. . . . One with pictures of dead people. At least I think they're dead—" In the background he heard Joe say that they had to be dead, which made him shiver a bit. "—they're just lying there with their eyes closed, blood all over them."

Luke lowered the walkie-talkie from his ear. A photo album of dead people? Bryce was an even sicker fuck than he'd imagined. The boys had stumbled onto a gold mine, and it meant they could go straight to the police. With photographic evidence, the police *had* to believe them, and they would be able to protect Amanda. But that evidence did something else as well: it told Luke that Bryce was incredibly dangerous. There was no telling what he'd do to get the album back if he discovered it was missing.

Without waiting any longer, Luke raised the walkie-talkie to his mouth. He was just about to press the button when he realized C.J. never said "over" to end his transmission. He waited a few more seconds, and when he reasoned that C.J. had just forgotten to say it again and didn't plan on continuing, he thumbed the button and spoke: "Joe, C.J. Listen to me, and listen very carefully, okay? You have to make sure you don't leave any signs of your presence behind. It's extremely important that Bryce doesn't find out you were in the house. Put everything back in its place and—"

That's when he saw the car screaming down the block. At first he couldn't distinguish the make, model, or even the color because of the reflection of the sun on its windshield, but as it drew closer and the reflection shifted, his deepest fears turned into reality. And by the speed at which Bryce was coming, it looked as if he were royally pissed off.

"It's him!" Luke shouted into the walkie-talkie. "It's Bryce! He's coming home! *Get out right now! Over!*"

"Sorry," C.J. said. "I didn't get all of that. Say it again? Over."

Before Luke could repeat himself, a child's voice spat out: "One, two, three. Ready or not, here I come!"

Luke cursed, wanting to strangle the child for interrupting. He hoped that C.J. remembered the procedure for third-party interference but waited on the channel for three seconds just in case he didn't. When C.J. didn't speak again, Luke switched to channel 36 and started screaming: *"Joe, C.J. Bryce is home! Get out as fast as you can! GetoutGetoutGetout!"*

To Luke's horror, Bryce pulled into the driveway, practically leaped out of the Mercedes, and rushed over to the door. He definitely knew something was up. But how? They had been so careful. None of them had spoken of the plan to anyone. Luke realized it didn't matter. What mattered was the boys' safety.

The second Bryce vanished inside the house, Luke popped out from behind the bush and ran across the street. He acted so instinctively that he didn't even think about what he was doing. He bustled over to the front door, grabbed the knob, and pushed. To his surprise, the door didn't open. It was locked from the inside.

That's when somebody screamed.

CHAPTER 57

The first thing Bryce noticed when he burst into the house was the mess on the living room floor. There were books and pieces of a broken—vase? pot?—scattered everywhere. He walked over to the clutter, fearing the worst. Sure enough, *The Bear and the Dragon* by Tom Clancy was among the books on the floor. He picked it up with a trembling hand, praying that the photo album was still inside. If it was, he could continue his fun and arrest the little bastard for breaking into his home (who else would have done it, if not him?). But if it wasn't there, and the little bastard *had* found it . . . well, that was something Bryce didn't even want to think about.

Finally, he opened the book, but slowly, fearing the worst. In doing so, he drew out the tension so much that when he finally discovered that the album wasn't in the hollowed-out section of the pages, he screamed loud enough to wake the dead.

In reply, there was a pounding on the front door.

"Open up! Open up right now!" the voice on the other side shouted. It sounded like it belonged to Crystal's ex-husband, and if he was knocking with such fury, then that had to mean the little bastard was still in the house! Bryce was glad he had locked the door behind him. It would keep Luke out and give him time to find that little fucker so he could get his revenge.

He let the empty husk of the book fall from his fingers and crash to the floor. He barely paid it any attention, rooting his eyes around the room for signs of Joe instead. The little bastard had to have left something behind: an overturned throw-rug, a footprint, hell, even a trail of breadcrumbs, kids were stupid. But none of these things were present. Bryce even strained his ears to see if he could hear where the little bastard was hiding, but all he heard were the chimes of the doorbell as Luke summoned them like a mad Quasimodo. Bryce ignored this distraction. They were Luke's feeble attempts at rescuing the kid, just like the feeble attempts he had made at trying to keep his marriage alive. Bryce had shown him just how easy it was to come between him and Crystal, and now he would show him how easy it would be to find Joe and kill him. He could get his gun—it was only upstairs—but he didn't want to give Joe a chance to get away. He pulled something out of his pocket instead and flicked his wrist. A blade appeared, catching the light, then he crept forward, moving with the careful deliberation of a cheetah creeping under brush. Joe was close—he could almost smell his fear in the air. Bryce looked behind the living room couch first and then moved to the dining room and looked under the table. Nothing so far, but that meant he had eliminated two spots. By process of elimination, he was two steps closer. Without giving pause, he moved on to the den. Almost immediately, Bryce noted that two of the locks on the sliding glass door were open. All that held it closed was the tiny pin at the top, which was bent horribly out of true, as though someone had forgotten about it and had frantically tried to pry the door open. That was a good sign. It meant the little bastard was close. It meant he had rushed into the den and tried to escape, only to find his passage barred.

While someone else might have called out "Come out, come out, wherever you are!" at this moment, Bryce remained silent, straining his ears, directing every fiber of his being to finding Joe. He slinked over to the television stand and peered behind it. Nothing. Then he slithered over to the array of potted plants in the corner. Nothing there, either. He was getting closer. He could almost feel it the way someone might feel their hair start to stand on end as they drew closer to a static electricity source.

Joe watched through the crack between the door and its frame as Bryce made his way toward the couch, where C.J. was hiding. (It wasn't the best of hiding spots, but C.J. hadn't had time to find a better one.)

There had to be something Joe could do to distract Bryce.

Think! he scolded himself. *Think!*

Time was dwindling. With each second that passed, Bryce was one step closer to finding C.J.

Joe squeezed his eyes shut, pressing his fists against his temples the way a child does when engaged in immense thought, and just like that, the answer came. It was so simple he almost hit himself for not thinking of it sooner. He had Bryce's phone number. Had it ever since Bryce staged that text message conversation that Amanda found. All he had to do was remember the name Bryce had saved it under. Without a second to spare, he dug his hands into his pocket and pulled out his cell, going through the texts. The conversation wasn't there. It had been over a month ago, and he had deleted it since. Cursing to himself, he manually went through his contacts, hoping he could remember the name when he saw it.

He got through the first six contacts when he chanced a second look into the den. To his horror, Bryce was already looking behind one end of the couch, his knife held out, ready to be used. Joe didn't have much time left. He went back to the contacts, frantically scrolling through them. He passed the *C*s and moved on to the *D*s, hating himself for having saved so many numbers he never called. He was just about to give up and do something crazy, like burst out the door so Bryce could chase him, when he came to the name *Daniel.* He knew two *Daniel*s, but had them stored in his phone under their last names to avoid confusion.

He called the number, praying it was the right one, as he watched Bryce move to the other side of the couch where C.J. was hiding.

Come on! Come on! Ring, damn you! Ring!

Finally, it did.

Just as Bryce leaned forward, about to look, the phone attached to his belt rang. He paused out of instinct, unclipped it, and looked at the caller I.D.

"Where are you, you little shit? I know you're in here!"

It was apparent that Bryce had stored Joe's number. That saved Joe the trouble of having to identify himself.

"You're right," Joe said, keeping his voice low so Bryce could only hear it come out of the phone's speaker. "I'm here, but not for long. I'm climbing out your bedroom window right now. I'll be at the police station soon."

Bryce stood up straighter than an arrow, his head tilted toward the ceiling, his eyes staring at it so intently that it almost looked like he was trying to peer through the drywall to see if Joe was telling the truth. "You're not up there," he said snidely. "You're still hiding."

"Fine," Joe said. "If that's what you wanna believe, then that's cool with me. Either way, I've got a nice new photo album that I'm sure your friends at work would *love* to see."

Bryce fought back an acid comment, using all his willpower to keep his voice calm. He knew yelling at this point would only make things worse. Kids were stupid, he reminded himself. They were like dogs—if you wanted them to do something, you had to be nice to them. "Joeeeee. Neighborrrr. Let's talk," he said as sweetly as he could. "I'm sure we can work this out. There must be *something* you want. Tell me what it is, and we can make a deal." As he said this, he slowly moved away from the couch, checking behind the treadmill and Kendra's wooden castle.

"Okay," Joe said. He thought about Amanda and Snowball and Luke and his car. "There *is* something I want, actually."

"See, I knew you'd come to your senses. What is it? You want me to finally leave you alone? I think that can be arranged. All you have to do is give me back my photo album, and the only time you'll ever see me is when I wave to you from across the street. How's that sound?"

"It sounds good, but that's not what I want."

"Then what do you want?"

Bryce moved from the treadmill to the basement door. Joe held his breath, not moving. Then, as calmly as he could manage, he said, "I want you to go *fuck* yourself."

Bryce had begun to slowly turn to knob. Now his tranquility snapped like a rubber band and he tried wrenching it open instead, screaming, *"You little shit! You're dead! Do you know that? Dead! When I get my hands on you, I'm going to press my thumbs into your eyeballs until they pop like grapes!"*

The door thundered in its frame. Joe didn't say anything. He just stood there in silence as Bryce wrestled with the knob.

"Open up! Open up, you little bastard!" Bryce pulled with all his might. Finally he realized the problem and threw back the deadbolt. Now the door flung open, crashing into the front of the treadmill and sending chips of plastic flying into the air. He thrust his head into the opening and turned on the light. "*Where are you?"* he screeched. *"Come out of there!"*

Joe couldn't believe his luck. In his fury, Bryce had temporarily lost the ability to think rationally. If Joe had been hiding in the basement then there would have been no way he could have locked the door behind him. But Bryce didn't seem to realize this. He just poked his head in farther, even took the first few steps down the stairs.

Joe realized he was never going to get a better opportunity. If he was quiet enough and quick enough, he could sneak out of the closet across the room and shove Bryce down the stairs. Then he could lock him in the basement until the police arrived.

He decided he'd do just that, and slowly began to push open the door. It opened maybe three inches before the hinges squealed like a pig. Joe cringed, biting down on his lip hard enough to draw blood. The coppery taste filled his mouth as he watched Bryce abruptly stop, then cock his head toward the sound. A moment later he was walking back up the stairs, his knife held out in front of him.

By now, Joe's heart was pounding loud enough to be confused with a snare drum at a rock concert. He bit down on his lip even harder, praying that Bryce wouldn't hear it. It seemed that his prayers were not answered: Bryce—either because of incredibly keen ears, or smelling Joe's fear—walked straight over to the closet and pulled it open.

CHAPTER 58

Joe did the only thing he could think of. He yelled. He yelled so loud that when Bryce pulled open the closet door, he jumped back as if a jack-in-the-box had just shot out at him. Bryce instinctively crossed his arms in front of his face to ward off the attack. Joe tried to scurry past, but Bryce reached out with his free hand and grabbed Joe's shirt, wrestling him to the floor. Joe was taller, but Bryce still weighed more, and years of lifting weights had made him stronger. He handled Joe the way a veteran crocodile wrestler handles a baby croc: tossing him around, rolling on top of him, and pinning him to the floor.

"Get off!" Joe shouted, fighting to get free and holding onto Bryce's wrists so as to avoid the blade of the knife.

Bryce answered by driving his right elbow into Joe's mouth. Joe's lip burst open, spilling blood onto the carpet.

Suddenly, there was a thunderous banging. Joe used the distraction to knock the knife out of Bryce's hand, and together they looked up to see Luke standing on the other side of the sliding door, pounding on the glass like a mime who's trying to gain entry through an invisible barrier.

Bryce's mouth twisted into a smile, exposing his filed teeth. He didn't seem to care that he'd lost his weapon. As deliberately as ever, he raised his fist so that Luke could see it, and then smashed it into Joe's nose as hard as he could. There was a horrible crunching sound, and Joe screamed, covering his face. Luke shouted something, pulling feverishly at the door's handle. It wouldn't open. The pin at the top, although horribly bent, still did its job.

Bryce returned his focus to Joe. Like the pistons in a motor, he began issuing blows, one after another. Joe did the best he could to block them, but the majority of Bryce's strikes found their way through his defense, bloodying his ear, the side of his face, and opening a gash above his left eyebrow.

"Your friend can't help you now!" Bryce shouted, laughing maniacally. He pinned Joe's arms against his body, securing them with his thighs. He looked up, wanting Luke to watch him snap the little bastard's neck, but Luke was already gone. It would have been nice to have an audience to watch the concluding act of his performance, but it didn't matter. What mattered was teaching the little bastard a lesson he wouldn't soon forget.

Joe thought Bryce's hands felt remarkably powerful, like the sides of a vice. When Bryce grabbed his face, he thought Bryce was going to crush the life out of him. He stared up into Bryce's eyes, saw the malicious look in them that so many of Bryce's victims had seen, and closed his own. Just before those powerful hands did their work, Bryce cried out in pain and flopped forward.

Joe snapped his eyes open, staring at the figure standing over him. It took a second for him to realize that it was C.J. He had the walkie-talkie in his hand, smashed, oozing out electronics from the cracked plastic.

"Get up!" he cried. "Get up!"

Bryce, sprawled out on the floor, moaned and writhed in pain.

C.J. dropped what remained of the walkie-talkie and reached out for Joe. "Goddamit, hurry!"

Joe didn't need to be told twice. He grabbed C.J.'s hand and allowed himself to be helped to his feet. The minute he stood, however, it felt like someone had altered the rules of physics. His head swelled to an incredible five hundred pounds and then almost instantly dropped down to the weight of a balloon filled with helium. He began to see black confetti falling from the ceiling as though it was someone's birthday, and he felt his legs almost give out.

"Fight it!" C.J. shouted. He'd played too many sports not to recognize the signs of a fainting spell. "You gotta fight it!" He grabbed Joe to keep him from falling. "Just take deep breaths. But hurry!"

Bryce was hurrying, too. He'd flopped onto his back, and now his hands dazedly explored the point of impact at the base of his skull. He felt the beginnings of a bump starting to appear. He had mediocre medical knowledge, and knew that if he'd been hit a little harder and a little lower he might have been rendered unconscious. He scolded himself for getting too cocky and dropping his guard—of course there had been someone else in the house with the little bastard. He felt like hitting himself for not realizing it sooner. The only thing he could do now was play his injury to his advantage. He writhed in pain a little longer, and then, like a possum, played dead.

C.J. stared down at him the way a zoologist might stare at a sick animal. "Wait a minute. . . . I think I knocked him out."

"Thank God," Joe said, grabbing his pounding head. It felt like he had been hit by an eighteen wheeler. The side of his face was on fire, his left eye swelling. The blood from the laceration above his eyebrow was leaking into it, making it sting. He tried to rub it but realized his hand was already coated in blood. Without thinking, he wiped it on his white basketball shorts, leaving a stain remarkably similar to the Nike swoosh.

"Come on," C.J. said. "Try to walk."

Joe did. The first two steps were difficult—his head was still swimming—but the second and third were easier. By the fourth, he didn't need C.J. to support him anymore. The black confetti that had started to fall over his vision had vanished. The party was over. Bryce was knocked out. Joe had the evidence he needed to show the police. Soon Bryce would be behind bars. It sounded like a good end to everything that had happened over the last few months.

Only one person didn't seem to think so.

The moment Joe and C.J. turned their backs on him, Bryce snaked out his hand and coiled his fingers around Joe's ankle like the tentacles of a squid. Then he yanked with all his strength and pulled Joe to the floor. Joe let out a startled gasp. C.J. cried out, too, but for a different reason: he saw the knife in Bryce's hand.

"Lookout!" he shouted.

Joe turned to his attacker at the last possible moment. Bryce's hand was already coming down, preparing to drive the knife deep into Joe's thigh, rendering his leg useless. Joe knew what would come to pass if that occurred, which was why he kicked out with all his might. Had his foot connected with Bryce's chest like he'd intended it to, he might have gotten away unscathed. Yet, just as Amanda had missed Tony's nose, Joe missed and kicked Bryce's shoulder instead. This slight miscalculation cost him greatly. Rather than driving Bryce back, Joe only caused him to twist, and the knife, already guided by momentum, buried itself into Joe's calf.

Joe released a blood-curdling scream that echoed not only in the den, but in his head as well. It was so loud that it seemed to rattle his brain. Suddenly his calf felt like it had been plunged into a cauldron of acid, the pain so unbelievable that he didn't think the human body was capable of it.

Bryce didn't let this mishap interfere with his duties. He jerked the knife free, ignoring Joe's anguished cries, and prepared to drive it down again, only a little higher. C.J. didn't let this happen. He shot forward and kicked the knife like a football. The weapon sailed through the air, turning blade over hilt, and lodged itself into the wall. Then he kicked out again and again, first connecting with Bryce's ribs and then his face. Bryce snarled, lashing out, but C.J. danced out of reach. He faked a kick to Bryce's head, and then landed another to his testicles.

Bryce felt like he was being ripped in half. There was a horrific throbbing sensation that began in his loins and raced all the way up to his head. It caused his throat to ache, his vision to double, his eyes to water, and his stomach to turn, clenching and unclenching, working to send its contents rocketing up the esophagus.

C.J. didn't waste any time. While Bryce turned over onto his hands and knees, coughing, he grabbed Joe and hauled him to his feet. "Come on!

Get up! We gotta get outta here!"

Joe responded by gritting his teeth. C.J. was right. They had to get out of there. But because of his ankle, running was out of the question. Therefore he leaned on C.J.'s shoulder, allowing himself to be lead away. It wasn't until he looked up that he realized C.J. was leading him to the basement. "Wait, we can't go down there."

"Why not?"

"Because there's no way—" But that was as far as he got. Bryce had already gotten up behind them. His kick connected with C.J.'s side, smacking him into Joe and sending the two of them down the basement stairs. They tumbled head-over-heels until they hit the bottom and split apart.

Joe was the first to sit up, moaning dreadfully. He watched Bryce appear in the doorframe at the top of the stairs, silhouetted in the light, the shape of the knife once more in his hand.

"Oh, shit!" Joe cried. "C.J., get up! Get up!"

C.J. didn't. He just laid there.

Joe reached out in the dark and shook his friend, trying to rouse him. C.J. didn't move. Now Joe started to worry. What if C.J. had gotten knocked out? Or worse . . . what if he'd broken his neck? With all the effort Joe could manage, he reached up, found the light switch, and looked at his friend.

He was lying beside him, his face resting against the thin carpet as if it were a pillow. With his eyes closed, he looked almost peaceful. That's when Joe noticed the blood. It wasn't a lot, but it was enough to make him worry.

He shook C.J. again, his nerves practically snapping. *"Wake up! Wake up! C.J., wake up!"*

At first he didn't think C.J. would, that he really *had* broken his neck, but then he groaned and opened his eyes. In their reflection, Joe could see that Bryce was already a quarter of the way down the stairs, purposefully drawing out his descent the way all killers do in bad horror movies. Unlike them, this scared the absolute shit out of Joe. This simple, routine performance somehow transformed Bryce into the pinnacle of his nightmares: a deranged psycho bent on destruction. It made Joe scurry to his feet—carefully putting all the pressure on his good leg—and pull C.J. up with almost super-human strength.

The scream that followed was the loudest he had ever heard, and when C.J.'s arm flopped out from beneath him, Joe echoed it.

What was once a powerful limb used to propel a basketball from a three-point line was now a broken piece of organic machinery. The skin between the elbow and the shoulder, where someone might get a tattoo, was split open. And instead of a tattoo, there was ink of another kind, this one redder than any crimson ever concocted by mixing a pigment and a carrier. It spilled out of the open wound, dripping down C.J.'s arm in a shower of capillaries. And poking out from the center, looking like a broken periscope, was the shattered end of C.J.'s humerus.

Joe sucked in breath and turned away.

In as derisive a tone as Bryce could muster, he asked, "What's the matter? Your friend get hurt? Did he—"

Bryce stopped when he noticed C.J.'s arm hanging limply by his side. The way the bone poked out of the broken skin instantly brought him back to the day of the bike trail from his childhood. All at once, he was standing over Charlie with his broken arm again. Yet, when he blinked, returning to the present, the sight of Charlie's arm came back with him, turning into C.J.'s. It made all thoughts of revenge slip from Bryce's mind. What took their place was the almost-primal urge to satisfy his iniquitous desire. So instead of tightening the grip on the knife in his hand in rage, he tightened it in a lecherous hunger.

Joe caught the deranged look in Bryce's eyes and knew what it implied at once. He pulled at C.J. again, ignoring his friend's painful shouts of protest, and hauled him to his feet and away from the stairs.

Now their roles were reversed, and it was his turn to lead C.J. to safety. He slung his friend's good arm over his shoulder and ferried him through Kendra's playroom, zigzagging around the toys that littered the floor like mines in a minefield, and around the back of the staircase, which stood at the center of the room. If he had any luck, he might be able to get Bryce to follow him so he could circumnavigate the staircase and lead C.J. back up to safety.

Unfortunately, he didn't get the chance.

"Keep going," he told C.J. "I've got a plan, and it only works if you keep going. We have to—"

That's when C.J.'s body grew incredibly heavy. When Joe looked over, he saw that he was practically dragging his friend.

"C.J.? C.J.!" He shook him again, trying to wake him up, but C.J.'s head only flopped to the side like a marionette whose strings have been cut. He was still breathing—the wheeze of his respiration confirmed this—but he was unconscious. Very quickly, Joe laid him on the ground and gave him another hard shake. When that didn't work, Joe slapped him across the face. He winced at the loud sound it made, but C.J. didn't seem to mind—he just lay with his eyes closed, as peaceful as ever. Maybe he had the right idea. Maybe it was better to face the end unconscious, without fear or worry; to one minute be straddling the line between the terrestrial world and the ethereal plain, and the next floating over it without any knowledge or pain. Bryce was going to kill them in the end anyway. Now that C.J. was unconscious, there was no chance Joe could heave him up the stairs. So why shouldn't Joe follow his example? Why shouldn't he run head-first into the wall until he knocked himself out cold? If he did that, he could at least rob Bryce of some of the satisfaction. One final *fuck you* before his spirit departed his body. He didn't understand the intricate workings of Bryce's unbalanced mind, but he understood enough to know that he was like a vampire. Only, instead of sucking blood, he sucked out fear, and savored that even more. Therefore if Joe knocked himself unconscious, Bryce would not be able to get what he wanted.

Joe thought about doing this, contemplating it more than ever, when Bryce's footsteps stopped, indicating that he had reached the bottom of the stairs. What made Joe decide against it was one word that echoed over and over in his head: *Amanda.* She'd been unconscious, too. Only inches away from slipping into that spirit world. But she had fought off the grim reaper for over a month so she could be with Joe. If she had done that for him, then Joe couldn't be selfish and not do the same for her. Bryce might be the incarnation of death, and Joe's end might be inevitable, but he still had to try to survive.

He drew in a deep breath, filling his lungs with life-giving oxygen, and let it out slowly. When Bryce came around the staircase Joe wanted him to see him standing defiantly in front of C.J., protecting his friend the way a lion might protect its cubs, ready for the attack.

There was only one problem. Bryce never came . .

CHAPTER 59

Joe waited for what felt like a minute. Then two. Then three. During that span of time, his eyes kept flirting with the edges of the wall that made up the back of the staircase. He expected Bryce to appear around one of its sides any minute. To Joe's alarm, he didn't. Somehow, his absence was even more unsettling than his presence. It meant that he could be anywhere.

Joe strained his ears, hoping they would bring him the slightest indication of Bryce's whereabouts. They brought nothing except the normal sounds of the house: the oil burner, the hum of the overhead lights, the beams creaking in response to a gust of wind outside . . .

Joe was listening to these mundane melodies when the lights clicked off, pitching him into an almost-complete darkness, the only light left leaking in from the spaces between the blinds of the small rectangular windows set high in the walls.

In response, he took a step backward. His foot encountered something soft. He nearly screamed, but remembered that C.J. was behind him, and let his breath out in a harsh, shuddering sigh instead.

I can't do this, he thought. *I can't. I—*

"Joeeeeeeeeeee?"

His name filled the darkness as if it had been uttered by the wind, the syllable elongated, stretching almost into oblivion before slowly fading away. Joe snapped his head to the left and then the right. Which direction had it come from? He strained his ears harder than ever, but only the click of the oil burner shutting off came back to him.

It was too much to take. Joe snapped, screaming into the darkness as loud as he could. *"Just leave us alone! I give up, okay? I'll give you your stupid pictures back if you just leave us alone!"* He shoved his hand into his pocket, dug past the disposable camera, and pulled out the album of death. One part of him knew he should keep hold of it on the off-chance that he and C.J. escaped, but the other part knew that as long as he had it Bryce would never let that happen.

His self preservation took over—he had to get back to Amanda, he couldn't end up a corpse in a basement—and he threw the album. He watched it tumble through the air until the darkness swallowed it. "There!" he shouted when he heard it crash to the floor. "You got what you wanted! Now leave us alone!"

He waited for a response, for movement, for anything. He almost didn't think it would come, that Bryce was going to remain where he was, slowly driving him insane with his absence. Then, out of nowhere: "You shouldn't take things that don't belong to you." Bryce's voice was more scholarly than ever, a teacher bestowing wisdom to a pupil. "Taking things without asking is a punishable offence."

And so is killing people! Joe wanted to shout, but he held his tongue. He knew you couldn't argue with a maniac. "I'm sorry," he said instead. "I was wrong. But I gave it back. Can you let us go now?"

Silence again. It stretched out for a full five minutes. During it, Joe thought he saw movement off to the left, and he whipped his head in that direction. He was squeezing his eyes into slits, desperately trying to see into the shadows, when somebody whispered a single word in his ear: "No."

Bryce was so close that Joe felt the moisture of his breath bead on his skin. He spun around, trying to face him, but it was too late. The next thing he knew, his body left the ground as Bryce lifted him in a tackle.

Joe didn't have time to think; all he had time to do was flail his hands and beat wildly at Bryce's back. It either worked, or Bryce tripped over C.J.'s unconscious body, because the next thing Joe knew, the both of them were falling.

Together they landed on something hard, and there was a splintering sound as whatever was under them exploded into a million pieces. Joe cried out, his wounds throbbing. Bryce only grunted, and then punched Joe in the face. Joe saw a burst of fireworks and then felt warm liquid pouring out of his nose again. He tried to cover his face and felt the blade of Bryce's knife scrape his hands over and over as he blocked the oncoming punches. He knew Bryce could kill him at any moment. It was with a sickening clarity that he realized Bryce was only playing with him. It made him feel worthless, like he was nothing more than a toy. Like how the shattered remains of the wooden thing under him had been a toy to Kendra. The clouds outside shifted, and the thin rays of light streaming through the little windows were just enough to illuminate the splinters of the doll house Luke had finished building for his daughter. Splinters that eerily resembled weapons. Joe snatched one of them up, a broken slat of wood that had probably once been part of a door or a table, and without thought drove it as hard as he could into Bryce's arm.

Bryce roared in a combination of pain and rage and immediately clapped his hand to the wound. In the process he dropped the knife. It clattered to the floor, and Joe snatched it up.

He had to kill Bryce, and he had to kill him now before it was too late.

He raised the knife, preparing to drive it into Bryce's heart, when Bryce grabbed his wrist. Thankfully, due to his wound, Bryce's strength had ebbed considerably. What had once been comparable to a hydraulic machine was now only that of a teenager. Joe used this sudden burst of good fortune to his advantage and tried to pry Bryce's fingers off his wrist. Before he could do that, Bryce found the wound in Joe's calf and thrust his thumb into it.

The pain was so intense that Joe nearly blacked out. He dropped the knife, fighting to remain conscious. It was an effort that nearly failed.

The only thing that helped him succeed was Bryce punching him square in the chest, driving all the air out of his lungs.

Joe gasped, struggling to suck in oxygen. When he finally managed to sit up, it was to find Bryce kneeling over C.J., the rays of light from the window playing over his face, transforming it into something hideous.

"Enough horsing around." Bryce held up the knife so Joe could see it. "I'm going to kill your friend right in front of your eyes. And then I'm going to kill you. But I'm not going to stop there. I'm also going to kill Luke, and then that little whore you fancy so much. Maybe I'll even fuck her first. How would you like that?"

Joe tried to say something, anything, to draw out the time. His mouth worked, but nothing came out. He even tried to stand, but the pain in his calf nearly crippled him. Bryce seemed to like this response the best. Grinning, he raised the knife over C.J.'s chest. Then he brought it down.

CHAPTER 60

Luke pounded on the glass of the sliding door as hard as he could. Through it, he could make out two figures rolling around on the carpet on the other side. He didn't need to guess to know who they were.

Suddenly, Bryce looked up, and when he saw Luke, he grinned a wolfish grin. Then he carefully raised his fist and brought it down on Joe's face.

"You asshole!" Luke shouted, pounding on the glass harder than ever. *"Open up! Open up, right now!"*

He tried pulling feverishly at the handle, but like the front door, it was locked.

It didn't take him long to realize that the only way in was through the upstairs bathroom window. Without wasting another minute, he rushed over to the barbecue and scrambled on top of it. His balance wasn't what it used to be (he'd put on weight since the divorce) and he nearly wobbled off. What kept him from doing so was the knowledge that Joe and C.J. needed him.

It took him a few minutes to clamber onto the roof—his back protesting each step of the way—but when he did, the going got easier. Unlike Joe, he didn't have a fear of heights, and the trek to the window was uneventful. He hoisted one leg over the sill and slipped his body in.

Once inside, he scurried through the bathroom, out into the hall, and down the stairs, noting the familiar layout of the house, but also the unfamiliar way the furniture was arranged. It was a little surreal, as if he'd stumbled into an alternate universe of his past life, and it made him feel a little bit unwelcome. Especially when he came upon the living room and saw the books scattered about the floor. Crystal had never read before, and he felt a little betrayed to see that she had adopted a new hobby the moment he was out of her life.

He reached down and picked up one of the books. It was by Tom Clancy. He'd never heard of the guy before. All he knew was that the book was heavy and decided to take it with him. He wasn't going to read it, but if anything, Mr. Clancy's book might still come in handy.

He made his way to the den, where Joe and Bryce had been rolling around. What had once been a carpet occupied by two bodies was now empty space. Luke quickly scanned the room, confirming that he was the only one in it.

"C.J.? C.J., are you there?" he said into his walkie-talkie.

No answer. It was only then that he spotted the black object lying on the floor. He picked it up and studied the remains of the smashed walkie-talkie before tossing it away. He was just about to panic when Joe's voice sprang up out of the basement: *"There! You got what you want! Now leave us alone!"*

Luke turned toward the open door, amazed that he hadn't noticed it sooner. The three of them were down there, and by the sound of it, Joe and C.J. were in trouble. He remembered that Bryce was armed, and knew that if there was any chance of rescue it had to be done by stealth. Which was why instead of flying down the stairs, heedless of the noise it would make, he descended them slower than he had ever descended them before.

The first thing he noticed was that the lights were off. The second was that Bryce was very close. He heard him talking about taking things without asking, then Joe pleading for Bryce to leave him and C.J. alone. Luke waited a full minute, forcing himself to count to sixty, before continuing. He was just about to resume his descent when there was a crash and a cry of pain. Throwing all caution to the wind, he raced down the stairs.

Bryce was kneeling over a motionless shape on the floor. "Enough horsing around," he said to Joe. "I'm going to kill your friend right in front of your eyes. And then, I'm going to kill you. But I'm not going to stop there. I'm also going to kill Luke, and then that little whore you fancy so much. Maybe I'll even fuck her first. How would you like that?"

Without waiting for an answer, Bryce raised his hands, and the meager light streaming in through the windows caught the blade of a knife. He held it up, preparing to plunge it down. As he did, Luke sprang forward. He swung the Tom Clancy book with all his might. Had he aimed for Bryce's head, C.J. might have been turned into a pincushion. As it was, he struck Bryce's wrists, and hard. The impact forced the knife out of Bryce's hands. It landed on the carpet and bounced somewhere off into the darkness.

Luke shouted, "Joe, grab C.J. and get out, now! Hurry!"

He didn't wait to see if Joe was following his directions. He swung the book again, this time brining it down on Bryce's neck. Bryce ducked the blow and kicked out at Luke's legs. Luke went sprawling to the floor, feeling a sickening pop in his back. Bryce didn't hesitate in the slightest. Like a ju-jitsu practitioner, he mounted Luke, pinning him to the ground. Luke balled his hands into fists and threw two quick punches, crying out in pain as he did. The first missed, but the next connected, shaking Bryce's head back and forth like a bobblehead doll. He tried to throw another, but Bryce was already punching back. Luke got hit once, twice, and after suffering three more blows to the side of the face, watched the world before him dissolve and a shadow swallow him whole.

While Bryce and Luke were engaged in their fight, Joe used the distraction to pull C.J. to safety. He grabbed his friend's good arm and dragged him around the wall of the staircase. He was just about to try to lift C.J. so he could haul him up the stairs when Bryce cried out in triumph:

"You're going to have to do better than that, Joe! Keep sending in your friends, and I'll keep knocking them down. It's no sweat off my sack. The minute I kill you, I'm going back and slashing every one of their throats. Just know that their blood will be on your hands."

Joe paused in front of the staircase, contemplating his escape. He knew he couldn't ascend the stairs fast enough, not with C.J.'s dead weight slowing him down. Which is why he chose to hide instead. Before he did, however, he stamped down on the stairs, pounding on them—loud at first, but then softer and softer—the way someone does when they want to pretend they ran up. The pain this brought his already-burning calf nearly made him want to cry out, but he bit the inside of his cheek to keep silent. When the pain subsided, he hoisted C.J.'s body and dragged him farther into the basement, to the door that opened into Luke's old work room.

Bryce heard the little bastard running up the stairs. He couldn't let him get away. As of right now he could still catch him, kill the others, and make up some twisted lie about how Luke had broken into the house to find Joe and his friend planning to molest Kendra. He could tell his police buddies that they had fought and killed each other. It wasn't the best of lies, but it was the first one that came to mind. Given time, he could think of a much better one. However, if Joe escaped, then all would be lost. Joe didn't have the photo album—Bryce had that tucked safely inside his back pocket—but if Joe went to the police and the police investigated, Bryce would have a lot of explaining to do. Especially if they ran his phone records.

No, letting Joe escape was not an option.

Bryce dropped to the floor, quickly searching for the knife in the darkness like a blind man. When he couldn't find it, he shot up and ran around to the staircase. He was about to ascend when something caught his eye. It was small, almost unnoticeable, but his police training had made his senses startlingly keen. Without taking his eyes off the drop of liquid, he flipped the light switch. When the overheads illuminated, the drop of blood came into focus.

Bryce scanned the rest of the stairs above it. Nothing. But there were more drops of blood on the landing below coming from around the staircase just like he had, pausing at the landing, and then leading away. So his quarry hadn't climbed up the stairs after all. Bryce knew the little bastard would be stupid enough to leave a trail of breadcrumbs. He followed it past a second play area scattered with toys, and to a door. The handle was smeared red. That didn't disgust Bryce. In fact, it turned him on. It meant that the little bastard had trapped himself, and the thought of him cowering in a corner, trembling in fear, was more appetizing than ever.

Joe wiped his face again. The blood from the cut over his eyebrow was still dripping into his eye, making it sting. It also made it hard for him to see, and he knew that his life might very well depend on his vision. He wiped it again, surprised to find that Luke's workroom still had all his tools in it. Surprised, but happy. When he was opening the door, he had been battling a fear that the room would be empty. Now, at least he had a place to hide.

He wove his way through a maze of boxes, past the huge band saw, and to the back wall, where the long counter stretched out, holding up the portable grinders and sanders. The first thing he did after hiding C.J. under the counter was unscrew the light bulb above it. On the off chance that Bryce didn't take the bait and run up the stairs, he wanted to make it as difficult as possible for him to search any further.

Joe moved over to the remaining two bulbs in the middle of the room. He had just finishing unscrewing the last when the door opened. It didn't open slowly, causing the hinges to squeal eerily in the darkness, and it didn't open fast, either, slamming into the wall and spraying bits and chips of plaster everywhere. It opened normally. For some reason, that was even scarier. It indicated that Bryce knew Joe was in here, and that he would find him and kill him.

Joe clapped a hand to his mouth, stifling a moan as he ducked down and placed the light bulb on the floor as quietly as he could. He heard Bryce flip the light switch up and down only to find that it didn't work.

Try to find me now, you jackass.

It occurred to Joe just then that he was playing hide-and-seek in Luke's house again. Only this time the ultimate version, one where there was only one winner: the survivor.

"Where are you, Joe?" Bryce asked, walking in.

Joe didn't say anything. He watched from his hiding spot as Bryce crept forward, pausing every now and then to check behind piles of boxes. Thankfully there were no windows in the workroom, and the light streaming in from the door was only bright enough to illuminate the first few feet. When Bryce passed this point, he held out his hands so he wouldn't bump into anything.

"I know you're in here," he continued. "Why don't you make it easy for yourself and come out?"

Not a chance, Joe thought. He wrapped his hands around his legs, pulling them into his chest to make himself smaller.

Bryce walked farther into the room, making his way blindly to the back wall. Joe listened as he ran his hands over the tools hanging on the pegboard, producing an eerie melody like a conductor out of hell, as chisels and screwdrivers clanged against the blades of handsaws.

Like Amanda's late brother, one of Joe's senses didn't work. He was glad that in this case, it was his sight instead of his hearing. He listened as Bryce plucked something off the wall and turned around.

"Fine," Bryce said. "We'll do it the hard way, then. To be honest, it's more fun for me anyway."

Joe didn't doubt him. By the sound of it, Bryce was having the time of his life. He took a step forward, then another, and then all at once the sound of his footsteps vanished. Joe listened carefully, trying to see if they would begin again, but the oil burner kicked back in, drowning out all sound. Now he was deaf as well as blind.

The silence stretched out.

One second.

Two.

Three.

It was maddening. Joe tried to focus, to keep his mind from imagining horrible fantasies, but it was no use. In one, Bryce found C.J. and cut his throat. In another, Bryce whispered something in Joe's ear again, then shoved an ice pick through his neck.

Joe squeezed his eyes closed. When he opened them, he was still alive and still in the dark.

He's going to kill you, the cruel voice told him. *You know that, right? He's going to kill you.*

Joe knew. As much as he didn't want to believe it, he did. If he sat there waiting for the end to come, it would. He couldn't just hope for a miracle. Just like in life, you couldn't hope that the scratch on your car magically buffed itself out, or that the busted headlight repaired itself. If Luke had taught him anything, it was that you had to make things happen for yourself. It had been true about his car, it had been true about getting Amanda to become his girlfriend, and now the same logic applied to staying alive. If he wanted to survive, he had to do something about it, rather than sit around hoping for a miracle. Like Luke coming to the rescue again, for instance. That first time with C.J. really had been a miracle, but by the sound of Bryce's earlier shouts of triumph, Luke had either been knocked out or killed. Now Luke's life—if it had not already been taken—was in Joe's hands. And if he didn't succeed, Luke could kiss it goodbye. Same with C.J. Same with Amanda. Same with him.

Slowly, and quietly, Joe closed his hand around the light bulb and raised himself up, peering over the tray of the band saw. On one side of the room he could make out the light streaming in from the open door, illuminating a few boxes and a nearby workbench. On the other side, nothing. He had a feeling Bryce would be hiding in the shadows, like a true grim reaper waiting to strike. Needing to know for certain, Joe drew his hand back and threw the light bulb into the darkness, hoping that it would do more than just explode, that it would startle Bryce enough to give away his location.

CHAPTER 61

Joe strained his ears, listening for the thin glass around the filament to burst into a million pieces. He expected the bulb to soar through the air and explode somewhere on the far side of the workroom. What he did not expect was for it to shatter on something no more than three feet in front of him. When it did, that something went berserk.

Bryce lunged forward, swinging in the darkness. The tool that he had removed from the back wall, now a weapon, sliced through the air like a knife. It only cut empty space. Joe felt the breeze from it as it passed through the air millimeters in front of his face, and instinctively jerked his head back.

Bryce anticipated the move and lunged forward a second time, grabbing onto Joe's collar with his free hand.

"Get over here, you little bastard!" he roared.

Joe tried to squirm free, but the fabric of his shirt wouldn't tear. It held his torso like a straightjacket and allowed Bryce to pull him forward. Joe fought furiously, turning away and grabbing the tray of the band saw for support. He used it for leverage, pulling himself backwards. Bryce knew an opportunity when he saw one, and struck out with the weapon. If he could hit Joe in the right spot—the carotid artery, for example—he could be done with the little bastard for good. Instead of hitting Joe in the neck, however, Bryce hit the drum of the band saw. He hit it with such force that the shock vibrated up his arm, forcing his hand to release the weapon, where it clattered to the floor.

That's when Joe got the idea.

He felt around the case of the band saw for the ON switch, Luke's words echoing in his head: *Got it caught in a band saw. . . . Sucked the sleeve of my shirt right in. The blade spins so fast it'll nip anything off in the blink of an eye, no hesitation.*

Luke had been talking about his finger. The band saw was a powerful piece of machinery, and if you didn't treat it with respect, it would disrespect you the moment it got a chance. The serrated blade was created with one purpose, and one purpose only: to cut things. To rip through whatever was shoved in front of it, severing it in half.

Joe knew it was his only hope. There was no way he could fight Bryce off by himself. He had to get the saw on and feed Bryce's sleeve into it so it could suck him in just as it had sucked Luke in. If he was lucky, it would do more than just sever Bryce's finger. It would sever the horrible connection between them. It was a long shot, but Joe knew from his mini golf experience with Amanda that sometimes you did make the long shots. He also knew that if he didn't act now, when Bryce was momentarily distracted, he'd never get another opportunity.

Joe's fingers flirted with screws, stickers, and a few imperfections on the side of the saw, but that was all. No switch. His heart plunged. He was just about to give up his search and come to terms with the fact that he would have to try to fight off Bryce on his own when he brushed up against it.

He had operated the band saw back in school and figured this one would be the same. It was. Suddenly the machine burst to life, spinning the rollers and turning the blade. It was slow at first, moving at a speed someone might be able to crank by hand, but then grew faster and faster, eventually spinning so fast that a high-pitched whine filled the darkness. It sent chills racing up Joe's spine as he thought of the infinite number of teeth cycling through the saw's invisible hungry mouth. Even if he could see, feeding Bryce's sleeve into the blade would be a difficult task (Bryce could buck or jerk his arm, which in turn might send Joe's into it instead). Now, in the darkness, it would be almost impossible. One wrong move, one slip, and Joe could lose his fingers, his hand, or even his arm. It was an unsettling thought, but the thought of Bryce going after Amanda was even worse, and it gave him the courage to do what he did next.

He reached out and blindly groped for Bryce's sleeve. The arm was easy to find—the hand attached to it was still firmly affixed to his shirt collar—but the sleeve was rolled up. Trying to pull it down while Bryce jerked him forward was more difficult than finding the band saw's switch. After a few attempts, he managed to grab it. The moment he did, Bryce wrenched his arm backward, pulling Joe forward. Joe pawed for the tray of the band saw again and caught hold of it just in time. The saw rocked up a quarter of an inch, but that was all. It was heavy and was as good as an anchor.

"Let go!" Bryce hissed. He tugged Joe's shirt again, harder than ever. There was a snarling sound as the fabric finally ripped. It made Joe fall backward. Had he not reached out and grabbed Bryce's wrist at that moment, he might have fallen into the saw himself. It was too close. The moan of the serrated blade was coming from no more than an inch behind him. It forced him to recognize the seriousness of the situation. It was either kill or be killed. Become the predator or remain the prey. And with that little bit of wisdom running through his head, he grabbed Bryce's arm and heaved it toward the hungry sound.

At first Bryce didn't do anything but try to pull his hand back. Then he *screamed.* It was as loud as thunder, so loud that Joe thought his eardrums had ruptured. There was a horrible whining. Then there was wet stuff hitting Joe's face. It felt like it was raining sideways. Then pouring. All at once Joe knew what it was: the saw had sucked in Bryce's sleeve, slicing through flesh and bone, starting with his fingers, devouring them, and moving on to his hand. It would have kept going, its never-ending hunger un-satiated, but Bryce yanked his arm back in a last-ditch effort to save himself. He crashed to the floor in a bloody mess, writhing in pain.

Joe was thankful the lights were off; he didn't think he could stand to see the extent of Bryce's injuries. By the amount of blood that had showered him, he assumed they were bad. Wondered, in fact, if Bryce was going to die right here and now.

In answer, a slimy hand clamped around his ankle. It pulled him to the ground with surprising strength—strength that only the clinically insane possessed. Joe tried to kick his leg free, but Bryce held it tight. He moved his hand up Joe's leg until he came to the spot where he had driven the knife into earlier. Then he *squeezed*, his fingers sinking into Joe's flesh the way someone's thumb might sink into a hot stick of butter. Joe uttered a loud, piercing cry. He saw stars appear in the darkness, and for a second, thought he was outside looking up at the sky. Then he kicked out with his free leg. It connected with Bryce's face, but Bryce didn't let go. Joe tried beating at him with his hands, but whatever they hit—Bryce's back? his arm? his shoulder? his head?—felt more like solid stone than flesh. Joe had heard somewhere, either in a movie or a book, that the dead pull the living down, and it seemed that it was absolutely true. The dead—or at least the dying, in this case—was going to pull the living down, after all, into that great abyss that opened up in the fabric of the earth. Joe couldn't let that happen; he had too many responsibilities to attend to. He had to make sure Luke was okay, he had to keep Bryce from finding C.J., and most of all, he had to protect Amanda. She was the most important one of all. He couldn't let Bryce escape so he could attack her again. Once was already too much. Bryce deserved to die for putting her in the hospital. He deserved the pain he was feeling now. And he deserved to have it intensify ten-fold.

Joe kicked at him one last time before deciding upon a better strategy than just throwing punches. He remembered how Bryce had dropped something metallic when he hit the band saw, and knew by the sound of it clattering to the concrete that it couldn't be too far off. Joe spread out his hands, searching for the weapon. He found a lot of dust, but that was all. He stretched out a bit farther, and the tips of his fingers encountered something long, thin, and cold. It was either a screwdriver or an ice pick. Joe didn't waste any time trying to figure out which. He reached out again, only to discover with a sickening dread that his arm wasn't long enough.

It was as if instinct took over. Just like Amanda had taught him, he contorted his hand into the letter *P* and shoved it into Bryce's eye. Bryce yelped and loosened his grip. It granted Joe the additional length he needed. He grabbed the weapon by its handle and shoved it into Bryce's forearm.

If he had thought Bryce's first scream had been deafening, then this second blotted out every sound in existence. He forced himself not to let it distract him. He knew if he faltered now, at this crucial moment, he might lose his life. For that reason, he pulled the screwdriver/ice pick out of Bryce's forearm and prepared himself to drive it into Bryce's neck.

Before he could, Bryce lashed out with his mutilated stump. Joe felt the wet slap and the slime of blood smear across his cheek. It caught him off guard, and he dropped the screwdriver/ice pick, which produced a musical note as it clattered to the floor. There was no time to listen to the rest of the symphony it might have made, because Bryce let go of Joe's leg and snatched up the weapon with his good hand, locating it entirely by sense of sound.

Joe didn't see it coming. He didn't see the evil leer on Bryce's face, either. All he saw was the darkness. If he *could* see, however, he would have seen C.J. staggering over, holding a mini sledge hammer in his good hand, his left arm hanging broken and useless by his side. He would have seen him raise it high, pausing as he tried to figure out which of the shapes entangled before him was Bryce. And he would have seen him bring it down.

The mini sledge didn't whistle through the air like an arrow or the blade of a sword. It just fell; heavily, soundlessly. That is, until it struck Joe's leg and there was a sickening crunch.

Bryce didn't miss a beat. He swung around, burying the screwdriver/ice pick into C.J.'s side. C.J. threw the sledge away, howling in agony. He staggered backward, tried to reach out for something to grab on to, failed, and crashed to the floor.

"Thought your little buddy could save you again, didn't you?" Bryce roared. "Thought he could come out of the dark and knock me out. Well, he can't. It's just you and me, Joe. Just you and me. And I'm going to teach you a lesson you won't soon forget."

Joe wasn't listening. He was too busy trying not to scream. It felt like somebody had packed fiberglass into his leg. It stung, burned, and throbbed all at the same time, each unpleasant sensation gnawing at the bone. It was torture to move, but he forced himself to anyway, knowing that if he stayed where he was Bryce would kill him in a matter of seconds.

With all the strength he could muster, he gritted his teeth and pushed himself backward. The torment this summoned was indescribable. He had never suffered so much in his life. He wanted to cry out but stifled the impulse by biting down on his lip. By now it was a ragged piece of flesh, and he couldn't even tell if it was bleeding anymore. He just inched backward, slowly pushing himself out of harm's reach. He got only a few feet before he realized he couldn't bear to go on, that it was too much, that death would be the only way to end the excruciating signals his nerve endings were sending.

Dazed, he found his hands wandering, inspecting his leg. It had to be broken. Absurd thoughts flashed through his mind: *Coach Heck's gonna be pissed at me. I'm not gonna be able to run anymore. I wonder if I can drive with a cast on?* They might have continued had he not felt the blocky shape in his pocket. He reached in, pulling out the disposable camera Luke had given him. It felt almost alien, an artifact from a time when he, Luke, and C.J. had been together and without injury. He turned it over in his hands, staring at it in the darkness, remembering that better time.

At the same moment, he heard Bryce move. Without thinking, Joe charged the flash and snapped a photo. He needed to see Bryce one last time, needed to see the hate in his eyes before he descended. Yet, when the flash illuminated, something Joe didn't expect happened: Bryce cried out, shielding his eyes. In the pitch black, it must have been blinding. The ice pick—it was an ice pick, Joe could see this now, its steel streaked with blood—fell out of his hand, clattering to the floor. It broke Joe's daze, snapping him back to reality.

Bryce moved forward, the afterimage of the flash swimming before his vision. He batted the air blindly with his stump as he clutched at his eyes with his good hand.

Joe pushed himself backward again, realizing for a second time that if he didn't move he was going to die. When he got as far as the pain would allow him, he charged up the flash and snapped another photo. Like lightning, the darkness lit up.

Bryce was even closer. He recoiled at the burst of light, snarling like a wild animal. By the amount of blood spilling out of his stump, Joe couldn't believe he hadn't died yet. He assumed it was because Bryce was powered by insanity. It was as if he were facing a machine instead of a man. Joe was trying to figure out how he could kill this unstoppable maniac when his hand encountered the mini sledge C.J. had brought down on his leg. Joe picked it up, feeling like Thor, the god of thunder. The sledge had power, and he intended to wield it.

He silently pushed himself sideways, moving out of Bryce's line of attack. If Bryce was anything like an animal, he would pounce, and when he did, Joe would be ready.

He waited. One second. Two. Then it happened. In the blink of an eye, Bryce was soaring through the air, the ice pick shooting forward. Joe didn't waste any time. He raised the mini sledge and brought it down. It struck Bryce on the back, and he let out a muffled cry. Bryce dropped the ice pick, but didn't stop there—he twisted around and seized Joe by the neck, coiling his fingers around his throat. Joe tried to pull away, but it was too late; already, it felt like he was sucking in air through a straw. Bryce kept squeezing, his grip tightening like pliers. Joe felt his head grow woozy, and watched the world waver.

Knowing what this implied, and knowing what would happen if he passed out, he clenched the muscles of his broken leg as hard as he could. The burst of pain was just enough to keep him conscious. It was also enough to force him to raise the mini sledge and bring it down on Bryce's head again and again.

~ ~ ~

Joe lay where he was, listening. Bryce had played possum once before, therefore he could be playing it again. Slowly, cautiously, Joe reached out with a trembling hand. His fingers flirted with the trench he had opened in Bryce's skull, then moved down to his neck, where he could check his pulse. He found the carotid artery and pressed.

Nothing.

He was just about to let go when Bryce moaned. Joe jumped back in surprise, screaming at the pain this abrupt movement caused. He frantically grabbed for the mini sledge, preparing to bring it down one last time, when the moan sounded again. It took him only a second to realize it hadn't come from Bryce.

"C.J.?" he called out. "Is that you?"

He was answered by another moan, this one stronger.

"C.J.?"

C.J. staggered to his feet somewhere off in the darkness. "Yeah," he said. "It's me." He sounded like he had a hangover.

Joe didn't blame him. He struggled to find his own voice as his body throbbed. "Are you okay?"

"I think so. Bastard got me pretty good. Think he hit the bone, though. Thank God for small favors, right?"

"Yeah," Joe said. He felt C.J.'s hand reach out and help him up. He remembered that ever since they had fought and ended their friendship he felt like he had been missing something in his life. He had originally thought it was C.J. Now he realized it was everybody, as a whole: C.J., Luke, his parents, Amanda. And it wasn't until he and C.J. teamed up to fight evil and help protect those he cared about that he truly felt complete.

Joe was about to thank C.J. for all his help when there was a gasp from upstairs. By the sound of it, Joe could tell it had come from a woman.

Then: *"Kendra, stay right there! Don't come in any farther! Bryce? Bryce?"*

Joe listened as Crystal quickly moved from the living room to the den and then down the basement stairs.

"Bryce? Bryce, are you down here? Did something happen? Is everything all right? Your books are all over the—"

That's when she screamed. Joe and C.J. had come out of the workroom, meeting her at the bottom of the stairs. All she had to do was take one look at C.J.'s mutilated arm and the blood pouring out of Joe's leg to faint. Joe tried to catch her, but he wasn't fast enough. She crumbled, dropping to the rug.

"Mommy . . . ?"

The pitter patter of little feet followed the voice, and Kendra appeared at the top of the stairs. Before she could even look down, Joe rushed up, grabbing on to the banister with both hands and hopping on his good leg. He ignored the resounding blare of pain this caused, and snatched Kendra into his arms.

"Joseph!"

"Yeah, Kendra. It's me," he said, hugging her, not daring to let go.

"Where's my mommy?"

"She's safe." He gave her a gentle squeeze, and then kissed her on the forehead. "We're all safe now."

CHAPTER 62

Joe turned the ratchet one last time until the bolt tightened. Then he slid out from under his car and found the five-quart bottle of oil. He opened the cap under the hood and poured it in. Changing his oil had always been a boring, monotonous job. Now it was different. Now it seemed almost cathartic, meditative, allowing him to concentrate on his positive thoughts while he purged the negative. And after everything that had happened last month, he had a lot of negative thoughts to purge.

He gave the bottle one last shake and then tossed it away, wiping at the sweat on his forehead. It was approaching summer, and the days were getting hotter and longer. Time stopped for no one. It buried the past, leaving only memories, and slowly those started to fade as well. Joe didn't think his would ever fade, though. All he had to do was look at the cast on his leg or run his finger down the bridge of his nose, and he would remember. The rest of his injuries—his lip, the superficial cuts on his cheeks, the purplish bruises on his neck, and the gash above his eyebrow, which had taken twenty-six stitches—had healed quickly and efficiently. His nose had been a different story. Like his leg, it had been broken. It was healing but with a slight protrusion where there had once been a gentle slope. Joe didn't mind. He thought it made him look more defined. But it was still a reminder of what had happened. Each time he looked in the mirror, he remembered that final struggle in the basement where Bryce had tried to kill him.

There was no chance of Bryce doing that now. He was buried in the Farmsville Cemetery on Larkstone Road. He supposedly had a family plot there. Joe didn't know for certain because he didn't go to the funeral or the burial service. Neither did Crystal. Not after Joe, Luke, and C.J. explained everything to her. At first she wouldn't listen, strictly denying everything, but after Joe pulled the photo album out of Bryce's pocket and showed it to her, Crystal nearly fainted a second time. It probably wasn't the smartest thing to do, but he was glad he did it, even if he did get scolded by the police for removing evidence from a dead body.

That was another thing. The police were as surprised and appalled as Crystal was, learning that their beloved captain had turned out to be the Craig's List murderer. Like her, Bryce was the last person they would have suspected. It just went to show you that it was impossible to truly know someone. That there's always a part of ourselves we keep locked away, because if we showed it we would become truly transparent, and that scares us more than anything. It was just unfortunate that the part Bryce kept locked away had been so dark and morbid.

Luke found out just how dark and morbid that part was the minute he got home. After spending two and a half hours at Crystal's house consoling Kendra and repeating his story well over five times so the police could get all the details right, he drove back to his apartment. He was expecting a nice quiet evening to catch up on his sanity. He got the complete opposite. Awaiting him, sprawled out on the floor in a bloody mess, was the body of an obese man. There was brake fluid on his arm and a pair of green-handled clippers in his back pocket. And that wasn't all. Sprinkled about the floor, under the giant paperweight of his body, were photographs of young women. Four were of victims of the Craig's List murderer. The last was of Amanda.

For the second time that day, Luke found himself surrounded by police asking questions. Unlike the first, however, he didn't have all the answers. No, he'd never seen the man before. Yes, he thought the brake fluid on the man's sleeve was from his car. No, he hadn't killed him. Yes, he recognized Amanda from the photographs but didn't recognize any of the other women. No, he didn't know how any of these things had gotten into his apartment, but he had an idea it had something to do with Bryce.

Luke stuck to his story even after the police learned the identity of the dead body. It was a man by the name of Chester Lancaster.

"That's my dad's boss!" Joe had said, shocked, when Luke called to tell him about it later.

"Your dad's boss?"

"Yeah, he's the guy who I bought my car from. My dad had him over for dinner not too long ago."

Luke told Joe about the brake fluid and the clippers. He also told him how he thought Bryce had planted Mr. Lancaster's body in his apartment in order to frame him. It didn't take Joe long to realize that Mr. Lancaster's body was the lumpy thing in the duffle bag Bryce had been struggling with to get into the trunk. It made perfect sense. Joe remembered Luke telling him about the bloody underwear he had found in his glove box and understood that Bryce had tried to frame him then, as well. This was just another attempt . . . or a continuation of it.

When Luke relayed this information to the police, they came up with a plausible scenario: Bryce wanted them to believe that Luke and Mr. Lancaster were working together as the Craig's List murderers. They had gotten into a fight over who would kill Amanda and Luke had killed Mr. Lancaster, but not before Mr. Lancaster had a chance to cut Luke's brake lines. If everything had worked out with Bryce's plan, Luke would have died in a car accident, the two "murderers" would have been dead, and Bryce would have been able to walk away scot-free. There was only one problem with this scenario: Luke was a mechanic and would have never gotten into his car after discovering the brake fluid and the clippers. But then again, Bryce was human, and humans often overlooked the small, crucial details.

"I just don't understand one thing," Luke had said to Joe. "Why your dad's boss?"

That was an easy one. Joe remembered the night Mr. Lancaster had come over for dinner in perfect detail. Bryce had been there, too, and had become the butt of Mr. Lancaster's jokes. At the time it seemed like Bryce had enjoyed the humor, but due to the way things turned out, it was obvious that he hadn't. He had made sure Mr. Lancaster got his in the end.

Joe shut the hood of his car and placed the used oil filter, the empty bottle of oil, and a few dirty paper towels into a plastic bag. He was just about to carry it over to the curb when he looked up. A car turned onto his block, the sun glinting off the windshield. Joe shielded his eyes, unable to determine the make and model. For one horrible moment, he imagined it was a white Mercedes and the past was coming back to haunt him. But as it drew closer and the sun wandered off the windshield and onto the roof, he saw that it was a Ford Taurus. It pulled over to the curb in front of Joe's car and killed its engine.

"Joseph," Luke said when he stepped out. He had lost some of the extra weight he had put on after the divorce. He wasn't as thin as he'd once been, but he was getting there. Joe thought that after a month or two of working out, his weight would be back to what it used to be. Unfortunately, that was the only thing that would return to the way it used to be. Luke had needed another back surgery after his scuffle with Bryce, and he and Crystal hadn't gotten back together the way couples did in fairytales. Crystal found a new boyfriend immediately after the ordeal: a teacher in his mid-thirties who didn't seem to have any fetishes for pain and fear. Luke didn't take the news so easily. Joe knew that Luke had assumed that once Bryce was out of the picture, he'd have a shot at getting back together with his ex-wife. As it turned out, that wasn't the case.

Things did, however, have a strange way of working out. In the court proceedings that followed, Luke got joint custody of Kendra, and he started seeing someone else as well: the secretary at the dealership where he worked as a tech. She wasn't as pretty as Crystal—or at least that's what Luke had told Joe—but she was honest and had a great personality and that's what counted.

Joe couldn't help but hide a smile when he thought about this, and watched his old neighbor step out of his car. "Hey, Luke. How's it going?"

"Can't complain," Luke said. "I'm taking Kendra to that new adventure park that opened up in Bayview. They've got a jungle gym modeled after a castle that she's been dying to play on."

Joe knew that Kendra was into castles. He remembered the one Luke had built her. "Sounds pretty cool," he said. "Hope she has fun."

"Me, too. I have a feeling if she does, I'm going to have to build her one of her own." He said it the way someone does when they're dreading the idea, but Joe thought he could detect some excitement in Luke's voice. After all, he liked building things, and it was a chance for him to bond with his daughter that he wouldn't pass up. "How are your parents?" Luke asked after a pause.

"They're all right," Joe said. "The vacation did them good. They came back happy for once. Didn't even argue. That is, until they learned about everything that happened."

"How'd they take it?"

"My mom still won't accept it. I think she thought Bryce was perfect. My dad tried to get her to see reason, but she only snapped. They're going to counseling now. I'm not sure if it's working or not. I don't think it is."

Luke bit his lip, remembering the telltale signs of divorce.

"At least he doesn't spend as much time in his home office as he used to," Joe continued. "He's been trying to get out more. Spending time with me. Shooting hoops and stuff."

"That's good, at least."

"Yeah. He's horrible, but it's cool to finally see him make the effort."

"How's C.J.?" Luke asked.

"He's taking it easy," Joe said. "Showing everybody his scars. He gets his cast off about the same time I do. He was pissed that he couldn't play baseball at first, but I think it worked out for the best. He's been studying instead and got a twenty-three hundred on his SATs."

"Is that good?"

Joe blinked. "It's *amazing.* I only got a nineteen fifty. I'm taking them again over the summer with Amanda."

"How's she doing?"

"Much better. She got the wires taken out of her mouth this morning. I'm going over her house to see her as soon as I shower."

"I'm glad to hear that."

"Same here. She hated not being able to talk. The whole sign language thing definitely helped. I think it brought us closer together. I might even take a few classes in it, try to learn a little more, you know?"

"That's pretty ambitious," Luke said. "Good luck."

"Thanks. C.J. said he might give it a shot, too. He and Amanda are friendly now."

"Really?"

"Yeah, I didn't see that coming. But after I told her how he saved my life when Bryce and I were fighting upstairs, she promised to be civil towards him, and they're growing on one another. I didn't mention he was the one who broke my leg. I didn't think that would go over well. He was pretty much traumatized when he learned he was the one who'd done it anyway."

Luke chuckled. "That's good that they're not at each other's throats like before."

"Definitely."

They stood for a minute or two, letting the silence pass between them. It might have been a hint of what was to become of their friendship. Joe remembered how easily they had lost touch over the winter, and he told himself that he'd try his best not to let it happen again, but he knew that senior year would be tough and college tougher still, especially if he went out of state. Either way, whatever came to pass, he knew that he and Luke would always have the memory of what happened this year.

"Well," Luke said, turning toward his old house. "I better go get Kendra. I don't want to be late." There was a car in the driveway. A blue Mitsubishi. "I'm supposed to meet Crystal's boyfriend today."

"Are you sure you're ready to do that?" Joe asked.

"To be honest, no. But, it's the civil thing to do."

Joe had to agree with him on that. It was certainly more respectful than spying. Joe was just glad Luke hadn't asked him to do it again. If he had, Joe didn't think he would say yes this time. The past had a purpose—you learned from it.

"Good luck," Joe told him.

"Thank you," Luke said. "I'll need it."

"You won't."

"Either way, I appreciate it. Good luck with Amanda. Tell her I said hi."

"I will," Joe said. "And thank you." But Joe knew he wouldn't need luck. The minute he pressed his lips against Amanda's and told her he loved her he knew everything would be okay.

AUTHOR'S NOTE

This is the part of the novel where I get to talk to you, the reader, about all the things I couldn't during the story.

What I'd like to talk about today is literary license. Some of you may have heard the term used as "artistic license." Either way, it means the same thing: I've taken certain liberties distorting fact in *Bryce* to make the story a bit more interesting.

As a note, I try to avoid doing this as often as possible. Nevertheless, I have done it this time.

First off, the ICU . . .

I've been to plenty of hospitals during the course of my life. I'd like to thank my good fortune that it has been because I've welcomed new members into my family rather than having an injury or illness. Be that as it may, I have not come across one ICU unit where the nurses have abandoned their posts, as they did when Amanda wakes up from her coma. I simply had the nurses do that to create a tiny bit more suspense.

Further more, I have never visited an ICU unit described the way I have described mine: a singular room with sheets separating the beds. I did, however, come across a photo of one very similar—I think it was a military ICU unit, but I could be mistaken—and I chose to model mine after the one in that photo to make the story a little more interesting. I hope I have succeeded.

I also took literary license when Joe tries to jump his car in the industrial area. Touching the cables of a jumper machine to the chassis of a car will in no way produce sparks (I know this because I have done it on a few occasions). But the thought of having him jump back, fearing he has turned the car into some nightmarish creature like Frankenstein's monster was too good an opportunity to pass up.

Maybe that's why I like writing fiction. Maybe I like to create things, characters especially. I certainly enjoyed creating Bryce. He embodies that neighbor who nobody truly knows. Like that guy next door, or the man down the block who always wears the baseball cap. We come across these people all the time. But we never get close enough to really know what they're like inside. All we do is wave, smile, and make the standard small talk. What if we *did* get closer to them, though? What if we were asked to spy on them for a friend? And what if they caught us doing it? What would happen then?

I wrote *Bryce* to find that out.

Thank you for sticking with me during another fun journey through my mind. Without you, I'd have nobody to share my stories with.

Until next time, keep an eye out for your neighbors. There's no telling what they might be hiding . . .

Vincent Bivona
January 29, 2012

ACKNOWLEDGMENTS

Although this list may change from time to time, my gratitude will not. The following people have contributed to this novel, either by giving a great idea to advance the plot, or by proofreading and editing the manuscript. I wish to thank them all in no particular order: Jay Teta, Nathaniel Vaus, Sarah Pandolfo, Nicole Slavik, Gina Suriano, Chris Bivona, Bobbi Weiner, Chris Crisera, Michael Zillmann, Nina Triolo, and Kenneth Wishnia.

As always, without you guys, this novel would not be what it is today.

A big thank you goes out to five very special individuals. Without them, Bryce would not have the cover it does today. Lauren Malec, Melisa Merlino, Marisa Wedlock, and Rebecca Farrell, you guys are awesome victims :P Antonino LaGattuta, your ideas for the cover surpass my appreciation.

I also owe a special thanks to some very generous individuals. If it wasn't for them, among others, the book in your hand would not exist: Dr. Michael A. LoGuidice, D.O., MBA; Jerry Riekert; Antonino & Jacqueline LaGattuta; Richard & Theresa McKillop; Joshua Delgadillo; Douglas Albert; Glenn Fiocca; Brian Lawson; Donald J. Martin; Anthony Sclafani; Anthony Dirusso; Debra & Richard Ginsberg; Tony Iwanczuk; and Adam Rains.

www.ingramcontent.com/pod-product-compliance
Lightning Source LLC
Chambersburg PA
CBHW030552310726
48979CB00011B/2123/J

* 9 7 8 1 7 3 5 1 0 1 7 9 8 *